THE IMMORTAL SERPENT

Book 1 of The Bloodstone Dagger

K.E. BARRON

Thank Rob

FFF

The Immortal Serpent

K. E. Barron

Published by Foul Fantasy Fiction, an imprint of Bear Hill Publishing
1843b Kelowna Crescent
Cranbrook, B.C. V1C 6L6
Canada
foulfantasyfiction.com

Cover artwork by Tyson Villeneuve

Paperback ISBN 978-1-989071-20-5

Hardcover ISBN 978-1-989071-00-7

Ebook ISBN 978-1-989071-21-2

*Dedicated to Tessa for going on this
long, epic journey with me.*

The Desert Tribe Lands

Holy City of
Thessalin

Naja Archipelago

Elmijel Province (Of Del' Cabria)

Ankarr

Empire of
Rangardia

Tezkhan

Tezkhan
Settlement

Sunil

Sunil Slot Canyons

Death Tribe Ruins

City of Herran

Temple of Sagarath

Herran

Burning Waste

The Dunes

Serpentine River

Odafi

Tradesmen's Guild Lands

Del' Cabria
Proper

Ludesa Province
(Of Del' Cabria)

East Del' Cabria

Ingleheim

The Barrier of Kriegle

Del' Cabria
Proper

Eanore

The Deep
Wood

Faineshome

Grove of the
Crannabeatha

Fae'ren Province
(Of Del' Cabria)

Ludesa Province
(Of Del' Cabria)

The Citadel

Credence

Earth gives rise to all things
The source of life gives way to progress
There is no progress without suffering
Suffering brings death.

Ruins become overgrown
Pain is washed away
Pestilence devours the living and the rivers run dry
The foundation collapses and all fall with it.

– Circle of Creation

I

One to Love, and One to Fear

Vidya's vacant stare hung over her mother's face. She studied the skin stretched tight and yellow around the mouth and eyelids, disfiguring her once flawless features. Exquisite cream-tinted wings laid to rest over her body, primary feathers freshly plucked. Dark, loose curls, just dusted with white flecks at her temples—the only perceptible indication of her fifth decade.

She was such a beauty . . . then who must this be? She didn't look real much less beautiful. Her slender neck was blackened with bruises and broken veins, the handprints of the one who inflicted such mortal injury now engraved upon her olive skin. Vidya's fists clenched and unclenched. Her cheeks burned with a sudden familiar heat from the smoldering fire in her stomach, making her want to vomit and scream at the same time.

Few women on the Island of Credence commanded the attention that Councilor Sarta once did. Even now, as her lavender adorned body lie stiff in rigor mortis on the marble slab before the Mothers' Assembly, she was monumental.

The island's most prominent mothers gathered around the Grand Altar to pay their respects and receive the words of the Archon Xenith who stood between the effigies of the Siren and the Harpy, waiting for all to arrive.

Vidya could no longer bear her mother's diminished form and turned her gaze to the sea instead. The swiftly fading sun cast fiery pink strokes across a heavily clouded sky that reflected down on the rolling water's surface, the wet beach glistening like stained glass.

When Vidya lowered her eyes to the crowd ahead of her, she gulped at its size. Not only was the Mothers' Assembly in attendance, but their daughters as well. Even some male faces appeared amongst the throng—most of them husbands, some of them military commanders and their lieutenants. The Citadel Plaza was almost full. Only a few stragglers, some slow-moving elderly, continued to plod up the white marble steps to take their places before the altar. The sun bathed half their faces in a warm glow, but its falling draped the other in damning shadow.

Her sister Demeter, standing beside her and left of the slab, darted her eyes between the corpse and the crowd every few moments, struggling to keep her expression stoic with little success.

"I had hoped to see her before they defiled her wings," she muttered with a venomous air.

"Such is required for the ritual," said Vidya.

Demeter pursed her full, red lips that matched the color of her wig. "Mother believed you were meant for great things—even said the Harpy in you was more of a blessing than a curse." She exhaled sharply through her nose as if repelling a sour odor and stretched out her pale blue wings as a not so subtle reminder of what she possessed that Vidya did not. "The opportunity has finally come for you to prove her right. See to it that you don't waste it." The conversation ended. Demeter again stood sentinel and stone-faced as if her sister were not there, or maybe it was just that she wished she weren't.

Vidya shook her head. She would never understand why Demeter despised her so much. But she didn't care anymore. There were more important things to worry about now; their mother's death was only the beginning.

A humid coastal breeze swept over the altar, blowing Vidya's mess of brown ringlets behind her and chilling her through her thin, linen ceremonial gown. Nerves hollowed her stomach.

It was time.

The Archon stepped toward the altar's edge. She wore a light orange wrap-around dress, spirals of gray hair in abundance, held in place with a gold headband. Upon fluttering her flaxen wings, the chattering crowd silenced and instantly fell under her rapture. For a woman nearly in her seventh decade, Xenith still inspired undivided obedience. Frailty was not yet a trait she possessed, which was partly why the Mothers' Assembly continued to elect her Archon all these years.

In a clear and disarming voice, she addressed the audience. "We are gathered here, at the altar of Yasharra, to mourn the horrific loss of our Mistress of Foreign Relations and Trade." Xenith breathed deep and lifted her chest to steady her next words. "Her siren's song forever silenced by a man from whom she had no reason to suspect ill will."

The crowd remained silent, but uneasy eyes glanced off one another as the woman's meaning sank in. "As your Archon, it is my duty to inform you, good Mothers of Credence, that Councilor Sarta was *murdered* by the Overlord of Herran, Nas'Gavarr."

The congregation erupted in frightful chatter. "No!" a Mother called out. "How could a *man* hold any violent desire toward a siren?"

"Impossible!" rang other voices.

Xenith beat her wings again and hushed the crowd. "Nas'Gavarr is no mere man. The desert tribes worship him. They call him the Immortal Serpent. He has lived for two hundred years. Maybe more. Somehow, he is able to resist the touch of a siren, and one of Sarta's caliber . . ." trailing off, Xenith turned her head away from her audience and frowned at the sight of the dead siren on the slab. Her gaze did not hold for long. "He is a threat, the level of which our republic has never before faced."

Gasps and frightened chatter picked up tenfold. Vidya glanced down to her mother's corpse once again. *She is a goddess compared to the likes of him. And he took her beautiful neck in his hand and crushed it like a thin reed.* Her nostrils flared, and she began to shake. Demeter's bottom lip quivered. *What does she know of fear—of rage!* Vidya thought. *She didn't bear witness to it. All she did was greet him at the gate along with Mother and I, then watch him disappear behind the chamber doors.*

Xenith continued, the fatigue of hard memories clear on her face. "Sarta wished to discuss peace terms with the invader. She took him to the War Council already in session, and it was there he murdered her in front of the entire Siren Council and our military leaders. 'Man will rise, and the Siren will fall. Your goddess cannot protect you now.' Those were his words of peace!"

Vidya closed her eyes tight. That single word clawed at her insides. *Protect.* She had joined the infantry to protect the republic from her enemies and yet in that moment, when Nas'Gavarr snapped her mother's neck with one hand, she could do nothing to protect her. The air in her lungs shook out of her. *After tonight, I will be set on course to avenge her.*

"Blasphemy!" women screamed.

"Why would he do such a thing?" shouted a siren, her voice on the verge of cracking. "The Herrani pulled back their fleet yesterday!" An older siren next to her wrapped a comforting wing around her.

With a steady hand to the buzzing crowd, Xenith calmly continued, "The recent attack on our ports was nothing more than a show of force and a distraction. Just a few months ago, Nas'Gavarr killed a Senator of Del'Cabria, and they have since declared war. It appears Credence is next."

"Does that mean we must join with Del'Cabria?" a prominent Mother of the assembly asked in horror.

The Mothers of Credence were anything but comfortable with such an alliance. For hundreds of years, the insatiable kingdom on the mainland had threatened to expand their dominion to the little island nation to the south, and they didn't allow women the right to their own lives let alone the right to govern.

"Absolutely not," Xenith reassured everyone. "King Tiberius will undoubtedly demand that we become another Province of theirs. No matter the protections offered, we will not accept. Even if it allows for peace tomorrow, the cost of such—our sovereignty, our way of life—is a price far too high. We can continue to rely on Rangardia in the event of an invasion."

"Well then, what do you plan to do about this, O Archon?" a father blared, a few paces from the altar.

"*That* is why the Siren Council invites you all here tonight!" Xenith said with a sudden fervor. "For we are not here to eulogize our departed Councilor. No! We are here to bear witness to Yasharra's true might. Tonight, good Mothers of Credence, we will prove just how false the Overlord's claim is. Our goddess will not only protect us. She will avenge us!"

A potent silence enveloped the crowd, making way for the harmonic and soothing voices of three young sirens walking up the altar steps. Three male prisoners in chains followed dutifully behind them. They were shirtless and unkempt, but tall and muscular. Enraptured by the sirens' song, they allowed themselves to be led to a large square pool filled with water before the Harpy's effigy. Vidya could taste the men's fear from where she stood a few feet away, but each was powerless to the wishes of the sirens who accompanied them. *And that power had no effect on Nas'Gavarr.* A tremor ran down her spine.

Xenith stepped toward the Siren's effigy to her left and gently grazed her fingertips along its base. The statue stood twelve feet tall, body and face immaculately chiseled in white marble with glowing wings raised into the air and delicate fingers playing the harp. "Yasharra has two daughters. The Siren, beautiful, wise, and just" she began. "She requires a man's total devotion. She keeps them contented and grants them purpose. As women, we must care for Yasharra's creation as we do our own children."

The Archon then walked over to the other statue on the right. The Harpy's effigy was crouched atop its pedestal, face contorted into a frenzied shriek forever fixed in bronze. Her wings extended as a menacing vulture, casting its shadow over the prisoners standing in the pool beneath.

Xenith stepped under its wing and placed her hand on its stone base. "Then there is the Harpy, wayward and fierce! She requires no such gifts of spirit like the Siren, only the flesh and blood of dishonorable men. For those who disobey Yasharra's will by disrupting her peace, the Harpy punishes them and thus restores order. . . . One to love, and one to fear."

"One to love, and one to fear," Vidya repeated reverently with the rest of the crowd.

And fear they will, thought Vidya as every Mother, father, and daughter before her squirmed in anticipation of what was to come.

"And by honoring that balance," Xenith said, "we honor Yasharra's creation. The status given to all womankind is because of the blood we share with her. In every Crede woman, there is a piece of her within us, be it the Harpy or the Siren . . . but only the Siren governs here."

"The Harpy shall never rule Credence again!" everyone declared in unison. Demeter's voice more manifest in Vidya's ear.

"We rely on the Siren for stable leadership. This stability is more important now than ever. But, it is time for the Harpy to wake from her slumber and inflict her wrath upon our enemies!"

The silence of the crowd was then swallowed up by an eruption of cheers. Demeter cast her eyes down to her mother, refusing to meet her sister's gaze.

Xenith turned to the three men, still kneeling in the Harpy's fearsome shadow, and lifted the middle one's chin to look upon him. His wide, bloodshot eyes begged for deliverance, but he said nothing. "These three dishonored warriors will give their lives and be absolved of their crimes. For the first time in one thousand years, the Harpy's power will be made flesh!"

Mothers cheered, the sirens sang, and the three criminals trembled. The young sirens assisted them to their feet and shackled their chains to the effigy's base above their heads. The Harpy needed her sacrifices to suffer, and the law was such that they needed to have committed violent crimes to warrant that suffering. These men were either rapists, murderers, or both, but the ritual technically required none of these. They need only be warriors. Unlike sirens who were born, harpies were made.

"Step forward, Vidya, daughter of Sarta," Xenith beckoned. Vidya's stomach flopped as she went to stand by the Archon. She kept her arms taut at her sides.

"Do you accept Yasharra's gift so that you may become her instrument of war?"

Amongst the crowd, Vidya caught sight of her two closest friends whom she knew from infantry training. Phrea gave her an encouraging nod, and Daphne waved awkwardly, not smiling, but not frowning either. Vidya nodded back to them while trying to keep her nerves under control.

"I do," she said as loud and clear as she could.

"And with the power she grants you, do you swear to only use it to serve and protect Credence?"

Every eye in the audience fixed on Vidya. She glanced back to her sister for reasons she wasn't sure. Demeter nodded subtly out of reassurance or acceptance. Vidya couldn't tell.

"I do." She bowed. "For Yasharra and for Credence."

The crowd erupted in cheers again. Vidya turned to the Harpy's effigy and the men shivering in the knee-deep water.

They had slumped over, hanging from their chains in defeat. One of them with tears streaming down his face, the other two shaking in terror as each siren stepped into the pool, knives in hand. A vacuum of silence fell over the audience once more. Standing before their sacrifices, the sirens made deep incisions to the femoral arteries of their respective charges, as they'd been trained to do when performing the annual sacrifice made to the Harpy. The prisoners screamed in pain but it didn't take long for them to weaken, and the sirens left the pool, exposing the men and their gushing blood to the audience.

Vidya watched the dark droplets sink to the bottom of the basin then disperse through the water like a faint crimson smoke. The sight of it paralyzed her. It brought her out of her body for a moment, and she barely registered Xenith's gentle hand coaxing her forward.

"Now enter the bath," she whispered in her ear.

Vidya snapped out of her stupor and made way toward the pool. She lifted her dress and stepped in, doing her best to ignore her own reservations and the agonizing moans of the dying sacrifices. The water was much warmer than she'd expected, giving her a stab of nausea. Uncontrollable shivers coursed through her, and she could no longer feel her hands and feet. Vidya was no stranger to gore since she had enlisted in the infantry. Even before then, she had enjoyed watching the men fight each other for sport. She also had contended with more than her fair share of that same violence inflicted upon her by her husband in Rangardia, and she upon him in return. Memories of her time there bubbled to the surface, and she was too anxious to send them back down.

Macabre images of a marble tub filled with bloody water flashed through her mind. *Don't look in it . . . it's too late.* A scream threatened to burst from inside her. Reflections formed in the glassy pink water, and she couldn't be sure they were her own.

Taking deep breaths, she tried to calm herself, but standing up to her thighs in a pool of blood only made her want to clamber back up to the altar and throw herself into the sea. *No, I must do this.* Vidya walked to the center of the pool then turned to face the audience. She forced a smile through tears overflowing from her eyes.

Xenith began to recite the invocations. "With the blood of three, she will be given the strength of three, the resilience of three, and the longevity of three."

Vidya kept her eyes closed as she knelt down in the water. The blood was slippery beneath her knees, the metallic smell overwhelming her senses. The water grew colder, now up to her waist. She swallowed hard, trying her best not to vomit before the Assembly.

"Their flesh and bone will become her flesh and bone," Xenith said.

The sacrifices passed out, and their whimpers were reduced to naught. Their once tanned, olive complexions rendered slate gray, their blood almost completely depleted. If they weren't already dead, they would be in a few more minutes. Their paleness brought back a flash of what she had found in the blood-filled bathtub of her past. *Don't look!*

Vidya snapped her head away from the drained bodies and watched one of the young sirens empty a bag of her mother's beautiful cream plumes into the pool. They floated around her, becoming stained instantly with blood. *It's all right. Mother would have wanted this.*

"And the siren's feathers will become her feathers," Xenith announced. "Tonight, let us sing our siren's song to the Harpy and may Yasharra's wayward daughter finally return home!"

With a mighty beat of her wings, she ignited the crowd once again. The cheers, mixed with the siren's ever-singing voices, danced across the Altar like a hallowed wind.

Vidya sat down in the water, now neck-deep. She closed her eyes, took a deep breath, and held it before laying her head back and letting herself be fully submerged. The symphony of voices turned into a distorted drone. Vidya's skin prickled, becoming numb as her mother's blood-drenched feathers clung to her body.

Then, the water took on a mind of its own as it whirled over and beneath her, pushing the feathers around to her back as she struggled to hold her breath. Her arms and legs started convulsing, forcing her screams into the thickening liquid.

Shrieks from her own memories ripped through her to join with the muffled ones in her present. *What did you do? You sick bastard!*

Vidya's chest heaved—*I need to get out!*

Bursting from the surface, she gasped for air, choking back the blood running down her face and gagging on its brackishness. She clawed for the pool's edge and dragged her limp, trembling body out of the water, her dress stained red and clinging to her like a second skin. Pain shot through every one of her bones, in her shoulder blades worst of all. She tried to get up, but her legs were too heavy, her arms were too weak to support her weight even on all fours. She collapsed to her stomach, blood dripping into the cracks between the marble.

Storm clouds swirled above the Harpy's effigy, and a thundering boom cracked through the sky. The audience gasped and murmured, all their fears returning at once.

The pain in Vidya's back grew insurmountable. Each muscle and sinew stretched and contorted inside her, making her wheeze with every agonizing breath. Her bones popped and snapped—she could not find the wind to cry out. A new appendage tore through the skin, then another, extending from her flesh, and reached for the thundering sky.

2

Nothing Can Offend a Fae'ren

(Seven months later)

The sun beat down hard and relentless on the rolling dunes, creating waves across the desert. Small gusts of wind blew swirling sheets of sand that rose and fell in impossibly perfect patterns. Jeth focused his eyes on the distant umber peaks and the valleys between them.

Then the subtle sound of sand falling to his right. A tiny reptile head, the same dusty color as the mound it peeked out of, slithered from its hiding place. The snake wound sidelong and sidled up against Jeth's long bow, set down next to him. It was small. A viper with plenty of growing to do.

"Hey there, little fella," Jeth said.

He snatched the snake up, quick and precise, and held it below the jaw as it wound its body around his forearm. It was unlikely the little viper would produce much venom at this age, but he couldn't be too sure. He slid down the dune a few feet and let it go. It lifted its head, mouth opening wide in a silent threat. Jeth couldn't help but chuckle. "You're a real menace, now aren't you?" It disappeared in a flash to safety under the sand.

Scampering back to the top of the dune, Jeth lowered to his stomach once again. When he adjusted his eyes back to the distant hills, a palanquin of blue silk and gold appeared on the horizon. *Finally.*

"I see them," he called out before taking his bow in hand.

A head popped up from behind a ridge twenty strides away. Keeping low, Olivier rushed to Jeth's side. "Where?"

Jeth pointed out the palanquin in the distance. The box was being carried on two horizontal brass poles, tied to two camels being led by two camel pullers. One at the front, the other at the rear. Ten mounted escorts rode at the sides.

"Those are Herrani warriors. This has to be the Saf."

"They're too far away. It could just be a mirage," said Olivier.

"Trust me, Oli." He raised an eyebrow and cocked his head.

"Right. It's about damn time." Olivier shifted uncomfortably in his sweat-stained uniform.

Jeth couldn't agree more. Donning blue and white buttoned tailcoats and tan wrap-around head scarves the desert folk often wore had allowed the soldiers to blend in with the sandy terrain while keeping the sun from frying their scalps. But he wasn't used to wearing this much clothing back in the tepid old-growth forests of Fae'ren Province, let alone in an arid desert climate. They had spent two excruciating days sitting in wait for the party that was now coming toward them.

"I'll notify the others." Olivier went over the dune's ridge and disappeared down into the rift where four other soldiers were hiding. Jeth took an arrow from his quiver, strapped to his lower back, and waited for the palanquin to get within range.

The entourage became clearer as they descended the first dip in the sand dune. Each warrior wore charcoal-colored brigandine armor and light, wide-legged pants with leather shin guards bound up to their knees. Massive, curved swords hung at their sides. He counted nine males and one female. The Herrani allowed women to fight in their armies if they wanted, but this was the first he'd encountered since enlisting. The thought of her up against one of their men made him queasy.

Olivier returned. "Everyone is ready and out of sight. We take out the biggest threats first, and in the confusion, Baird and Tobin are going to rush them. They'll chase them further down the dune where Loche and the major will cut them off while we cover from up here."

"Sounds like a plan," said Jeth.

"I still don't see why the sorcerer can't just—" Olivier shook his hand in the air above his head "—put them all to sleep or something." He brushed the wind-blown sand from his ginger mustache, only to leave more behind.

Jeth shrugged. "Apparently, the most powerful wizard in Ingleheim needs to save his energy to fight the Overlord."

"That means it's up to us bowmen to handle everything, as always."

"Don't mind. I plan on earning my keep."

"Why?" Olivier scoffed as he got his bow ready. "So the urlings will see you as their equal? Keep dreaming, my Fae'ren friend. You can single handedly win Del'Cabria the war like the Great Gershlon before you, and they still won't let you near their women."

"Pfft. Urling women don't do much for me, anyway. They're so strange looking, I mean . . . what's the point of having such long pointy ears if they don't give them a hearing advantage?"

The palanquin disappeared between the dunes. Jeth hoped it would reappear on top of the next ridge in a few moments.

"I don't know, I kind of like them," Olivier said. "Besides, there's more to a woman than her ears, for Deity's sake."

"Yeah, like her eyes. Why are theirs so far apart?"

"For someone with such good eyesight, you can't see real beauty when it's right in front of you." Olivier chortled.

"It's not that they're not beautiful, just no more than human women. If the urlings didn't keep them so far out of reach from men like us—not that I blame them—they wouldn't seem so great. If you want the next best thing, get yourself a Fae. They look a little like urlings but with smaller ears, and there're no laws against them cozying up to a human every now and again, just as long as you treat them nice."

"You're speaking from experience, I take it?"

Jeth chuckled. "More from outside observation. Fae women don't touch fellas like me."

"Why? Because you're a scrawny varmint who doesn't treat them nice?" Olivier said snidely.

"I'm not scrawny, and I do treat them nice . . . or I mean, I would . . . " Jeth paused, not wanting to divulge his life story while waiting for their targets to get in range. "I've got a girl in Ludesa Province . . . if things go right out here, that is."

Memories of Lady Hanalei's soft red hair and mischievous green eyes drifted through Jeth's mind.

"Ah, say no more." Olivier patted him on the back, shaking sand loose from the folds in his scarf. "There is nothing like the ladies back home, I tell you. I got one waiting for me there myself."

"Then, let's get this mission over with so we can return to them, aye?" Jeth said, patting Olivier on the back in turn. *If she hasn't agreed to marry someone else while you're gone, otherwise these last seven months will have been for nothing.* He pushed the thought from his mind.

The palanquin's golden tip lumbered up the next ridge. Jeth wiped the beads of sweat from his brow and tucked a wayward lock of matted brown hair back under his head scarf.

Olivier harrumphed in good spirits. "If this doesn't turn into a suicide mission you mean, then yes."

The palanquin began to make its descent down the second dune.

"Guess we'll see, won't we? Our targets are in range."

"Alright." Olivier picked up his bow and ran back to his vantage point.

Jeth nocked an arrow and drew it back on his bowstring. He honed his eyesight, bringing the front Herrani warrior into stark focus apart from the others. His eagle-like vision, and his total control of it, came in handy in identifying targets, almost as if he were peering through a spyglass.

"I got the shot. Prepare to take out the big fella on the right after I get the one on the left," he shouted over to Olivier.

"Right," Olivier returned and took aim.

Jeth could no longer feel the dry desert heat as he blocked out all other senses save sight. He and the target were all that existed. With a deep breath, he exhaled and let the arrow fly. It cleanly pierced the warrior's forehead, knocking him off his saddle with scarcely a sound.

Before the Saf's entourage could react to the first death, Olivier's arrow zipped through the air and hit its target in the armored shoulder.

"Dammit!" he griped.

Jeth already had his second arrow nocked and shot the warrior in the side of the neck, finishing the job.

"Don't steal my kills!" Olivier spat.

"Sorry. Hey, there goes Grunt Number One and Grunt Number Two." Jeth brought Olivier's attention down to Baird and Tobin, rushing out to attack.

Tobin expertly dodged a sword swipe from one of the warriors before finding an opening and thrusting his spear through the man's side. Baird, on the other hand, didn't wait for an opening. He drove his into the horse's neck, killing it first before impaling the female rider trapped underneath. The horse's agonizing screech ripped through Jeth's ears, and he had to scale back his hearing to concentrate. *The urling doesn't fight fair, but at least he's effective.* He couldn't help but grimace.

The pullers tried to direct the camels as far from the violence as possible only to find Major Faron and Master Loche approaching from the other side. Two more Herrani warriors from behind the palanquin rode to meet them, where they clashed tulwar to long sword.

A dismounted warrior rose from the sand where Tobin had left him. "Hey, Tobin's man is getting away . . . he's coming in behind Loche."

"Got him." Olivier aimed and released in a single movement, hitting the Herrani in the throat, the older swordsman left unaware of the danger he had scantily avoided. "We're still outnumbered down there."

"Not for long," Jeth said.

He shot off another arrow to take out one of the warriors surrounding Baird, but those fighting Faron and Loche were moving about too sporadically for Jeth to fix his aim on any one.

His assistance this time would prove unnecessary. A Herrani's throat was slashed near to the bone and another's skull cracked. The older camel puller tried to join the fight, but soon had his torso run through with a spear. The soldiers dispatched all who remained, leaving only the rear puller standing. The young man dashed to the front camel, but Tobin restrained him in a bear maul. Baird stuck his spear into the sand and strode to the halted palanquin with his chest goosed.

Olivier threw down his bow and stretched his arms behind his head. "There. Our job is done. All the warriors are dead, and Baird's got the bride."

Baird climbed the brass poles and reached into the palanquin. As soon as he put his head behind the silk curtain, he went flying back out and landed flat on his ass.

"I wouldn't say that yet," Jeth quipped.

A young, white haired woman, draped in sheer blue silks, face covered up to her eyes in a glittering veil, and armed with a tulwar, sprang from the palanquin. As Baird attempted to get up, she tackled him, sat herself astride him, and raised her blade high, preparing to drive it through his chest. Loche grabbed her by the arm from behind and pulled her off. She spun around and sliced open his forearm, then kicked him away. Baird rolled to his spear, yanked it from the ground, and came at the woman.

"Do not hurt her!" Faron warned.

Spinning around, the Saf slashed at Baird. The blade bit into the wooden shaft of his spear that he used to block her attacks. The big urling held the weapon crossways and gave it a good spin, wrenching her weapon from her hands before pushing her hard with the shaft. The Saf gasped for air, then fell backward and rolled up to her feet with a burst.

Baird came at her again; this time she was ready. She grabbed hold of his spear, brought herself close, and kneed him hard in the groin. Now it was Baird gasping for air as he released his weapon to her and collapsed to his knees. With his own spear, the Saf whacked him across the head and proceeded to wail on the other surrounding men.

Major Faron sliced the spear in two with one swing of his sword, knocking both pieces from her hands. Jeth watched in awe as the now unarmed Herrani woman leaped and rolled away from each soldier's advances, the blue silk tails of her top billowing behind her, creating a spectacularly elegant image amongst the chaos.

Tobin tried to trap her from behind with the shaft of his spear, but she elbowed him in his sunburnt face and flipped him overhead. Faron came at her again. The Saf kicked up her tulwar from the ground to her hand, then cast the sand into Faron's face with a flick of the blade. Jeth laughed out loud, more out of disbelief than in humor.

All four men circled the woman. She stood in a defensive stance, breathing hard, her steel pointed out. As Faron began to speak low, Jeth honed his hearing to listen in. ". . . not going to hurt you. Put the sword down and cooperate."

It then dawned on Jeth, a non-violent way to end this.

He nocked an arrow.

"What are you doing?" Olivier said with a start.

Jeth shut the world out again as he focused on the Saf's silk tails trailing along the ground behind her. He let go of the bow string. The arrow pierced through her garments and into the sand at a diagonal. She gasped and spun around, stared at the arrow as if unsure what to think and gave the tails a tug. The men capitalized on her confusion and all advanced at once. She roared and swung her sword, but Faron blocked it and disarmed her. From there, they subdued her while she attacked only with curses.

"Great shot!" Olivier exclaimed, jogging over to Jeth.

Faron forced the Saf to her knees while Tobin went to tie her wrists and ankles. She looked around furiously before settling her gaze on the two archers at the top of the dune. Rage blazed through her pale blue eyes. They were her only visible facial feature, yet they had the power to make Jeth's spine tingle. He grinned and waved, but his gesture only increased the severity of her angered stare.

"Hah! Now there's a woman who will never touch you." Olivier slapped him on the back before sliding down the dune. Jeth chuckled and gulped thereafter.

By the time he reached the rest of the task force, the palanquin had been taken down from the camels, and the Saf's hands were tied to one of them. Her feet were bound together, so she sat sideways between the two humps. He'd never seen a Herrani woman this close before. The ones he had come across were from the poorer villages, wrapped head to toe in robes to protect their skin as they worked in the glaring sun. The Saf, however, wore sheer fabrics adorned with glittering garnets but left much of her honey brown skin exposed. His gaze poured over her ample bosom and drew down to her exposed midriff. It was only seconds before her furious glare found him again, and he immediately averted his eyes.

The portly horse master Roscoe came out of hiding with the team's mounts. He transferred some of their heavier gear onto the other camel's back, along with the Saf's belongings, including silken pillows, clothing, and accessories, as well as her weapon. The young puller's life was spared so he could manage the camels. Olivier, who was also the field medic, went to bind and treat Loche's wounded arm with alcohol.

The old man ground his teeth in pain.

"You're lucky, sir," Olivier said. "The gash isn't too deep. It should heal on its own well enough."

"I sure hope you're right, lad." Loche took a swig of the liquor himself and wiped the excess drops from his graying stubble. "I've had plenty of cuts and scrapes in my day, but this one stings worse than a fair lady's rebuff."

"That's probably the alcohol." Olivier took the flask from Loche's hand and placed it back in his medical bag.

Loche waved him along, muttering a thank you, and went to review his maps.

The Mage from Ingleheim, Meister Melikheil, rode up on his white steed. He wore dark desert robes over his tailcoat and vest, yet he didn't appear uncomfortable in the heat. Jeth stared at him, one part with wonder and another with nervous caution. The man's imposing presence set shivers down his spine on the best of days. He spent most of his time meditating and standing watch over nothing in particular, staring out into empty spaces with an air of superiority like a conqueror acquiring great nations in his mind. *Although, what do you expect from a man whose people worship an active volcano.*

"Master Loche, how far is the nearest watering hole?" Faron asked the navigator.

Tobin turned from readying his mount to scoff to his fellow spearman beside him. "A watering hole? Near these dust mounds? Hardly."

Loche pointed to his maps and said, "If we keep heading northwest, we will reach Sunil territory by nightfall. It's relatively neutral ground and a little less destitute. There's a lake formed by runoff from the Serpentine River."

"Finish watering your horses, soldiers. We have a long trek ahead of us. Tobin, keep an eye on the hostage." Faron mounted his bay gelding and went to the front of the party.

"I'll keep two eyes on her, Major." Tobin winked at the girl who narrowed her own eyes in disgust.

"And if she tries anything, I'll keep more than my eyes on her," Baird added. He took her pant leg and rubbed the sheer fabric between his fingers. The Saf kicked him square in the face with both feet.

Baird staggered back, clutching a bloody nose. Olivier shook his head and went to tend to it, but Baird jerked away from him and turned back to the captive. "Bitch! How would you like to be tied to the underside of that camel!"

"Stand down, soldier!" the major called down the line.

Melikheil nudged his horse away from the men. The epitome of disdain.

"Aye, Major." Baird spat blood onto the sand.

When the major turned away, Olivier held a handkerchief out to Baird. He snatched it, wiped the blood from his long hook nose, and stormed off. Olivier made a face and Jeth couldn't stop himself from snickering.

Baird spun right back around. "What are you laughing at, bowman?"

"Definitely not you getting knocked about the head for the third time today, that's for sure." He cringed. *Why can't you say nothing for a change? Nothing is always better.*

"You need to learn to shut that filthy gob of yours."

"You know, I was just thinking that. . . ." he replied with a nervous chuckle.

"I will quite enjoy wiping that shit-eating grin off your face, Fae scum," growled Baird as he took steps toward him.

"Fae scum? No, Fae are the pointed ear people of Fae'ren. I have round ears."

"You dare correct me?" Baird seized Jeth by the scruff.

"I just mean, if you're going to insult me, do it right, that's all." He winced again. *Take the urling oaf's advice and shut your gob!*

"Don't bother with him," said Tobin. "Nothing can offend a Fae'ren. Despite all our efforts to civilize them, they remain shameless. One cannot insult something with no shame."

"Immune to insults? What about sound beatings?" Baird raised his fist, and Jeth flinched. This time his mouth stayed shut. A punch in the face was preferable to being caught fighting an urling way above his station, regardless who started the brawl.

"Sir Baird, you shouldn't over exert yourself after that blow you took to the gonads. Are you sure you don't need me to take a look at them for you?" *Oli, always with the perfect timing.*

"Excuse me?" Baird let Jeth go and stared at Olivier like he had just told him the sky was brown.

"He's a medic," said Jeth, readjusting his scarf. "He wants to make sure your balls are all right."

"Where do you two get off speaking to me this way?"

"Soldiers!" barked Faron. "Mount up and move out!"

"Major, these humans need to be reminded of their place."

"All of you stop prattling on like petulant children and get back on your bloody horses!" He narrowed his severe gaze at all four men, his angular features tautening, his lips forming a hard, thin line.

"Aye, Major," the soldiers said in unison. Baird flashed both Jeth and Olivier a dirty look and climbed his mount.

As the task force rode, the bowmen fell farthest back while the spearmen rode in the middle with the camels. The swordsmen, horse master, and sorcerer rode up front. The Ingle Mage moved his hands about, pulling at the air as if playing an imaginary harp. A mist began to form and lift as clouds above the soldiers' heads. Sprinkles of water coated Jeth's sweat-stained skin as he rode underneath them. For all the unease the Ingle Mage brought, it was all worth it for his water magic ability alone.

"Thanks for your help back there, Oli," Jeth said.

"Don't mention it. Boys like Baird and Tobin need to be corrected sometimes . . . too bad that often results in a beating for those doing the correcting."

"Not sure I understand your methods, though. Talking about a man's testicles wouldn't be my first choice to diffuse a situation."

"As a medical professional, I was legitimately concerned for the poor man's injury." Olivier laughed.

"It's nice to know that our balls are safe in your hands."

Olivier's freckled face reddened as he cleared his throat. "Alright, that's enough now."

"I'd let you examine my balls, Oli." He grinned. He always got a kick out of how easy it was to embarrass Del'Cabrians, even the human variety from Ludesa Province.

"I should've let Baird knock you around a bit. It would do you some good."

"I'd let you treat my *wounds*," he said, feigning offense.

"I'll give you some wounds if you don't shut it."

The two men got their laughs out as Tobin and Baird shot frequent glares in their direction.

The sand gave way to dry, rocky plains as the task force came upon the Sunil territory. Towering sandstone formations materialized on the horizon, an otherworldly backdrop that could never be reached no matter how long they rode toward it. The temperature cooled considerably as the sun started to set, but the winds only picked up speed.

Jeth welcomed the change of climate and took the opportunity to remove his headwear, allowing his brown fairy locks to tumble down to his shoulders. He dropped his reins and let his horse follow the herd unguided as he wrapped a few of the front strands from either side around the others and carefully tied them together to keep the matted sets from flailing in the wind.

As Loche had indicated, the task force came upon the watering hole around nightfall. The small basin was located at the center of an expansive arena of red castle-shaped cliffs, hoodoos, and plateaus.

The men all dismounted and started making camp for the night. "Jeth. You take first watch." Faron said, passing him by with a crate of supplies in hand. Jeth rejoiced inside at not having to help with the tedious nightly routine and took off to the top of the highest reachable plateau he could find. From there he had an excellent view of the Sunil Tribe Lands.

The sun set, and a brilliant yellow light streaked across the entire horizon. Out from the desert edge, the clouds shifted from yellow to the brightest oranges he had ever seen, a disquieting sight. He was trapped in this barren landscape, so dry and hot that the sky burst into flames each night.

"All there is out here is death," he whispered to himself. For a split second, he felt a longing for the sights and smells of his forest home, but pushed those sentiments back down where they belonged. "There's no going back. It's not your home anymore."

When the sun had sunk beneath the earth, the night swallowed up all but the stars. The one full moon, and the second crescent moon, emitted just enough light that he could possibly make out travelers below, but there were none.

A few hours later, Olivier joined him on the plateau with two oil lamps. "You should go get some gruel before it's gone."

Jeth's stomach growled audibly at the very mention of food. "Thanks. Good luck seeing anything out there." He started off toward the path.

"Jeth, wait!" His friend held out the second lamp to him, brows cinched with a smirk on his face. "You'll need this to light your way . . . ?"

"Oh, right. Thanks." Jeth took it from Olivier and made his way back to camp. As valuable as his eyesight was for seeing long distances, it didn't help him much in the dark.

When he arrived at the pot of bean stew brewing above the fire pit, he had to scrape the last bits from the bottom. On his way to find a seat, Baird accidentally on purpose bumped him, knocking his bowl to the ground.

"Real nice, Baird."

"Sometimes the man on watch misses out on dinner. . . . Ever so sorry." Baird brushed past him to take a seat by the fire, leaving Jeth staring down at his fallen meal. *Most of it should still be good,* he thought. With shrugging sigh, he recovered what he could from the ground.

"Oh look, he's going to eat it anyway," Baird jeered. "I keep forgetting that dirt is a delicacy where he's from."

Roscoe snickered as he slurped down his stew, making such revolting smacks, Jeth was forced to scale back his hearing. The camel puller, mending the camels' saddle blankets, made eye contact with him as if to say—*Are you going to take that from them? Aren't you supposed to be one of them*—?At least, that's what he imagined the young Herrani was thinking.

A myriad of backhanded responses were at the ready, but Loche was sitting there already giving him a reprimanding eye. Swallowing hard, he plunked himself down on the rocks opposite of Baird and Roscoe and shoved a spoonful of stew in his mouth to ensure that no words would come out of it.

Roscoe snorted through his pig-like nose. "How do you find it, Fae'ren?"

He gave a broad grin, his mouth full. "It's your best batch yet, Roscoe." The grit of it made him want to gag. "In fact, it could use more sand." He took some from below the rock he sat on, daintily sprinkled it into his stew and followed up with another bite. The jarring crunch of the particulates was unpleasant, but it was worth it just to witness the disgusted look on Baird's face. Roscoe snorted with laughter and shook his head.

"You're lucky you're proficient with that bow. Otherwise, they'd have you cleaning out the chamber pots at the prisoner of war camps with the rest of your ilk," Baird huffed.

"Luck has nothing to do with how proficient one is with a bow, just as it's not with your spear," said Loche. He had finished eating and was now sitting by the water basin cleaning and redressing his wound. It had swelled considerably since they set out from the dunes. A hint of rot hung in the air. *That's not good.*

"Of course, Master Loche, all I meant was . . ." Baird stammered.

Loche pointed to Jeth with his thumb. "This lad here might be the best archer this army has. Pay respect where respect is due, will you?"

An awkward hush fell over the campfire. Flames popping under the cast iron pot were the only replies Loche received. The swordsman returned to wrapping the bandages around his arm, his teeth grinding and eyes watering.

"You need help with that, sir?" Baird's voice was demure.

"It'll be fine. Needs more alcohol. Excuse me, lads." Loche rose to his feet with a groan, nodded to Baird and Roscoe—not Jeth or the puller—and lumbered toward the tent he shared with Faron.

The remaining three men ate in silence. Jeth couldn't bear to finish his stew now that the jest was over. "Where's Tobin?" he asked, trying to break the tension Loche left behind.

"Sir Tobin," Baird corrected, "is guarding the desert bitch." He motioned his head toward one of the far tents behind him.

"Tell me, Sir Baird." Jeth made a slight bowing motion with his head. "Do you call every woman you come across a bitch or just the ones that kick you in the face?"

Baird put down his stew, jaw tight, but Loche's warning must have had some effect on him. He didn't move to attack this time.

"That white-haired vixen is a daughter of our enemy, the most wicked sorcerer of our age. Don't think for a moment she wouldn't cut our throats in our sleep if she had the chance. Desert people possess reptilian blood, you know? They can't be trusted."

"Sure, but Fae'ren have the blood of fairies, and urlings the blood of the ashray. Most of us can trace our lineage back to some ancient being or other, so what's the difference?"

"For one thing, the ashray are pure, enlightened beings, the naja are savage beasts, and fairies probably don't exist."

Jeth snorted into his bowl. "Alright then." *Don't ask the Fae'ren sitting right next to you or anything*, he thought.

Baird continued is haughty rant. "Del'Cabrian ladies are dignified and carry themselves with poise. They dress modestly and strive to be pure in the eyes of the Deities That Cannot Be Named. Now, recall how the Saf was about to present herself to her betrothed."

"Doesn't leave much to the imagination," Roscoe said as he licked his bowl clean.

Baird looked over to the slobbering human beside him and turned up his lip in disgust. Roscoe belched. "I'm going to make sure those horses are good and pegged down for the night. See you lads in the morning." And with that, he was gone.

Baird continued, "Desert women are all a bunch of obnoxious, self-serving whores that dare to fight as men do. I say, if they refuse to act like ladies, then I will address them accordingly."

Bringing his attentions back to his bowl, Jeth rolled his eyes, wondering how many desert women Baird had the pleasure of meeting before he came to such a conclusion. He was satisfied with leaving the subject alone until a small male voice peeped up.

"Women of Herran have as much right to fight for their tribe as anyone else," said the camel puller.

"Did anyone say you could speak, desert dog?" Baird snapped.

The puller cast his eyes away and continued washing the blankets, yet all the while Jeth heard the puller's heart rate pick up at an alarming pace.

Just then, Faron burst from his tent and marched over to the campfire. "Sir Baird, you're replacing Olivier on watch tonight. Send him to my tent immediately."

"Aye, Major." Baird tossed his bowl aside and went to task.

"And Jeth," said Faron as he walked over to him.

He stood with a start and nodded. "Yes, Major?"

"You will spend the night watching Meister Melikheil."

Faron's order caused a tingling sensation at the base of his spine. Since their operation began, there had been no need to guard the Mage. Why now all of the sudden?

"Come." Faron motioned for him to follow. "As you know, our mission is to prevent the union of the Herrani and Tezkhan tribes by abducting the bride. But she also serves as our means for drawing out the Overlord to do combat with Meister Melikheil."

"Right here at this camp?" He gulped, trotting along to keep up with the taller man's stride.

"He intends to use his spirit magic to confirm when the Overlord will arrive. Once we know of his location, we will return to home base and leave the Saf here with him. It will be your job to monitor him while he performs his spell and report his findings back to me. Understood?"

"But how does he know Nas'Gavarr is going to—?"

"Is that clear, soldier?"

"Aye, Major." Jeth saluted and scurried off, only to realize that he was heading toward the Saf's tent. Spinning on his heels, he made way to the pavilion at the south end of camp.

Reluctantly, Jeth peered through the flaps to find the statuesque man sitting in a chair in the center of the tent, long black hair tied back, and mustache and goatee freshly trimmed. His eyes were closed, both hands placed over top his brass walking stick. Melikheil had removed his desert garb and wore a black buttoned tailcoat and cravat. He appeared even more out of place than usual. A cold sweat started to trickle down Jeth's back.

"M-Meister?" he peeped as he stepped inside.

The Mage opened his dark eyes languidly and proceeded to stare through him like he were nothing more than an apparition. Melikheil wouldn't answer, so he resumed. "Have you started without me?"

"No, I'm gathering essence aura to prepare," he replied in his severe Ingle dialect. He then stood, towering above Jeth almost twice over, hence the extra tall tent to accommodate him.

"Great . . . uh . . . Meister . . . or do you prefer Herr Wizard?" he blurted with a nervous chuckle.

Melikheil's daunting gaze narrowed down at him as if considering whether he should crush him like a bug. *Yes, let's attempt to jest with the most powerful Mage in Ingleheim and Del'Cabria combined.*

"Meister is fine," Melikheil stated, blunt as a hammer, then turned away, allowing Jeth to exhale. "I assume your major informed you of why you are here." Melikheil moved the chair from the middle of the tent.

"Sort of. . . ." he said. "He told me you can track Nas'Gavarr with magic. But permission to ask how?"

Melikheil grabbed his bed roll and started laying it out on the floor. Just then, a little brown serpent slithered out from beneath it, running straight into Melikheil's boot. Without hesitation, the Mage squashed its head with the end of his staff and flicked it out of the tent.

The glint in the Mage's eye made the breath catch in Jeth's chest.

"Yes," he replied. "His daughter would have a rapport with him as would all his children. She would have reached out to him the moment we captured her. I will be projecting my spirit into the Spirit Chamber where I will be able to sense him."

"Right, right." Jeth nodded, not having a clue what the man was talking about. "And you need me to watch you do that?"

"Spiritual projection is difficult and dangerous for any Mage. If my spirit roams too far from my body, it can become lost forever." Melikheil took a seat and motioned for him to sit in the chair. "If you see me convulsing at any point, hit me as hard as you can in the chest. That should bring my spirit roaring back. Understood?"

"Convulsing, hit you, got it."

"I've done this many times before. I don't anticipate you having to do anything, but it's hard to say how far my spirit must roam."

"What if Nas'Gavarr doesn't come—sends someone else to retrieve his daughter on his behalf?"

"He won't," Melikheil said. "Through their rapport, he should be able to sense my spirit in her vicinity. He knows who I am. He knows what I am here to do. And he will face me." Melikheil laid down on his back.

"Do you really think you can beat him on your own? I-I mean, not that I doubt you, it's just . . . the Overlord is immortal and that."

Sitting back up, Melikheil ran his tongue over his teeth. Jeth feared he was getting on the Mage's nerves. "You are smart to doubt, young herr. No Mage in history has come up against Nas'Gavarr and lived to tell of it. However, I'm the first one who truly understands his power. No man is immortal, but some can find ways to live unnaturally long lives. Nas'Gavarr is the only Mage known to hold dominion over all three components of existence . . ."

"Essence, spirit, and flesh," Jeth finished.

Melikheil nodded, raising a black eyebrow. "Ah, the Fae'ren people are not ignorant of magic, I see."

Jeth shrugged. Back in Fae'ren forest, the fairies taught him about the essences of fire, water, wind, earth, light, and life force. All he remembered, however, was that some people were in tune to the auras that those essences emanated. Those people were known as Essence Mages. He didn't know much about Spirit or Flesh Mages, only to be extremely wary of them.

"I believe Nas'Gavarr uses a combination of essence and flesh magic to keep himself alive, making him near impossible to harm," Melikheil said.

"But you can harm him, right?"

Melikheil brought in hand his staff, adorned with a sapphire clutched in the talons of a brass raven. "I have discovered how to concentrate essence aura in such a way, that I have stored years' worth of it in this sapphire that otherwise could only have stored enough for a few days if I'd absorbed it naturally."

"Really? How?" Jeth stared at the tiny blue gem, wide-eyed.

The Mage placed it on the ground beside him and waved a long index finger. "Enough. All you need worry about is making sure nothing happens to me or this staff while I'm out, or we are all doomed." He laid back down, clasped his hands over his stomach, and closed his eyes.

Jeth sat and stared at Melikheil lying there in his black suit like a cadaver awaiting its funeral.

After a few moments, he whispered, "Are you projecting yet?"

There was a long silence before Melikheil uttered a curt, "No."

"How do you even do it?"

The Meister sighed again, this time louder. "By making my spirit strong enough to exist outside the body. It comes through a process known as spirit breaking."

"How do you break a spirit?" he asked, not sure if he wanted to know.

"Years of self-torture."

Jeth said nothing after that. Was the Mage making it all up to intimidate him? People from the Mountain Ranges of Ingleheim were known to be as intimidating as they were tall, and they were certainly tall.

He managed to remain silent for the next half hour, only honing his hearing to listen to Melikheil's strong, droning heartbeat.

Eventually, he felt brave enough to get out of his chair and walk over to the vacant Mage. *There's really no spirit in there. You're looking at a live body with no sentience; you could probably do anything to him, and he wouldn't be aware . . . anything but hit him in the chest.* He waved his hands inches from the man's face. "Meister. . . . Meister Melikheil . . . ? Herr Wizard?"

No reaction. *You better find something to occupy yourself. It could be a long night.*

He spent the remaining hours sharpening his arrowheads and repairing damaged fletching while the wind whistled through the hoodoos, and dried shrubbery rustled against the rippling canvas of the tent. He allowed his thoughts to wander along welcome memories of Lady Hanalei's soft red hair and captivating smile. Then came the not so welcome memories. The fairies and how they callously—

"Three days," a deep croak sounded from beside him.

"Gah!" Jeth threw his carving tool.

The cadaver rose from its coffin, erect and silent. Jeth's heart pounded in his chest.

"Nas'Gavarr . . ." Melikheil looked straight ahead at nothing. ". . . is three days from here."

3

The Pecking Order

"So, how did you end up in Ludesa anyway?" Olivier asked with a heave as he and Jeth lugged a tin basin sloshing with fresh water from the lake.

Now that the task force knew when Nas'Gavarr would be upon them, they spent the next day preparing supplies. The two were busy packing the lake to take home with them. Or at least that's what it felt like. Without Melikheil to provide water, they would need as much for the long journey home as they could carry.

"To find work, why else?" Jeth replied. They hoisted the basin between their shoulders and carried it up the sandy embankment. "I break horses and herd cattle at a ranch there."

"I've heard lots of your people are laboring on Ludesan farms," Olivier said. "I always wondered why they'd leave the communes that supposedly provide for their every need."

Jeth scoffed. "Maybe a long time ago. Now, it's plagues, poverty, and other gifts from the good ol' Confederation Period."

"The Second Wave passed almost a decade ago." The men lowered the basin near Faron and Loche's tent. "Is it still that bad living there?"

"A question only a *true* ignorant imperialist would ask." He chuckled.

"You do realize my province was also swallowed up by urling expansion."

"Sure, a hundred years before Fae'ren and by will of its own. Not a drop of blood spilled if I remember the tales." He grabbed a bundle of empty waterskins piled near Roscoe, cooking the day's lunch, and handed some off to Olivier.

"True, Del'Cabria never had to invade Ludesa with swords or bows, but they invaded all the same. Most of us didn't like it any more than your people did," the red-headed bowman replied. "We did have more time to adapt to urling rule, I suppose."

"And now your province is the second richest in the Kingdom."

"That'll happen when you produce most of the Kingdom's food. Maybe Fae'ren should do something similar," Olivier said with a toothy grin beneath his mustache.

"Like what? Provide the Kingdom all its drinking water? No, wait, Elmifel Province has the monopoly on that . . . as well as all the wine." Jeth winked.

"You got all that wood." Olivier bent down to start filling the waterskins along with Jeth. "If your people didn't worship all the trees, you could cut a few down and make a fortune."

"We don't worship them. . . that much . . . just one really, and it's a very impressive tree, mind you."

"I bet it is." Olivier grinned.

Jeth often enjoyed his and Olivier's political discussions, even when they trod on sour territory. Ludesa Province was home enough for him, its people, for the most part, warm and accepting. No one paid too much mind to where a man came from as long as he understood his place and worked hard. For Jeth, any place at all, even at the bottom, was a step up from where he had been.

When they returned with full waterskins over their shoulders, Major Faron was talking to Baird just outside the Saf's tent. Faron was stone-faced as always, and Baird bit his cheek with anxiety and nodded repeatedly. "Go retrieve Sir Tobin from watch and come to the Meister's tent for a briefing," Faron finished.

Baird did as he was told and Faron approached Jeth and Olivier. Both lowered the waterskins, and Olivier erected himself, taut as a bowstring. "We're right behind you, Major."

"No. You need to tend to Master Loche again, his wound is getting worse." The major swallowed hard and wiped sweat from his glistening cross-cropped hair that made his pointed urling ears appear even longer.

"Aye, Major." Olivier marched to his patient's tent.

"Jeth, you will watch the Saf. She hasn't eaten or drunk a thing since we arrived. See to it that she does. I don't want her dropping dead of dehydration before the Overlord gets here."

"Aye, Major," he repeated with a curt nod and left.

Faron called after him, "Oh, and don't talk to her any more than you have to and absolutely no touching her unless to prevent her escape." He then turned on his heel and was gone.

Jeth's nostrils flared as he stretched his neck to the side with a crack before picking up one of the waterskins. *Tell that to your spearmen, for Mother's sake*, he fumed within his mind.

Still shaking his head, he went to Roscoe at the fire pit to grab a bowl of stew and headed for the square, floorless tent where the Saf was being held. He walked through the rolled open flap and found her curled up on two cushions, her wrists and ankles bound with a rope tied to a metal peg, embedded deep into the ground underneath a chair. The tent's canvas filtered the blazing sun's light and gave the entire space an apricot hue.

He placed the bowl of stew on the small table near the sleeping hostage, and she immediately jerked awake. "Wha . . . ?" Her voice was muffled under the veil she still wore. It no longer lent her an air of opulence or mystery. It was just something she hid behind.

Jeth put his arms up and backed off. "It's all right, it's just food."

"Oh," she muttered, glancing at the bowl then waved it away with her bound hands.

"Suit yourself." He unscrewed the cap on the waterskin's spout and held it out to her. "You do need to drink something. You're in a desert."

The Saf gave him a dry, *'I know. I live in one, you moron'* glare.

"Alright then, more for me." He cast his head back and drank the refreshing liquid in obnoxious gulps until it ran down his face.

The Saf stared up at him, blinking furiously. "Stop that!"

"Oh . . . you want some?" he offered.

The Saf snatched it out of his hand, and he chuckled to himself as he sat in the chair. She put the skin under her veil to drink, but the cumbersome material got in the way. With a grunt of frustration, she unclipped it from her hair band and tossed it aside. She drank with such urgency the skin deflated into a crumpled hide. Breathing hard, the Saf wiped her mouth and threw the skin back at him where he plucked it out of the air. His gaze caught her unveiled face, and he fumbled it before it hit the ground.

Her skin, decorated with tiny iridescent gemstones around her cheekbones and temples, illuminated like bronze. Her soft, youthful features, full lips, and ice blue eyes made her look both innocent and wicked all at once. A powerful combination.

"F-feel better now?"

The Saf didn't move or say a word, only continued to stare at him with eyes like frost in the desert heat. Jeth's pulse quickened.

"You're the archer that put a hole through my wedding garments," Her Herrani dialect made the words sound like a river flowing off her tongue, a river that could pull Jeth under and drown him if he weren't careful.

He nervously scratched at his scruffy beard and shrugged. "Shouldn't matter now, because you're not getting married anymore. Though, I suppose you'd rather be with your new husband than tied up by enemy soldiers."

The woman pursed her lips and narrowed her unsettling gaze. *When did you start sweating so much?* Jeth thought.

"And look on the bright side," he continued. "It's rumored that the Tezkhan Chief already has about . . . ten wives he stole from other tribes so . . . you can probably do better."

After a few blinks of her long white eyelashes, her features softened, and she appeared about to grin. She didn't.

She ran her hands down the blue silk material of her pants, stopping at the tear made by his arrow. "He is a barbarian, no doubt about that, but lucky for me, I get to contend with eight more right here. I think I would have preferred the company of Chief Ukhuna of the Tezkhan raiders."

"Ouch." Jeth mimed being shot in the heart, and then bent down close in his seat as if to tell her a secret. "In your present situation, it might be hard for you to believe, but we aren't *all* bad."

"Oh?" She raised a white eyebrow in feigned interest and leaned into him with a matched conspiratorial tone. She spied around the room and flashed him a dangerous smile before continuing at a whisper, "Last night, the blonde one with the sunburn insisted on watching me urinate because he thought I might try to escape. As if I could make a run for it mid-stream with an armed soldier holding the rope tied to my ankles." Her smile slanted to a scowl that paralyzed him in his seat. "So, if you were wondering why I refused to eat or drink . . . now you know."

Jeth released a drawn-out sigh. "That's uh . . . sorry . . . and they're supposed to be the civilized ones."

His stomach churned, recalling how he too had contended with numerous brutes like Baird and Tobin for most of his life. He relied on his quick-witted remarks and good humor to distract them from the notion that he was dirt beneath their feet. "Don't worry. You won't have to put up with us much longer."

She scoffed and drew her gaze down to her hands. "Isn't that Mage you brought with you going to try to kill the Overlord?"

He scratched his head again. "Uh . . . you know, I shouldn't be talking to you."

She shook her head and before long, came breathy laughter.

"What's so funny?"

"Your wizard is doomed." The Saf giggled like it was a joke she alone understood.

Jeth could only shrug in response. If anyone could defeat the Overlord of Herran, it would be Meister Melikheil, but he was not about to explain why to the hostage.

"Are you going to eat that?" Jeth leaned over to pick up the bowl of now cold stew on the table.

The Saf grabbed it and held it away from him.

Jeth sat back in the chair as the Saf finally ate a few bites of her meal. In the meantime, he took out his knife and started cleaning small granules from his fingernails. Twenty minutes later, the Saf was done.

She wiped her mouth and asked, "Where are you from, Del'Cabrian?"

Squirming in his seat, he said, "Oh no. I'm not telling *you* that."

"Why not?"

"Because anything I say to you, I might as well be saying to your father.

And I'm not especially comfortable with him knowing where I'm from." Jeth slid his knife back in his scabbard.

"Do you really think the Overlord cares where you're from?" She snorted. "As if you're that important, he'd waste his precious time tracking *you* down."

"He's got all the time in the world."

The Saf pouted, saying nothing more as she slumped against her propped up pillows. Jeth tapped his fingers on the armrest, resenting the silence until she looked up at him from under long lashes, eyes round. *What's the Overlord going to do to your home? You're never going back there,* he thought. "Why do you even care where I'm from?"

"I don't know. . . ." she began in a softer tone, smoothing out her pants. "You're different than the others. You don't speak like them or look like them. They don't seem to accept you as one of them, and yet you fight alongside them. That is very curious to me."

Her frost-blue eyes continued to blaze into his, generating a heat within the tent of which the scorching sun outside was not the source.

"I've been told I can be very intriguing," he said. No one has ever told you that, not once.

The Saf bit her bottom lip to stifle a giggle. "I see." She then became serious. "You don't owe those men anything. Why fight for their way of life? For their king?"

Jeth thought back to all the abuse he'd been subjected to since enlisting. Despite his archery skill, which allowed him to be a part of this integral mission—one that could win Del'Cabria the war—he feared his achievements would still go unrecognized. *You probably should have stayed on Talbit's ranch.*

"I was told that the only way a man like me can move up is through military honors."

"Move up what?"

"In status—the pecking order."

"I don't understand that." The Saf shook her head.

"You don't have social statuses in Herran?" he asked with surprise.

"You mean a system in which the privileged on the top rule over others based on some made-up standard? No." She looked him straight in the eye. "For you to risk your life out here for a chance to move up in this silly *pecking order* means that it must be very hard on the bottom."

"Not so bad," he said, rubbing the back of his neck. "Back where I'm from, everyone is relatively equal. Everyone contributes, and has a voice . . . well, almost everyone." He cleared his throat, not wanting to get into why he couldn't be a part of that because of some inane superstition.

"Then why desire to move up at all?" She inched closer, looking up at him from her knees.

"Some of us have to play by other people's rules to survive." He crossed his arms over his chest and shifted away.

"And that is why they will never change," she said. "So, stop playing the game."

"You think it's that easy, do you?"

She nodded. "In Herran, Sunil, and Odafi, all men and women are free to do as they please and will bear the responsibilities that come with that freedom."

Jeth raised an eyebrow. "Like the freedom to choose who to marry for instance?"

"Freedom to marry at all."

"To be clear. You're *choosing* to marry Chief Ukhuna of the Tezkhan raiders and are in no way being forced to by your father," he said with suspicion.

The Saf laughed out loud. She was missing one of her upper molars, but it did little to challenge her beauty and, in fact, added to her charm. "Yes, I'm choosing to marry the Chief, but only temporarily."

"Huh?"

"Your major didn't tell you, did he?"

"Tell me what?" His nerves fluttered about in his stomach. *You shouldn't be talking to her for this long, you goat.*

"I'm not a daughter of Nas'Gavarr," she said.

"What? Are you a decoy or something?"

"Nas'Gavarr has no use for decoys. I'm a thief, posing as Saf'Raisha, intent on robbing the Tezkhan Chief of something extremely valuable."

"Why are you telling me this?" His eyebrows cinched together as he cocked his chin to the side.

She closed the last small gap between them and whispered, "I can be persuaded to split my part of the earnings with you. If . . ." she bit her lip again and shrugged, ". . . you let me go?"

He leaned back and chuckled deep in his chest. *Of course,* he pushed his tongue against the inside of his cheek. This was not the first time he had been manipulated by someone who saw him as a fool. He could smell it in the air before she opened her mouth. Yet there was something about her proclaiming she was not the real Saf that gave him pause.

"You don't want to keep fighting this war, do you?" she said in breathless wonder. "You deserve much better than this. These Del'Cabrians will never accept you into their society. In the desert, the lowest of men can find whatever it is they seek. Be it riches, respect . . . *pleasure.*" A wicked giggle escaped her at that word. "But it will not come to those who are unwilling to take it."

It would be easy for Jeth to take her up on her offer, even knowing if he helped her today she would betray him tomorrow. Might be less infuriating than being seen as shit under a horse's hooves or less futile than trying to prove himself worthy in the eyes of Hanalei's father.

He hissed aloud at the last thought, which sounded too much like the fancies of a young girl. The Saf kept her eyes on his but didn't say a word.

Voices rang from outside. Faron, Baird, and Tobin left the Mage's pavilion. The major flicked his hand at Tobin, sending the blonde urling up the hill for watch before ducking into Loche's tent with Baird.

Jeth's attention was pulled back to his charge when she put her hand on his knee, her eyes glossy.

"Please," she begged. "Your major won't listen. You have to help me. You will be a wealthy man if you do."

"Hold on." He got up to leave.

"Where are you going?" she asked, grasping his pant leg. He took her wrist and pulled it aside to check her bindings. The peg was secure. He started for the exit again.

"Stop! I want to ask you something."

He groaned. "What?"

"That older swordsman. The one I cut. Haven't seen him up and about. Is he all right?"

"Why do *you* care?" His brow furrowed.

Baird burst out of Loche's tent and proceeded to kick over a carton of rations. He clutched at his head, running his hands over his brown, sweat-slicked hair, breathing hard.

"I'll be right back," Jeth muttered.

After asking Roscoe to keep an eye on the Saf, he approached the frustrated spearman. "What's going on?"

Baird snapped his head around, eyes red with dark circles underneath like the last hour had been more strenuous than every day since the start of their mission combined. He squatted down on his heels and rested his forehead against his thumbs. "Master Loche . . ."

Jeth stared down at him, listening to Baird's heart pump thick blood through his chest, his own growing heavier. "You two have history?"

Baird stood back up and wiped his dry nose. "You can say that. We've been fighting together since this blasted war started. I've seen him cleave through hordes of naja without breaking a sweat. And a little scratch by some bitch's blade does him in? It doesn't make any ashray-licking sense." He stood back up and stormed off toward the lake.

Jeth entered Loche's tent to find Faron and Olivier kneeling over the navigator, now sickly white and covered in rivers of sweat. The stench of rot and burnt flesh was overpowering. He scaled back his sense of smell, but the thickness of the air lingered, along with a sharp, foreign odor.

"Cauterize it again," Faron commanded.

"I've done it twice already. It's not working," protested Olivier.

"Then perhaps you are doing it incorrectly."

"With all due respect, Major. I learned how to cauterize a wound before I ever picked up a bow. Some kind of desert pathogen must have infected his wound."

Loche opened his peeling lips and rasped, "Don't even think about putting that hot poker on me again. You should all be getting ready to leave this place. Get as far from here as your horses will take you." He leaned his head to the bag of whiskey in the tent's corner. "Leave me a bottle, and you boys take the rest. Have yourselves one good night. I'll be fine here."

Faron slowly rose to his feet and exhaled heavily through his nose. His tired gaze finally fell on Jeth standing there. "Why aren't you guarding the Saf?"

"She's claiming she's not. But a thief posing as her," Jeth replied.

The major rolled his eyes and led Jeth out of the tent. "Do not believe a word that woman says." He pointed at him with a rigid forefinger.

"What if she's telling the truth?" Jeth said. "Don't you find it strange that Nas'Gavarr would send his daughter to meet her betrothed with nothing more than ten of his warriors and two camels? Why wouldn't he escort her himself if this marriage is so important?"

"She has the marking on her back that all of Nas'Gavarr's daughters have. I checked as soon as we secured her. The Meister confirmed her father is on his way. She is without a doubt, the Saf. You will not leave your post again unless it's an emergency. Is that clear?" Faron's voice stiffened even more, his tone low. Jeth began to tremble.

"Aye," he said, so quiet he wasn't sure a sound came out at all. He bowed and started to walk back.

"Wait," Faron said. "She obviously sees you as an easy mark. *I* will watch her."

"Uh . . . alright. What will you have me do instead? Should I help Olivier?"

"Get some sleep. I need you to watch the Meister for one more night. Be prepared to set off at first light."

Something's wrong here, you know it, he thought. It felt prudent to press the issue of the Saf's identity. Make Faron listen. He tried to force the words out, but they wouldn't come. "What about Master Loche?" he asked instead.

Faron's jaw tightened, and his hard, blue gaze broke before replying, "He will not be returning with us."

The major, in his purposeful, stiff fashion, walked toward the Saf's tent.

4
The Antidote

Every inch of earth under Jeth's bed roll was an obstruction to his sleep. He tossed himself over and over in the sweltering tent and eventually gave up on the idea of resting before his duties with the Mage. He couldn't stop thinking about the Saf and how convincing she was, how close he had come to considering her offer, even knowing it was all deception. *Maybe the major's right not to trust you.*

The sun set on the Sunil Tribe Lands once again. Groggy and overheated, Jeth lugged himself to the fire pit and dished up on some fresh stew. Drunken laughter from Baird, Tobin, and Roscoe made his head pound as he ate his meal in silence. Apparently, Olivier, not in the mood to drink, had gone on watch, leaving Jeth with no one to talk to yet again.

The sound of Major Faron sharpening his sword in the Saf's tent rang through the camp. Her promises of 'riches, respect, and pleasure' still fresh in his mind. And that laugh of hers. *Lies. . . . It has to be.*

Done eating, he went to Melikheil's tent. This time the Mage didn't say a word and set to preparing his spirit mediations straight away. He appeared calm for someone nearing an epic battle to the assured death of one or both parties. But something in the silence made the air heavy.

The night drew on, and the discomfort in Jeth's gut only grew, thinking about the Saf's story and Loche's condition. He could still smell the stench of decay in his wound while stringing his bow. He wanted to confide in Olivier and offer assistance. He wanted to do something for the old navigator who came to his defense at the campfire. Loche was one of the few urlings who didn't treat him like dirt, and now he was going to be left alone to die in the desert. The whole situation made him sick to his stomach.

A desert pathogen should require a desert cure, he thought. In Fae'ren, before the Del'Cabrians came, every ailment, or close to it, could be remedied with herbs found in the forest itself. Why not in the desert? *The Saf must know something. Why else ask how Loche was faring?* He cursed himself for not pressing her when he had the chance. Perhaps he should bring it up with Faron, but he didn't want to be reprimanded for leaving his post again, especially if his hunch turned out to be nothing.

When the moons were high and full in the night sky, Faron retired for the evening, leaving a semi-drunk Roscoe to guard the Saf. Roscoe sat down in front of the tent rather than inside it. As soon as Faron was out of sight, he pulled a bottle out from behind him and continued to nurse it, gazing out into the star-speckled sky.

The camp remained quiet for nearly an hour—even the mutterings of Baird and Tobin had drifted off. Then came a carrying on from the Saf's tent. Jeth peeked his head out to investigate. Roscoe was inside now, and Jeth honed his hearing to listen closer.

"Come on, girl, do you want to go or not?" Roscoe said, voice rough from drink.

"Not with you. I want the younger one with the matted hair."

"He's busy. You got me for the night, now let's go."

"Don't touch me!" she hissed.

"Then you can wet yourself for all I care," Roscoe griped.

Jeth glanced over to Melikheil, completely vacant in the middle of the tent. *He'll be fine for a minute or two. This might be your only chance to talk to the Saf before it's too late.*

With his bow and quiver strapped to his back, he ducked out of the Mage's tent and jogged all the way across camp. Baird and Tobin were preoccupied with humiliating the camel puller to pay Jeth any mind. He shook his head at Tobin wearing the man's headscarf and butchering his Herrani dialect.

"You're just going to stand there and watch me wet my pants?" the Saf screeched as Jeth strode in.

"Roscoe, I can take her if you guard the Meister for me."

The horse master looked between the Saf and Jeth and grumbled, "Oh, all right. Get me when she's done."

Once Roscoe was gone, Jeth went to untie her rope from the peg.

"Thank you," she whispered with relief.

"Don't try anything, alright?" He took her under her arm and helped her to her feet.

"I'll be good," she cooed with a small sideways grin, making his skin flush.

There was just enough slack in the rope around the Saf's ankles for her to shuffle along while Jeth held the lead behind her. They circled her tent and gradually made way toward a roughly dug latrine past the camels and horses.

When they reached their destination the Saf asked, "Before I squat down and relieve myself with you standing there, might I at least know your name?"

Scratching at his beard in hesitation, he relented, "Jeth." *Doesn't matter now.*

". . . Jeth?" she looked back to him, her face scrunched.

"Short for Jethril," he blurted, then instantly cursed himself for revealing his full name. He never told it to anyone out of fear of people using it. It was not common practice for Fae'ren to refer to themselves or others in their full name.

She seemed to relax upon hearing its long version, though. "Have you given any more thought to my offer, Jethril?"

He was compelled to correct her, but something about the way the 'r' rolled off her tongue was pleasing, so he let it go. "You're mad if you think I'm going to free you. Now, get on."

She groaned and shambled to the ditch, and he kept his back turned. He scaled back his hearing a bit so not to listen to her urine soaking into the sand. After a minute or two, a foul smell wafted through the air. "Hey! Are you *shitting*?"

"I might as well while I'm out here . . ." she said between grunts.

He groaned.

"I hate to break it to you, but women do occasionally defecate. Plug your nose or something."

He did just that and brought his hearing down to near nothing.

The Saf finally emerged, smoothing the sash she wore over her sheer pants. As she moved past Jeth, he pivoted, grabbed her shoulder, and stood in her way.

"Wait," he said. Her body tensed, so he continued with haste. "To answer your question about our navigator earlier, he's probably not going to make it. Do you know why his wound won't heal? Any desert remedy you can think of?"

After a long silence, the Saf's eyes drifted to the ground. "My blade is laced with a small amount of naja saliva. Ancient Herrani warriors used to apply it to their weapons, but the practice was stopped when the naja first went extinct . . . before the Overlord brought them back."

"Sweet Mother Oak!" He let go of her shoulder and pushed back his hair. Looking up at the sky, his hands slid down the mats as he gave a silent prayer.

The Saf lifted her eyes to meet his. "When a naja bites you and by some miracle you survive, the saliva will cause the wound to fester and death is a guarantee."

"Were you ever going to let us know?"

"If I told any of the others, what do you think they would have done to me?" she posed.

"But you're telling me . . ."

"I have the antidote made from naja blood. It will neutralize the poison, and your navigator should recover."

"Where? In your things?" He looked back to the mounts and the pilfered items from the Saf's palanquin. "Help me find it."

He began to pull her along, but she rooted. "Only if you promise me something first."

"I can't help you escape!" he exclaimed. "But, Loche is a good man. He doesn't deserve to die!"

Scuffing footsteps came from behind. He had forgotten to bring his senses back fully and hadn't noticed the liquor infused scent of Baird and Tobin permeating the air around them.

"What is this we're hearing?" Baird said before taking a swig from his near empty whiskey bottle. "You have a cure for our good Master Loche?"

Jeth immediately stepped up to the two stumbling spearmen, keeping the Saf behind him. "She was just about to tell me. Let me handle this."

"I'm your superior officer now, and you will defer this matter to me," Baird replied. "Now hand her over."

"You're both drunk. We should inform the major first." He stood cocked, but his pulse raced out of control.

Baird tossed his whiskey bottle over his shoulder with an echoing clink. "You dare disobey my order, Fae?" Baird's nostrils flared, and his protruding jaw steeled. Jeth gulped and balled his fists.

"Out of the way!" Baird grabbed him by the coat collar and shoved him to the ground. The Saf on his lead went with him.

"Don't!" he yelped.

Tobin snatched the rope out of his hand. Then Baird kicked him in the head. Jeth tried to shake off the blow, but Baird grabbed him by the hair and snarled in his ear. "Was I interrupting something between you two? Did you take her out here to piss or to get a taste of that reptilian cunt?"

"By the Unnamed Deities, man, what did your mother do to you?" Jeth rasped. *Wrong thing to say.*

Baird smashed his face into the dusty earth. Once. Twice. Sharp grains shot up his nostrils and filled his mouth. Another bracing kick to the back of the head left him seeing white. He wiped the blood dripping from his nose and choked out gobs of coarse, black dirt. Through his disoriented haze, he watched Baird lumber to the Saf, propelled only by rage and drunken, drifting inertia.

"Rope. Give it." Baird yanked it from Tobin's hand before he could reply. "Tell us where this antidote is, desert bitch!" he snarled into her face.

She tried to scream, but Tobin muffled the noise with his meaty palm. "That's not a good enough answer," the blonde spearmen said.

"Maybe she needs a little more convincing." Baird flipped the rope around her neck and yanked her onto her back. He wrapped the slack around his hand and trod toward the horses. The Saf gasped, kicking furiously with her bound legs creating billows of dust as she skidded behind her tormenter.

"Stop!" Jeth croaked. The moons and stars spun in circles above the tilting horizon. He tried to find his feet, but he lost his balance, and fell hard on one elbow.

"Tobin, go find that tulwar!" Baird barked. Tobin ran past his accomplice. Reaching the bag, he searched by throwing items haphazardly until he located the curved blade.

Snatching it from Tobin's hand, Baird loosened the rope around the Saf's neck and put the tulwar to her red raw, throat. She gasped for air. "If I were to cut you with this, would you be able to cure it?"

Her eyes scorched. "Cut me and my father will annihilate all of you!"

"We will be miles away before your father gets here, and our Mage will see to his end. We don't care what happens to you thereafter," Baird hissed.

He took hold of her arm and put the tulwar against it as Tobin clasped his hand over her mouth from behind once again. The wrath within her ice blue eyes turned to terror.

"You have one last chance. Where's the antidote?"

The Saf tried to speak through Tobin's hand. He released her and she gasped. "It's in my hair piece."

"What?"

"Let go of my arm and I will give it to you."

Baird did so and put the blade to her bare stomach instead. The Saf pushed out one of the garnets from the band holding her hair up. It wasn't a gem at all, but a tiny vial filled with a brown liquid. The urling wrenched her wrist and forced the vial from her slack grip.

"Now, leave me be."

Baird tossed aside the tulwar and placed the vial in his pocket. He didn't move.

"Let's get that to Master Loche," said Tobin.

"Not yet," said Baird with a dark sneer. "This desert whore tried to kill one of ours. She needs to pay."

"Hurt her and I'll report you to the major," Jeth warned, standing up on tottering legs.

The two spearmen guffawed. "Go wake him up then if you're so inclined and leave the *real* men to their business."

Baird clutched the Saf's face in his one hand and shoved her to the dirt. His other hand tautened the rope around her neck, making her gulp for air that would not come. He then smacked her across the face with the back of his hand.

Jeth's ears popped. Every grain of sand sang below his feet. The breeze scraped against his dry skin. Aromas separated, distinct and vibrant as color. Something visceral ignited deep in his belly as his eagle vision focused on the men in the dark. All his fears and self-doubt extinguished.

He grabbed the first blunt object he could find—the bottle of whiskey and raced to Baird. The bottle cracked over the back of his skull.

The glass shattered, its remnants slicing Baird's nape while the strong-smelling liquor splashed into the fresh cut.

Baird growled, "You son of a boar!"

He lunged forward, grabbed the broken bottle in Jeth's hand, and attempted to wrench it from his grip. Jeth was flung to the ground and rolled into a resting camel. It gave a pitched groan, almost pulling its stake out of the earth as it moved away.

Still on the ground, Jeth kicked Baird's legs out and threw himself on top of him. Tobin was busy keeping the Saf from wriggling away, allowing Jeth to focus his entire wrath on Baird alone. Not recalling where the broken bottle had gone, Jeth punched him in the face, then again. Again, and again. Each strike satisfied a long overdue need to cause him pain. Before another fist could land, Baird shoved him over.

Both men shot up, and Baird tackled Jeth back down. But in his intoxication, he tripped up and fell with him. *When did Baird find the bottle?* It didn't matter. He was intent on driving it down into Jeth's face. Jeth grabbed Baird's arm, struggling to keep the jagged glass away, but the urling's strength was overpowering his. Both men's teeth gnashed at the effort.

Jeth let go and rolled to the side before the bottle became embedded in the sand inches from his left ear, more glass pieces breaking off.

Whether it was the adrenaline pumping through his veins or the drink still affecting Baird's reflexes that made Jeth so swift, he didn't know. But he soon found his own hands around the bottle and was walloping Baird in the face. The urling staggered, eyes dashing about, trying to focus on his assailant. The bottle smashed to pieces on the third strike, bits of glass biting into Jeth's right hand. Now he only had his fists. Upon a strike to his midsection, Baird doubled over, but Jeth wasn't finished. He struck Baird with an uppercut so hard the urling fell straight on his back. Then a sickening crack. Blood splattered across the sand. The back of Baird's skull had landed squarely on the camel peg sticking a little too far out of the ground. His mouth twitched for a few agonizing moments before locking in place.

Jeth stood paralyzed over him, watching the blood gush from the back of his head, forming dark puddles in the sand. Panic jolted through him like a lightning strike grounded at his sternum.

"B-Baird?" Tobin sputtered. His bloodshot eyes were fixed on his friend. One hand still over the Saf's mouth and the other clutching her arm in a white-knuckled grip.

Jeth could only stare blankly at Baird's unmoving husk, mouth agape, color draining from his face as quickly as the blood from his skull.

5

Innocent

Tobin jumped up, his hands clasped over his head, and his eyes glued to the body of his fellow spearman. "You killed him!"

"I-I didn't mean to."

Jeth felt like he should do something. Run for the major, run for the medic, run for his life. Anything. But all he could do was stare dully at the soldier falling apart in front of him.

"Shit! Shit!" Tobin sucked in a trembling breath. "I need to get the major." He started to run.

With a jolt, Jeth lunged for him, wrapped his arm around his neck from behind, and kept his head still with the other. "Don't!" he pleaded.

Tobin struggled, elbowed him in the jaw, and knocked him down next to the Saf.

"Major!" Tobin yelled as he ran back toward the petering campfire in the distance.

Without a thought, Jeth took his bow from his back, an arrow from his quiver, fell to one knee, and pulled back the bowstring. His head spun. No time to aim at the ever-darkening figure gaining distance from him. Pure instinct took over.

Tobin made it a few paces from camp before the arrow pierced through his back and into his heart. A throat rattling wheeze escaped the spearman, and he collapsed face first onto the sand right next to the Saf's tent. Silence followed.

Jeth released a shaking exhalation. Nothing stirred in the camp. *Someone must have heard something*, but it was hard for him to assess the range of others' hearing apart from his own. He gripped his bow tightly in his left hand, his heart pounding, head throbbing, but he was unable to move.

"Jethril . . ." The Saf's calm voice brought him out of his paralysis.

She was still on the ground, hair disheveled, pants specked with blood, and the tiny jewels from her left cheek ripped from her skin. He grimaced at Baird's gaping corpse right next to her. One second ago the man was both her and Jeth's biggest threat. Now he was just an empty shell.

"I didn't want—I didn't mean to . . ." he whispered, struggling to keep from vomiting.

"I'm glad you did," the Saf said as she held her bound wrists out to him. "Now, if you would cut me loose."

Still reeling, he barely registered her request. He pawed at himself in search of his knife that had never left his scabbard.

"Never mind." She sighed, took Baird's knife, and expertly went to work cutting her ropes.

Once free, she pulled off his scabbard and fastened it around her own waist. "Thanks for the new knife, urling pig." She spat on the body before adjusting the straps of the belt to fit her more curvaceous hips.

"I'm a murderer," Jeth sputtered.

The Saf waved him off. "You've killed before."

"That was different. These were my brothers in arms." He began to pace about in the dark.

She stepped in front of him and took him by the shoulders. "Listen to me. There was no telling the horrors they would have subjected me to, and they would have *killed* you. You did the right thing. So, snap out of it and help me."

"What?" Jeth backed out of her grasp. "Murdering my own men and letting you escape? That's treason!"

"Which is why you need to leave here at once."

He shook his head and started pacing again. "No, I-I have to go to the major—"

"And tell him what?" the Saf asked in a shrill whisper.

"The truth. Baird and Tobin attacked you. I did what I had to do. He'll understand." His guts twisted at his own words.

"A human and a daughter of the enemy are responsible for the deaths of two high standing urling soldiers. Are you certain your *urling* major will understand?"

Roscoe was supposed to be the one guarding the Saf, not you, he thought.

"Maybe not," he said. "But running will ensure he never does. Let me tie you back up, and I can figure this—"

The Saf grabbed Jeth's arm, jammed her hip into his midsection, and flipped him on his back. Now on top of him, she put the knife to his throat. "Touch me with those ropes again, and your body will join Sir Horse Face's over there."

He gulped beneath the blade's razer edge. "Easy now."

"Don't think me ungrateful for what you did, but I will kill you if I have to. However, I'd much rather return the favor. Escape with me, and you might live through this."

"I'll be hanged if I run."

She brought her face closer to his. "Even if they spare your life, there is nothing for you here, and there never was. How will you climb your silly social ladder when you're in prison or dishonorably discharged? You will never be a free man again. Come with me, and you have a chance at a future. But, if you choose to stay, I will not be staying with you."

Through Jeth's heavy breathing, he felt the cold steel begin to break the skin. He looked into the Saf's icy eyes and knew she was right. Even if by some miracle, Faron believed that killing members of his task force were justified, the fact remained that he chose to leave his post to take the Saf outside of camp. Baird and Tobin could just as readily have been there to stop him. It was his word against their cold, dead lips.

"Alright. . . . What do we do?"

With a relieved sigh, the Saf got off him and said, "Get the bodies out of sight. I will prepare the horses."

"The antidote!" He rushed over to Baird's body. Trying to ignore his ghostly face, he fished through his pocket and found the vial.

"There's no time," the Saf said as she started saddling a chestnut mare.

"I won't have Loche's blood on my hands too!"

"If you aren't ready when I am, I will leave without you. Is your navigator's life worth your freedom?" she posed.

Jeth started toward the camp, then stopped, turned, and took a few steps back. He reached up and ran his fingers over his head and pulled at his locks. "I-I need to give it to him."

He didn't wait for the Saf to respond as he ran back to camp, and past Tobin's body, not stopping until he reached the fire pit. Loud snoring could be heard from Melikheil's tent. *Roscoe must have passed out watching him.* With the tiny brown vial in hand, he cautiously made way for Faron and Loche's tent. He halted, not having thought his plan through.

Will you apply it to Loche's wound yourself? No, he'll wake up for sure and Faron will be right beside him. Give it to Olivier, explain what it is, then run like mad. That sounds better.

He scanned the plateau to the southwest, hoping to catch sight of Olivier's silhouette against the moon, but found no one.

Then, the familiar croak of a stretching bowstring. His heart stopped, and he slowly turned around. Olivier emerged from the shadows with an arrow nocked and pointed at his head. *Damn your timing, Oli!* He thought. "Oli, let me explain."

"There's no need," said Olivier. "It's surprising what you can hear echoing off the rocks from up there. I came down to find that the Saf wasn't in her tent, and then Tobin was shot dead by an arrow right outside it."

Slowly putting his hands above his head, Jeth said in a shaking voice, "I had to do it. They were hurting her. I tried to stop them, but they wouldn't. .

. . You've got to believe me. I didn't mean to kill them."

"Them?"

"Baird. He was an accident, and Tobin—I-I panicked. . . ."

Olivier eased on his bowstring but kept the arrow pointed at his friend. "Those two were trouble from the start. It was only a matter of time before something like this happened."

The relief Jeth felt upon hearing that his fellow bowman was on his side slipped away when Olivier looked past him. "The major's awake."

With a glance over his shoulder, Jeth saw the glow of Faron's oil lamp through the light-colored canvas. He turned back to Olivier, his heart beating a hole through his chest. "Please, let me go. No one will know that you helped me."

"Are you insane?" Olivier said. "We will explain this to the major. It's going to be fine, Jeth."

"People like me get thrown in jail for *looking* at urlings the wrong way. It's not going to be fine!" he said as he took a trembling step forward.

"Don't move!" Olivier demanded, his drawing arm quivering.

"Listen to me." He nodded toward his left hand where he held the vial. "The Saf gave me this to treat Loche's wound."

"The Saf? Where is she?"

"With the horses."

"If we catch her, this mission can be salvaged. We can figure this out together, Jeth, but you have to trust me." The fire-headed man's voice nearly squeaked as he spoke.

"Oli . . . we can't." Jeth's eyes welled. "I'm a dead man, and you know it."

A horse snorted in the darkness.

Olivier glanced behind him, lowering his aim mere inches. Jeth acted without a second thought. He tackled him to the ground, separating him from his bow. Positioning himself behind him, he wrapped his arm around his neck, locked his head in place, and cut off his airway.

"I don't want to do this," he murmured. Olivier kicked his legs about, but Jeth maintained a fast grip. He stared at the shadow of Faron moving about in his tent as Olivier's heart slowed to a crawl and he sank unconscious in his arms. After a few more seconds, he set Olivier down gently. "I'm sorry, friend," he whispered.

The Saf led two chestnut mounts behind her with bulging saddle bags, her tulwar strapped to her back. She looked down at Jeth with something akin to sympathy or disappointment. He couldn't tell.

"Let's go," she said as she handed him the gelding's reins and climbed upon the mare.

"What's going on out here?" Faron barked, exiting his tent. His eyes landed on Jeth and then the Saf. The next few moments lingered on for an eternity. Jeth's heart stuck in his throat.

"Soldiers! The Saf is escaping!"

With a groan, the Saf took off on her horse. Jeth hastily placed the antidote in Olivier's unconscious hand. It twitched as he began to come to.

"Jeth, move away from him and get on your knees!" Faron hollered.

The escaped hostage was almost at the lake, soon to be swallowed by the desert night. He looked up to meet the smoldering coals in Faron's eyes. "Sorry, Major."

Jeth jumped on the gelding and kicked it into a frantic gallop after the Saf. He was partly out of the camp before Faron's bellow rang out. "Traitor! Soldiers! After him!"

He was thankful for the head start, but his heart was heavy as he caught up to the Saf halfway around the lake. It was not long before a set of hooves gave chase.

With his hearing at maximum, he listened for how close Faron was getting. Then came the hooves of a second horse. The now conscious Olivier had mounted his steed and joined in the pursuit, bow in hand.

"We have to get out of range!" Jeth shouted to the Saf ahead.

"We can lose them in the hoodoos," she called back. They had little choice as they neared the lake's west bank.

The two escapees pushed their horses harder, forcing them between the towering pillars of sandstone, growing more numerous the deeper they rode. The Saf's glowing white ponytail, flowing out behind her, acted as a beacon to help him navigate through the crowding rock formations. It reminded him of running through the massive oaks in Fae'ren's Deep Wood at night. Only he had never done it on horseback. His cattle herding experience also came in handy, steering sharply through the twists and turns.

An arrow cut through the air and struck a sandstone structure just behind him. They kicked their horses more furiously. The hoodoos became a blur of shapeless obstructions in the darkness. The horses whinnied and tossed their heads as they were forced into tighter spaces and around sharper twists. There was no way out of the endless city of stone towers.

In a few moments, Jeth lost sight of the Saf.

"Shit!" He lashed his head around, but he was now alone. Even his pursuers had vanished.

"Jethril!" The Saf called from a ridge a few feet above the path. "This way!"

He backtracked and found the narrow incline to take him to her, all the while whispering pleas to not be spotted. They continued to ride between even narrower passages. The horses shook with anxiety at the uneven ground, but battle bred, continued to cooperate. Soon enough, one of the moons came into view, peeking through the cluster of towering rocks, proving there was a way out after all.

The Saf kicked her horse into a faster gallop leaning over the neck, her hands out almost to its ears. Jeth did the same only to find the earth swallow up both her and horse.

The way out of the hoodoos happened to be a sheer drop onto a sand dune. Jeth braced for the jump. The Saf's horse landed awkwardly, then came a jarring snap. The mare collapsed face first into the sand, catapulting the Saf off the saddle. She rolled several paces before coming to a halt in a bundle of dry bushes. Jeth's horse managed to land without breaking any bones, and he was able to circle around. The Saf stumbled out of the bushes, pulling dried leaves and twigs from her hair.

Swinging off the horse he rushed to her side. "Are you all right?"

Brushing off sand from her once sparkling garments, she answered, "Nothing feels broken. Can't say the same for that horse though."

The mare struggled to get to its feet, but its front left leg was mangled beyond repair. Its piercing screeches echoed off the canyon cliffs as it writhed in pain. They had lost Faron and Olivier in the hoodoos, but the horse's cries would lead them straight there in a short while. The Saf appeared to have already had that event in mind as she unsheathed her tulwar and took steps toward the broken steed.

"Allow me," he offered as he reached for the bow at his back. He had enough experience in putting down lame steeds back at the ranch, only he normally used a flintlock rifle to make the process as humane as possible, as loud and cumbersome as the weapons were.

"I've got this," said the Saf.

She approached the horse carefully. It jerked its head from side to side, screaming in agony. As soon as she laid her hand upon its withers, it stilled. The beast blew out labored bursts of air before she put the tip of her sword to the base of its skull. With a grunting effort, she pushed it through, rendering the horse limp in an instant. Using her foot for leverage, she yanked the sword out, blood splashing vertically into the air. She then wiped her brow with her left arm, the other covered up to the elbow in red.

The Saf wiped the blood from her tulwar on its hair then sheathed it. Jeth gave her his scarf to wipe it from her arm and helped hoist her onto the saddle behind him.

"Continue west. We should come upon the Serpentine River at dawn," she said.

Still numb, he kicked the horse in that direction.

In a couple of hours, the morning light trickled over the horizon, painting the distant canyons fiery red while the moons still hung large and white in the dark violet sky. A streak of water glistened in the distance, and a few minutes later they reached a slow-moving tributary. The Saf didn't wait for them to come to a complete stop before jumping down and running to the river's edge.

She started ripping off her rings and bracelets, dropping them one by one onto the sandy bank where Jeth came to join her. The horse ambled alongside him and began drinking its fill.

"Let's replenish our water, wash up, and keep moving," he said as he began to do just that. "Melikheil's spirit is probably searching for us right now."

"If I were him, I would be concentrating on the Overlord. As for the others, they would have given up pursuit in the interest of saving their navigator. We have plenty of time," she said as she dipped her toes into the glimmering liquid and let out a relaxed sigh. "Oh, the water is perfect. I can't go meeting the Tezkhan Chief in this repulsive state, now can I?"

Despite her tousled hair, scrapes, and bruises, she was positively glowing. She smiled contently as a farmer satisfied after a good harvest. Jeth was anything but comfortable as the night's events sank in, keeping adrenaline ever present under the surface. *You just ran away with the Overlord's daughter . . . and he's on his way here now!*

"I can help you get somewhere safe, but afterward, I'll need to take the horse and go . . . I'm not sure where, but far from here would be a start."

"Are you stupid?" She eyed him wryly while rinsing the dried horse blood from her tulwar. "A light skinned person like you won't survive a day out there on your own. Even *I* wouldn't attempt such a thing."

"Better to be a dried husk out there than a live body in the hands of a Flesh Mage! What do you think your father is going to do to me when he finds us? Sure, he might be grateful I helped you, but I'm sort of the reason you needed help in the first place—how long until he gets here?"

"How should I know? I told you, I'm not his daughter." She shrugged as she unclasped her jeweled hair band. Silky white tresses shone silver and gold simultaneously in the light of the dawn as they tumbled down to the small of her back.

"You were telling me the truth?"

The Saf nodded as if that were obvious. She removed the belt and scabbard she'd pilfered from Baird, letting it drop to the bank with her other accessories.

Jeth scratched at his beard. "But . . . our Mage sensed Nas'Gavarr was on his way to rescue you."

She giggled. "He's probably escorting his *real* daughter to the Slot Canyons of Sunil where they are supposed to meet Chief Ukhuna, which happens to pass close by where we were just camped."

"Who are you?"

"A thief. I told you." She turned away and started to untie her pants.

"I know, not . . ." Jeth paused, clenched his fists, and cracked the knuckles. "What is your name?"

"Anwarr."

"No Saf attached to that?"

Another breathy giggle accompanied a shake of the head. "Saf means child of the Overlord, and I am not one of those, I assure you." She stepped out of her pants, revealing dark and shapely legs, shimmering like bronze, beneath nothing more than the wrap around sash over her pelvis.

"Hold on." His head was still reeling. He set his bow and quiver down and planted himself on a rock at the river bank. "If you really aren't his daughter then why do you have the marking of one?"

"Oh, you mean this old thing?" Anwarr turned around and gathered her hair over her shoulder to reveal her partially bare back. A black and green tattoo of two entwined serpents mimicked her hourglass shape, snarling at each other at the shoulders. "This is why I was hired for this job in the first place. I once worked as one of Nas'Gavarr's harem attendants. My connections there helped me find someone to tattoo me. Only four inkers in all of Herran know how to make the unique patterns just right."

Jeth honed his eyesight to get a closer look. If he could touch Anwarr's back, he imagined it would feel like real snake skin. He wished he were close enough to do so, though she'd likely knock him off his feet and drown him in the river if he tried.

"All of Nas'Gavarr's daughters get that?"

Anwarr nodded, and cast her hair back over it, shielding it from view. "They represent the Serpentine Gods: Sagorath and Salotaph. They complete each other, as do day and night, pleasure and pain, male and female, and life and death. It is different for every tribe, but in Herran, it means all are born equal, and all will die the same."

"All that just for some Tezkhan treasure?"

Anwarr turned her head back to him with a devilish glint in her eye. "I've had it for years. It helps get me into places forbidden to most people. Useful for many lucrative heists, but detrimental for others. And this isn't just some treasure. But the Emerald of Dulsakh."

A blank stare was Jeth's only response, and she continued, "Legends say that it holds the spirit of the first naja created by the Serpentine Gods. It will also fetch a price so high, my crew and I won't have to work for a year."

"Crew? The ones we killed. . . ."

"No, thank Sagorath," she replied, unclasping the rest of her top. "They were Herrani warriors loyal to the one who hired me. He won't be happy they're dead, but receiving the emerald ought to make up for it."

At those words, she tossed her entire top onto the bank and dove into the river, splashing him in the process. He sat frozen on the rock, not even moving to wipe the water dripping down his face.

Anwarr burst from the river in another location, whipping her long white hair back and gasping in delight. Rising sunlight illuminated the water droplets as they glided down her bouncing curvature, so slow and smooth, it was as if even the elements reveled in the feel of her skin and refused to let go. She made no attempt to cover her breasts as she stood waist deep in the water directly in his line of sight. He was invisible to her.

Reflexively, he turned away. "Sorry, I'll be over here." He got up and walked a few paces from the water's edge.

Anwarr let out a shivering sigh. "It's much colder than I thought but nice. Hurry up and get in."

"Sure. Uh. . . right after you're done."

"Oh, come on, now's not the time to be shy," Anwarr said in a teasing tone that made his whole body flush and stiffen all at once.

"You've nothing I haven't seen before." He scoffed while turning slowly around to find her neck deep in the water. He sighed in both relief and disappointment.

Anwarr sprang from the water again, combing her fingers through her wet hair. He snapped his head up to the red sky.

"Oh, I see. . . . Is there a woman back home?"

"She's not . . . my woman," he muttered. His gut wrenched upon realizing he might never see Hanalei again.

"But you fucked her?" Anwarr asked bluntly.

Jeth was taken aback. "No, no, she's a proper Ludesan lady. You need to wait until marriage for that kind of thing."

Anwarr let out a mischievous giggle. "By the wiles of Salotaph. Del'Cabrians really are as repressed as they say." She finally covered herself with her arms and said, "So, you've never been with a woman."

"That is *not* what I said." He tried to laugh it off, but his reddening face betrayed him. All he'd ever been able to do was steal a few kisses from Hanalei behind the barn when her father wasn't around. Anything further would have been against Del'Cabrian law.

"How old are you?" she asked, sinking into the water again.

"Old enough to be in the Del'Cabrian forces. . . ."

"I should have known. There is something so innocent about you."

Jeth wanted to dig a hole and sit in it. "*Innocent?* I just killed two men in cold blood!"

"Get in the water. It'll help, I promise," Anwarr said more seriously before submerging herself once again.

She's killed enough men to know then? With a groaning sigh, Jeth undressed to his underthings and dove into the cool river. He had to admit how great it felt to wash away the week's sweat and grime, but confusion continued to haunt him. What did Anwarr want from him? *This woman will shit in front of you, so what does she care if you see her nude? This sure isn't Del'Cabria.*

Once clean, they returned to the bank and redressed.

"Where do we go now? Do I take you back to your crew?" Jeth asked.

"Oh no. There is still a job to finish."

"How?"

"I gave myself a three-day head start for this reason. Saf'Raisha is still at least a day from the meeting point. All I have to do is get there before her, convince the Chief that I am his bride, and he will take me back to his tribe lands."

"That's cutting it close."

"Even on one horse, the two of us can cover more ground than an entire retinue could."

"The two of us?" He turned from the horse to face her.

"Yes. I was hoping you'd come with me. The offer I made you last night still stands."

Rubbing the back of his neck, he said, "Traitor and thief . . . ? I'm not so sure about that."

"What else are you going to do?" she said. "Return home and hope the woman you left behind holds preference for murderers?"

A stabbing pain shot through his chest. *She would never marry you anyway. You would always be the Fae'ren help to her.*

He then thought about his forest home and the fairies, which came with the all too familiar ache in his gut. But it was the only place where he knew who he was or at least where not knowing didn't matter so much. *They may not want you to come back, but why not return anyway? The forest is big enough.*

Anwarr said, "The choice is yours, Jethril. If you wish to return home then the next caravan we see, you can go with them and find your way back. But, I doubt your future is behind you."

He furrowed his brow as he climbed onto the horse. One thing he knew was he couldn't return to the forest. The loneliness would kill him, his people believed him to be a bad omen, the object of his affection thought him beneath her, and his country now wanted a noose around his neck. At least Anwarr was offering a life. For only a month, a week, or maybe a day. It was something.

Beyond the water, everything was so dry. Empty. *Can you really live here forever?* "Why do you care if I stay or go?"

Anwarr approached the horse and looked up at him thoughtfully. "Right now, I need someone to get me to Chief Ukhuna. I intend to marry that barbarian, and I *will* make it out with the Emerald of Dulsakh. I know I just met you, but I feel like I can trust you. I'm not often wrong about people. It's one of my many talents."

He bit the inside of his cheek and remained silent for a time before putting his hand out for her to take. "How can I help?"

She grabbed hold of his arm and used it to pull herself on the horse behind him. "Watch my back. And . . . keep me entertained on the way."

"I can be pretty entertaining," he commented.

"Good, because it will take a couple days to get there, and I bore easily."

Jeth nudged the gelding forward. "And when we get the emerald, what then?"

She held onto his waist from behind and shouted over the rhythmic triple beat of the horse's cantering hooves on the unyielding earth. "Whatever the future holds. And that we cannot know."

6

Play Your Part

A caravan stretched along the Serpentine River heading south. The first sign of life Jeth and Anwarr had seen after a long day's ride through the beating desert sun.

"Don't get too close, they may be unfriendly," Anwarr cautioned.

Jeth focused on the line of people traveling on horseback, camelback, and on foot. "They don't look like fighters, just a group of robed men and women. A peaceful tribe maybe?"

"You can make that out from here?" She raised a suspicious eyebrow.

"I have really good eyesight," he said without lifting his gaze from the procession.

"Good to know. Tell me then, do they wear their hair in braids?"

Inspecting further, he found each man wore a peculiar square hat, their light-colored hair hanging in a single braid down their backs while the women wore two braids, tied in bundles off their necks.a

"Yeah, how'd you guess?"

"They are Sunil servants. These lands are named after them. Their interpretation of the Serpentine involves the balance between master and servant, and serving others is the most honorable role a person can take in life."

"Does that mean they will offer us some supplies?" he asked.

Anwarr giggled. "They won't serve *anybody*. Only those willing to pay their exorbitant stipend."

Jeth moaned in disappointment.

"They may part with some water, but we need much more than that." Anwarr urged him to ride behind a rust-colored sandstone formation, where they dismounted. "It would be wise for you to replace that uniform with something more suitable to the region."

"You want to steal the robes off some humble servant's back?"

"And the horse he rides upon," Anwarr said with a wink. "These people are extremely protective of their Order and would never give their sacred robes to anyone no matter how nicely one asks. Besides, I prefer to take things as opposed to having them given to me."

"Makes sense. So, what's your plan?"

Anwarr peered around the rock to the passing servants. "First, take off that uniform. Then wait here, watch, and learn."

Not giving him a chance to respond, Anwarr darted off toward the caravan and waved her arms above her head. She tripped over a gnarled shrub and rolled down the sandy incline, crying out with every tumble.

One of the men riding a flea-bitten gray veered off from the rest of the group. *She's baiting him.* A lightness percolated in Jeth's chest, and a smile crept across his face. He honed his hearing to listen to what was being said.

"Please! Help! I need water—anything. Please. . . ."

The servant rode up to Anwarr but didn't dismount. "What happened?"

"Del'Cabrian attack."

After a few moments, the man sighed and took out a canteen from his saddle bag. "Where are these Del'Cabrians?" The Sunil's eyes darted about then up to Jeth. He snapped back behind the rocks, sure he'd been spotted, but the servant continued as before, "Have they invaded our lands as well?"

Jeth peeked out again as the Sunil held out the canteen to Anwarr. She grasped for it with both hands, but instead of taking it, she seized the man's arm and hoisted herself up onto the horse's rump.

"Hey! What are you doing?" the Sunil cried out.

With her blade at his throat, she said, "Ride forward, toward those rocks."

Not giving the poor Sunil a chance to protest, she kicked his horse into a gallop while holding the knife steady.

"Shit!" Jeth hastily began to undress. He had just stepped out of his sand-encrusted trousers when Anwarr and her captive rode up. As the gray steed slowed down, she jumped off, bringing the man down with her. Jeth caught the passing horse's reins and brought it to a halt. Already, a number of Sunil riders, having witnessed the altercation, galloped to assist their distressed member.

Anwarr pushed the servant up against the rock wall and held her knife up to his throat again. "Take off your clothes and give them to my partner, here."

The Sunil's lips quivered, but his light hazel eyes remained resolute. His cold, tranquil expression made Jeth's pulse hasten along with the pounding hoof beats getting closer.

"Do what she says."

A thin red line formed along the Sunil's skin under Anwarr's blade. *Would she actually kill him? An innocent man?* He touched the recent scab on his own neck. The Sunil untied his belt sash.

"This is a sacrilege," he growled, removing his yellow silk embroidered robe and tossing it to Jeth, followed by his cream-colored smock and trousers.

"It is for the greater good, don't you worry," said Anwarr.

Jeth jumped into the comfortable wide-legged pants, tapered at the ankles, and threw on the smock that hung loosely from his torso, fitting much more comfortably than his restricting military vest had. He finished putting on the heavy silk robe, but there was no time to figure out how to tie the green belt sash. Three more Sunil, armed with long, curved tulwars appeared from around the rock formations.

"Time to go." He snatched the square hat from the servant's head while Anwarr collected the curly-toed shoes he kicked off. They ducked the swings of the Sunil's blades and jumped back on their steeds.

The Sunil gave chase for a minute or two, but likely not wishing to waste their energy on a single horse and uniform, turned back.

After gaining considerable distance, Jeth and Anwarr stopped their horses by the river.

"As convenient as it would be to travel on two mounts," said Anwarr, "it's more important to blend in. Your Del'Cabrian tack will cause undue suspicion among the Tezkhan."

"Right." He collected the weapons and supplies from the chestnut gelding and transferred it onto the gray. Anwarr ensured his Sunil attire was worn properly and set to tying the length of his locks into a single braid that reached just past his neck. It felt strange whenever someone else touched them, like a peaceful forest grove being disturbed. Yet, he welcomed it all the same.

"Your hair is quite interesting," said Anwarr. "How do you get it to separate like this?"

"Provided we don't comb it, it does it naturally. Although, we do have to do some maintenance to keep the mats uniform as they grow."

"We?"

"The Fae'ren people."

"Never heard of them." She shrugged.

"That's refreshing."

"Why?"

"When people, urlings in particular, find out I'm from Fae'ren, it's all, 'you're dirty, lazy, and copulate with wild boars. . . .' dare I continue?"

"Is all that true?"

"Of course not, well—some go months without bathing, but I'm not one of them." Jeth's powerful sense of smell made such unhygienic practices a non-option for him.

Anwarr cackled. "And thank Salotaph for that."

She tied off the braid and stretched the hat over the rest of the frizz at the top of his head. Stepping back, she put her hands to her chin and studied her handiwork. "It will have to do."

"What? I don't pass for a Sunil servant?"

"Not in the strictest sense." She mounted and adjusted the stirrups to her liking. "Luckily for you, they've accepted Del'Cabrians into their Order before. Once contracted, a Sunil is sworn to serve their master until they die or the contract is ended by the master's own will. They must follow every command without hesitation unless that command would bring shame to their Order or put their master in harm's way."

"I think I can handle that," he said.

This time, he got on the back of the horse. Anwarr took the reins. In control, the most natural state he'd seen her in yet.

Red sand and stone ceaselessly surrounded the two thieves. Dust clouds swirled about by the winds blustering through rock formations that had eroded into rippling crimson waves. Jeth and Anwarr reached the falls that marked the entrance to the Sunil Slot Canyons by the next day. According to Anwarr, a yearlong drought had turned the once majestic waterfall of the upper canyons to the single trickle that now fed into the sandy lakebed.

People camped at the water's edge. Jeth counted about thirty men and horses and not a single woman among them. They were thickly built, short of stature, yet their faces were gaunt with full beards and wiry, black hair sticking out from rolled-up headdresses. Their worn, dust-crusted smocks were made of various hides and mismatched fabrics.

"These must be the Tezkhan raiders. Looks like we made it on time," he said as they rode into view.

Several men from the shaded area of the canyon stood and made haste toward the unknown riders, heavy axes, and mallets in hand.

"You go the wrong way, woman," one of them warned, looking up at Anwarr and shielding his eyes from the sun.

Jeth dismounted from the back of the horse, inciting the raiders to point their weapons at him.

"Stop right there," barked the tallest one in front.

Putting up his hands, Jeth bowed. "Friends, there is no need to be wary," he began, in a voice he imagined a humble servant would use to address such rough looking folk. "I present to you, Saf'Raisha, the daughter of my master and Overlord of Herran, Nas'Gavarr."

Anwarr gave him a quick nod of approval and added, "Forgive our lateness. I am ready to meet my betrothed, the esteemed Chief Ukhuna."

"You look not like a daughter of the Overlord," jeered the Tezkhan up front, his dark, leathery face cracking around the mouth and temples. Jeth feared that after a day of riding in the blazing sun absent the rain clouds made by Melikheil, his much fairer skin might look the same.

"If you are the Herrani bride, then why do you come before my brothers in such untidy appearance?" boomed a voice from behind the group. The men stepped aside to accommodate a much larger man, marching forward. He towered above everyone. His barrel chest made more prominent by a dusty breastplate with a running horse insignia, the only one among them wearing armor at all. His long scraggily hair was tied back and growing on his wide face was a black beard braided down to his chest in three sets. The hulking man scowled, small dark eyes scrutinizing.

Anwarr began, "I can explain—"

"And who is this little man? Why does Nas'Gavarr insult me by not presenting his daughter himself?" the Chief spouted whilst chewing on an overpowering, putrid-smelling substance. Jeth tried his best to scale back his sense of smell accordingly, but it still left him nauseated.

"To insult you was not his intention, Great Chief," Anwarr said as she descended from the horse. "Our retinue was attacked by Del'Cabrian invaders. They wish to prevent this marriage. My father stayed back to fight in order to protect our union and the Sunil Tribe Lands from the pointed-ear threat. I came here as swiftly as I could, to return to your lands where our invaders will be unable to follow."

"Then who is he?" Ukhuna narrowed a suspicious eye at Jeth before spitting a dark green gob on the ground. "He is pale-faced like a Del'Cabrian."

"This is Baird, one of my father's most trusted Sunil servants," Anwarr said without pause. Jeth's stomach lurched at the name, but there was no correcting it now. "He was ordered to take me to safety unbeknownst to our attackers. He may look Del'Cabrian, but the Sunil Order accepts any and all who wish to devote their lives to the service of others."

He stepped beside Anwarr and bowed obligingly to the Chief. "I am sworn to serve Nas'Gavarr and Saf'Raisha until my dying day."

Ukhuna grunted and crossed his arms over his immense armored chest. "Prove to me you are the daughter of Nas'Gavarr and we may proceed."

Anwarr smiled sweetly. "With pleasure."

She turned her back to the group of men and slithered out of her top, granting them view of her tattoo.

All the raiders ogled until Ukhuna waved them away. "Cover yourself, Raisha, soon to be my eighth wife. Welcome!"

Nestling back into her shirt, Anwarr turned to face her husband to be. "It is a great honor to finally meet you, and I look forward to our coming union. I only pray that it will be soon."

"We have waited here long enough. If it does not insult the Immortal Serpent, let us prepare to set off at once. We will be wed in the morrow before the Equestrian Gods," Ukhuna thundered for all to hear. He took Anwarr under his massive arm and started leading her back to their camp. Jeth, with the horse, began to follow.

The Chief turned. "You may return to your master, manservant. Report to him that his daughter is safe and that a Tezkhan and Herrani alliance has been attained."

Jeth cleared his throat. He glanced at Anwarr then the Chief. "Uh . . . my orders are to stay by Saf'Raisha's side until after the nuptials, to ensure it takes place firsthand."

Letting go of Anwarr, Ukhuna took sweeping strides toward him. "Does your master not trust in our agreement?"

Anwarr said, "If it is no trouble, I would prefer to keep Baird with me in any case. Returning before the job is complete will bring great shame to his name and his Order. You understand."

With another grunt, Ukhuna placed his arm around Anwarr again, then spit more goop on the ground. "As the father of the bride cannot be witness himself, I will allow you to accompany her until after the festivities."

"Thank you, Great Chief." Jeth bowed again, feeling at home in the new role he was playing. "I will return to the Overlord with pleasant tidings of a long and prosperous cooperation between your two tribes."

Were it not for the drought, the way through the slot canyons would be impossible to traverse. Today, the path through the constricting caverns was filled mostly with packed sand and a few ankle-deep puddles.

The canyon walls were a dry crimson ocean. Smooth sandstone sediments were lit ablaze by the sinking sun on the western horizon, igniting them in a flame-red radiance. The passages became so narrow at one point that the riders were forced to take their feet out of the stirrups and place them up onto their saddles. The horses whinnied with aggravation as they were forced single file through the winding crevasses.

As the caverns opened up toward the end of the trek, Jeth could ride side by side with Anwarr. The Chief and his band rode further up ahead and out of earshot.

"Is this the only way to the Tezkhan Tribe Lands?"

"No, but it is the only way for them to get to the Sunil Tribe Lands," she replied. "For thousands of years, the Tezkhan raiders have rampaged through much of what is now Sunil and Herrani territory. They were arguably the most successful tribe and one of the few that stood to threaten the naja that ruled most of the desert at the time. Our ancestors drove away the naja, and not long after, the Tezkhan. These slot canyons have protected the Sunil from their raids ever since. The West Serpentine River and the Burning Waste separates them from Herran."

"The Burning Waste?"

"Another tale for another time," she said. "Needless to say, the Tezkhan have been rather isolated from the other tribes for the last two thousand years, leaving the impoverished Ankarr tribes along the western coast the only regular victims of their marauding."

"Is that why they don't have white hair like the rest of you?"

"Yes. They have not interbred with any other, except some unfortunate Ankarrans, most of whom have dark hair as well."

"And Nas'Gavarr wants to ally with the Tezkhan, adding hundreds of horsemen to his forces," he said, trying to hide the nervousness he feared was plastered all over his face.

Anwarr nodded. "This alliance is not solely based on marriage, but a promise that the Tezkhan can settle on conquered territory. I suspect that Nas'Gavarr will use them to raid the Del'Cabrian strongholds and force them out of the desert. They will have to promise not to raid allied tribes, and therefore set their sights on your people instead," said Anwarr, her voice low.

"Making it all the more imperative for the task force to capture the real Saf'Raisha. I'm all for murder and theft, but indirectly causing the future suffering of innocent Del'Cabrians . . ." He took a swig from his canteen.

"I wouldn't worry about that," Anwarr whispered. "After we take the emerald, it will ruin any chance of an alliance for the foreseeable future. It is passed down from chief to chief. Without it, the entire Tezkhan's, as you say, pecking order, will collapse and the raiders will scatter." Anwarr gave her breathy giggle that he was starting to get used to hearing after nearly every sentence.

"Great," he said, sitting up straighter in his saddle. "I enjoy a good power structure collapse."

The canyon began to narrow again to the point where their legs brushed against one another's.

"Stay by my side, my Sunil servant, for I have much to teach you." She giggled again and smiled before nudging her horse further ahead. Her face shifted from his sight, and the light peeking around the fiery-red canyon walls went with it.

At dusk, the train of riders emerged from the canyons into a wasteland more barren than the sand dunes of Herran. Rough sun-bleached terrain and dry, gnarled bushes littered the landscape far into the horizon. Shockingly cool winds ripped across the plains from the north, giving Jeth a respite from the stifling heat.

An hour's ride took them to a massive settlement just off the West Serpentine River. Wide and treacherous, the river's rapids flowed from the higher altitude canyon regions to make its final stretch toward the far ocean.

As they neared the camp, crowds of people gathered around the incoming party, waving and hollering good tidings to their chief and his new bride. Women, with their faces shrouded, peered out from their large cylindrical tents the Tezkhan referred to as yurts. Their children ran about near naked and browned from the sun.

The women surrounded Anwarr as soon as they saw her. They blathered excitedly, touching her hair and her clothing. Some shook their heads in disapproval as they dragged her away.

"Where are they taking her?" Jeth objected.

Ukhuna patted his shoulder with a powerful hand, and he staggered sideways. "Leave the women folk to it. As for the rest of us, we will feast. Does your Order frown on drink?"

"I'm going to say no?" Anwarr never mentioned anything about a Sunil's propensity for drinking while on duty. At this point, it probably didn't matter.

The men went to the center of the camp where grilled antelope meat was being cooked on a rotisserie over a massive fire pit. A lanky boy deposited a clay cup of fermented horse milk into Jeth's hand without a word and ran off. It smelled vile but to keep up appearances, he downed as much as he could. Every sip of the sickly warm liquid made his stomach churn, and he ended up throwing the remainder over his shoulder when no one was paying attention. Ukhuna took out a sinewy green substance from his pocket and bit a piece off, releasing that strong stench that made Jeth's eyes water. *You might have to chop off your nose if you plan on staying here much longer.*

"May I ask what that is?" he said, trying not to gag.

Ukhuna replied, "This is khat leaf; good for focus. It grows only in the most desolate Tezkhan plains. I'd offer you some, but it's too rare."

Jeth shrugged. "Not to worry, Great Chief. You've been so generous already." He breathed a sigh of relief. *If it smells this bad, the taste would probably kill you.*

The sun fell not long after, and he retired to a yurt housing the tribe's slaves. He didn't get to see Anwarr until the next morning when he found her making her horse ready for the wedding ceremony at the edge of camp. He arrived to a crowd of people gathered to watch. Anwarr was tending to the buckskin mare she had ridden in on. She was dressed in the dusty wraparound robes and sash the other women wore, her hair and face shrouded. Her ice blue eyes were the only visible feature to identify her.

"Do you know the whereabouts of the emerald yet?" he murmured into her ear, close behind.

While adjusting the stirrups, she whispered back, "I finally got one of the wives to talk about it last night. He keeps it on his person at all times."

"Really? Where?"

"Hiding in plain sight. On the pommel of his sword."

He went to put on the bridle and subtly glanced at Ukhuna's scabbard worn at his left hip, chagrined at not having noticed the massive shining gem festooned to the end of his sword's grip before now.

"I thought it would be bigger . . ." he said.

"To trap an ancient spirit, the size of the emerald is less important than the power of the Mage that put it there."

"In my experience, separating a man from his sword is no easy task."

Although her smile remained hidden beneath her shroud, the twinkle in her eyes gave it away. "Well, my experience is to the contrary."

Ukhuna mounted his black steed and boomed, "Are you ready, my Beauty? I will give you a head start."

"What's happening?" Jeth asked.

"A Tezkhan cannot wed a woman he has not captured from horseback," Anwarr said as she mounted her buckskin.

"Yes," Ukhuna added. "Although Raisha is already promised to me, the Equestrian Gods will not approve of our union before this is done." He directed Anwarr along with a sweep of his arm, and she kicked her horse onto the empty plains.

Chief Ukhuna sat on his mount, watching his bride galloping toward the horizon. Then, with a sharp whistle, he sped after her.

For such a heavy man, his horse didn't appear at all hindered by his weight, and he gained on Anwarr in a few moments. She zigzagged out of his reach, but the Chief kept right on her tail.

Ukhuna got right up next to her and snatched Anwarr out of her saddle before she could steer away. She screeched as Ukhuna threw her over his horse's withers. As the two of them loped back to camp, Ukhuna held her around the waist with one arm and managed the reins with the other. He whispered in her ear, which made her throw her head back in laughter. Jeth scratched at his beard, irked by how effortless Anwarr played the part of the excited bride to be. *It's just an act . . .*

Cheers rang out as the people ran to meet their triumphant chief. He dismounted before turning to assist Anwarr from the saddle.

"Gather around, wives of mine, sisters, and brothers." Ukhuna's steed pushed against his shoulder, and he quickly pulled him back by the reins, laughing heartily. "Not you, Sandstorm." A slave rushed up and led the horse away so the Chief could continue. "I will now disrobe my captured bride before the Equestrian Gods!"

The people cheered again as Jeth looked around for someone to explain what was about to happen. He began to sweat as Ukhuna unraveled Anwarr's belt sash. He then yanked off her robes with a mere flick of the wrist. Jeth's heart skipped a beat, but instantly relaxed when he found her to be wearing a form-fitting two-piece dress of red silk and yellow lace trim underneath. The Chief removed her head and face covering, revealing her shining white hair in a high bundle. A formless woman approached and placed upon it a red headdress with yellow beads that hung down jingling in front of her face.

"Raisha, daughter of Herran's Overlord, I take you as my eighth wife. Before the Equestrian Gods and your father's representative." He motioned to Jeth, and he replied with a deferential nod. "Do you swear to honor Chief Ukhuna of the Tezkhan?"

Anwarr glanced at Jeth also before she turned to her groom and lowered her head, the beads clacking together. "I promise to honor you as your wife, Great Chief."

"We will exchange gifts now," Ukhuna announced, beaming from ear to ear.

He snapped for one of his brothers to bring the buckskin horse they had just retrieved from the plain.

Anwarr took the reins and brought it beside her. "I thank you a thousand times for this wonderful gift," she said. "I give to you now, a weapon of my tribe, a traditional offering to all husbands of Nas'Gavarr's daughters."

The cheering quieted to a murmur when Anwarr motioned to a slave girl to carry an item wrapped in a soft hide and present it to Ukhuna. He attentively folded back the hide to reveal Anwarr's tulwar.

Ukhuna's eyes widened. He grabbed the hilt and swished his new blade above his head a couple of times before nodding in approval and handing it off to his own slave.

The Chief roared, "Now we celebrate. Let the games begin!"

One of the games Ukhuna referred to, Jeth soon learned, was a competition to tame an untameable steed. The first man to catch, mount, and break it would be given the horse and their choice of any of the Chief's concubines. They saddled up a particularly feisty dapple gray, having advanced in age to the point it should be untrainable.

While the women prepared the night's feast and the slaves pampered the Chief and his new wife upon their cushions, near twenty men chased a bucking mare across the plains. They rode in tight circles to keep it from escaping. Every few seconds, groups of riders randomly shot out into the circle, crisscrossing their paths, confusing the mare, and blinding it with clouds of kicked-up dirt while attempting to catch it around the neck with their lariats.

Jeth laughed at the men flying through the air after every failed attempt to mount the mare. Ukhuna turned to him. "Does this game entertain you, Manservant?"

"It does," he replied. "I'm curious, though, why couldn't that horse be broken when it was younger?"

Ukhuna spat another green gob and grinned, showing his crooked green-tinged teeth. "There are mares, just as there are women, who have a fire within them near impossible to snuff out."

"What happens to those that can't be tamed? Are they slaughtered for meat? The horses that is, not the women . . ."

"Foolish foreigner." Ukhuna shook his head. "To kill a horse of the Tezkhan for such a reason is an affront to the Equestrian Gods and punishable by death. Nothing of the sort happens to the untameable. Even the most stubborn of mares will one day succumb to the right rider." He nudged Anwarr, and she responded with a good-natured laugh then rolled her eyes as soon as he turned back to Jeth. "Do you not wish to partake?"

"It is not my place . . . is it?" Jeth turned to his pretend mistress.

"A Sunil is higher than a slave, fit to sit at their master's table if they so desire," Anwarr replied. "If the Chief allows it, you may have a go at the untameable steed."

"Do you know much of horse taming?" asked Ukhuna.

"As it happens, I was a horse trainer for my Order."

Ukhuna snapped his fingers for the nearest slave. "Saddle up another catcher and find a lariat pole." He turned back to Jeth. "Make haste and mount that mare before one of my brothers beats you to it."

Anwarr gave Jeth an encouraging nod. He wasn't expecting to join the Tezkhan in their celebratory games, but he didn't want to turn down the opportunity either. "I'd be delighted, what's the worst that can happen?" He chuckled, then muttered more to himself, "Other than breaking my neck."

Within minutes, Jeth was riding in the dizzying circle alongside the others. Once the group had whittled down to nine men, the barrier weakened, turning the game into a free for all.

The horse veered straight for him. He threw out his lariat with a flick of the pole, but it came nowhere near the steed's neck. One man cut in front of him and jumped onto its back, but it jerked away. The man landed hard on his face, leaving a splatter of blood amongst scattered teeth on the bleached earth. Another rider flung his lariat over the mare's neck and leveraged himself onto it with more success. The men cheered him on as he took hold of the reins and pulled back. The horse violently shook its head from side to side, kicking and bucking to such a degree, dust billowed into the air, causing many, Jeth included, to cough and hack. When the dust cleared the rider was nowhere to be seen. The horse bolted to the side and then came a sickening snap followed by a high-pitched wail. The horse had trampled him under foot. Everyone else grimaced.

"It's not worth it until someone breaks something," said the rider next to Jeth who he recognized as the first man to speak to him and Anwarr upon arrival.

He was reminded of the ranch and the many training methods he had experimented with in an attempt to limit the number of untrainable horses that would have been turned into food for the herding dogs. One tried and true way was to tire the beast out, if one could stay on its back long enough for that to happen. Once Jeth realized the Tezkhan were doing just that, a competitive flame ignited deep inside him. *You can win this; You will win this! You just have to do it your way.*

First thing to do was sabotage.

Another lariat caught the mare around the neck. Before the man could make the leap, Jeth smacked the horse on the rump as he rode by. It kicked its legs out and chucked the man to the dirt.

A moment later, someone absent his pole jumped and made it onto its back. Jeth turned his horse in front of the bucking mare. It reared, dancing on its hind legs until the rider slid off. *Down to five.* Soon, four more men were out, leaving only him and the man who spoke to him earlier. *This one looks like he's biding his time too.*

Both men chased the mare through the plains, kicking up copious amounts of dust and trampling down the dry foliage. Still, the untameable horse showed no signs of tiring and yet Jeth could sense his own mount petering. He wiped the sweat pouring from his brow, shocked that his Sunil hat had not come off. He looked ahead to the West Serpentine River. *That's how you'll finish this.* A new energy invigorated him.

Tossing away his lariat pole, he called over to his competitor, "Hey, what's your name?"

"Genkhai," he called back.

"I need you to help me force this mare to the river, Genkhai."

"Why should I help you? The horse is mine." He veered to the right and led the horse back east, away from the river. Jeth groaned and rode toward the flank to turn it back south.

"Give me a chance to win the horse, and I'll let you have the concubine. Otherwise, I won't even attempt to get on, and I'll wait for you to get bucked off instead."

"I was with you when you said concubine." Genkhai grinned. He immediately turned to the mare's left flank and forced it to keep galloping south. Jeth kept at its right, bringing it closer to the raging river ahead.

He stood in the stirrups and steered in tight. At the right moment, he launched himself onto the mare's back. Just as he hoped, the shock of his landing made it buck out of control and straight into the rapids.

"Are you trying to drown it?" Genkhai halted his horse at the river bank.

Jeth jerked on the reins, spinning the horse around, so it faced the rapids flowing eastward. The mare struggled to stay above water, fighting the rapids with determined fervor. It continued to jerk its head back and forth, but Jeth had no trouble staying on while it was swimming. The cool rapids were refreshing but did nothing to dampen his or the horse's adrenaline. He kept nudging it toward the embankment, but it continued to fight him, shrieking all the while.

"Come on, you stubborn beast, figure it out or drown," he muttered and yanked the horse to the left.

Genkhai sat still on his own steed, staring blankly at him and the mare thrashing about in the river for several minutes. The horse's movements eventually slowed and it became more receptive to Jeth's directions. It climbed back onto the bank, both of them soaking wet and exhausted.

"Are you ready to listen to me now, you stubborn thing?" He patted its damp neck as it lumbered up the embankment and back onto flat ground. The tired mare didn't give him any more trouble as it made the walk back to the camp. Even after he dismounted onto unsteady legs, it stayed by his side, blowing hard out flaring nostrils.

He stroked the horse's white face, and it nickered deeply. "You're all right."

Jeth hadn't noticed all the spectators cheering for the foreign victor. As good as it felt to earn the respect of so many, Anwarr's reaction to his triumph gave him more pause. She jumped up and down, clapping and screeching. Dragging him over to the Chief by the arm, Anwarr beamed. "Do I have a talented Sunil or what?"

Jeth was too out of breath to respond.

"That was most impressive, indeed," Ukhuna rang. "My concubines await you. Be the first manservant to ever sample one of my beauties."

He stepped aside to present a line of five women, all veiled head to toe. He told them to reveal their faces so that Jeth could choose one of them. After looking briefly at each, Jeth was relieved he had made that deal with Genkhai. *You've yet to be with a woman, but with faces like those you can afford to wait.* Only two of them were absent lesions around their mouths and cheeks, or other deformities, and that was only because they appeared well below bedding age.

"I am honored you'd offer a humble servant like myself such a beautiful gift, but I cannot accept."

"Why?" Ukhuna snorted, hands slapping his protruding belly. "Do Sunil not have man parts?"

Jeth huffed, "What? Of course, we do. We——"

Anwarr smothered a giggle in her hand.

With a calming exhalation, he pointed to Genkhai tending to his own horse. "I have forgone this prize already to this fine rider here. Were it not for him I wouldn't have won."

Ukhuna grumbled a bit, but nodded in agreement. "Very well. Genkhai, take your pick. Baird, you may keep the steed. What name will you give her?"

"Oh uh. . . ." Jeth looked back at the wild dapple gray. It looked right back at him, and the name suddenly came to him like the rapids slapping him in the face. "Her name will be Torrent."

As soon as the sun set, the camp erupted in celebration. Several fires blazed at the center of camp, men blasted horns, and women played long string instruments, the music from which sounded distorted, but strangely beautiful. All men were shirtless, and the women unveiled, no longer concerned with the hot sun on their skin.

To avoid having to drink more of that fermented milk, Jeth retired to the horse pens to tend on his prize. He was unsure how long it would take Anwarr to complete her task; he needed to keep establishing trust so he could mount the horse again at a moment's notice.

He was in the midst of brushing the dust off her coat when Anwarr, still wearing her red silks and beaded headdress, appeared just outside the pen. He dropped the brush and dashed over to her. "Did you get the sword?"

"Not yet, but soon," she said. "When it's time for the consummation, I need you close to the yurt."

"Consummation?" He gulped. "Y-you'd actually go that far . . . with him?"

"I'd rather not, but he is my husband after all." Anwarr gave a sardonic smile.

Jeth just stared at her, not sure how to respond.

"What?" she asked.

"N-nothing, it's just . . . you actually married a man for an emerald."

"Does that bother you?" She crossed her arms over her chest.

"Where I come from, when two people decide to . . . copulate, it's forever . . . or long enough for the children to grow up at least."

Anwarr giggled, placing a soft hand on his face, running her fingers down his cheek, then tugging gently at his sideburns. "What a precious boy you are. I am not here to fall in love and give birth to his future horde. He's my target, and nothing more."

"We can figure out another way. The two of us together can take him."

"If he strikes either one of us just once, it's all over. Not to mention an entire camp of loyal riders will chase us down with the fastest horses in the known world. What I need you to do is sneak into the yurt, snatch his sword, and make headway to the canyon entrance to wait for me."

"Are you sure you want to do this?" Discomfort rooted in his gut.

"Your first lesson: know the target's weaknesses as well as you know your own capabilities. Some men respond to threats, others to flattery. Sunil servants are far too disciplined for my . . . persuasion tactics to work, but men like Ukhuna refuse to acknowledge that they have weaknesses at all. That is what I live to exploit."

"I don't doubt that . . ." Jeth muttered.

Anwarr flashed a self-satisfied grin. "He is already drunk, and I intend to make him more so. The faster he passes out, the easier our getaway is going to be."

"It will take a lot of horse milk to bring a man of that size down."

"Leave him to me. One way or another, he won't even know you're there."

Jeth was speechless. He couldn't decide what was worse, stealing from a man who had shown him nothing but hospitality since arrival or the thought of Anwarr consummating her fake marriage to him.

Anwarr reached over the fencing and took him by both shoulders, forcing him to look at her. "Are you still with me on this?"

"As a Sunil, I am sworn to do whatever my mistress commands, aren't I?"

"You play your part well," she said with a relieved sigh.

"I'm always playing a part," he replied. "This is nothing."

Her smile widened enough to showcase her missing molar. "Good. Now I must play mine. Wish me luck."

He nodded dumbly and watched her scurry back to her husband.

Jeth spent the next half hour securing an escape route while ensuring both of their horses were saddled with food and water and that their weapons were packed. It wasn't until midnight when Ukhuna announced his intentions to take his new wife to their marriage bed.

"Continue your feasting and merry making," he boomed with drunken levity. "I will return to you all by mid-day."

The Chief cast Anwarr over his shoulder like a sack of potatoes, and she screeched in laughter as everyone else cheered, the men most of all. The burly raider staggered into one of the more elaborate yurts, released the hide door flap, and let it roll down to the ground.

Even as the festivities grew louder and rowdier, Jeth's sensitive ears picked out the various grunts and giggles emanating from the Chief's yurt. Anwarr sounded as if she were legitimately enjoying herself and he couldn't decide whether that was a good or bad thing. He ambled closer, waiting for a chance to enter without anyone noticing.

One of Ukhuna's brothers chasing a tittering woman scurried by Jeth. He ducked away from the yurt's entrance. *You shouldn't be doing this. The Tezkhan would probably take you in as one of their own and the Del'Cabrian army would never find you here.* He halted his gait and shook the thought out of his mind. Despite his temporary acceptance into the Tezkhan fold, he couldn't imagine selling out Anwarr to join a group of raiders whose way of life involved terrorizing tribes and collecting slaves. He still didn't know if he could trust her, but he couldn't trust a man like Chief Ukhuna either. He had come too far not to see this plan through. Ill-advised as it was.

Returning to the yurt, he honed his hearing for a sign of it being safe to enter.

"I wish to take you now, Raisha. Enough with these games you play," grunted Ukhuna.

"First, let me soothe your aching muscles. All that riding you've done lately—"

"Never have my eyes fallen upon a beauty such as yours. I've waited long enough."

"And never have you experienced the pleasures that a Herrani woman can give. Relax and allow me to show you," cooed Anwarr. A drink sloshed before the two shuffled about the room. "Lay upon your stomach and close your eyes."

She knows you're listening. This is your chance.

Taking a few deep breaths, Jeth surveyed the area one more time for potential witnesses and finding none, soundlessly slipped between the flaps. Inside, he found Ukhuna shirtless, oiled, and face down on his bedding. Anwarr was astride him, topless and facing away from the door with a bottle of oil in one hand. Jeth crouched down so the braziers wouldn't cast his shadow in front of them. The torch's light ignited the intricate details of Anwarr's tattoo. Escaped wisps of hair from her tousled bun danced upon her shoulders. He stopped dead, near forgetting what he came in for. Anwarr motioned her head toward Ukhuna's clothes upon the floor, his sword and sheathe among them.

As Jeth crept along the ground, Anwarr continued to rub the oils on Ukhuna's hairy back. His moans of pleasure were loud, allowing Jeth to sift through his heavy hides without him hearing.

The hilt of the Chief's sword sparkled in the lamp light. He slid his hands along the belt and worked at unbinding the scabbard. Ukhuna stirred and Jeth peeked up to find him facing his direction. If the man were to open his eyes, it would be all over. Jeth froze.

Anwarr bent down to kiss her husband, temporarily blocking his possible view of Jeth. With quivering hands, he continued to untie the scabbard while Ukhuna turned over onto his back and brought Anwarr on top of him. Jeth froze again, his heart thudding into his throat. Anwarr fell to Ukhuna's left side so that he would turn to face her, and Jeth used this opportunity to retrieve the sheath and make way for the exit.

So anxious to get out of there, he neglected to stay crouched low enough. A shadow of the top of his square hat cast itself on the far wall, directly in Ukhuna's line of sight.

"What's that?" he mumbled.

Jeth dropped down flat on the floor, hiding his shadow, but it would only be a matter of seconds before Ukhuna glanced down to find a member of the Sunil Order and trusted servant of the Overlord with his priceless sword in hand.

7

The Serpent's Philosophy

Anwarr grabbed the Chief's bearded face and sharply turned him toward her. "I am finished waiting. Take me now, husband."

"You are a fickle woman," Ukhuna replied as he began to undo his pants.

He dove on his new wife, turning away from the door. Jeth snuck the rest of the way out of the yurt, trying not to focus on what Ukhuna was about to do to his accomplice.

Adrenaline surged through his body as he emerged outside. Keeping to the shadows of the camp, he made his way back to the horse pens and found Torrent. Rowdy hollers from the festivities continued. A few stumbling men with women under their arms passed by the pens, none of them taking notice of Jeth securing the emerald adorned weapon to his saddle bag.

Now was his chance to mount up and ride off into the night, but a dreadful weight still clamped down on his chest. He glanced back to Ukhuna's yurt where he and Anwarr were still together. *You can't just leave her in there. . . .*

He found Anwarr's horse and tied its reins to one of the posts then proceeded to open the pen's gate before hopping on Torrent's back. She pranced underneath him for a few moments but soon conceded to his control. He cantered around the pen, chasing the other horses out, namely the colts and the fillies. The resulting chaos caused all the horses to whinny and carry on into the night.

"The horses got out! Get the lariat poles!" came male shouts from camp.

Jeth rode alongside the stampede, pretending to herd the horses back toward the pens, but Torrent wasn't cooperating completely, as he expected she wouldn't. In a few moments, the Chief emerged from his yurt, partially robed and scowling.

"What's going on out here?" he bellowed.

Anwarr appeared from the yurt a few seconds later, wrapped in a large burgundy robe and hopping into her shoes. She bolted for the horse pens while her husband was distracted. She found her mount tied to the post, unable to escape with the others. Once she was in the saddle, she met eyes with Jeth for a moment. She gave him a curt nod and took off eastward. Jeth circled the camp with the other horses to get out of Ukhuna's sight, then broke away to follow Anwarr into the blackness. In a few minutes, he caught up with her and the two of them rode hard for the entrance of the slot canyons.

When they arrived, Anwarr lit her Sunil lantern, festooned on a short pole, and followed Jeth into the crevasse. "Didn't you think to bring a torch? Or can you see in the pitch black as well?" she asked.

"Unfortunately, no. My night vision is as good as yours."

"Then perhaps I should lead. I can't promise I will remember the way we came, though. If we take a wrong turn, we could run into a dead end, and there won't be enough room for our horses to turn around."

"That's all right, just keep the lamp on, I can get us back through," he said.

"Are you sure?"

He was almost too embarrassed to say more. Where excellent vision was impressive to most, a hound-like sense of smell was often a little disconcerting. "Uh . . . I can smell where the horses from yesterday have been."

"How?"

"From their manure, mostly. Let's just say I can retrace our steps out of here."

"You are turning out to be quite the useful travel companion," said Anwarr. "Do all Fae'ren have heightened senses like yours? Naja can smell a drop of blood from a mile away; it would do the Del'Cabrian army good to have people on their side who could do the same."

"Yeah, that would be something." He chuckled. "As far as I'm aware, I'm the only one. But fairy's senses are far better than mine. My people can trace their lineage back thousands of years to fairies who abandoned their duty to the forest, were stripped of their wings, and became mortals. Much of their abilities have been lost over the generations, but for some reason, our matting hair was one trait that stuck. That and pointed ears in those who call themselves the Fae."

"You think some of those fairy abilities are left in you, even though you are not a Fae?" Anwarr wondered.

"Maybe, I don't know. I didn't even realize I had better senses than other people until I started coming in contact with them."

"You're saying that, at one point, you were not in contact with any people?" Anwarr asked. The canyon widened for a stretch, and she sidled up next to him.

"I had a rather abnormal upbringing," he said with a sideways grin.

"What is abnormal where you come from?" She matched his smile with one of her own, hardly discernable in the dark.

"Not having parents. Well, ones that abandon you in the forest to be raised by fairies. I didn't get to meet another human being until I was fourteen."

"That sounds lonely," Anwarr said.

"Not that fairies don't make good company. It's just . . . they don't feel the same range of emotions we do. They don't have the same sort of nurturing instinct—at least not for humans. In that way . . . it was pretty lonely, I suppose."

He swallowed a lump in his throat as they silently navigated a tight curve in the canyon.

Anwarr was the first to resume their conversation. "I know the feeling."

"You're an orphan too?" Jeth turned to face her, only to find her closing in behind him as the path ahead narrowed.

"No, my parents are still alive. My mother is ill of mind, and my father was hardly ever around. I had so many siblings it was easy to become lost. Even in a large family like mine, it can feel like you have no one at all."

"Do you get to see them often?"

She turned her head away. "Never."

Jeth wanted to ask her more, but something about the coldness in her voice told him not to pry any further.

Silence draped over them, and they soon left the canyons behind. They watered their horses at the pond and galloped south, far from the river and into the open desert plains of Sunil to best avoid crossing paths with the real Raisha's retinue.

Both moons were full in the night sky. Thousands of stars lit up the landscape, so they no longer needed the lantern. The sheer openness in every direction left him vulnerable in a way he wasn't used to. He hated not being able to rely on his eyesight to determine if anybody was approaching from the blackness. When they stopped to rest for the night, he kept scanning the horizon for shadows against the star-speckled sky but found nothing, which did little to relieve his anxiety.

Then Anwarr lit a fire.

"Put that out! Someone could spot us."

"Like who?" She presented the vast openness with her arms. "The Del'Cabrians likely stopped looking for us. They have the Overlord to worry about. We need this fire to stay warm. Sunil can be frigid on nights like this."

"I'm more afraid of the Tezkhan finding us," he said as he lugged over a heavy stone to hold the horses' leads down for the night.

"They won't be able to get all their horses through the canyons tonight anyway. But, thanks to you, they will head out at first light in search of what they now know we took." Anwarr took out Ukhuna's sheathed sword from Torrent's saddle and waved it in front of Jeth.

"Thanks to *me?* I was following *your* plan!"

"The plan was to take the sword and meet me at the canyon entrance, not to create a commotion."

"I did that to help you."

"Yes, except I didn't need your help. I had Ukhuna under my control. He would have passed out cold where I could have then made my escape quietly. It would have been well into the afternoon before any of them woke to realize what happened, and we would be miles into Herrani territory."

Jeth took off his hat and stuffed it in his saddle bag. "I'm sorry, but I couldn't just sit there and wait for Ukhuna to . . ." He bit his tongue.

"For Ukhuna to what?" She crossed her arms over her chest.

He sighed. "I was just trying to protect you."

"It is not your job to protect me. Next time, trust in my abilities just as I trust in yours." Anwarr took the small blanket from the back of her horse's saddle and fanned it out on the ground near the fire.

"N-next time?"

Anwarr stood straight but didn't fully turn around to face him. "You have a lot to learn, but I believe you would make a fine addition to our crew."

"You don't want to get rid of me yet?" he asked with a nervous grin.

Meeting his eye, her expression softened. "I'd rather keep you around a bit longer. That is unless you'd rather return to your family of fairies."

"Not a chance," he said in a flat tone, taking a seat on the blanket.

"Are they really that bad?" Anwarr sat down next to him, crossing her legs and holding her knees to her chest.

"No. They have a duty to preserve the forest and don't generally associate with mortals unless it's to play the odd prank when bored or chase out those they believe a threat. Other than that, they are peaceful creatures, but very protective."

"But they accepted you into their fold. . . ."

"They raised me to honor my mother's prayer to the Crannabeatha, or the Mother Oak as my people call her," he said. "She gives life to all of the forest and the fairies. They kept me from the other humans so that I wouldn't catch the plague that broke out. When it ran its course, and I could more or less take care of myself, they made me leave."

Anwarr's usual cheerful expression turned sorrowful.

"Little did they realize," Jeth continued, "the Fae'ren people wouldn't have me either. Orphans are considered cursed. So . . . they shunned me."

"That is too cruel—to blame a child for the death of its parents," Anwarr said in a hushed voice.

"Orphans aren't something my people were used to dealing with before the increased number of adult deaths in recent decades. In the past, a mother never died giving birth, a father rarely went to war—families were small and manageable. Since the Del'Cabrians took over, a lot of that has changed." He shrugged.

"Do you miss it there?" Anwarr asked while drawing serpents in the sand with a thin stick.

Jeth fiddled with the small twigs around him. "I miss the Deep Wood where I grew up, not the communes. I didn't mind the solitude that much. I was close to a pixie named Serra. She was there for me for as long as I can remember. But, she did her duty, kept me alive until I was old enough to chase out of the forest like any other human." He flung one of the small sticks into the fire. It landed with a pop.

The two stared into the dancing flames for a few moments. Jeth could still hear the last words Serra said to him right before he left the Deep Wood for good.

"It's my sacred duty. I can never leave this forest, but you can, and should. You belong with other humans, not with us. Now leave."

"Or what?"

"There is no 'or what?' You either leave, or we make you."

He sniffed and wiped his ever-drying nostrils.

Anwarr broke the silence. "All for the best, I say."

He snorted. "Haven't you been listening?"

"The past only serves to keep you from truly being free. I live by the Serpent's Philosophy," she began as she completed her drawing of a winding snake in the sand. "Just as the serpent will not slither backward, neither will I. Whichever direction I face, it is always forward."

"Is that why you won't go home to your family?" he asked, staring at the picture she drew.

"They are the past. The only thing that exists is this very moment. Everything before is gone forever." Anwarr's eyes darkened as she mixed the sand with her hand, erasing her snake from existence.

"But that's just it. The past isn't gone, it's stuck. In here." Jeth picked up another stick and tapped the point to his own head. "How do you just forget about it?"

"By looking to the future; the infinite possibilities of the unknown. That is far more exciting than dwelling in the painful memories of yesterday."

"In theory." He threw that stick in the fire as well.

"Look up there." Anwarr pointed to the two full moons in the south. "The larger moon represents the light of Sagorath. He is domineering, strong, and feared. He is the bringer of death and yet he protects us all. The smaller and brighter moon is Salotaph. She is elegant, wise, and nurturing, the creator of life. She gives us hope. The two spend many years apart, lost in their own struggles. Then, for a few wonderful nights they come together to merge their light. As you can see, Salotaph is going to catch up with Sagorath and soon they will become one, as they inevitably do."

The moons' brightness stung Jeth's eyes. He found more comfort watching Anwarr describe them, her eyes as two glowing moons in and of themselves.

"Their union marks the Lunahalah, a glorious festival where any new experience imaginable is undertaken without consequence. When Salotaph parts from her lover's embrace, all is forgotten, and she embarks on a journey anew. Not even the might of Sagorath can hold her back. It is she who chooses to return to him."

"Are you like Salotaph?" he asked.

A cool breeze blew between them, twirling Anwarr's silver strands around her ears as she hugged herself. "No, she faithfully returns, but not me. Like I said, the serpent does not slither backward and neither do I. That is what you should do." Anwarr's eyes now blazed into his. "Find your bliss, take it, live it, and when it suits you, forget about it. Make room for great things to come into your life and in time all that you drag behind you will fall away. That is the meaning of the Lunahalah, and for me, the meaning of life itself. Death comes for us all, no matter how far back you run. You might as well enjoy yourself while you can."

"Can't say I hate the sound of that," Jeth said as he lay back with his hands behind his head. "There's only one problem. Careening head first into the future doesn't change what happened in the past. It doesn't make me any less of a traitor."

Anwarr moved her legs to the side and propped herself up on one arm, better showcasing her full figure, apparent even under her thick robe. "This is what I'm talking about. You were a traitor, you are not one now, nor will you be as long as you stop giving power to a word that other people use to define you. Those same people would call you Fae scum, and is that who you are?"

"No, but I actually am a traitor by definition."

"Not even by definition. How do you betray something you were never loyal to in the first place?"

"I swore an oath to serve my country."

Anwarr waved her hand in dismissal. "Just words. Admit it. You swore only to serve yourself. To move up the status order or whatever it is."

"True, but . . ." He scratched at his chin and sighed.

"It's all right," she said in a softer tone as she lay down on her side, keeping her head up with her arm and stroking the blanket fibers with the other. "We all serve our own self-interest. A selfless man would have left me with those brutes in reporting them to his superior officer. My temporary suffering would be a necessary cost to end the suffering of war. Lucky for me, that was not the case."

"You're saying, I killed my own men, betrayed my country, and ruined my life because I'm selfish?"

"What other reason is there?" She shrugged.

Jeth let out a dry cough into his left shoulder and chuckled darkly. How does she do it? he wondered. Looking to the sky, he said, "Do you want to know the truth?"

Anwarr nodded as she loosened her bun and let down her long, white tresses.

"You're right. I didn't kill my own men out of the goodness of my heart. I did it because . . . I wanted to. In that moment, I wasn't thinking about following orders, about winning the war, or saving you. I just wanted those urling bastards dead. I'm glad they are, and I'm glad I'm the one who killed them."

"And they deserved it," she added.

"It's not for me to say whether they did or didn't. All I know is that if faced with the decision to do it again, I would. I guess . . ." He sighed deeply as he cracked his knuckles under his head, "that makes me the animal everybody thinks I am."

Anwarr shook her head. "It makes you human. Good, bad, it all balances out in the end. The only thing that matters is that you are true to yourself and nothing else."

"So how does one go about doing that?"

"You already are. It's why you chose to run with me instead of leaving your fate in the hands of lesser men."

Jeth sat up, leaning on his left arm and casually resting his other on his bent knee. "You know, Del'Cabrians have another word for fate. They call it the Way. The Deities have preset all of our paths in life, and one must accept it before one will ever know peace."

"Forget peace. What do you want your *Way* to be?" Anwarr flicked her hair off of her shoulders, allowing the moonlight to reflect off every twist of her body beneath the robe.

Jeth bit the inside of his cheek before uttering a response. "I haven't thought that much about it."

"Bullshit." Anwarr sat up and looked him straight in the eye. "Everyone has desires. What do you want?"

His pulse raced in response to how Anwarr looked at him, ardently awaiting his answer, her partially exposed bosom muddling his thoughts. "R-right now?"

"Right now," she repeated, bringing her face closer to his.

The musk of Ukhuna's sweat surrounded her, but Jeth could make out her own sweet scent beneath. It made him hesitate. Yet, the firelight dancing in her glowing eyes encouraged him. He leaned in to kiss her only for her to turn away, letting out a soft chortle.

Jeth's skin flushed as he remained frozen, his advance unreciprocated, and his stomach twisting in knots. Anwarr didn't move completely away, but she didn't move any closer either. He could hear her steady heartbeat inches from him while his own fluttered in his chest.

"What do you want from me?" he whispered.

Anwarr opened her mouth to reply, but a searing light shone straight into their faces. It was brighter than the flames and the moons combined, and it was emanating from a figure on camelback galloping toward them. *Dammit, man, your senses should have been directed elsewhere!*

The camel came to a stop several feet from the fire, and the bright light was extinguished, casting the rider in shadow.

"Anwarr?" came a deep, feminine voice.

The figure dismounted and stepped into the firelight, revealing an ebony-skinned woman with shining blue eyes, wearing a tan colored tunic and hood. She carried a large gnarled stick with a sapphire embedded in grooves along the top. Her clothing was masculine, her bare arms muscular, her build sturdy, but her lips were full and eyelashes long.

"Istari!" Anwarr jumped to her feet. Wrapping her arms around the dark woman's neck, she gushed, "How did you find me out here? You were supposed to wait for me at the river crossing."

Istari dropped her staff, took Anwarr's arms from her neck, and held them in place. "I was, but you were supposed to meet me there yesterday. I had no choice, but to go wandering the desert in search of you. What in Sag's name have you been up to all this time? Did you get the emerald?"

"Of course, I got it. We were just on our way to you. Have you lost faith in me so quickly?" Anwarr cooed, tickling Istari's arm with the tips of her fingers.

"No, but it's also not like you to be behind schedule. I was afraid that barbarian uncovered our ruse and killed you." Istari uncrossed her arms and drew Anwarr's hips toward hers.

Anwarr took down Istari's hood to reveal white wooly hair, trimmed short, showcasing the elegant shape of her head.

"I have much to tell you. But, first, come here." Anwarr ran her hands over the back of Istari's head and pulled her in for a kiss.

Jeth sat on the blanket stunned and invisible while the two women joined lips in a passionate embrace. *Is this the reason she spurned your advance a second ago?* He was unable to stop gawking but eventually found the wherewithal to stand. Istari pulled herself away from Anwarr to regard him suspiciously.

She stepped in front of her and said, "I see you've made a new friend, Ana. A Sunil? Can we afford him? How much is his contract?"

Anwarr laughed. "It's a disguise, silly. This is Jethril, a Fae'ren who helped me out of my predicament. He's agreed to join our team."

"Call me Jeth," he said with a finger-wriggling wave. Istari scrunched her face in response, and Jeth placed his arm down awkwardly at his side.

With her arms still wrapped around Istari, Anwarr said, "This is Istari, the crew's Light Mage from Odafi and a woman I've missed dearly."

Istari gently nudged her aside so she could better size Jeth up. "He's Del'Cabrian. We can't trust him."

"Will you let me worry about who we can and can't trust?" Anwarr said.

"He will not disappoint."

Jeth picked up Ukhuna's sword from where Anwarr had left it on the blanket and tossed it to Istari. "This is the stone we've picked up. Where are we taking it?"

Istari marveled at the emerald on the sword's pommel before responding, "That's not for you to know."

"Why not? Aren't I on the team now?"

"Hah! Not until the entire crew agrees that you are." Istari pointed her thumb back at Anwarr. "This one likes to think she's in charge, but decisions like this require the unanimous agreement of all members."

Anwarr groaned. "Stari, you're making the poor boy nervous. You have nothing to worry about, Jethril. I know you will impress the others just as you did me. We are selling our bounty to Snake Eye, the most influential buyer of stolen goods in Herran."

"And failure to bring it to him is not an option," Istari joined. "Which is why I'm so glad to have found you, Ana."

Anwarr motioned toward Jeth. "Then be glad I found him."

Istari gave Jeth a reluctant, yet grateful nod and went to get her things from the camel.

The two women slept in a bedroll, giggling together while Jeth lay upon the rough blanket a few feet away. Sleep did not come easy for him that night.

A week's ride took the thieves to the City of Herran, or more like the city of chaos. Unlike Del'Cabrian settlements of similar size, there were no predetermined locations for people to walk, for horse-drawn buggies or caravans to tread, vendors to peddle their wares, or street performers to showcase their talents. Wherever one desired to go or whatever one wished to do was fair game in Herran's most bustling metropolis.

They rode through the narrow streets, which branched out in a seemingly nonsensical fashion. Ramps and stairs led to thoroughfares above and below, making it difficult to distinguish which level travelers were on or how many levels there even were. It was reminiscent of the winding forested paths of the Deep Wood, only here, the crowds were stifling, making Jeth sweat more than he had while traveling back across the dunes in the days before. Luckily for him, the trio had come across a caravan of merchants where they obtained new clothing and headscarves.

An old man with a bushy blonde beard and wearing a ragged smock reached for him. "You there! For a reasonable price, I will guard your horse, so that you may walk more freely."

"Uh . . . what do I do?"

"Pay him no mind, Jeth," Istari warned, riding atop her camel beside him.

"A trustworthy vendor is one you seek out on your own."

Past the old man, more people rushed to him, holding their trinkets, beads, and various fruits in his face. They shouted details of their wares all at once, their words sounding as incoherent babble. He nudged Torrent into a trot to keep ahead of them. Had he carried any currency, he would have felt mildly guilty for not stopping, but neither Anwarr nor Istari gave the pushy merchants the courtesy of a glance.

After a while, the trio turned down a narrow thoroughfare that curved downward around a building and emerged underneath the street they had just been riding on. There they dropped their mounts off at a small stable that the two women seemed to trust and continued on foot.

Around the corner, three men in the crowd leaned against a market stand, staring and motioning toward the group, Anwarr in particular. She wore loose pants and a form-fitting halter that showcased her arms and midriff. Plenty of other women in the street wore far less than she, and yet the men seemed especially fixated on her. Two of them were young and baby-faced, wearing identical embroidered red tunics, and tightly wrapped hats adorned with a golden cobra-shaped crest to hold it in place. The third man was bearded and muscular, wearing the similar headwear and a brigandine vest etched with the same insignia.

"Over there." Jeth nodded toward the strange men. "Snake Eye's men?" All three of them snapped their heads away and started conversing with each other.

"I don't recognize them," said Istari.

Jeth honed his hearing to make out what the two young men were saying. "That Odafi woman must be the Essence Mage, but what of that pale fellow she's with?"

"Well they're talking about us," he cautioned. "They seem to know you, Anwarr."

"I've never seen them before. We should lose them to be safe," she said, without giving them so much as a glance.

The three walked past the mysterious strangers, and just as Jeth expected, they slowly ambled along behind them.

". . . And they're following us," he said.

Istari put her arms around both Jeth's and Anwarr's shoulders as she walked between them. "Keep walking. I'm going to take care of this."

As the three strode along, the strange men stopped. They scanned around, craning their necks to see over the throng. The large one came right up to stand in front of Jeth. He froze, but the man looked right past him. Not before long, the three strangers turned down a different road and scurried out of sight.

"What happened?" he said, just now remembering to breathe.

"I bent the light around us so they could not see us."

"That could have come in handy a week ago." He turned to Anwarr while pointing to Istari with his thumb. "And you didn't take her on your last mission because . . . ?"

"Sal knows I wanted to," she replied, peering adoringly into her lover's eyes. "But I couldn't guarantee her safety among the Tezkhan."

"Odafi and Tezkhan tribes have clashed for decades," Istari began, returning her loving glance. "The merchant fighting force, known as the Bahazur, drives them out of the Ankarr Tribe Lands every few decades. As a result, the Tezkhan are extra ruthless when they do manage to raid one of my people's communities along the border. Had I come as Saf'Raisha's companion, it would have been much harder to gain Chief Ukhuna's trust. Instead, I utilized my abilities to intercept the messages between him and the Overlord to change the meeting day to when Ana was supposed to arrive." Istari then pursed her lips at Anwarr. "She claimed she would be fine with her ten warriors."

Anwarr scoffed. "A lot of good they did me. Jethril alone took out, how many of them?"

"Three, if I recall."

"Three Herrani warriors is no small feat, I suppose," Istari said nonchalantly. "But you're no Steinkamp soldier."

"No, I am certainly not a nameless and faceless killer. Thanks for the reassurance," Jeth said with a shiver.

The reputation of Ingleheim's most specialized soldiers, trained since childhood in the art of death, more than preceded them. It was told that Ingleheim often sent them after their own defectors. Lucky for you, you're not an Ingleman, he thought.

They turned another corner to a darker, narrower road under a crumbling overpass. Animal hooves pounded on the road above as cart wheels squeaked, shaking small bits of dirt loose. Waiting at the end of a street, with hands behind his back, was a Sunil servant.

"I think that man is waiting for us," said Jeth.

"That is Yemesh, the Sunil contracted to Snake Eye," replied Anwarr.

As the trio approached, Jeth realized how tall Yemesh was. His long slender body appeared lithe enough to mount a camel as easily as any horse. Despite his gangly build, he had a handsome, clean-shaven face save a small blonde goatee trimmed close to his chin.

The Sunil nodded in greeting. "Good day to you, Anwarr, Istari, and who is your new companion?" Yemesh narrowed his piercing blue eyes at him.

He introduced himself as cordially as he could, and Yemesh nodded in response, but maintained his suspicious countenance.

"He is a potential recruit, but never mind that. We have the artifact for your master," Anwarr said.

Yemesh presented an even tighter alley between two buildings. He allowed

Istari and Anwarr passage but stepped to block Jeth. "Only those known to my master may pass this point."

"Seems like I'm being denied at every turn these days," Jeth muttered.

Anwar spun around. "Sorry, Jethril. When you join our crew—"

"If you join our crew," corrected Istari with her arms crossed over her chest.

"I promise I will introduce you to all our contacts, but for now, it would be best if you wait out here."

"That's all right, you ladies go ahead and get paid, I'll be fine."

"We won't be long."

At that, everyone but Jeth disappeared through a small door into the left building. He took a seat on a shaded bench under a storefront awning, clasped his hands behind his head, and settled for people-watching to pass the time. Folks with skin tones ranging from lightly tanned to near charcoal walked by with eyes of various hues of blue, green, and even yellow. A striking and shapely woman was studying him from afar. He caught her eye and smiled, but she scowled and walked away. Then, a group of four women distracted him. All were shrouded head to toe in bright colored garments, tittering away as they passed. None of these women need an escort? He pondered. Further down the street, beyond the shrouded women, the two chubby youths in red tunics wandered about. Them again! Jeth stood up with a start.

They didn't seem to notice him as they continued to look about the street in search of their quarry. The two parted ways, one of them ducking between buildings a block away from where Jeth stood.

Without a second thought, he followed. When he reached the alley, the man in red was walking down it with his back to him. He rushed over, grabbed him from behind, and dragged him into the recess of an old doorway. Jeth spun him around and shoved him up against the wall, clamping onto his arms.

"What do you want?" the man cried before he could get a word out.

"That's what I was about to ask you? Why are you following us?"

The man yelped, but Jeth muffled his cries with a hand over his mouth. "Tell me what you want from her, and I promise you won't get hurt."

He nodded, and Jeth carefully lifted his hand. A rapid shuffling came up behind him. He turned around just in time to block a punch from a much larger assailant. Jeth staggered by the blow and the follow-up strike sent him spinning face first into the old wooden door. Bouncing off it, he landed on his backside in the dirty alley. An old lady opened the door, only to witness the large bearded man lift Jeth up by the scruff and throw him overhead. The woman screamed and slammed the door shut while the younger man scampered off.

The armored brute loomed over Jeth, unsheathing a fittingly large tulwar.

"Jeth, close your eyes!" yelled Istari from behind. Confused by the strange command, he hesitated. A blinding light erupted in the dark alley, and both he and his opponent cried out in pain. A hand around his arm pulled him to his feet and led him back out onto the street.

"So far, I am less than impressed with your sit there and wait ability, but I see potential in your capacity for getting your face smashed in," said Istari in a dry tone.

Jeth groaned and rubbed his stinging eyes. "Those mystery men came back. I was trying to find out what they wanted. Deities damn my eyes!"

"A little blinding spell, it'll wear off momentarily." Istari patted him on the shoulder. "Those men seem to be gone now. Did you find out anything?"

He shook his head, blinking profusely while trying to bring the dark blur of Istari into focus.

She harrumphed. "Oh well, it was probably members of a rival band or Sag forbid, goons hired by Ezrai."

"Who's Ezrai?"

"Oh, just a cud stain we used to work for years ago. People in our occupation tend to make a few enemies. That's why it's important to look out for each other."

"All the easier when I get my eyesight back."

A blurry vision of Anwarr appeared next to them. "I got our notes!" she squealed in delight, flapping about five small sheets of parchment.

"Don't wave those around," Istari chastised as she snatched hers.

Anwarr handed Jeth a parchment with a signature over a Serpentine watermark and the amount of five thousand gold etched into it. Had this been in the form of Dels, Del'Cabria's currency, five thousand was a big enough number that someone of Jeth's status would likely never see it.

"I-is this . . . all mine?"

Anwarr nodded triumphantly. "Yes, it is. These notes are signed by Snake Eye, who has connections with a few coin changers in Odafi where we can have them traded in for real gold. As promised, you get half of my portion."

"Thank you, but you really didn't have to give me this much—unless this isn't as much as I think it is."

"We earned forty thousand gold between all five of us. That is enough for us to lay low for a year, maybe more if we scrimp." Anwarr grinned wide enough to reveal her missing molar then tucked three of the notes between her breasts.

Jeth was speechless while staring at his own note. *Your future is definitely not behind you*, he thought, excitement percolating within him.

"Ready to be a part of our crew, Jethril?" Anwarr asked.

Stuffing his note into his shirt pocket, Jeth nodded eagerly. "Put me where you want me."

Anwarr raised an eyebrow. "Oh, I intend to."

8

Shoot Fast and Don't Miss

Later that day, the women took Jeth to a giant marketplace. Like a city within a city, it had its own streets resembling hallways with hundreds of shops serving as rooms in an enormous mansion, permeating it in an endless array of colors and smells. Every type of hat, scarf, and rug, pottery, jewels, weapons, spices, and perfumes were on display. No one tried to push their wares unless one showed a legitimate interest, making him more comfortable than he had been in other parts of the city.

"What is this place?" he asked, gawking up at the unlit lanterns hanging overhead.

Anwarr replied, "This is the Great Bazaar of Herran. Only the finest vendors are allowed to operate here. It is also where our base of operations is."

"A thieving crew working out of a marketplace . . ." He nodded. "Convenient."

Istari gave him a warning eye. "We don't shit where we eat."

"Neither do I. Despite what you might have heard of my people, we keep our shit reasonably far from our food."

Anwarr giggled. "What Istari means is that the people here are part of our community. We never steal from them."

"Oh . . . makes sense." He coughed into his shoulder.

"Our home is just ahead."

Soon, the cluster of outdoor kiosks transformed into colorful sandstone buildings, all with shops and other businesses inside. A three-story structure with green spiral designs painted on the walls marked the spice shop the thieves called home.

They rode into the small attached stable where a skinny, shirtless boy excitedly waved the ladies in. His wide grin revealed horrendous teeth, many of them missing. He looked similar to the slave boys of the Tezkhan.

The boy threw his arms around Anwarr's waist and hugged her tight. "I missed you too, Khiri." She rubbed the boy's shaven head before giving it a kiss. "I trust things have not fallen apart while I've been away?"

Khiri silently shook his head, then greeted Istari in a similar manner but not with the same enthusiasm he had Anwarr.

"Not much for words, is he?" Jeth commented.

"Khiri is an Ankarran boy we rescued on a job off the coast of Odafi," said Anwarr. "He can't say much on account of his tongue having been cut out. Now, he helps out in the shop and looks after our beasts of burden." She motioned to a dark brown draft horse, another camel, and a donkey in the stable with them.

"He is also becoming quite the talented pickpocket," Istari added.

"Who would cut out a child's tongue?" Jeth's forehead creased.

Anwarr said, "The Ankarr tribes still partake in slave trading and are known for their barbarous treatment of them. Nas'Gavarr will soon unite them under his sphere and put a stop to it, I'm sure."

"Nice to meet you, kid." He offered his hand, but the boy only stared at it in confusion. Rubbing his little head instead, he left the mounts for him to deal with.

Inside the shop, Istari announced, "Lys, we're back."

An unassuming, middle-aged man with a dark, thin beard, looked up from counting his coins to acknowledge the crew members walking in. "Anwarr, you had us all very worried," he said in a disapproving tone.

Although the shopkeeper was dressed in the basic smock and head covering of a desert man, he possessed dark brown hair, a lighter, more olive skin tone, and a prominent bone structure. *He must be a Rangarder. Though, his dialect is strange.*

"Lay your worries to rest, Lysandros. I come bearing lots and lots of gold . . . the promise of it anyway." Anwarr took the parchments from her cleavage and smacked them down on the counter.

"I'll set off for Odafi first thing in the morning to cash them in," Istari said.

Lys's brown eyes widened as he rubbed his hands together with glee. "Very good. I will record these now."

He unlocked a drawer under the counter and brought out a leather-bound ledger. In the meantime, Jeth amused himself with the various bins of bulk spices, all combining a confusing, yet pleasing collection of scents. He took in hand a few granules of a red powder and sniffed it. The dust shot up his nose, and he sneezed violently. Everyone turned to stare at him. The older man appeared most annoyed.

"Please do not touch what you don't intend to purchase, young man."

"Sorry." Jeth wiped the red spice on his pants. Anwarr laughed and went on to explain to the shopkeeper who he was and why he was there.

"Oh, very good," he muttered and returned to his accounting.

"Lysandros owns this shop, which he uses to clean our coin as it were. He keeps our cover, and we keep his," said Anwarr.

"Cover for what?"

Istari explained, "He is an escapee from the Island of Credence. We've had to shoo away a few of their bounty hunters in the past. But not for a while, eh Lys?"

Lys shook his head without looking up from the ledger. "I just may be in the clear."

Jeth raised his eyebrow. "Credence?"

"You know," Istari went on. "The female-governed island south of Del'Cabria."

"I've heard of Credence, but I thought it was a fantasy paradise where great warriors hope to go when they die to be serviced by the most beautiful women imaginable. If such a place exists, why would you ever need to escape?"

"I was castrated and then forced to do hard labor," Lys said, barely looking up from his writing.

Jeth grimaced, scratching the back of his neck. "Oh, uh . . . that's rough . . . can I ask what you did to deserve such a dire fate?"

Istari tsked with disapproval. Lys put his quill and book away, then replied in a casual manner, "I hit a woman."

Jeth couldn't help but guffaw. "Like a queen or something?"

Lys shook his head. "No, a Mother."

"Well, I hope she deserved it," Jeth quipped, cringing at himself, but unsure what else to say to someone in Lys's particular situation.

"Very much." Lys nodded and went about tidying up the small spice jars behind the counter, humming all the while.

"Great." Jeth clapped his hands and rubbed them together. "Anyone else for me to meet?"

"Where's Ash?" Istari asked Lys.

"He just returned from a small job and is upstairs asleep."

"And the incessant chatter down here just woke me up," came a deep and raspy voice from the far-right corner of the shop.

Lumbering down the sandstone staircase was a groggy, tattooed fellow of enormous proportions, even bigger than the man Jeth had fought in the alley. He wore dark red, wide-legged pants, and an open vest, exposing an impossibly sculpted chest, tattooed with a giant red scorpion, its tail traveling up his sternum and the stinger nestled in the hollow of his clavicle.

The man, who Jeth assumed was Ash, shuffled his massive frame onto the shop floor, yawning and stretching his muscular arms above his head. Each one was tattooed with a blue and black serpent that wound around his biceps, over the shoulders and up the neck, to come to two hissing hooded heads on each side of his face, accentuated by the rings he wore in his earlobes and nose. He was bald except for a long tail of white hair, bound in sets reaching the small of his back.

"Please tell me you found her, Star," he said.

Anwarr, hiding behind a shelf, waited for Ash to pass by. She leaped onto his broad shoulders and started strangling him with one arm around his thick neck.

"Gah!" he yelped, flipping her overhead. She screeched and laughed as he spun her around, nearly knocking over a couple of barrels of spice in the process. Lys flinched.

"For the love of Sal, Ana, you are one crazy bitch!" he griped upon putting her down. A smile soon crept across his face, the jaws of each hooded snake widening eerily as he did so.

Anwarr hugged him, squealing. "Doesn't matter because we're rich!"

"I ought to knock another one of your teeth out for making us worry. What in Sag's name took you so long?" he said, still holding her. *Is she with him too?*

"A girl is late by a couple days, and you all act like the world almost ended." She shoved Ash, but he barely moved an inch. Jeth winced at the thought of him knocking Anwarr's tooth out.

Holding onto Ash's arm as a lady does her lord, Anwarr turned to Jeth. "Jethril, this is Ashbedael. He is the team's muscle." She gave the bulbous bicep a firm squeeze. "He used to be a member of the Bahazur, which means he's quite good with the tabar."

"I should have come with you as your bodyguard," Ash said, looking down at her with concern.

"It was a good thing you didn't," she said, gazing up at him from below his hulking shoulder. "Every one of the warriors was killed by Del'Cabrians."

"Like the one you just brought in here?"

Anwarr went on to explain everything to Ash that she had Lys, only with more detail about the task force that interrupted her mission.

Ash put out his huge hand, tattooed with the pattern of a net over the back of it. "I suppose you have my thanks, for keeping our girl safe."

"Don't mention it." Jeth tried to shake it at the same time Ash gripped his fingers and held them in a fist. The entire event ended up as an awkward attempt for both men to correct themselves until they each gave up.

"Somebody teach this boy how to greet a Herrani properly," griped Ash.

"You'll have plenty of time to do that when he joins our team," said Anwarr.

"No. No Del'Cabrian is going to be a part of this crew."

"He has more than proven himself."

"Oh, I'm sure he has." Ash glared at Anwarr with an accusing eye.

"What is that supposed to mean?"

"I think you know what it means." He narrowed his green gaze.

"I don't know what it means," Jeth piped up.

"Shut up. This doesn't concern you," Ash snapped.

"Doesn't it, though?"

Anwarr said, "Give me one good reason why he wouldn't be useful to us."

"We can't trust him for one thing. What if he never truly defected?" Ash turned to Jeth as if posing the question to him.

"You got me." He threw his hands up. "You figured out Del'Cabria's master plan. Send me as a spy to infiltrate one tiny thieving crew because that will surely win the war."

Everyone fell silent, save Ash cracking his knuckles. Lys, in an impassive voice, said, "The young man has a point. Give him a chance."

Anwarr nodded in thanks to Lys and then turned back to Ash. "I saw him defect with my own eyes. We can trust him."

"What do you have to offer then, traitor?" posed Ash.

"Other than being a general pleasure to have around, I'd start with archery." Jeth pointed to the bow and quiver still strapped to his back.

"We can find archers anywhere." Ash crossed his arms over his chest, closing the gap between him and the ceiling a few inches.

"How many can say they've never missed a shot?" Jeth stepped up to meet Ash's posture. *You liar.* He had missed plenty of targets, but usually during his own experimental practice sessions.

"You expect me to believe that?" Ash looked to Anwarr. "Where did you find this kid?"

"I haven't seen him miss one yet," she said.

Ash grunted. "Alright, boy. Let's put that arrogance of yours to the test. Lys, time to close up shop for the afternoon. We're going to the archery grounds."

A mile outside city walls, Herran boasted an impressive battle training camp, available to anyone for a fair price. Ash was happy to pay the way for all of them to enter the grounds, situated between two massive sand dunes exposed to the sun.

The sweltering heat and blinding brightness of daylight ensured the archery grounds were empty when the crew arrived. They rode up to the five splintering wood targets set up along the side of a dune at equal distance from each other and at varying heights. Liquid heat waves flowed over them, making them appear as specters in the sun.

"Hit each of these targets' bullseye, and we will talk about you joining us," said Ash. Everyone dismounted from their steeds, and Khiri led them to a trough to drink.

Jeth adjusted his headscarf then drew an arrow from his quiver. He took aim at the far-left target first, focusing his vision to find the bullseye through the rippling air.

As soon as he fell into his usual engrossed state, he released his first arrow and grabbed the second before the first one even struck. He had released the second by the time he noticed where the first one ended up and was already aiming the third. In five seconds, all five arrows had struck a target square in the bullseye.

Anwarr clapped, Ash nodded, and Lys said, "Very good."

"Beginner's training," jeered Jeth. "Frankly, I'm a little insulted."

Ash's face lit up. "We are just getting warmed up, boy. How about you hit them again from horseback."

Rolling his eyes, Jeth trudged over to Torrent at the trough. "With this new horse of mine, this might actually be a challenge."

Upon mounting his steed, he circled the grounds to take her in hand before charging past the targets at a gallop. In many ways, he found archery from horseback easier than standing still. There was no time to flinch or to second guess the aim. He, the bow, and the horse were a single entity. Another five arrows released, each one finding the bullseye with ease, right next to the others.

When he trotted back around and dismounted, Ash met him. "You didn't split the first set of arrows in half."

"And destroy perfectly good shafts? Only the most careless of bowmen split their own arrows for no good reason."

"Are you satisfied, Ashbedael?" Anwarr asked.

Ash grunted again. "Perhaps, but we came all this way, and I want to get my coin's worth. Are you up for more, boy?"

"I haven't even broken a sweat yet," he said, wiping that very thing from his brow.

"Glad to hear it. Come on, everyone. Let's go to the fighting pits."

"Pits . . . ? For fighting in?" The knot in his throat bobbed up and down.

Anwarr protested, "Were those last two demonstrations not enough? Now you expect him to fight you?"

"I'm with Ana on this one," Istari said. "I already saved his ass from a gigantic brute earlier today. Believe me, he's not up for it."

"Come on now. I could have taken him had you—"

"Quiet, I'm trying to keep you from being smashed into the dirt . . . again."

He threw up his arms in frustration. "Alright, you want to fight me, Big Fella? Fine. Let's get this over with."

Ash laughed heartily, the serpent maws on his cheeks grinning along with him. "You're not going to fight me, as entertaining as that would be for everyone." He gave Jeth a stinging slap on the shoulder. "I just want to see how far your archery skills can take you when your targets are moving and numerous." He motioned to the wooden targets. "Collect your arrows. You're going to need them."

Audibly gulping, Jeth, with the help of Khiri, scrambled up the dune to collect his arrows. Afterward, they followed everyone else to a rectangular hollow in the center of the grounds, dug deep into the packed down sand. Ash whispered something to Lys and he, hesitant at first, ran off to one of the huts. After a couple of combatants were done their set, Jeth was instructed to climb down into the pit while Ash halted another man from going down with the intent to challenge him.

Minutes later, Lys returned with a large basket, the contents of which were hissing with a fever pitch.

"What's in the basket?" Jeth's stomach flipped over itself.

Ash took the basket and held it out over the pit. "You better shoot fast and don't miss. These are silent cobras, the most venomous of their kind and are known for their tendency to attack in groups."

"Ashbedael, I'm serious. Do not put those down there with him!" Anwarr scolded.

"Not to worry," Lys said. "These ones just had their poison extracted to make antivenom . . . at least most of them . . . I think."

"Go and get some!" Anwarr screeched, sending Lys running for the huts again.

Not waiting for the Crede man to return, Ash turned the basket upside down. The lid fell into the pit with several blue-black cobras to follow. They hissed and spat to such a degree, they drowned out any other noise. Not so silent after all. Jeth shook his head in despair, then collected himself. You have to do this.

"Jethril, just climb out of there, you don't have to do this," Anwarr pleaded.

"Hey, what happened to trusting in my abilities?" he said. *Do you even trust them yourself right now? Climb out of here, you cocksure twit!*

The serpents bundled in the far corners, not yet realizing where they were. He seized the opportunity to get situated. Needing his entire peripheral vision, he unraveled his head scarf and tossed it aside. He slid his hand down the shaft of one loose lock. "Cannabreatha, steady my hand," he prayed and nocked an arrow. As the cobras uncoiled, a couple broke from the group, and he released, pinning one snake against the wall but missing another.

"Dammit!" He grit his teeth.

"Oh look, he missed," Ash pointed out to the many people starting to congregate around the pit.

"Quiet!" Jeth barked.

Everyone complied, including the cobras. The snakes, without a sound, slithered all at once toward their only perceived threat. The movement of the sand beneath them was imperceptible as if they floated across it.

He took to one knee and breathed in deep. When the snakes fanned out, he counted.

"Only eight, all right," he murmured, waiting for them to get closer, and allowing him to anticipate their winding movements more accurately. With all heading in the same direction, he began shooting down arrows in rapid succession.

One, two, three. Arrow after arrow impaled the shining black skin of each cobra as they advanced. The two snakes remaining picked up speed. Jeth backed up, narrowly avoiding one snapping at him. Both Anwarr and Istari gasped, but Jeth was able to shoot another two arrows, both piercing the cobra's spade-shaped heads.

"Sweating yet?" Ash asked with a chuckle.

Jeth wiped his saturated brow, taking in heaps of air. "I may have a slight glow about me. Is that all?" *Don't tempt the man, you dunce.*

"I don't know, is that all?"

A tingling sensation ran up his spine. For him, the number of arrows loosed was usually equal to the number of dead targets, but he had missed one. He nocked another. *Damn these silent cobras!* Every one of his senses was maximized as he hoped the eighth snake escaped the pit somehow.

A black serpent amongst the throng of identical serpent corpses wriggled in his periphery. He spun around to a crouch. The cobra sprang from the sand, its fanged mouth open and coming straight for his face. It moved in slow motion, the spit from its hissing orifice floating through the air, and yet, he was ready for it—more focused than he had ever been behind his bow. He let the bow string go and the arrow sluggishly released.

Then, everything hastened. The arrow ripped through the cobra's mouth, into its throat, and out through its body in milliseconds. Jeth dropped his bow and collapsed onto his hands and knees, his heart pounding a hole in his chest. Drops of sweat fell from the tip of his nose and were soaked up by the sand. None of the spectators uttered a word. Ash's reverberating applause broke the silence.

Wheezing, Jeth looked up at Ash, grinning maniacally. "Have I earned my spot yet?"

Ash laughed out loud. "I agreed to consider you after the second demonstration. I just enjoy watching arrogant pale-faced boys like you sweat in the desert heat. I suppose we can use you for a while."

With that said, the enormous thief turned and walked away.

Lys nodded with a, "Very good," then followed.

Anwarr's eyes were wide and her smile wider. She laughed between sighs of relief. Jeth laughed right along with her as his heart calmed. Istari could only glare at the two of them, her lips pursed in a subtle scowl before she turned to follow the others.

Night had fallen, and the crew relaxed back at the spice shop. After having trimmed his unruly facial hair, Jeth decided to take advantage of a hot bath on the covered terrace behind the building, tucked between hedges and hidden from the Bazaar crowds. The spice shop had once served as a bathhouse, and a few of the round pools remained. Lys had shown him how to fill one of them and heat it with oil flame in vents beneath to bring it to a perfect temperature.

He let his fairy locks loose and fully submerged himself in the water. Resurfacing, he proceeded to separate and smooth each set, one at a time, before pushing them back off his face.

Letting go of all of his senses, he laid his head back on the cool tile, glad to be alive, venom free, and finally clean. He hadn't realized just how important it was to him to gain acceptance among the thieving crew until earlier that day. He knew a large part of that was because of Anwarr.

Thinking of her brought to mind her sweet scent of which he had grown accustomed on their travels. Soon, he realized that he wasn't recalling it but smelling it for real. She was in the doorway, her hair up in a haphazard bun, wearing nothing more than a thin silk robe that she held closed at her navel. His body jolted as he tried to cover himself in the water.

"You're a hard one to sneak up on," Anwarr said as she took the few steps down to the terrace.

Pointing to his nose, he said, "It's much harder to turn this thing off as opposed to my other senses."

Anwarr grimaced. "Are you implying that I need to bathe as well?"

"N-no, no, you smell fine—better than fine, but uh—unless you want to bathe. I'm finishing up here."

He was about to grab his towel when Anwarr said, "I won't chase you out. Surely this large bath can hold us both."

Before Jeth could utter a clever retort, Anwarr dropped the robe at her feet, the entirety of her curvaceous naked body in plain view. Jeth's blood ran hot in his veins, the steaming water cool against his skin. He involuntarily averted his gaze, cursing his whole being in the process.

"This is nice tile," he said as he ran a finger along the edge of it.

The water displaced as Anwarr submerged herself. She let out a pleasure-filled moan before laying her head back and stretching her arms across the bath's edge. The water obscured her bountiful breasts, but it was all he could do to hide the erection forming between his legs.

"Nothing like washing away the filth from a previous job," she said with eyes closed.

"You're telling me. That sand really gets everywhere, doesn't it?" He shifted in his seat.

Anwarr chortled, still not opening her eyes. "I was referring to my night with the Tezkhan Chief, but yes, sand is a troublesome nuisance in these parts."

"O-oh . . . I'm sorry you had to do that."

Her eyes opened, and she said, "I do what I must to finish the job. Besides, between you and me, the Chief had a little difficulty performing. There were many attempts, but no serious results."

"Impossible," Jeth said. "What man could ever have trouble performing around you?"

"You'd be surprised," she said, putting her arms under the water and becoming a floating head. "But you don't seem to have that problem, do you?"

Anwarr's frosted eyes drilled into his, sending chills of excitement through his body. "I-I wouldn't know. You already guessed that I've never been with—"

"Not that." She splashed him with a flick of her foot. "Earlier today. I've never seen anyone move that fast before. Both yours and the serpent's movements were invisible to the naked eye. How did you do that?"

"Uh . . . adrenaline, I guess." Jeth didn't exactly know what happened down in that snake pit. All he remembered was how slowly the cobra moved through the air and his reaction. *You've seen fairies move as fast as she's describing.*

Anwarr glided over to Jeth's side of the pool. "Either way, I'm glad you are on our team."

"No regrets on this end," he replied, now able to make out the distorted image of Anwarr's breasts under the water.

"Do you remember that night when you asked me what I wanted from you?" she asked in a softened voice.

"Before we were literally blindsided by your Light Mage lover? Yeah, I remember."

Anwarr sidled up so close, her nipples ever so slightly brushed up against his arm. "Well, I'm going to answer that for you now."

"Yeah?" He was now out of breath and hardly able to get out a sentence. "What might . . . that be?"

She bit her lip wickedly, and a soft sensation ran up his left leg. A hot jolt of excitement rushed over him as Anwarr's fingers traveled up his thigh. The next thing he knew, she had those fingers wrapped around his ever-hardening shaft.

"Oh, my." Anwarr gasped in surprise as she glanced down. "Sagorath has blessed you, hasn't he?"

"I'm not sure what that means, but I'll assume it's a good thing?" he sputtered.

"Good for me." Anwarr was suddenly astride him, her body pressing firmly against his, her soft breasts tepid against his chest. His upper back bit into the hard tile, but he didn't dare move. She brought her lips to his, so soft at first, he was paralyzed by them. When her tongue found his, an electric warmth spread throughout his entire body. Everything was happening so fast. He became all too aware, his senses taking in far too much.

"W-why now?" he murmured between kisses. "Aren't you with Istari?"

"Does it look like I'm with Istari?" Anwarr replied before taking his earlobe in her mouth.

"No—I mean, yes!" he shouted in such a high pitch he offended his own ears. "You two seemed really close before, not that I'm bothered by it. Whatever you girls like to do is all fine by me. . . . It's just if she sees us, won't she be mad?"

Anwarr put her finger to his lips to stop their nervous flapping. "I don't belong to her. I belong to no one. Now, do you want to touch me or do you want to keep talking about Istari?"

Not giving him a chance to respond, Anwarr forcibly grabbed his hands and placed them over her breasts, nipples hard against his palms. "Who's Istari?"

"That's better," she whispered and kissed him again.

With the supple softness of her breasts in both hands, Jeth let go of any and all control of his own faculties. He was lost in the taste of her lips, the sensation of her warm wet skin, and her hips rhythmically gyrating upon him, building a pressure in his loins to an insurmountable level. He knew they should slow down; he prayed to the Deities for it not to be over so soon and yet he was powerless beneath her.

She grabbed his cock and started to reposition herself. *This is it. This is happening.* Her touch alone drove him wild, and he wasn't even inside her yet. *Oh no, no, no, no, not yet.* He tried to pull away, but it was far too late. The pressure that had built so high since the moment they met capsized and a release of pleasure radiated through him, hotter than the water they sat in.

At that moment, time stopped. Jeth deflated, and a flood of reality started rushing in. Anwarr floated off of him, looking at him with concern and confusion. His skin flushed as he struggled to think of something—anything to say to make this moment less mortifying.

"I'm sorry, but uh . . . you seemed so impressed with how fast I was before, I just thought . . ."

Anwarr blinked a few times before she threw her head back in laughter. She splashed him. "You fiend! I suppose we will have to reconvene later."

One second ago, he couldn't imagine being more ashamed than he was then, but Anwarr's fun-loving reaction to the situation invigorated him like never before. *She might be the one!*

He took her by the waist and pulled her through the water as she screeched in surprise. Pressing himself against her, he kissed her hard on the lips.

Anwarr giggled and playfully pushed him away. "I'm going to enjoy keeping you."

She rose to her feet and stepped out of the pool. Water beaded off her perfect form, the torchlight illuminating every part of her rich brown skin. Jeth unabashedly watched her pick up her robe and drape it around herself with an untold grace. Looking back to him from the doorway, she said, "Let me know when you are ready to try again."

At those very words, Jeth could feel the stirrings of a new arousal. "I'm ready now," he blurted.

Anwarr raised her eyebrow in disbelief, smiled, and then said. "If you say so. I'll be in your bed."

His heart leaped into his throat at hearing Anwarr utter those words. She sashayed back into the shop, and then flashed him an irresistible grin before disappearing around the corner.

"Wait." Jeth scrambled out of the water, grabbed his towel, and followed her upstairs. "Where is my bed?"

9

Pretty Things

(Three months later)

"Khiri fought well today," Ash remarked.

He and Jeth watched the eleven-year-old boy swishing one of Jeth's new scimitars about the busy streets. The three of them had just left a small combat facility located within the city and were now on their way back to the Bazaar.

Soon after Istari had exchanged Jeth's note for its amount in gold, one of the first purchases he made were two khopeshes as a close-quarter alternative to his bow. Ash had agreed to accompany him to the arenas from time to time and even gave him some pointers on how to dual wield the unusual sickle-shaped scimitars. On the last few trips, they thought it a good idea to bring Khiri along so he might start his own training.

"I should show him how to use a bow pretty soon too," Jeth said.

"Careful now. With skills in shop keeping, swordsmanship, archery, and pick-pocketing, the boy will only need to uncover a magical inclination before he can replace us all."

Jeth nodded. "Fair point."

The three of them turned down a winding ramp and emerged upon a lower level road, more shaded from the mid-afternoon sun.

"You're becoming quite skilled with those blades yourself, although I have yet to see you move as fast as you did that time in the pit," said Ash.

"I don't know." Jeth sighed, tightening the ties that kept his bundle of fairy locks in check, having grown past his shoulders. "I've been trying, but I haven't been able to do it again. I might need to be in a life or death situation."

The crowds grew denser. Khiri, however, was still swinging the sword around without a care, causing a few people to yelp and duck out of the way.

Jeth jogged up to the boy and took the sword out of his hand. "Alright, Khir, time to give that back. Can't have you slicing the arms off passersby."

Khiri rolled his eyes and groaned, unable to put his frustration into words.

"Sorry, kid. You'll have your own someday soon, I promise."

The boy continued on, dragging his feet and kicking up dust from the street.

"Maybe the pirate spawn is about ready for his own blade," said Ash.

Jeth nodded but didn't give Ash's comment any further thought as they started to cross a wide canal bridge. Vendors swarmed each side of it, brandishing their wares. Immediately, he spotted a slender woman of ebony skin, covered head to toe in every jewel and precious metal one could dream of, layers of necklaces, and earrings piercing all the available space on her lobes. She wore rings, chains, and charms up the entire length of her arms and legs and on every finger and toe, and had garnets sewn into her clothing. People gathered around her to purchase the treasures right off her body. Jeth's eyes honed into a stunning armlet around her bicep, a shining white gold serpent with two heads about to devour each other. *You know where you've seen that before.*

"Maybe you're right, Ash." He stepped out in front of Khiri, knelt to his level, and took out his knife. "What do you think of this? It's authentic military-grade steel from Del'Cabria. You can have it—"

Khiri tried to grab it, but Jeth kept it away. "Only if those phantom fingers of yours can snatch me that Serpentine charm off that lady's arm. Do you see it?" He pointed to the jeweled woman, and after a moment or two, Khiri nodded eagerly.

He patted the boy on the back. "Go get it, and I'll make you a trade."

The little pick-pocket kept his eye glued to the target as he wandered about the bridge while Ash and Jeth pretended to take an interest in the other vendors across the way. Khiri stopped and made jerking motions toward them with his arms.

"What is he doing?" Jeth gestured toward the target with his head.

"He wants us to provide a distraction," said Ash.

"Oh, right." Jeth stroked his beard in contemplation. "I wonder what we should d—"

Ash shoved him back hard, casting him over the side of the bridge and into the water below.

"Man off the bridge!" Ash called, getting the attention of everyone passing by. Jeth splashed to the surface, spitting out a fountain of dirty, brown canal water.

"May Sag take your balls, Ash!" he griped as he made the swim to dry land amongst raucous laughter from everyone on the bridge. When Jeth reached the lower sidewalk, Khiri was there to assist his soaking wet body from the water. As he did so, he slipped the armlet into Jeth's pocket, which he hardly felt despite being well aware of the boy's aptitude for sleight-of-hand.

He removed his belt and scabbard and handed it to the successful thief. "You earned this, kid. Take good care of it, now." Khiri's face lit up as he belted his new weapon around his scrawny waist and immediately started playing with the blade.

They met Ash and his mocking serpent grin at the end of the bridge. "Be glad I didn't decide to push you into the rickshaw of camel shit that was passing by."

"There is all sorts of shit in that canal!" Jeth grumbled as he wrung out his pants followed by his heavy locks.

"Then you should feel right at home." Ash patted him on the back, making squishing sounds between his meaty palm and Jeth's wet shirt.

He flashed Ash a cantankerous look, and the trio continued. They soon came upon a group of children playing in a fountain, where Jeth stopped to wash the filth off himself as best he could, starting with his hair. *Damn it all if you return to Anwarr smelling like Herran's arsehole.*

Later, they came upon the bustling Bazaar, and he felt it safe to fish the armlet out of his pocket. He bit down on it, the softness between his teeth indicating the gold was true enough. Istari had recently taught him that trick.

While Jeth was admiring the rubies that made up the serpent's eyes, Ash said, "It's an impressive piece, but it won't suit you."

"No, it won't." Jeth put it back in his pocket. "But it may suit someone else."

"Istari?"

"Guess again." He chuckled as they came up to the shop entrance.

Khiri sped straight in while Ash turned to block Jeth. "I know that what I am about to say will be difficult for a Del'Cabrian-born male like you to understand, but allow me to give you some advice."

"Uh . . . sure . . . ?"

"No matter how many trinkets you steal for her or how many times she polishes your rod, it won't be enough."

"Do I sense a hint of jealousy there, Big Fella?"

Crossing his arms over his scorpion tattoo, Ash grunted. "I've been fucking Anwarr since before you could hold a bow, but she is no more mine than she is anyone else's. There is no reason for me to be jealous."

"Are you sure? How long has it been since she's 'polished your rod?' Dare I guess about a month? It's all right, she bores easily, you know?" He patted the hulking thief on the shoulder and attempted to duck under his arm. Ash brought it down lower.

With a frustrated exhalation from his broad nostrils, he said, "Listen to me. Anwarr is a free woman of Herran, not some Del'Cabrian floozy who you can buy with pretty things. She will never belong to you. You'd do well to remember that, Fairy Boy."

Ash ducked inside the shop. *He just can't handle the fact that she prefers you.* Although the more Jeth reflected on Ash's warning, the less confident he felt. He shrugged it off and continued into the shop. After nodding a greeting to Lys at the counter, he followed the voices of the others to the second floor.

He caught up with Ash lumbering up the staircase, and the two of them entered the dining area together. Anwarr and Istari were cuddled close, feeding each other various finger fruits from the table and giggling amongst themselves. Khiri was already half way through a bowl of spiced lamb and rice.

"Girls, please tell me you celebrate our return and not our absence," Ash said.

"Boys, you're back," Anwarr squealed as she waved them to join her and Istari at the low table. As soon as Jeth sat down cross-legged on his usual cushion, he began to gorge on flatbread smeared with butter. "Jethril, you're all wet. Did Ashbedael work you into a sweat again?"

"No to it being sweat, but yes to it being Ash's fault," he returned with a playful punch in the Bahazur's massive shoulder.

"I'm so glad to see you two getting along." Anwarr took a sip of her wine. She then waved everyone in to listen what she had to say. They all waited for her finish swallowing before she began, "I have news. While you three were gone, I received a message from Snake Eye. He has a new job for us!"

"Already?" Ash said. "Whatever happened to laying low for a year? It's not like we need the gold."

"Silly, silly, Ashbedael," Anwarr cooed, holding her cup of wine close to her lips, but not taking a sip. "This is a question of want, not need. When you hear how much he is offering, we will all want for nothing."

"How much are we talking?" Jeth inquired.

"Forty thousand." Anwarr finally took a sip and then let out a satisfied exhalation.

"That's the same amount we pulled on our last job," said Ash.

"Oh, did I say total?" Anwarr put down her cup. "I meant . . . each."

From that point on, the dining area erupted in hoots and hollers. Wine was poured, and sips were had by all.

Jeth called down, "Hey Lys, did you hear that? Forty thousand gold each!"

"Very good!" he called back in a manner only slightly more jovial than normal.

"Make that very, very good, my Crede friend," hollered Ash.

When the ruckus quieted, Istari said, "Snake Eye wants to meet with all of us tonight to provide details. This is it. This is the job that will make us legends."

"And rich beyond imagining," Anwarr cheered, putting her cup out for everyone to clink. Wine splashed up and spilled over everyone's hands on impact, but no one seemed to mind a little of the expensive liquid going to waste now.

Once they had downed their drinks and eaten their fill, they shuffled off to prepare for the meeting that night. Before Anwarr could scurry up the stairs to the third floor, Jeth took her by the arm.

"An."

"Oh, Jethril, isn't it exciting?" she gushed, throwing her arms around him with such force, his back hit the wall. "Your first real job as a part of our crew and it's our biggest one yet. We need to get you out of these wet clothes. You can't meet Snake Eye looking like a drowned cat." Anwarr started unraveling the sashes he wore crossways over his shirt with his sleeves rolled up to the shoulders.

"Wait, wait, wait, I have something to show you." He held out one hand to brace the overeager thief and presented the armlet to her with the other. "I saw this on a street vendor and thought of you."

Her widening eyes sparkled with the armlet's reflection. "By the wiles of Salotaph, is that white gold? Do you know how rare that is?" She was about to take it out of his hand but hesitated. "Unfortunately, you are aware I find no fun in gifts."

Jeth's heart sank. *Idiot, what were you thinking?*

"Gift? This?" He dangled it in front of Anwarr. "I just said it made me think of you. I said nothing about giving it to you."

"Liar." She snorted.

He backed away. "If you want it, you'll have to steal it from me."

Anwarr bit her lip, narrowing her gaze at the armlet. She snapped her hand out for it, but he yanked it away from her. She tried to snatch it again, but he backed further away. Chasing him around the table, she tried to trap him in the corner, but he ducked and spun out from around her.

"Sag curse your reflexes," she complained through animated laughter.

Jeth led Anwarr up the stairs and into his room. He let her tackle him onto his bedding where she tried to overpower him. Squeezing him between her legs, she reached to the left and then to the right for the glittering prize. Eventually, she fell over top of him in exhaustion. As soon as he wrapped his arms around her waist, their lips joined, and the piece of jewelry in his hand became an afterthought. That's when Anwarr reached behind her and swiped the armlet before rolling off of him. "Got it!"

"That's not playing fair."

"Know your target's weakness." She smirked while clasping it around her upper arm.

"You sure know mine."

Anwarr marveled at the white gold adornment on her arm for a few seconds then took it off, her glowing smile transforming into a sudden frown.

"What's the matter? You don't like it?" he said, sitting up on the bed.

"It's gorgeous, but it doesn't fit right." Anwarr hesitantly put the armlet back into his hand.

"It looked like it fit perfectly—"

"It's uncomfortable."

"I-I don't get it." Jeth's mind clouded with confusion.

Anwarr touched his hand. "I'm sorry. I hope you didn't go through too much trouble for it. An excellent find, otherwise."

"Alright." He gripped the armlet in his palm and muttered, "I guess I'll sell it somewhere."

Anwarr gave him a peck on his cheek and stood up. He took her by the hand to keep her from leaving. "You don't have to go."

Her hand slipped out of his as she used it to gather her mess of hair off her shoulders. Jeth liked how she wore it lately, tied under a bandana, braids intermingled with flowing loose strands. He stood up to run his hands through it, but she stepped just out of his reach.

"I have to . . . help Istari with something." She flashed a weak smile and left the room.

Jeth fell backward onto the bed, letting out a deep sigh of frustration. He dangled the armlet above his face, confused thoughts racing through his mind.

On some days, Anwarr was insatiable. It was as if she couldn't get enough of him and on others, she'd leave him yearning for her while she directed her affections elsewhere. But he didn't always mind. He understood that Istari fulfilled desires for her he never could. Ash was a whole other matter, but Anwarr almost always came to Jeth first when she required a man's touch. Although, it drove him mad on the nights she didn't. *Del'Cabrian, Fae'ren, Herrani, it doesn't matter, you'll never understand women.*

That thought was followed by one darker. It's because she will never love you.

You're cursed, even here.

That night, the core team, consisting of Anwarr, Istari, Ash, and Jeth met Yemesh at the narrow alleyway beneath the overpass. This time, the Sunil allowed Jeth passage. He led the team through the dark wooden door and down a steep and narrow set of stairs into a basement dwelling. Years' worth of scents permeated the walls, getting stronger as they descended, and made Jeth sick to his stomach. The bottom floor was clouded with colorful smokes emanating from groups seated on pillows around tables smoking water pipes. Men and women blew smoke into the air through their mouths or nostrils as the crew passed by.

"What exactly is this establishment for?" he asked.

"Snake Eye is an ashipu, or what you'd call a healer," Anwarr said. "He also happens to be a collector of rare artifacts he claims assist him in his occupation. His methods are . . . unconventional, so after someone has been healed, they smoke certain herbs that make the whole experience . . . *fuzzy*."

"Also, people come here to get high," Istari added.

"I can get behind that," Jeth said, reminiscing on the grass-smoking huts back in Fae'ren.

Yemesh led the crew to a doorway, parted the hanging curtains, and allowed them entry. In the intimate space beyond was a poised man lying casually on a plush collection of silk pillows and decorative rugs. He held a water pipe and was sharing it with two stunning women who swayed back and forth, eyes glazed over, and completely unaware of the thieves strolling in. Yemesh presented the crew to the man who Jeth assumed was Snake Eye. He gracefully nodded as they approached, his visible eye an unusual golden yellow accentuated by a dark liner. His head was shaved on one side, and on the other, covering the other eye, smooth white tresses cradled his firm, yet, elegant jaw line.

Upon closer inspection, it became more difficult to determine whether he was a man at all. He wore a thin shirt with no sash, and pants that tapered below the knee, leaving little doubt of his male physique, but the refined sensuality of his every movement made Jeth more uncertain.

"Welcome, welcome, find a cushion. How is my favorite band of thieves?" The smooth lightness in Snake Eye's voice sounded even more feminine than Jeth had expected. *He has to be a woman, but . . .*

Anwarr said, "Snake Eye, it is a pleasure to see you as always. You can imagine upon receipt of your message we are in exceptionally high spirits."

"I thought that would get your attention," he said, then held up his water pipe spout. "Anyone?"

Ash and Istari waved their hands in refusal and Jeth was too anxious to make a sound. "Anwarr, my Doll, come sit." His yellow gaze honed in on her as he patted the spot next to him. Jeth cringed. To his disappointment, Anwarr shrugged and took a seat on his large cushion, displacing one of the other girls lounging there.

Snake Eye offered her the mouth piece, and she accepted without hesitation. Everyone else sat down on other pillows splayed along the rug, leaving Jeth to shuffle about awkwardly. This captured the ashipu's attention.

"Ah, you must be the new blood I've heard so much about." He beckoned him to come closer in a quasi-seductive manner. "Come here. Let me get a good look at you. Don't be shy."

With his guts doing somersaults inside him, Jeth did what was asked and sat down at Snake Eye's right. The likely man rubbed one of his matted locks between his fingers. "Magnificent! The hair of fairies. You are far from home, aren't you?"

Jeth shook his head in response. "My home is here in Herran."

"Is it now?" Snake Eye grinned. "You're an archer too. That reminds me of a tale I've heard, about the Great Gershlon, Champion of Archers, surely you know of him."

He nodded. "Every Fae'ren knows of him. Before we became a province of Del'Cabria, he fought alongside them and took down the war golems of Ingleheim in the Golem Wars."

"Yes, and because of his heroic efforts, your people answer to the pointed ear devils as opposed to ruthless Golem Mages from the mountains."

Jeth shrugged and nodded, impressed a Herrani knew anything about Fae'ren heroes long dead.

Snake Eye passed the pipe spout to Jeth. He was afraid to refuse, so he inhaled a mouthful and gave it back. The flavorful smoke was sweet on his tongue mere seconds before he began choking. Snake Eye patted him on the back, the force consistent with a man's strength.

"Mm, you are quite young, barely a man."

"I assure you, he is." Anwarr tittered.

"Ah, and I'm willing to wager it was you who ushered him there, you saucy thing."

"Maybe we should talk about that job you have for us," Jeth said, his face reddening. Snake Eye pushed back his hair that had been covering the right side of his face. His right eye blinked sideways, the pupil a thin, vertical slit, resembling that of a serpent. The left eye, although shared the same golden color, was entirely human.

"Whoa!" Jeth pointed to it. "That's why they call you Snake Eye!"

The awkward silence dampened the room like the smoke from the water pipes. Ash put his shaking head in his hands, and Istari turned herself invisible. Even the semi-conscious women stopped to stare at him like he was a simpleton. After coughing into his shoulder, he said, ". . . which I already knew and is completely normal. . . ."

Snake Eye's half-reptilian gaze was unnerving, but when Anwarr snorted back laughter, he let out a pitched laugh of his own. "Eyes like this are not so normal anymore," he said.

Anwarr cut in, "Some Herrani people still exhibit characteristics of our ancient naja ancestors. The human-naja hybrid race was said to all possess the serpent's eyes. Some even maintained a modest number of scales."

"You mean it's true that desert folk actually descend from those . . . things?"

"The naja of old were not the monstrous, oversized reptiles that exist today," Snake Eye began. "They were once beautiful and intelligent, capable of forming societies but brutal nonetheless, and powerful in the ways of flesh magic. They were called the Najahai." He put his arm around Anwarr to offer her another puff of his water pipe.

"So, who thought it would be a good idea to mate with them?" Jeth asked.

Snake Eye turned back to him. "The Najahai of course. They had enslaved the human tribes for millennia. They were too slow in propagating themselves, coveting the humans' reproductive ability. So, they impregnated slave women with their spawn."

"I can't imagine that being much fun." Jeth grimaced. Anwarr shook her head in agreement.

"Not for the slaves to be sure," said Snake Eye, "but even less so for the Najahai later on. The hybrids were more human than reptile. But, they were strong, lived longer, and were not so quick to submit to their slave masters. Their humanity gave them access to essence and spirit magic, and the reptilian in them gave them access to flesh. They used it all to fight back. The rise of the Immortal One, banded the tribes together, using their superior numbers to beat the Najahai back. And to better combat the hybrids, the Najahai transformed ninety percent of their population into the ferocious yet dimwitted beasts that we have seen today. This only made the creatures more vulnerable to spirit manipulation, and thus the era of naja enslavement by the tribes began."

Snake Eye blew out smoke rings from his lips. "Now, most of them have been driven to the driest desert plains, succumbing to death faster than they can reproduce. They should have gone extinct, but they have risen again. . . ."

Everyone nodded, understanding that Nas'Gavarr had amassed an entire force of them. It was not known exactly how many naja he had under his control.

"As much as I love listening to you talk about ancient naja history, Snake Eye, I seem to be growing bored." Anwarr yawned.

He took her chin in his hand and softly caressed her cheek with his thumb. "Oh, you poor, poor thing."

Watching Snake Eye touch Anwarr so intimately made Jeth's head spin. *What history do they share? Does he require her to perform sexual favors in exchange for jobs?*

Snake Eye took his arm off her and said to the dazed women near him. "Ladies, you're healed now. Time to leave." They moaned while slowly picking themselves up and left.

He then sat up straight and grew serious. "An opportunity has presented itself, relevant to the history I just told you." He took a puff and blew some more smoke rings into the air. "There is an artifact, one that dates back much further than the Emerald of Dulsakh, and I simply must have it in my collection."

"You've captured my interest," Anwarr said, sitting up perky and cross-legged.

"The Bloodstone Dagger." Snake Eyes eyed everyone in the room in turn. "It was used by the Najahai in their human sacrifice rituals. Scholars don't believe it exists, but the Magi of Sagorath know it well. They say it can absorb and hold the blood of a hundred bodies." Snake Eye flicked his long hair over his shoulder, revealing a twinkle in his reptilian eye. "Now, if that treasure does not trump all treasures, I don't know what does." He rested his ringed hand on Anwarr's knee, and she made no attempt to move it.

"Who are the Magi of Sagorath?" Jeth asked, finding it hard to concentrate while the ashipu's hands were on Anwarr.

"In the time before Nas'Gavarr's reign, the Death tribes occupied most of what is now Herran. Their magi, or priests as you would call them, believe that Salotaph is a minor Deity and that Sagorath rules supreme. It just so happens Sagorath is the God of Death, so not much fun. Most of them were killed in Nas'Gavarr's campaign to unite the tribes. . . ."

Jeth's ears picked up on a heart skipping a beat. . . . Maybe Snake Eye's?

"But you happen to know one who has seen this . . . magic dagger," Ash finished.

"I have a little bird who told me that it rests in an ancient Serpentine Temple belonging to the last surviving Death tribe."

"Didn't the Overlord burn them all to the ground?" asked Istari.

"Not this one. It is the only one untouched by the Burning Waste that contains it."

Ash slapped his knee. "Well that explains the generous reward."

Snake Eye waved a dainty hand. "I wouldn't dream of sending my best thieves across such dangerous terrain if I didn't think you could do it." He pointed to Istari. "My Blackest Star, have you been practicing water magic?"

"Yes. I can see myself and maybe two others across the dunes, but I don't know about the Burning Waste. I'd need a lot of water aura."

Without taking his attentions from Istari, Snake Eye snapped for his Sunil. "Yemesh, bring the sorceress Gizelle's Sapphire from my safe if you please."

"As you wish." Yemesh bowed and left the room.

"It is the largest and purest of sapphires in my possession. It should provide more than enough essence storage for you to get your team there and back."

Istari nodded graciously. "Thank you. I will return your treasure as soon as the job's complete."

"I know where to find you if you don't," he sang with a chilling closed mouth grin.

He then turned to Ash. "And you, my giant fellow, do sharpen your tabar." Then he put a hand on Jeth's shoulder. "And you, bring as many arrows as you can carry. The temple will be rigorously guarded by the magi—oh, and watch out for giant scorpions as well, nasty things."

Ash nodded while cracking his netted knuckles in each fist. "Will do."

"Kill whoever and whatever you must to gain access to that temple. My spy will join you just beyond the waste to guide you."

"Alright, I've got to chime in here," said Jeth with his hand raised. "You want us to trek through a desert wasteland—that I'm assuming will burn us—and fight our way through Deity knows what sort of peril for a bloodstone knife that we aren't sure will even be there?"

"You're right to fret, my little Gershlon," Snake Eye said, gripping his knee in the same fashion he did Anwarr's earlier, confusing him more. "This will be the most challenging job any of you have ever done."

"There is a risk of death on any big job," Ash said.

"And I'm all for taking risks, you know I am, but not without some guarantee."

"Snake Eye does not give advances, Jethril," said Anwarr.

The ashipu cut in, "The boy has a reasonable concern. So, let me tell you all now. This job is not just about my propensity for collecting rare oddities. There is, believe it or not, a more noble purpose behind it." He leaned in closer, inciting the others to lean in as well, his voice lowering in register. "Imagine what could happen if any of them, particularly a dagger that holds the blood of a hundred men, fell into the hands of a Flesh Mage."

"What?" Jeth asked in near whisper.

"For a Flesh Mage to possess the blood of that many men would allow him to control the blood of those men and anyone who shares a similar bloodline," Snake Eye replied.

"You're trying to keep these artifacts from the Overlord," Istari concluded.

With a clap of his hands, Snake Eye said, "The Odafi witch is correct. In my hands, these treasures are nothing more than trinkets, but to Nas'Gavarr—well, the world should never have to witness what he could do with them."

"Part of his alliance with the Tezkhan was to secure the Emerald of Dulsakh, wasn't it?" Jeth guessed.

Snake Eye tugged at his sideburns and gave his cheek a friendly tap. "You're very astute, my boy. Yes."

"Have you thought of what you will do when he finds out you took them?" Anwarr posed, her brow lining with worry.

"Do not concern yourself with such things, Pretty Doll." Snake Eye brushed a strand of her hair off her shoulder. "I have ways of avoiding detection."

"So, that's it then," said Jeth. "You just want us to steal the dagger before Nas'Gavarr finds it?"

Snake Eye shook his head, his reptilian eye blinking sideways. "Oh no. He's found it. You're going to steal it away from him."

Silence cloaked the room. Only the thumping of six hearts remained. One, in particular, reverberated like war drums on Jeth's skull. He looked to the source of the frantic rhythm. And for the first time since they'd met, he saw true fear in Anwarr's eyes.

10

Something to Remember You By

Jeth spent the next morning mucking the stables while Khiri helped Lys deal with a rush of customers. Welcoming the distraction, he took the time to groom his own horse, starting by picking out the dirt lodged in her hooves.

When done, he brushed the dusty sand from her mane. "Wish I could take you with me, Tor, but Star won't waste her water aura keeping us both alive in the Burning Waste. Khiri'll take good care of you while I'm gone." Torrent responded with a low nicker.

"It's sweet how you talk to her," Anwarr said, standing at the doorway.

Jeth's skin prickled, not realizing she had returned. The time he spent with horses made the rest of the world fall away, just like aiming an arrow.

Anwarr giggled as she ambled over to Torrent's stall and rested her arms on the wooden railing. "Now kiss," she dared.

Jeth puckered his lips and brought them toward the horse's snout.

"No, don't!" With a cackle, Anwarr reached over the railing, took hold of Jeth's shirt, and pulled him away from the horse before his lips could reach the tip of her nose.

"I wouldn't have done it," he lied.

They laughed, and Jeth almost forgot he hadn't seen Anwarr all night.

"When did you get back?"

"A few minutes ago."

"So," he began with a sigh. "What did Snake Eye want from you that we couldn't be present for?"

"Just plans for future jobs. He also gave me some maps of the Burning Waste and the temple lands. Ash and Stari are looking through them now. You should too."

"And that required you to spend the entire night?" His gut twisted at the thought of what Snake Eye might have wanted from her. It was different than when she seduced Ukhuna or slept with Ash. There was something more intimate between her and the effeminate ashipu that rattled Jeth to his core.

"Those strange men were wandering about the street outside Snake Eye's after you all left. I thought it safer to stay over."

"I've seen you take on four armed soldiers by yourself," Jeth argued.

Anwarr rolled her eyes. "Yes, and you remember how that turned out. For that reason, Snake Eye said I shouldn't accompany you three on this job. Given how dangerous it is going to be, I won't be much help to you out there."

"Of course, you will," said Jeth as he collected the horse grooming supplies into a bucket. "Snake Eye just thinks we might die, and he wants to make sure you live so he can add you to his collection of rare treasures." He ended with an exaggerated impression of the probable man.

"Don't be ridiculous." Anwarr went over to the post outside Torrent's stall and leaned against it as Jeth hung the bucket on a hook. "He wants me to live because there are other artifacts he'd have me look for. Searching for new targets is where my talents are best put to use."

"I wonder what other talents of yours he wants to put to use," Jeth muttered.

Crossing her arms over her chest, Anwarr pursed her lips. "Not that it is any of your concern, but Snake Eye has no interest in me beyond a friendly touch."

"I find that hard to believe," he said, closing the gate to the stall.

"We go back a long time. He's like a brother to me." Anwarr paused to mull over her words. "A strange, sister-like brother."

"I think he may feel differently about you," Jeth said, scratching at his sideburns.

"Remember when I told you I was a dancer for hire after I quit the harem?" she asked.

Jeth nodded, recalling that a month ago, she had mentioned she'd hoped to make her fortune in the profession rather than tending to the needs of Nas'Gavarr's many wives and daughters.

"Well, a few years ago, Snake Eye hired me to dance for him in one of his shady establishments. I wasn't just there to perform but to steal some of his highly sought-after treasures. Back then, I was inexperienced but too confident to know any better. I thought I had that man-woman's full attention while Istari used her cloaking spell to sneak by. That simple ruse always worked for us in the past, but not with Snake Eye. We thought he was going to kill us right then and there. But, he took us into his fold instead. It was because of him that Istari and I were able to leave our previous employer and become independent thieves. He knows I owe everything to him and not once has he taken advantage of that."

Jeth sighed, realizing that he perhaps was being irrational. Her story did incite another question, however. "This old employer of yours . . . was his name Ezrai?"

Anwarr blinked several times and broke eye contact. She began playing with one of her bronze hooped earrings. "Did Istari tell you about him?"

"She told me he was a cud-stain. Anything I should know about him?"

"Like what?"

"Like if he's going to be sending any more men after you."

Anwarr waved a dismissive hand. "Ezrai's in the past and might as well not exist."

The way Anwarr avoided the subject made the strange dread in the pit of Jeth's stomach return in full force.

"Sorry, I know how much you hate looking backward, but promise me you will at least watch your back while we're gone."

"I always do. Those men were gone by this morning, and I made sure that I was not followed here. The shop is our safe haven."

Exhaling heavily, Jeth nodded. *It's your own arse you should be concerned about, not hers*, he thought.

He did one final check to ensure Torrent had everything she needed and started to go inside. Anwarr stepped in his way.

"Something you want?" he asked.

She stared at him for a moment, her breath growing shorter.

"Did you sell that armlet from yesterday?" Her voice was disarmingly soft. Jeth fished it out of his pocket. "No, why?"

Anwarr took it from him and put it on. She looked upon the white gold charm around her bicep with the same fear in her eyes Jeth had seen in them the day before. Then they met his, and she smiled.

"Chief Ukhuna was right. You are a fickle woman," he said.

"I thought it would be nice to have something to remember you by." She moved so close he could feel the heat off her skin, the thudding of her heart echoing in his ears.

"I'll be gone for less than a week, An." Jeth chuckled despite the twisting in his gut. "Nas'Gavarr isn't going to be anywhere near the temple, remember? Snake Eye said he and his armies are moving against the Del'Cabrian front at the Odafi and Herrani border."

She started smoothing out the sashes over his shirt. "I know—I know that. It's just . . ." A tear glistened against her brown cheek.

Jeth instantly took her head in his hand and wiped the tear with his thumb. "An . . . ?"

"I'm fine." She sniffed, putting her head on his shoulder. "I always worry when you all go on jobs without me."

"Then I won't go," he said, drawing her toward him by the waist. "They don't need an archer. I can stay here with you."

Anwarr lifted her head. "I'd love nothing more, but you have to go. It's your first real job . . ." Her words caught in her throat and her bottom lip quivered.

He rubbed his thumb along it. "There'll be other jobs."

She shook her head back and forth, eyelashes fluttering. Jeth took hold of her face and brought his lips to hers. Her immediate response was to pull herself flush against him, kindling all five of his senses. As their kiss grew in passion, Anwarr's captivating scent enveloped him, hers and no one else's, which gave him much needed peace of mind.

Then Ash's booming voice rattled his skull. "Hey, Jeth! If you're done making love to that horse, you should get in here and review these maps with us!"

Their kiss abruptly ended, and Jeth's senses withdrew. "Not now, Ash!" he called back.

Anwarr pressed her forehead to his while tugging on his beard. She whispered, "You've more than proven yourself to me. But this is your chance to show the others what I've always seen in you. Go on this job, and when you return, I can show you more of what our world has to offer."

She kissed him again, making his whole body weak. It took all of his strength to let go of her and head inside.

Great pillars of flame billowed into the air, creating black sheets of smoke across the horizon. Jeth, Istari, and Ash rode their camels across the crusted, ash-laden terrain of the Burning Waste.

"What exactly is burning?" Jeth yelled through his breathing mask.

Istari, riding her own camel between the two men, replied, "This land is rich in oil, like the kind we use in our lamps, only what is found here is far more unstable."

"Why is it here?"

"Not sure," Istari said. "This land was used by the Death tribes a hundred years ago before Nas'Gavarr went to war with them. It is told that he used earth magic to lift up the sands and with fire magic, lit the oil ablaze, rendering their villages and temples to ashes. This place has been burning ever since."

"For one hundred years? Sweet Deity." Jeth wiped the sweat running down his brow.

"As the oil continues to rise toward the ground's surface, it will burn until nothing is left."

The roar of the flames drowned out their own voices and the gargling bleats of their mounts. The hot stench was so overpowering, their filtering masks could do little to dilute it. Jeth struggled to keep down his stomach contents.

After a time, the smoke surrounded them and the floating ash lessened their visibility. The party stopped to secure breathing apparatuses on their camels as well. Istari's was not too keen on it, but the other two, having been trained for traversing the waste, didn't fight them. From that point onward, Istari concentrated all her magical efforts on blowing the smoke aside so they could see. She kept their waterskins filled to pour over themselves periodically while still leaving enough to drink. They found small respites in pockets of land where the smoke wasn't so thick, only for the wind to shift and close up the openings a short while after.

As the sun set, the smoke became denser, and the winds picked up. Istari struggled to keep the winds under control while maintaining a bright light on her staff to pierce through the darkness. The trio came upon a large pocket of earth that appeared to have burnt out some time ago, and there they made camp for the night.

All they had were small bedrolls and blankets to cover themselves from the falling ash. Lying down, Jeth said, "At least we don't have to worry about starting a fire to keep warm."

While hammering in the metal spikes each camel would be tied to, Ash said between grunts, "Star, how about whipping up an ice bath for us to sleep in."

"Oh, believe me, I would if I could," she said as she gathered the near-empty waterskins. "It's taking longer for me to condensate the water from the air."

"I've honestly never been so hot in my entire life," Jeth complained. "I long for the dunes. I just want to feel a breeze that isn't on fire! Sag, I'll take no breeze over this."

"When we get out of this mess, I promise to douse all of us in freezing rain. It might take me a while to do it, but I will damn well try," said Istari.

"I keep telling you to get sapphire-laced tattoos." Ash pointed to his chest. "The artist who did my scorpion has marked countless Essence Mages. I could get you a good deal."

"Forget it, Ash. I'll keep my sapphire outside of my body, thanks." Istari shivered despite the roaring flames around them.

"Well, get to filling auras then," he said.

With a grumble, Istari took out her knapsack that held the large antelope-shaped sapphire from Snake Eye. She placed both hands upon it and closed her eyes. Jeth understood the process as she had explained it to him once. She pulled water essence from the air and into the gem while absorbing what she needed from it into herself. But no matter how intently he studied her as she did this, he could see no sign of her doing anything out of the ordinary.

Ash pulled his rough blanket over his head and went to sleep. Jeth tried to do the same but falling asleep while wearing the uncomfortable breathing mask proved difficult. *If only you had full control over your sense of touch, you could numb yourself from this heat,* he thought before eventually dozing off.

Jeth was jerked awake by an ear shattering male scream. *Just a nightmare,* he thought. But then the scream returned and was joined by two others. The first faded into an impossibly low and agonizing moan. *The camels!* Jeth shot up to his feet while Ash and Istari were just beginning to stir.

The wind had carried the black smoke across their camp, limiting visibility, but the excruciating bleats of the camels led Jeth straight to them. Two were pulling back on their leads to free themselves. The other was lying on its side, unmoving. Through the smoke, Jeth sensed a presence around the still camel. The crunch of flesh being cut and the dull moans made him lose sensation in his legs. A hint of blood and entrails hung in the air, strong even through the filtering mask.

"What in the name of . . . ?" Jeth panted, bringing a khopesh in hand.

Then, the cutting stopped and was replaced by a scuttling. Something burst from the black smoke, and a massive stinger swung down at him. He yelped and jumped backward, tripping over loose rocks, and falling to the ground. He scrambled along the scorched earth as gigantic brown pincers snapped at his feet.

"Scorpion! Giant scorpion!" Jeth screeched.

"Watch out!" Ash came in fast, bringing his pole axe down hard between the arachnid's mandibles, slicing crossways through its bulbous, central eyes, and crushing its head in one brutal motion.

The scorpion squealed, its eight legs thrashing about before its body jerked to a halt, and its tail hit the blackened earth. Struggling to catch his breath in his mask, Jeth staggered to his feet, unable to take his eyes off the enormous creature. It was wider than the camel it had just fed on, its tail thicker than one of Ash's arms. Jeth patted him on the shoulder. "Thanks, Big Fella."

"My pleasure." Ash flicked the brown scorpion blood from his axe blade.

Istari walked over to Jeth. "Do you hear any others?"

Honing his hearing as far as he could and not sensing more, he shook his head.

"Scorpions don't hunt in groups, but we should keep moving before the camel corpse attracts more of them," suggested Ash.

Istari looked over to the fallen camel. "No, please, no." She knelt down at the animal's mutilated carcass and exhaled with relief. "Oh, thank the Serpentine Gods, it's not mine."

"Whose is it?" Jeth asked, still breathless.

Ash yanked one of the pegs from the ground. "Well, mine is right here, so it must be yours."

"Sag damn it!" he griped.

Istari freed her camel and got on its back. "You can ride with me the rest of the way, I suppose," she offered.

"Thanks." Jeth sighed and climbed on behind her.

With only an hour or two of sleep, the trio pushed through. Istari was unable to produce any more water, and they had to conserve what little they had. Jeth grew dizzier as time went on. He intermittently fell in and out of consciousness on the camel's back. A few times, Istari elbowed him in the ribs when he fell forward onto her shoulder. He shook his head and slapped his own face to stay alert.

A shadow loomed above. Looking up with a start, he found nothing. Only a flicker of movement in the black smoke clouds cloaking the sky. The subtle outline of a winged creature glided above them. Then it was gone.

"Are the vultures out here giant as well?" Jeth asked warily.

"No bird can survive out here, not even vultures," Istari replied.

"But I saw—"

"The fire and smoke are probably making you see things. Keep an eye on the ground. Vultures won't kill us, but scorpions will."

Jeth took a small sip of his water, the hot liquid scarcely quenching his violent thirst. Soon, the smoke cleared and the morning sun lit up the ground a few feet away. He was quickly disheartened to find it was just another pocket and not a very large one at that.

"Let's rest here for a bit," Ash said, his camel barely offering him a chance to dismount before folding its legs underneath itself.

"I'll try to make more water." Istari got down and retrieved the sapphire from her sack.

Ash took out the map and compass. "I hope we aren't going in circles. This smoke is too thick. If we don't find a way out soon . . ." He failed to catch enough breath to finish his sentence.

A bright orange wall of flame was closing in around them, and Jeth said, "We need to—"

The winged shadow flew by, and again, there was nothing more than black smoke when Jeth looked above. *Something is for sure up there,* he thought. "We need to move now!"

Istari returned the sapphire to her bag. "Ugh, forget the water. I need to push these fire walls back and clear a path for us to go straight through. It's all this going around them that is slowing us down. Which way is west?"

Ash checked the compass and pointed due west.

Istari took her staff in hand and placed her free hand in front of her. She breathed hard through her mask. The winds picked up around them, and slowly but steadily the smoke and flame in the west began to part. Istari stood there, shaking, sweat dripping down her forehead.

"Dammit, I can't . . ." She gasped. The black smoke closed in even tighter. The fires raged at all sides.

Istari shook, struggling to change the course of the blinding smoke. "It's too much. I don't have enough aura!"

"Do something, Star! There's nowhere else to go!" Panic rose in Ash's voice.

Then, Jeth heard it—more scuttling coming from every direction, but the smoke was too thick to see the source.

"Scorpions again!" Jeth took out his bow and Ash his axe. All three thieves took position at each other's backs, waiting for an unknown number of arachnids to jump out at them.

A wall of flame moved in, and the scuttling grew louder. Jeth shot an arrow out into the abyss. There came a shrill screech, but the scampering continued. Another arrow launched and hit nothing.

"I can't see shit!" Jeth grunted. The scorpion's advance was being drowned out by the howling wind in his ears. The smoke whipped around them, swirling in a tornado of ash and scorched sand. Three giant scorpions were taken up into the cyclone, whirled about, and flung away. Something else was riding along with the dark winds above, but Jeth couldn't make out what it was before it disappeared into the blackness.

"What's going on?" Ash hollered.

At that moment, the mysterious cyclone widened, pushing the fire wall back and parting the black smoke all the way to the western horizon.

"You did it, Star!" Jeth patted her on the back.

The Light Mage collapsed to her knees, hanging onto her staff with both hands and gasping for air. "I-I didn't do any of that."

More scuffling behind them. Jeth spun around with an arrow nocked. A giant scorpion scurried across the sand straight for them. It halted, screeched, and shook as it was sliced from behind. Its tail tore off with a sickening crack, and the creature collapsed dead.

A tall olive-skinned woman with a strong build and heaps of tight brown curls, partly tied back, tossed aside the giant scorpion's tail and stepped around the carcass.

The mystery woman said in a casual tone, "You all seem to be lost."

I I

Like a Champion

Where did she come from? Jeth wondered. He instinctively took a step back and placed a hand on the hilt of his sword. Istari did the same with the knife strapped to her side.

Ash took off his mask and wiped the sweat from his bald head. "Who are you?" he asked, a subtle smile forming on his face.

"My name is Vidya," the woman replied in a blunt fashion while eyeing the trio up and down. "Snake Eye told me you were coming, but I grew tired of waiting. I figured you were having trouble getting here. Not many people traverse the waste successfully without an adequate Water Mage present."

"Judging by your impractical attire, I'm guessing you're a pretty good one then?" Istari said, still out of breath.

Vidya wore no filtering mask, no face or head covering, and rode no mount. All she possessed were brown leather slacks and boots, an armored leather corset, and a brown shoulder cape. She had two short blades strapped to her forearms and dual flintlock pistols holstered at each hip.

"Oh, I'm no Mage," she said. "But I have a way with wind."

Istari removed her breathing mask, revealing a confused expression.

"And a way with scorpions as well," said Ash with a playful glint in his eyes.

"Follow me." Vidya walked past them. "It's not far to the end."

The thieving crew exchanged glances, but no one put up any arguments. It was no more than an hour before the way ahead was clear of smoke. Vidya led them across a dry plain until they reached her small camp in the shade of a crumbling rock formation. There, a muddy stream trickled between the cracks in the stone. Jeth let it run into his hands before slurping it up, the dull, metallic taste not bothering him in the least. With the blunt end of his axe, Ash busted off chunks of rock until the stream flowed more freely.

As Jeth splashed a handful of water over his face, he gazed back into the raging red abyss surrounding them and dreading having to go through it all again once they'd found what they were looking for.

"So, Vidya," Ash began. "How did you get through the waste on your own without a mount?"

She sat down on a shaded stone surface, leaning back on her arms. "I don't require beasts of burden."

Swaggering over and sitting down beside her, he leaned in. "Ah, but have you considered riding a beast for pleasure?" He lifted both eyebrows and lowered his green gaze on her.

Vidya narrowed her own, glaring at him with pure contempt.

Without a word, she rose to clean the scorpion blood from her arm blades at the stream, leaving the big axe man to grimace at himself. Istari rolled her eyes, and Jeth guffawed. "Ash, that was pure brilliance."

"You liked that, did you?" He threw a handful of sand at Jeth who spun out of its way just in time, snickering all the while.

He turned to the new arrival and said, "Well, Vidya. I don't care how you got here or how you manipulated the essence of wind without being a Mage. I'm just glad you did. . . . So thank you on behalf of all of us. I'm Jeth, Star, and this is our beast of burden Ash."

Vidya gave a casual nod and continued to clean her blade. Ash grunted, shook his head, but otherwise ignored Jeth's insult. Finding his own shaded spot, Jeth lay down on his back and closed his eyes, enjoying the slight breeze drifting over the plains to caress his blistering skin.

The next thing he knew, Ash was kicking him awake. The sun had moved, and he was now lying on scorching stone. The crew had already filled their waterskins at the stream, and Istari had replenished her aura and looked refreshed.

The three thieves, with Vidya as their guide, left the two camels to eat and drink their fill and continued west. They soon came upon desolate ruins. Skeletal remains, human and animal, hung from gutted and crumbling stone buildings. Hundreds of skulls, from adult to infant, lined the road on each side. The only signs of life were hideous vultures perched upon what remained of cylindrical stone towers and walls, their beady black eyes following the group as they passed.

"What is all this?" Jeth muttered.

Istari said, "I think this was an old settlement of a Death tribe."

Jeth tensed while looking at the eye sockets of each skull on the ground. The strange patterns in which they were arranged appeared intentional.

"This isn't a Death tribe settlement, but a graveyard," Vidya said. "They had built entire cities dedicated to keeping the dead. This is the last of them."

"How do you know that?" Istari asked.

"I've been watching the Magi of Sagorath for a while now. They don't believe in burials. Many a sad or sickly wretch who still holds these old beliefs, traverses the waste to find the last temple. They ask the magi to put them out of their misery, and their remains are laid to rest in these ruins to be vulture or scorpion food."

The crew continued on, leaving the graveyard behind and entering a towering canyon. They trekked through the maze of yellow sandstone walls, having been smoothed by years of erosion and were now dry as bone.

"We are almost there," Vidya announced.

"I don't see a temple," said Ash as he spun his axe around in his hand, attentions fixated on Vidya walking ahead.

The canyon walls to their left transformed into yellow sandstone pillars. Intricately carved archways presented dozens of windows and ledges, crafted right into the stone, a beautiful and simple structure despite its desiccated appearance.

"This is it?" Ash asked as the crew stopped in front of it. "Where are all these magi Snake Eye warned us about?"

"They're watching us now, but they don't see us as a threat yet," said Vidya.

Three and four stories high, Jeth spotted movement in six of the arched windows. Bare skulls peered down at them. The hairs lifted on the back of his neck.

In a few moments, the giant temple doors groaned open, bits of sand falling from between them as if they hadn't been moved in years. A man of undetermined age, wearing gray and black robes emerged, his hood obscuring most of his face. He stopped a few feet from the party, lifted his head, and brought down his hood. He was bald with dark tattoos around his eyes, cheeks, and lips creating a hollowing effect in his bleached, off-white skin. Even his hands and feet were tattooed to look like bone.

With milky white eyes, the magus scrutinized the group before saying in a gravelly, monotone voice, "Who among you longs to die on this day?"

The thieving crew exchanged glances. "Uh . . . none of us?" Istari peeped.

"All who come to this place must bring an offering to Sagorath. If you do not have one, turn back the way you came."

The magus started to put his hood back on before Ash said, "If we give you an offering, will you allow us inside the temple?"

Canceling his motion, the magus nodded. "Sagorath awaits inside for those who long for death. Make your choice."

Jeth heard bowstrings drawing from the other magi in the temple windows. Before he could think of an idea, Ash grabbed him by the shoulder and forced him to stand in front of him. "We offer this one. He came all the way from Del'Cabria to die."

"Ash, come on, what're y—?"

Ash whispered into Jeth's ear, "Think of this as your official initiation. Get in there, kill him, and come out with the prize while we wait out here." He pushed Jeth down to his knees at the magus's feet.

From closer up, Jeth noticed the dark tattoo ink was sparkling blue in spots. *Sapphire! This man's an Essence Mage.*

As frustrated as Jeth was for being singled out, Ash did propose a fine plan. With a quiet groan to himself, Jeth said, "That's right. I came here to die so, please, won't you kill me . . . inside the temple?"

The magus narrowed his gaze. "One among you may bear witness to the sacrifice."

Ash and Istari looked at each other, neither of them volunteering to go in with him. Vidya spoke up, "I will."

Both Istari's and Ash's eyes widened in surprise, then they shrugged. The magus put his hood back on and beckoned Jeth and Vidya to follow him.

On their way into the temple, Jeth whispered, "Why are you coming with me? Not that I don't appreciate it, but you already did your duty in getting us here."

"My duty is not to your crew, but to Credence."

Jeth was stunned. "What is a Crede woman doing all the way out here?"

"I have something of my own to find in this temple. When we take care of the magus, you go your way, and I go mine. Got it?"

"Fine by me."

They followed the magus up the wide steps and into the temple, the smell of blood and death flooding into Jeth's nostrils before he even stepped over the threshold. It was too dark to see inside until the magus lifted his arms and several hanging braziers ignited at his will. The large atrium was a macabre sight of carved skeletal depictions on the walls and metal cages suspended by chains above with human corpses left to rot inside. Jeth covered his nose with his scarf, trying not to vomit. Vidya grimaced but did nothing to block the stench for herself.

The magus took them to the atrium's center where an eighteen-foot stone statue stood, surrounded by an empty circular pool. Jeth's gaze traced the coiled serpent's body of the statue, transforming into the chest, arms, and head of a domineering male figure, wearing a cobra headdress, and holding a massive hanging brazier.

"This must be Sagorath," Jeth muttered.

Another magus joined them in the atrium from a stairwell to the left. Both magi looked almost identical, with the same skeletal tattoos, gaunt face, and robes.

The second magus circled around the duo and stopped between them and the door. He said, "Each of us before you specialize in one of two essences: fire or water. Water is the essence of Salotaph. We are all born in it, and some choose to return to it."

The other magus who stood nearest to the statue continued, "Fire is the essence of Sagorath and purest of them all. For those who can withstand its scorch will earn his eternal favor. Which do you choose?"

"Hmm, death by drowning or burning alive, both really solid choices." Jeth stroked his chin. "Can I pick something else?"

"How you wish to die is up to you, but we must warn that only through fire or water can your spirit be returned to the Serpentine Gods."

"I was thinking about a good old-fashioned stabbing. Perhaps . . . with a dagger. It has to be a special one though, one with dark and magical properties. Do you have anything like that . . . lying around here . . . maybe?"

"We sense your motives are impure. Do you wish to die or not?" said the magus nearest to the door.

"You spend your days in the making and handling of rotting corpses, and I'm impure?"

"If you will not choose an essence, an essence will be chosen for you," the first magus stated firmly.

He raised his arms, and the flames leaped out of every brazier along the walls. The fires whirled around his body, turning from orange, to green, then to blue, giving off unbearable heat. Jeth backed away, only to find the other magus forming water from the air and concentrating it to such a degree, it formed an electrical charge between each palm.

"We know what you ask after," the water magus said. "But you will not find it here, only death. That is all."

Before Jeth could figure out a way to dodge the magi's flame and lightning attacks, an echoing bang rang out, bringing a reverberating pain to his ears. Both magi were knocked violently back, chests exploding simultaneously. The fire was put out, and the only light that remained streamed in from the still open door and through the small hole in the roof above the statue.

Vidya stood there, arms outstretched, and holding her two flintlock pistols, one for each of the magi who'd met an abrupt end.

After blowing the smoking barrels, she took out a tiny sack filled with black powder and carefully reloaded her pistols, one at a time.

While Vidya was jamming the ramrod into each barrel, Jeth said, "I guess this is where we split up. What are you looking for anyway?"

"Not the Bloodstone Dagger," she replied as she put both loaded pistols back into their holsters.

"Figured that one out on my own," Jeth said. "If you want to keep it a secret, fine." He changed the subject. "How long have you worked for Snake Eye?"

"I don't work for Snake Eye," she said and headed toward the staircase, leaving his question unanswered.

"Uh . . . right then. Nice chatting with you too," Jeth muttered in annoyance. *There's something off about that woman.*

When she was gone, he started to search the atrium first. "If I were a Bloodstone Dagger in a temple of death, where would I be?" he sang to himself.

Taking the steps down into the empty pool, he circled around the statue, checking for clues or hieroglyphs at its base. The statue's male likeness blended into a female on the opposite side. The half snake, half woman, was holding an enormous decanter directly under the hole in the roof.

"Oh, Snake Eye. I didn't see you come in," he joked to the statue.

"Just here to check on my little Gershlon and grope some corpses," he replied to himself, doing his best impression of the plausible man as he sashayed around the statue.

Just then, the temple doors slammed shut, making his heart leap from his chest. The atrium was now almost completely in shadow. He brought his bow in hand and slowly edged around the statue with an arrow nocked. The braziers spontaneously lit up again, revealing just one magus. Other than being taller, he appeared no different than the others, save for how the entire room's atmosphere shifted with his presence. He ambled across the atrium, toward the empty pool. The astringent odor of smoke from the waste emanated from him.

Drawing back his bowstring, Jeth stepped into view and warned the advancing magus, "Stop right there."

The magus did just that. He reached into his wide sleeve and brought out a small curved knife. It was made of polished green stone with a bone hilt.

"Is this what you seek, young Fae'ren?" the magus said in a temperate yet commanding voice that made a shiver run up and down Jeth's spine.

"I think so," he said, his bow hand quivering. "Toss it over, and I won't put an arrow through your heart."

The magus responded with a chilling grin but made no move to give up the dagger. Without another warning, Jeth released his arrow, sending it exactly where he threatened it would go. The magus grunted, staggered back, and doubled over. He didn't drop the knife.

Jeth put his bow away and took out his khopeshes, then marched up the steps to finish the magus off. "Sorry about this," he said. He lifted the sword above his head and brought it down hard on the magus's neck. Instead of slicing off his head, the blade bounced off with a clang. Jeth stared at the sword as if it had betrayed him.

The magus shot up and grabbed Jeth by the scarf with one hand, the thin material tightening around his neck by the man's unnaturally strong grip. He choked as the magus ripped the arrow from his own chest and tossed it to the side.

"No need to apologize," he said and flung Jeth away with incredible force, sending him flying into the statue's coiled snake base, and he landed face down in the empty pool.

Pain shot through his shoulders from where his bow bit into him on impact. He dragged himself up and tried to regain his dropped weapons, only to find the stone beneath his feet liquefying.

"What the . . . ?"

He sank up to his shins before the ground hardened again, and he was stuck. *He knows earth and fire magic,* he thought with alarm.

The magus pulled off his robes, revealing the pants worn by Herrani warriors and a bare torso. Rib and collarbone images tattooed on his chest shone with sapphire accents. Around his neck, he wore a bronze plated brace with a string of fanged-tooth adornments hanging below it.

Jeth shook in horror as he met the magus's gaze. A kaleidoscope of green and red stared back at him, pupils replaced by vertical slits.

No, it can't be him! The magus's bleeding chest wound closed up before Jeth's eyes, and all his denials were swept away at once.

"Shit!" he mouthed, unable to make a sound. He tried to pull his legs out from the floor as the Overlord of Herran took deliberate steps down into the empty pool with him.

Even though it was hopeless, Jeth didn't stop struggling. Terror sweat dripped from every pore. Tremors rippled through him. "Y-you aren't supposed to be here," he stammered, trying to stall in any way he could. All he had now were his wits, not that they would do any good against an Essence, Spirit, and Flesh Mage all wrapped in one.

"I'm not?" Nas'Gavarr raised his white eyebrow, difficult to distinguish through his skeletal facial tattoo. "This temple is my home. You're in my house."

"You're a Magus of Sagorath?" Jeth sputtered, desperately trying to keep the Mage focused on talking rather than killing.

"Yes. In my youth."

"But you wiped them all out."

"Only those who refused to change. Not that I was surprised. Death never changes. Sooner or later it comes for us all," the Overlord said, mirroring words Anwarr had said to him months ago. Thinking of her brought him a flash of courage.

"But not you," Jeth said. "That's why they opposed you. Because a man who refuses to die is an affront to everything they stand for."

Nas'Gavarr nodded, taking slow steps toward him. "Once I complete my task, I can embrace death as everyone should, but that time has not yet come."

He now stood only inches from him. Jeth could make out a marking on his forehead of an upside down 'U' shape with tiny dots around it. Where have you seen that symbol before? Then, his attentions drew down to the Bloodstone Dagger still in Nas'Gavarr's hand. "You look like you got a good handle on that dagger there," he said shakily. "You should keep it. If you can just release me from this . . . floor . . . I can be on my way, and you'll never see me again."

Nas'Gavarr wrenched Jeth's head back roughly by the locks while bringing the tip of his knife to his face. "Please, please, I'll go. J-just—I'll go!" Whatever courage he'd found flew out of him as he closed his eyes. The Overlord pushed the knife into the skin. Blood trickled down his cheek. Then it was over.

He opened his eyes, the dagger mere inches from his face. He watched his own drop of blood absorb into the dagger and float upon its surface as a red fleck against the dark green stone. Nas'Gavarr put the tip of his finger to the blade's point, and the red spot floated up toward it and remerged as blood on his fingertip. After studying it for a few moments, Nas'Gavarr brought the blood to his tongue. His eyes lit up. A terrible smile stretched across his face.

Jeth's stomach churned, and his legs buckled, but the stone around his shins wouldn't let them give way. "H-how do I taste?"

The Overlord's reptilian eyes blinked sideways before he replied, "Like a champion."

Jeth trembled, his eyes welling with tears that he couldn't stop no matter how hard he swallowed them back.

Nas'Gavarr began to circle him. "You are very far from the forest, Jethril."

"How do you know my name?" His heart was now humming in his chest. "Did you get that from my blood?"

"Do you think it's by chance that you came to be at my temple, that you came to be in Herran at all?"

"I chose to come."

Nas'Gavarr twisted his head side to side like a snake. "What makes you so sure that you have a choice in anything? Did you choose to be born into a culture that casts out orphan children? Were you in control when you murdered your own brothers in arms? Were you not lured to a life of thievery by the wiles of a beautiful woman? You didn't even choose to enter this temple today."

Don't let him get into your head!

"I still made a choice. I wanted to—"

"Ah, want." The Immortal Serpent paced away, shaking his head. "The lie we tell ourselves so we can further cement our illusion of control. No man, woman, or child knows what they want. It's why they turn to beings more ancient and more powerful than them to give them purpose, to help them escape their true natures. Like all humankind, you are enslaved."

"And you're going free us all?" Jeth gulped.

"Not me alone. You too have a role in this."

"Me?"

"Yes. . . . And her." Nas'Gavarr lifted his gaze to the ceiling, to the subtle jostling of one of the cages hanging directly above them.

Vidya's black powder sack dropped from above and landed in the empty pool. A second later, a giant bird with expansive brown wings, burst out from between the cages and hurtled for the closed doors. The Overlord shot out his palm, and a blinding lightning blast followed, sending shockwaves of electric current through the escaping creature. It fell from the air and landed hard on the grimy stone floor. It was Vidya. Her curly hair was made wilder by the jolt, her cape now tied around her waist, and in its place, enormous feathered wings sprouted from her shoulder blades, flapping spastically on the ground.

Nas'Gavarr marched toward the disoriented woman as she tried to get up. Grabbing one of her wings, he flipped her onto her back and wrapped his fingers around her neck. He lifted her straight off the ground and started walking back to the statue. She attempted to fly off with him, but he fused his feet to the ground.

"It is not yet time for you, Vidya. However, I am glad to see that your transformation was successful."

"You killed my mother . . ." she croaked. With her forearm blade, she sliced open his, but it did nothing to weaken his grip. His blood streamed down his arm and dripped onto the floor as the wound closed up. Her wings continued to flap as a helpless bird struggling to escape a lion's claws.

"Yes, I did, and had I not you wouldn't be here as you are. Now you get to experience what your mother did in her last few moments."

In a last-ditch attempt to free herself, Vidya grabbed for her pistol. Nas'Gavarr never gave her a chance to fire it. With a sharp clench of his fingers around her throat, he snapped her neck, and her pistol fell to the floor with a clank. The Overlord threw Vidya's limp body to the ground where it landed with a thud.

The image of the winged woman splayed lifeless upon the grimy stone floor made Jeth's airways seize. He did that with one hand . . . just one hand. . . . he thought.

You're not getting out of here alive!

12

Always Forward

"I preserved this temple for its historical significance," the Overlord began, but Jeth could only stare at Vidya's corpse on the floor.

Carelessly stepping over her body, Nas'Gavarr continued, "This is the first Serpentine temple ever built. It belonged to the ancient Najahai before they were driven out by the Immortal One. Their gods became our gods. Sagorath stands before you and Salotaph behind him. Your Way has brought you to this effigy; brought you to me. There is no reason to be afraid, only to accept what is to come."

"Why would you believe in the *Way*?" Jeth asked, still trembling.

"When you've lived as long as I have, you begin to know things as they truly are. Your Del'Cabrian oppressors happen to be right in this case. The Way is real, and as long as our world is subject to the will of their Deities That Cannot Be Named, we will always be ruled by it."

"If you know so much about it, then what is my *Way*?"

Nas'Gavarr took his dagger in hand once again and walked purposefully toward him. "To take part in humankind's salvation."

Jeth's legs gave way, and he fell on his back side, the tendons in his knees straining. Never had he felt so impotent. All those times he had been ridiculed by urlings, rejected by women, told to leave and never come back—it all seemed so trivial now.

The Overlord took him by the shoulder. He flipped the mythical dagger over in his hand, his eyes studying Jeth like a butcher deciding that day's choice cut. The Flesh Mage soon made up his mind and placed the tip of the blade at the soft tissue of Jeth's right side.

"Wait. No!" Jeth struggled against his fast grip. Images of Anwarr flooded his mind, the sound of her laugh, how good it felt to fall asleep wrapped in her scent. *'I can show you more of what our world has to offer.'*

Then, an echoing bang reverberated through the atrium, and bright light from outside poured in as the heavy temple doors flew open. Nas'Gavarr whipped his head around in annoyance.

All was silent for a moment as Jeth tried to look past the Overlord, hoping, just maybe, his crew had come for him, but he couldn't see a thing. A single set of boot steps sounded, and another sound, a third tap after every other step. . . . *A walking stick.*

"Immortal Serpent!" a deep, ominous voice echoed.

Nas'Gavarr let go of Jeth and turned to face the mysterious guest. A strained relief showered over Jeth at the sight of him.

"Raven Sorcerer, at last we meet in the flesh," Nas'Gavarr said to the man with long black hair tied back, wearing a tailcoat, vest, and cravat.

"Meister!" Jeth screamed.

Melikheil brushed past his plea and said, "Your time has come, Gavarr."

"You should not have come all this way." The Overlord put away the dagger and walked up the steps to address the Ingle Mage.

As soon as his tormenter moved out of reach, Jeth took a stuttering breath and surveyed the room. He found nothing around him that could be of use, save for the arrows in his quiver and three dead bodies on the floor. No. Two. The body of Vidya was gone. *Where did she go?*

Melikheil's stoic voice brought his attention back to the Mages. "I was hoping we could do this at the battlefront, but when I got there, I saw you slithering off to your burrow like the snake you are."

"Why this animosity?" the Overlord asked, hands behind his back as he walked around Melikheil to size him up. "I have done nothing to you or your people . . . at least not yet."

"You know why I'm here." Melikheil rested both hands on the top of his staff.

"I know the King of Del'Cabria wants me dead, to end the war that he declared on me."

"A war you instigated with the murder of a senator."

Nas'Gavarr gave a knowing smirk. "Yes, it would appear that way. . . ." A chortle rumbled from under his breath.

"Why do you laugh?" Melikheil hissed.

"From what I've been able to sense thus far, the power you wield is impressive, but your motivation is paltry, as was that of all the others who dared challenge me. You want to be the most powerful sorcerer in the world. But you cannot begin to comprehend what that means. Now that you're here, I will be glad to show you."

Melikheil glared deep into Nas'Gavarr's reptilian eyes and smiled ever so slightly. "I am counting on it."

A knot rose up from Jeth's stomach as he watched the sorcerers circle each other. He wriggled to free himself one last time, but it was as futile as before.

"Meister Melikheil," Jeth pleaded. "You can use your earth magic to free me, please!"

His desperate cries went unheeded as Nas'Gavarr pulled the flames out of the braziers, formed a cyclone of fire in the air, and hurled it at the Ingle Mage. Melikheil defended with an ice blast that canceled out the flames. He followed up with a frost spell so powerful, Nas'Gavarr's flames sizzled out, and he was pushed hard against the wall, ice crystallizing around his body and forming a block in mere seconds.

With his adversary frozen to the wall, the dark wizard finally acknowledged Jeth stuck in the stone. "You're the Desert War Traitor. Stay right there. When I'm finished, I will be turning you over to the Del'Cabrians."

Jeth's heart sank to the bottom of his chest.

A loud sizzling noise brought their attention back to the block of rapidly melting ice, a bright flame growing beneath it.

"Forget my past deeds and let me go. Hurry, before he gets free!" Jeth called, tears streaming down his cheeks.

"Quiet!" Melikheil snapped. A penetrating yellow flame burst through the ice. He shielded it with more ice, but it melted too quickly. Melikheil turned the ultra-hot beam around onto Nas'Gavarr, and soon the two Mages were shooting the same ray of fire and light into itself. It shone so bright it pained Jeth's eyes even while shut tight, and his tears steamed off his cheeks. His exposed skin began to peel as he gritted his teeth in pain. Before long, the Mages lost control of their beams, shooting them upward, and melting some of the chains holding up the cages dangling from the ceiling. One cage fell on top of Nas'Gavarr, but with a wave of his arm, he rendered it to dust. Then came a loud clank from above. Another cage came loose. Jeth threw his body to the side and covered his head with his arms as the cage came crashing down just a few feet from him. The impact of the heavy iron structure cracked the old stone almost all the way to his right leg. He frantically tried to pull it out, but it still wouldn't budge.

The Mages cast themselves into the air with wind gusts and grappled each other. They flew about the atrium, Melikheil hanging on to Nas'Gavarr's bare shoulders and Nas'Gavarr clutching Melikheil's face until Nas'Gavarr pushed his adversary away. Melikheil went hurtling head first into the wall, the stone liquefied on impact, and he bounced back out uninjured.

"Hey, do that over here, but for me!" Jeth begged.

Nas'Gavarr returned to the ground and said, "There is a lot of life force within you, Raven."

"As is with you," Melikheil replied.

"You haven't had several generations to build it up. How is it that you have so much?"

"I have my methods."

"The only way you could have accumulated that much life force in such a short amount of time is by taking it from countless others." He sneered in disgust. "I doubt they have given it to you by choice."

"Don't tell me you have not done the same to stay alive for these last two hundred years," Melikheil shot back.

"All the life force I have ever gleaned was from willing participants. In this temple of death, those who chose a painless end outside of fire and water, allowed me to take what little they had left. For decades, I slowly built it up through physical mastery of my body. Don't dare compare youself to me, covetous child!" He spat on the floor.

"Fight me in the Spirit Chamber, and we will see how powerful you really are."

"I don't doubt your spirit is strong," Nas'Gavarr began, gripping the naja teeth around his neck. "I've felt it in my dreams before you ever came to the desert." His voice deepened and became raspier. His skin bubbled and peeled, replacing itself with red and green marbled scales. His arms grew longer. Bloodied claws emerged from under his fingernails, breaking each one off in their wake. Monstrous fangs pushed out from his gums, as he spoke. "I will be happy to show you my power, but it will not be by my spirit, only my flesh."

Jeth cowered. A fearsome naja stood in Nas'Gavarr's place, his hissing roar ripping through the atrium. Melikheil shot out a lightning bolt, but the Overlord leaped backward, jumped off the wall behind him, and sprang up amongst the hanging cages above. He vaulted from cage to cage, and they knocked together with a deafening clatter.

Melikheil spun around in circles, his dark eyes wide and fearful. The man-sized reptile remained hidden in the shadows of the ceiling.

"Meister, behind you!" Jeth yelled.

Nas'Gavarr bounded down the wall and pushed off it at incredible speed. Melikheil came down hard on his face, the naja on his back. He tore at his jacket with his claws and sank his fangs into the meat where his neck met shoulder.

The Ingle wizard bellowed as Nas'Gavarr yanked at his skin, stretching the flesh before it ripped off the bone. He swallowed it whole before Melikheil zapped him with a lightning bolt and staggered to his feet. Blood squirted through his fingers, holding his neck, and dripped down his arm and back. The wound began to heal itself, and soon enough he stopped applying pressure to it.

Dizziness overwhelmed Jeth. *Don't just stand here and watch these maniacs tear each other apart! Think of something!*

He scanned his surroundings again, forcing himself to stay focused this time. The fallen cage had created a crack in the stone, one of his khopeshes was to his left, just out of reach, and Vidya's fallen bag was in front of him . . . filled with black powder . . . which was highly explosive . . .

He bent forward as far as he could toward the tiny sack, but it too was out of reach. *Wait. Not quite!* His bow was still strapped to his back. Using it as an extended arm, he dragged the bag over to him. After fumbling it open, he found a sizable amount of powder inside. Whether it was enough to blow him out or blow him up, he didn't know. He checked on the Mage battle.

Melikheil had removed his blood-stained tailcoat. "You waste time. My life force will continue to heal my body, so bite and claw at me all you like," he rasped.

Nas'Gavarr's scales shed away, and he reverted to his human form. "I'm aware of that. But are you not aware of how flesh magic works?" He took slow steps toward the Ingleman. "I now have your flesh and blood inside me, and with that, every part of your body is at my mercy."

Melikheil tried to respond, but his words were caught in his throat. He leaned on his staff, legs buckling, and collapsed to his knees. The already pale Mage whitened the closer Nas'Gavarr got.

"I control how your blood flows through you—when it reaches your tissues. . . ." Melikheil clutched at his chest, gasping for air, and turning a startling blue.

I'll take my chances with blowing my legs off, Jeth thought, and he poured the contents of the sack into the thin crack nearest to him. He took an arrow from his quiver to use as a ramrod in packing down the powder into a smaller area.

"You still . . . can't . . . kill me," Melikheil gasped from the floor.

"I can control its coagulation, its pressure, even its volume."

At those words, Melikheil began to regurgitate blood. It dripped from his nose, his ears, and even from behind his eyes. Jeth did everything he could to concentrate on packing the powder down and not on the gruesome sight of Melikheil and the puddle of blood forming beneath him.

"I possess your skin," Nas'Gavarr continued. "I can stretch it, contort it." He shrugged. "I can do away with it altogether."

With a wave of his hand, Melikheil's skin was ripped away with such force, his hair, clothing, and every accessory went with it, blood splattering in all directions. A sour, metallic smell overpowered Jeth's senses, distracting him from his task. The Ingle Mage's agonizing shrieks flooded the atrium. The daunting, ominous presence that had once been so intimidating was rendered to a bleeding, trembling, mass of meat and bone, unrecognizable as anything close to human.

Vomit rose to Jeth's throat, and he swallowed it back down and looked away. He needed something to ignite the black powder and fast. The closest source of flame was the brazier hanging from Sagorath's fist just above him.

Nas'Gavarr loomed over Melikheil lying there quivering in a bloody pool upon the floor and whimpering like a premature animal ripped too early from its mother's womb. "Without skin, most men die in seconds, but your life force won't let you. It won't heal you quick enough either, so you are forced to suffer." Some of Melikheil's skin reformed on his hands and feet as he attempted to crawl away, leaving a trail of bodily fluids behind him.

Jeth aimed an arrow at the large bowl of lit oil and released. The impact caused the brazier to rock, but nothing more. *Come on, tip over. . . .* He shot out another one, timing it just right so the bowl swung near vertical, spilling some oil, but without adequate flame to go with it. "Shit!" A breathless cry.

"I have your muscle as well," Nas'Gavarr went on in the foreground. "Now they too, work at my will." Melikheil was on his feet and forced back against the wall near the door. His shrieks were nothing more than gurgling wheezes. His arms scraped against the stone, forced to outstretch to each side.

"Your veins, capillaries, and nerves, I took a piece of them all when I bit into you. . . ." Melikheil's bleeding veins and arteries moved from beneath his muscles. Thin, sinewy ropes ripped out of him and wrapped tightly around his arms, legs, and torso. His whimpering howls alone sent painful tremors up and down Jeth's spine. *How is this happening? No man can survive that!* Jeth choked back a sob as he nocked another arrow.

"I can't imagine the agony you must be in," Nas'Gavarr said, wrapping Melikheil's own nerves around his throat and choking off his cries. "If only you did not possess countless lifetimes within you."

Jeth's arrow released, the brazier capsized, and the contents dumped onto the floor, narrowly missing him. Some of the flames fell through the fissure where an explosion instantly rang out. The stone cracked, and Jeth hit the ground hard. Pain shot through his entire right leg, but he didn't care. Amongst the rock dust and the ringing in his ears, he managed to yank that leg out of captivity. His other was still held fast, but the rock around it had crumbled a little. With his bow, he dragged one of his swords over to him and used the pommel to bash against the stone holding his left leg in place. The Overlord smiled at Jeth as he tried to escape, but didn't appear to care enough to leave his adversary and stop him.

"No amount of suffering, outside of eternal, will make up for the atrocities you've committed to gain the power you have. But I am willing to do you one kindness." He strode over to Melikheil and whispered near where his ear should have been. The adrenaline pumping through Jeth kept his senses in tune to what was being said. ". . . I will end you in such a way that no amount of life force can ever bring you back."

The sinews strangling Melikheil's limbs tightened and pinched his left arm right off, and the other was about to suffer the same fate. Jeth kept banging against the rocks around his foot until enough of it crumbled away for him to pull it out. Despite the aching of each ankle, he scrambled for his second khopesh and made a run for the door.

With a final wave of his arm, Nas'Gavarr tore the skinless wizard apart from the inside. Blood and viscera splashed in every direction, saturating Jeth as he ran past. He caught a glimpse of a misshapen head of what used to be Melikheil, falling to the ground, his organs and tissues having been flung against every wall. Nas'Gavarr was as clean as when he first came in.

Jeth ran into the light of the outside world, feeling a stunted sense of relief of being released from the temple of death, yet the stench remained with him, dripping down his face. He bounded down the temple steps, nearly tumbling over them in his desperation to get away. "Ash, Star!" he screamed, but there was no one there except a few dead magi.

Right then, Jeth's legs wobbled, and a dreadful weakness came over him. His chest tightened, and he collapsed to his hands and knees. Nas'Gavarr emerged from the darkness of the temple, his hand raised toward him. He still has a drop of your blood! Jeth choked in heaps of air, but it didn't do any good. His arms and legs were useless, his heart crawling, the exhaustion too great.

Mother Oak, help me! His mind begged as the world around him began to fade into a sea of flashing lights before his eyes. Jeth fought against his impending unconsciousness with all of his mental might. He cried out with every movement as he dragged his enfeebled body along the ground. Then something sparked within him. His heart picked up pace, warmth returned to his limbs, and he miraculously found the strength to get up.

"You . . . No!" Nas'Gavarr's roared. Jeth was on his feet and running with every ounce of strength he had left.

The canyon was a yellow blur in Jeth's periphery as he sprinted through it. It was as if he were on the back of Torrent, wind whipping back his blood drenched locks. The scenery swiftly changed from canyon walls to skeletal ruins, his focus solely on the clouds of black smoke in the distance that signified his way out . . . or his final resting place.

When Jeth realized how far he had run in such a short amount of time his body began to slow and the shooting pain of his right leg returned in waves. It wasn't until he reached the rocks where he and his team had rested earlier that his body attempted to give way. His ankle was swollen in his boot, but it didn't seem broken. He managed to limp to the trickling stream where he collapsed onto his hands and knees.

The putrid stench of Melikheil's remains only worsened as the hot sun beamed down on him. Coagulated blood mixed with chunks of flesh and innards caked Jeth's hair, gluing the thick strands together. The blood drenched sand lodged under his nails, the stink of it up his nostrils, and the taste of it in his mouth, made him retch. He violently expelled his stomach on the rocks while fighting the urge to pass out. His pulse was still racing, his head spinning. *I have to keep moving. . . . The camels.*

Jeth limped around the rocks to find them gone. Not even a waterskin was left behind.

"Star!" Jeth yelled as he wiped the vomit from his lips. "Ash!" *They* left.

. . . They left you here to die!

He turned to face northeast, the direction he and his crew had come, hoping beyond hope that they were waiting there for him—that they wouldn't just abandon him. There was nothing but rising pillars of smoke in the distance.

Scanning the flaming horizon, what he found to the southeast made his pounding heart freeze. Around one hundred mounted, blue-coated men were standing in their battle formations. *You're hallucinating. Surely that many Del'Cabrian soldiers could not have come through the waste.* Then he remembered Melikheil's words back in the temple. *'I was hoping we could do this at the battlefront. . . .'*

Melikheil had brought an entire contingent with him, but why leave them behind to combat Nas'Gavarr one on one? Why risk bringing a hundred men through the waste, only to trap them here in the event he died? Unless he was that confident he'd be victorious. *Or . . .* A paralyzing fear swept through Jeth.

Straight east, a lone Herrani man with a white braided beard, atop a jet-black steed, and wielding a long trident spear, charged for the Del'Cabrian line. It all happened so fast. The rapid movement accompanied by low growls and distant screeches resounded from the Burning Waste. An army of giant armored reptiles sprang through the black smoke, taking up the charge behind the lone warrior. *Nas'Gavarr brought a contingent with him too!*

Jeth stood between the advancing forces, and all his limbs went numb. Surrounded by enemies, his only hope would be to fight through the rampage and run like the wind. He would never survive the waste without a mount or a mask. Even with an Essence Mage to assist, the soldiers still must have brought masks with them.

Taking out his bow, Jeth scanned the galloping cavalrymen in the front line. When he spotted one who had his breathing mask and canteen hanging visibly from the saddle, he took aim. Tuning out the monstrous roars of the naja heading toward them, he let an arrow fly, killing the unfortunate rider. He ran to retrieve the horse, trying not to think about the dead Del'Cabrian. *This is survival now, pure and simple. With their Mage dead, none of these men are getting out of here alive.*

The roar of the cavalry galloping at full speed came at Jeth fast. He ducked several spears and sword swipes, choking on the sand kicked up under the horse's hooves. When the naja army clashed with the cavalry, chaos erupted, and he soon lost sight of his target. He found himself in a hopeless mesh of clashing steel, agonizing screams, whinnies, and reptilian snarls. Naja flew overhead, taking down rider and horse as men on the ground hollered into battle. Jeth lost his unmounted horse, but found several more, galloping frantically about. As he went toward one, a spear came at his head from the left. Jeth sliced the spear in two and kicked its wielder down, only to have a naja take the man's shoulder in its jaws and drag him off screaming. Ducking beside a fallen horse, Jeth searched it for a mask and was disheartened to find it was under the heavy beast.

"Sal have mercy."

Another naja leaped at him, and he ducked. It flew overhead and took out a soldier behind him. With more adrenaline pumping through him, Jeth searched for any horse he could wrangle. Just as he focused in on another, a naja pounced on it and tore it and its rider to shreds in seconds.

The whistle of arrows cut through the air. Hundreds of black lines filled the cloudless blue sky. Del'Cabrians put up their shields to catch the rain of arrows. They pierced into the naja's thick scales but did little to faze them. Jeth dove behind a pile of bodies where he raised his swords over his head to deflect the stragglers.

An unmounted steed came galloping toward him. He sprang for it, grabbed its saddle, and pulled himself up. Checking the saddle bag, he found the mask secure and a canteen about half full. *Thank the Deities.*

With one khopesh readied, he took hold of the reins and turned the horse back through the droves, trampling dead bodies into the sand, and blocking any attacks that came his way.

As he ran by a ring of naja feeding off a pile of corpses, two of them caught his scent. In seconds, the blood-thirsty reptiles gained on Jeth's mount, pounced onto its hindquarters, and dragged their claws down its rump. The horse shrieked and fell backward. Jeth flipped out of its saddle before he became crushed beneath it. The pain of his ankle on landing made him cry out. An ear-splitting screech pierced through the carnage, and a naja leaped upon him, hardly giving him a chance to ready his swords. The stench of blood and decay from its breath was revolting. Its open maw of multi-rowed teeth came at his face.

"Get off!" he wailed.

More arrows rained down, piercing the creature's tough hide. It glanced over to the source of its irritation, partially lifting its weight off Jeth. With only one sword at his disposal, he slashed it across the naja's throat. The scaly flesh tore open, pouring red-orange blood onto his torso. It collapsed on top of him, trapping him beneath it.

With all his strength, Jeth tried to push the naja off, grunting with every pained effort, only to have another bounce off its back, embedding him deeper into the blood drenched sand and pushing the air further out of his lungs.

This thing weighs as much as a horse! Jeth's ribcage bowed under the dead mass, his entire body as weak as it was when Nas'Gavarr controlled his blood flow. Pounding horse hooves shook the ground overhead, naja shrieked, and arrows continued to pelt down. More bodies, almost all of them human or urling, fell screaming all around him, their blood pooling into the sand as naja ripped into them, and left them lifeless.

Closing his eyes, Jeth shut off every one of his senses. Seas of green replaced the arid plains of death. He lay on a bed of moss, with the pollens dancing in the breeze while hundreds of birds sang their morning song in the trees.

Jeth couldn't stop the tears from flowing as he lay upon the forest floor after the green sparks struck him in the side, taking his breath away. It felt like thousands of pricks from tiny thistles under his skin. All he had wanted to do was grab onto Serra's legs as she flew away so she'd take him with her.

"Fairy sparks can't harm you, they only sting for a few moments," Serra said. She was right, the pain was already subsiding, and Jeth calmed down.

"That's better. No need to leak water from your eyes," she said, wiping the tears off his face then immediately wiping her wet hand on herself. "I'll never understand why you children do this so much."

"We don't!" he lashed. Flushing with embarrassment, he ran into the bush, the forest fading into a bright white the farther he went.

Jeth was back in the desert, the terrible weight upon him having been lifted. A beautiful woman appeared. Her skin glistened like honey, and her hair shone like the moons. . . . "Anwarr!"

"Always forward, Jethril."

She took him in her arms. Her hands were rough and stank of blood and black powder. She spun his limp body around, and gripped him under his arms and firmly around the chest. He wheezed from the pain in his ribs.

A powerful wind blew out into the battlefield all around him, and the ground fell away. The massacre spiraled down below him, getting smaller and smaller before the nightmare vanished from sight.

13

Unscathed

Vidya left the mass of death and gore behind and flew back over the ruins holding the blood crusted Fae'ren to her chest.

They landed on a high tower close to the canyon, granting a view of the carnage below in its entirety. Vidya set Jeth down, letting him crumple to his knees and take in heaps of air while she made a more controlled landing beside him.

"W-what's happening?" Jeth wheezed. His eyes found their way up to her face, and his mouth gaped. "No. Y-you're—how are you . . . ?"

Vidya crouched on the edge, overlooking the path through the canyon. "We'll wait here until Nas'Gavarr leaves the temple," she said.

"You came back for me . . ." His red puffy eyes darted about.

"I never left," said Vidya, still looking downward for signs of the Overlord. "I waited on the temple roof for Nas'Gavarr to kill that Ingle Mage and finish whatever ritual he planned to do with you. I had hoped to gain some insights into his true motivations." She turned a suspicious eye toward Jeth. "But, here you are, completely unscathed."

"Unscathed? Is that what you think?" He let out a dark chuckle. "I'm sorry my survival disappoints you."

Vidya stretched her wings before folding them behind her back and turning to face him. He looked like a wild mongrel who had scavenged through killing fields his whole life. Dried red flakes stuck to his skin, burnt and peeling beneath.

Vidya said, "I saw him using blood magic on you, but you still got away. . . . *How?*"

The Fae'ren shivered like one would when bracing against a cold wind. "I don't know. He only had a drop of my blood. It probably wore off or something."

"Not that fast," she said. "Had he the blood of any Fae'ren, it would have been enough to kill you, or at least cause significant damage. The more similar the bloodline to his subject, the more power he wields over that subject." The Fae'ren kept shaking his head like an idiot as she talked. *How did such a weakling like him make it out of that temple?* Her patience was starting to wear thin. "For the Overlord to have even one drop of your blood means you should be dead."

"Just lucky, I guess."

He began to chortle while grinning dementedly, his round hazel eyes bloodshot and crazed. He's lost it!

Grabbing him by the arm, she snapped her fingers in front of his face. "Hey, stop fooling around and listen to me!" She clutched him by both shoulders and shook him hard enough to promptly cut off his laughter. "What manner of being are you?"

Jeth struggled to free himself from Vidya's grasp, but her grip was that of three warrior men. "I can ask you the same thing. I watched him electrocute you, snap your neck, and uh . . . there's something else odd about you. . . . Oh, right—wings!"

Vidya sighed and released him. "I suppose, I can't fault you for not knowing what I am. . . . I'm a harpy."

"Is every Crede woman a . . . a harpy?"

Looking back over the ledge, Vidya said, "No, just me. Although, I'm not the only one with wings. There are sirens too, but that's not important right now. I told you what I am, so what are you?"

"I'm a Fae'ren human, nothing more," Jeth maintained.

"No human being could run away from that temple as fast as you did. Did you take something before you came here? Are you some kind of forest sprite? Come on, just . . ." She took a breath and calmed the growing irritation inside her. ". . . Help me out here."

The Fae'ren shook his head with the blankest of expressions.

Vidya harrumphed before her attentions were drawn to movement below. "Look." She pointed downward. "He's leaving. The naja have overrun the Del'Cabrians, so he's likely going to take his beasts back to the Odafi front."

They watched the Overlord gallop his black steed toward the ruins. Jeth dropped down flat on his stomach as if trying to hide himself from the Mage passing far below the tower. Nas'Gavarr continued right by them to meet the man leading the naja horde.

"Who's that?" he whispered, even though neither men could possibly hear him from so far away.

"I think that's Saf'Ryeem, one of his sons, and a powerful Spirit Mage in his own right. Nas'Gavarr deferred control of his naja to him. Now's our chance to get back in." Vidya unfolded her wings.

"Are you insane? The last place we should be is back inside that madman's house!"

"We have to," she replied doggedly.

"We? No." Jeth pushed himself to unsteady feet. "I need to get back to the City of Herran."

"That's unfortunate. I suppose I should let you down here, and you can make your own way across the waste. See if you can catch up with your friends." Vidya smirked.

"You saw them?"

"While searching the upper floors, I pushed some magi out the window and spotted Nas'Gavarr riding up. They took one look at him and bolted." She raised an eyebrow. "Smart thieves."

Jeth weakly leaned against the crumbling stone bastions, putting his palm to his sweating forehead, dried blood flaking off in his hand. "They sure are, and I'm the fool."

Vidya stood up with a sigh. "Help me find what I came here for, and then I can fly you over the waste."

She figured she could use the extra hand, and she wasn't prepared to let him run away to his death without finding out how he avoided that very thing at the hands of Nas'Gavarr.

"What exactly are you looking for?" he asked.

Vidya clenched her fists as she continued to glare after the Overlord and his son riding off into the black smog parting before them. "The thing that allowed Nas'Gavarr to invade the inner sanctum of our island. He killed a Councilwoman and tried to incite dissent in our men."

". . . Was that Councilwoman your mother by chance?" he asked in a somber tone.

Vidya didn't meet his eyes, only touched at her neck, recalling how easily it snapped in the Overlord's hand. . . . . *A harpy's bones should not be so readily broken as a siren's.* Her teeth clenched as rage throbbed in her chest, making it hard to breathe.

"I see," Jeth continued. "He killed one of our senators too. Why is he starting wars with both nations?"

"That's what I'm here to find out. Credence doesn't have the numbers for war that other nations do. We possess only the siren's diplomacy, and now, the harpy's vengeance."

Vidya kept her eyes glued to the blood drenched sand, and the heaps of corpses in the battlefield, many of which were being gnawed on by naja fangs. She could hear hundreds of men's flesh ripping from the bone along with their last moans before death, all the way from her perch.

Something deep inside her began to stir, some flickering spark of recognition. The carnage below gave her a sick sense of serenity. Satisfaction in a punishment well executed and deserved, giving her a morbid kinship to the killer reptiles for a split second. *They kill so quickly and completely*, she thought almost reverently.

A familiar coarse-grained voice whispered sinisterly into her ear, *"That's what we have to do if we are going to defeat them."*

She glanced over to the Fae'ren, and he returned a cautious look but appeared unaware of the creature speaking to her, though she assumed as much. She had first heard the voice a month after her transformation.

A dark silhouette of a vulture against the sun circled above the battlefield, then descended upon a soldier's corpse. Vidya inhaled slowly while watching it, unable to make out its true shape outside of the sun's glare obscuring it by shadow in broad daylight. The winged creature made no attempt to consume the human's remains. It only stared at Vidya, amplifying her thirst for retribution in a single shiver down her spine. The voice spoke again, only this time it was distinct in her mind like a separate presence outside her. *"We must bring back the Harplite!"* And with those words, the winged shadow was swallowed into the light.

"Alright then, let's make it quick." Jeth groaned, bringing Vidya back to herself.

With a nod, she grabbed him from behind and summoned the winds. She spread her wings and leaped off the edge, gliding between the canyon walls and back to the temple roof. Once through the open skylight, they landed in front of Salotaph. Jeth brushed his hand over his blood-caked locks, looking around nervously.

"I didn't get a chance to search the basement floors." Vidya tucked her wings behind her back and started walking toward a downward staircase on the west side of the atrium.

The Fae'ren followed close behind. "Care to tell me what I should be looking out for?" he asked, his voice echoing off the sandstone.

"Keep it down. There are still magi afoot," she hissed.

The Fae'ren's mouth twitched as he scratched at his crusty beard. He remained silent while limping behind her.

Down the staircase, they came upon a series of dark hallways. Faint torchlight from skulls fashioned into sconces cast frightening shadows on every wall. They twisted and curved, endlessly circling, then branching off into a daunting labyrinth. More than the skeletal shadows and confusing corridors, it was the unnatural hush that disquieted Vidya the most.

"This place is a maze," Jeth said, his voice now a welcome distraction.

Vidya started scraping the stone walls with her forearm blades as they walked. "We should mark the halls we've already been down to guide us out."

"There's no need for that, I've got a good sense of direct—" Jeth grabbed her hand to halt her. "Wait, stop that."

She jerked her hand away. *How dare he touch me without permission? I should—* Her attentions were then drawn to a cloaked figure disappearing around the curvature of the hallway ahead.

"It's a magus," Jeth said, taking out his bow.

I bet he knows where the gate is, thought Vidya. Without a word, she dashed down the hall. Jeth groaned and limped after her.

As they turned the corner, they came to an open corridor, diverging into three hallways with no one in sight.

"Yasharra damn him, where did he go?" Vidya whispered through gritted teeth.

Jeth put up his hand to silence her. She was growing to hate the little shit more every second. He took an arrow from his quiver and ventured down the middle hallway. "This way," he said.

"Are you sure?" she whispered back. He didn't answer her and kept moving. *Is this man really human?*

Soon enough, his hunch paid off. The two pursuers now had the hooded magus in their sights, remaining far enough behind as not to alert him to their presence.

They soon reached another corridor with two branching hallways to their left and a large set of stone doors, guarded by two more magi. Those magi turned and pointed straight at Vidya and Jeth. The one they had been following spun around, flames from a skull sconce whirling into his hands. Jeth shot an arrow straight into his throat while Vidya gunned down a magus at the door with her one remaining pistol.

The bang reverberated sharply off the walls, and the Fae'ren covered his ears. Skeletal faces emerged from the shadows of the hallways in reaction to the noise. Jeth shot down the last guard and two of the advancing magi. He switched to dual scimitars as the others came closer. Three of them attacked with wooden staffs, but he dodged each strike, slid between them, and sliced two through the gut with his sickle-shaped blades before stabbing the third in the midsection with the pointed edge. *At least the man can fight,* Vidya thought.

She didn't bother to dodge the two magi that came after her. One of them brought his staff down hard over her wings, and it splintered on impact. She scarcely felt it, but her wings reacted anyhow. They snapped open and knocked both of the magi onto their backsides, and she finished them off with her arm blades. The corridor was silent once again.

Vidya turned to Jeth and said, "You're not too bad with that bow."

"You have no idea, lady," he replied, limping over to the double doors. Arrogant too. But that didn't bother Vidya as much. *I'll take pride over cowardice any day.*

There were no handles or knobs on the doors. Much like the temple's front doors, they needed to be pushed open. The Fae'ren put all of his meager weight behind the heavy sandstone and grunted in pain.

"It won't budge," he moaned. "What's the point of guarding these doors if they can't even open from this side?"

Vidya rolled her eyes. "Probably because Nas'Gavarr is one of the few strong enough to do so, meaning something important to him is behind them."

She bumped Jeth out of the way to get to the door herself.

"Hey, watch it, will you?"

Ignoring his whining, Vidya strained herself against the doors as dirt started to tumble down between them. The scraping stone against stone echoed down the corridors. With a beat of her wings, the air rushed in behind them, and the doors flew open and bashed against the wall on the other side.

"Whoa there." Jeth jumped back a foot. "Was that really necessary?"

"They were in my way," Vidya said dryly.

"Remind me to never get in your way."

With a smirk, Vidya stepped through the door and into the room beyond. Dozens of braziers wound up the length of several pillars and hung from the high arches of the ceiling. They lit the yellow sandstone to brilliant gold, draping the skeletal serpent depictions upon the walls with an ancient grandiosity. Standing in the center of the great room was a massive vertical ring of dark granite, laboriously smoothed and polished to resemble the intricate details of a snake's skin. The two serpent heads met at the top. Golden light from the braziers reflected off its black surface making the monument ghoulishly beautiful.

Vidya gasped as she ran across the room. "This is it!"

"What is it?" Jeth murmured, gaping up at the enormous structure.

"This is the warping gate Nas'Gavarr used to get to Credence." At home, the one and only gate was made of marble adorned with a carved siren's head and wings, a stark contrast the one before her now.

Vidya strode up the base's steps, across the round dais, and crouched down at its center. Pulling open a sliding stone door on the ground revealed the glistening yellow, jug-sized gemstone nestled in a tight cubicle.

"And what's that?" Jeth asked, now joining her on the base.

"This is warp stone, the substance that powers this magnificent piece of machinery," she said.

"I honestly never believed these things existed."

"There was a time when this stone was plentiful. For thousands of years, naja, sirens, and even humans used it to travel great distances. But, the warp stone became scarcer and now only trace amounts can be found off the coasts of Rangardia and Credence, the only two nations that can still warp."

"That doesn't seem to be the case anymore," Jeth said as he ran his hands along the carved granite ring.

"The desert depleted its warp stone deposits a thousand years ago. If Nas'Gavarr found any at all, this is likely all there is," she said. "That's why I'm taking it."

"Why not just warp here from Credence, or use this one to warp back?"

"That would be convenient." Vidya took the warp stone out of the hole in the base. "But, we've sealed away our stone to prevent Nas'Gavarr from coming back to finish what he started. We couldn't use ours to come here because he had done the same."

"So how did you know it would be here?"

"The warping gate that is used to travel to another must be turned to the direction of the destination to create a pathway. I simply set off in the direction he set ours to when he escaped through it. I found this temple, spied on the magi for a few months, and figured it out." She pulled an empty sack from her back pocket and placed the stone inside.

Jeth walked along the dais which resembled a massive sun dial independent from the base. He indicated to the triangular pointer with his foot. "Do both gates have to be turned toward each other in order to warp between them?" he asked.

"Not necessarily," replied Vidya. "To warp to somewhere, the gate must face the other one, but the other gate doesn't have to be facing it for the pathway to complete."

"So, according to this, Credence is straight west." He pointed in the direction that the dais was turned.

"You can tell where west is from down here?" Vidya came over to inspect the dais more closely.

"Growing up in the thickest forests in the world, you either develop a sense of direction, or you're never seen again."

A chill ran up Vidya's spine. "Credence is southeast of here."

She unwrapped the warp stone and nestled it back into its cubbyhole. "I need to find out where he was last. Over there." She pointed to the metallic crank sticking out from the side of the gate. "Start turning that as fast as you can. We're going to check for a pathway."

"Uh . . . right." He took hold of the granite handle as she secured the stone. At her indication, Jeth spun the crank. The grinding of gears below their feet started turning the warp stone beneath. Soon, a throbbing hum along with a pulsating yellow light emanated from it, slow at first, but picked up frequency the faster the cranks were turned.

"That's it," Vidya said. "The stone has sensed another one in this direction. The other gate's stone should be reacting to ours, alerting whoever is there to begin turning their crank."

Vidya cracked her knuckles in her fists as the pulses of the stone smoothed into a steady buzz. The stone's light then erupted into a bright translucent energy that trapped itself within the confines of the granite ring. Beyond the ring appeared as a dark hallway with figures moving about, but the distortion made it impossible to determine what was happening on the other side.

"You can stop," she told Jeth. "The two stones will feed each other. There should be enough energy for me to go there, find out what's going on, and come back. If the energy fades before that happens, you will have to turn the crank when the stone starts humming again. Otherwise I'll be stuck."

Without waiting for a reply from Jeth, Vidya walked through the field. Her skin prickled and a weightless sensation came over her for a split second.

She was now inside an enormous building, the climate much less arid, but no less hot. Grinding cogs powered by rushing water deafened her as conveyer belts moved massive chunks of glowing yellow stone into crushers. Men moved about leading horse drawn carts, brimming with the stone, and dumping it onto the conveyors.

"Señora! You cannot be here," said the man who had been turning the crank to allow her entry. *He's Rangardian!*

"Where is this place?" Vidya stepped into the man's view and flexed her wings.

"You are from Credence," he said with eyes wide. "How did you—?

"Where is this?"

"Venerra District."

"The warp stone mine," she concluded. "But there has never been a gate here before, has there?"

"It was built a year ago, to ease delivery between our other islands."

"May I inquire as to your business here, Señora?" said a second man walking up onto the platform. Unlike the other workers, he wore a vest and pants with dark hair trimmed short. He appeared to be the one in charge.

"Has this operation been supplying Nas'Gavarr in warp stone?"

"I beg your pardon?" The man's brow furrowed in confusion.

"I came from his gate in Herran. This was the last place he's been."

"I assure you, that desert serpent has never come through this gate," the manager insisted.

The voice in her head screeched, *"This man knows more. . . . He lies. . . ."* Vidya's guts twisted.

She was about to grill him further but decided against it; she had a task to complete. She went back through the gate to find Jeth pacing about. He rushed up to meet her. "I thought you weren't coming back. I was considering jumping in there after you."

"I must return to Credence!" Vidya bent down and lifted the warp stone from its cubby. The distortion imploded into itself with a crackling splash.

"So? Where did you go?"

She put the stone in her bag and stepped down from the platform. *I should destroy this gate*, she thought, patting herself down in search of her black powder. "Dammit," she grumbled, almost forgetting where she had left it. "We have to find my black powder in the atrium so I can blow up this ring."

Jeth gave Vidya a sheepish look as he scratched the back of his neck. "I sort of used it all to escape. Thanks for dropping it by the way."

"It was either that or risk getting hit with fire or lightning and blowing to bits," she huffed and started heading out the door. *I am no closer to finding the*

Overlord's weaknesses than when I first set out. I can't go home empty handed. . . . I just can't, she thought.

The Fae'ren kept pace behind her. "Are you going to tell me what in Mother's name is going on?"

Vidya spun around. "I just discovered that Credence's only ally may be aiding our worst enemy."

Flying above the Burning Waste was the best respite from the day's terrors Jeth could ask for. Vidya refused to fly him north toward the City of Herran because she needed to reach the nearest desert port to the south. The two opted to go straight east toward the Serpentine River, in Herrani territory, where they would go their separate ways, hopefully bypassing any combat from the front.

By nightfall, they found accommodations at a bathhouse in a small town acting as a Herrani military outpost. Jeth headed straight to the outdoor showers while Vidya retired to the women's dormitory.

The baths were nearly empty. The few people in the tubs eyed Jeth suspiciously, some holding their noses and cringing. Jeth had already become desensitized to the smell of smoke and entrails, and Vidya hadn't commented on it for the entire trip there. He had almost believed his powerful sense of smell made it seem worse than it was. Now he knew better.

Behind a tiled wall, a man, finishing up his shower, took one look at Jeth and rushed out, leaving him alone. Only removing his weapons, scarf, and boots, Jeth found the nearest spout and pushed down the water pump with his foot a few dozen times until the blast of lukewarm water hit him. The sensation of it against his blistering skin took his breath away. He grabbed a well-used stone of soap and began to furiously scrub himself clean, clothing and all. He slowly peeled away his blood-stained rags and let the water cascade down his bare body, the liquid turning a sickly brown as the bloody grime flowed into the ducts and out of sight. When the water depleted, Jeth pumped more out, picking through every matted lock and finding all manner of human tissue therein. As the pieces of flesh washed away, he couldn't stop shaking. He pulled out what appeared to be a finger bone and stared at it for a long time. *How is this possible? You talked to this person, traveled through the desert with him for months, and now you're wearing him!*

Jeth doubled over and dry heaved. He collapsed against the cool tile and slid down it. The water poured over him until it was gone. Dragging his wet hands down his face, he sat there for several minutes, willing his heart to slow and for his wind to return. *Everything's fine. You're alive. He didn't get you . . . .* Despite that, breathing still didn't come easy. *You just need some sleep, then come tomorrow, you'll be on you way home. You'll have a hot meal in your belly and Anwarr in your bed. Everything will return to normal.* The thought of normal left Jeth with an uncomfortable lump in his gut that wouldn't relent. The image of Nas'Gavarr tasting his blood and the words *'Like a champion'* were still fresh in his mind.

"Some champion," he muttered weakly.

After a few more minutes, Jeth's chills persuaded him to get up. He gathered his wet clothes and weapons, wrapped himself in a towel, and found an unclaimed cot in the men's dormitory.

He woke the next morning and headed to the mess hall. Although much more rested compared to the previous day, his stomach was still in knots. Periodically a rush of panic would come over him as he stood in the lineup for food only for it to leave as quickly as it came.

He grabbed a handful of dried fruit along with a pomegranate and went to find a place to sit. At a far corner table, Jeth was surprised to see Vidya sitting on her own, eating flatbread with stew.

"I thought you'd be up in the sky by now," Jeth said as he dropped his food on the table and planted himself down on a seat across from her.

She looked up from her breakfast with disdain. "Move it along or . . . Oh—it's you."

"Forgot about me already?" Jeth said as he threw a few dried apricots into his mouth.

"With you all cleaned up like that, I hardly recognized you."

"A temporary state, I assure you," Jeth quipped, his mouth half full. "I should thank you, for saving my life . . . again."

"I couldn't have the only person known to survive a run-in with Nas'Gavarr die needlessly in battle, could I?"

Jeth smirked and tossed another apricot into his mouth, trying to forget the heart-stopping weakness that had overcome every muscle fiber, and the ferocious energy that had broken him out of it.

"Be that as it may . . . I owe you one. Good luck in getting home, alright?"

Vidya shoved her dry bread and mostly finished stew aside and looked him dead on. "You can come with me."

Jeth nearly choked. "You mean to Credence?" Vidya nodded, not taking her intense brown-eyed gaze off him. "As fun as it would be to visit the island of winged ladies, I can't—"

"You have a connection to Nas'Gavarr, though you may be unaware of such." She leaned in and continued in a lower register. "There is a reason you were at that temple—that both of us were."

"The reason was for me to steal a dagger and for you to find a warping gate. That's all."

"I heard what he said to you."

"Ramblings of a madman who has lived far too long." Jeth jammed his pocketknife into the pomegranate and pried it open.

"Don't take me for a fool. The Overlord *knew* you!" She banged one hand on the table, making it jostle violently, and her soup bowl spring up and spill over. The other patrons peered over and whispered to each other.

"Look. I know I just said I owe you, but be reasonable. I'm not going to be of any use."

"I can think of a few uses for you," Vidya grumbled, sitting back on the bench with her arms crossed.

"Well, I'm flattered, really, but my priority right now is not giving the Overlord more of a reason to paint his walls with my blood, but getting back to my crew."

"Like they need you." She scoffed, then leaned over the table again. "Your crew abandoned you."

"They didn't have a choice," Jeth countered, although he wondered if that were true. *Ash was so eager to make you go in that temple alone . . . then Nas'Gavarr happens to show up?*

"Given the chance, I'd give my life in aid of those I care about," said Vidya.

"As would I." Jeth picked up one of the halves of his fruit.

Vidya shook her head. "Not them—not for you—and I think you know that deep down."

Jeth stared at the pomegranate in his hand and watched the dark red juices drip down his arm. Flashes of Melikheil's flesh ripping from his bone, the sound of it, the stink, all came rushing back. He set down the fruit and wiped his hand on his pants, no longer in the mood to eat.

"Help me stop Nas'Gavarr," Vidya said in a hushed voice.

"You don't get it," Jeth snarled, smacking the two halves of fruit off the table. "There is no stopping him. I only got away because of stupid, blind luck. Melikheil was the most powerful Mage that both Ingleheim and Del'Cabria had to offer, and I just finished washing him out of my hair! I watched him kill you! I'm sorry, lady, but if you go after him again, he will make damn sure you stay dead." He fell back against his chair and tried to catch his breath.

Vidya stood up from the table, hanging her sack over her shoulder. "Don't be sorry," she began in a cold voice. "I should not have expected much from a small-minded, weak-willed man. You Del'Cabrians are all bravado and no follow-through. That's why you'll lose the war. Run back to your loyal crew and perhaps you will forget about ever meeting Nas'Gavarr, but something tells me he will not forget about you."

"I'm glad you think of me as a man," was all Jeth could say in response.

"Good riddance then!" Vidya stormed off, roughly pushing aside chairs on her way out of the mess hall. *Forget her,* Jeth thought, his heart beginning to pound in his throat. *Just get home.*

14

Stuck

You made it. Jeth let the relief wash over him.

After having stolen fresh clothing from the outpost and finding something to bind his ankle, Jeth had set out on his journey home on a camel borrowed from a merchant caravan. Four days later, he arrived at the City of Herran, and the sight temporarily pushed the memories of his horrid experience from his mind. They all but faded when he came upon the spice shop an hour thereafter.

Heading to the stables first, Jeth found his dapple gray munching on hay in her box stall. "Tor, my girl," he gushed, scratching behind her ears. "I told you I'd be back." Torrent greeted him with a low whinny.

Khiri poked his head from behind Ash's horse and came running over with a guttural exclamation. The boy hugged Jeth so tight the air was forced from his lungs.

"Hey, good to see you too, kid, I can't express how much. Thanks for taking such good care of Torrent." Khiri let Jeth go and nodded, tears of joy in his small dark eyes.

"Where is everyone else?" Jeth asked as he plunked his weapons down in Torrent's stall.

Khiri beckoned him inside and ran over to Lys, cleaning out some of the spice bins. He tugged on the Crede man's robes who snapped up from his work ready to scold.

Once he caught sight of Jeth sauntering into the shop, Lys's eyes widened, and he dropped his rag. "You're back."

"I know, I can't believe it either."

"They told me you were dead," Lys said.

"You shouldn't believe that of someone until you see their cold, dead remains for yourself. . . . Actually, not always in that case."

A brood of rowdy children burst through the front entrance of the store followed by their dour mother, beckoning Lys's attention. "Yes, very good," he said with a pat on Jeth's back. "The others are upstairs. They will be overjoyed to see you."

Will they? Jeth wondered, a sudden queasiness coming over him. He swallowed the lump in his throat. *All that matters is An. You can deal with Ash and Star later.*

Jeth bounded up the stairs to the second floor. The smell of antelope meat and yams cooking on the stove wafted into his nostrils, making his stomach growl. Anwarr giggled from the outdoor patio that served as the cooking area. He froze.

"Woman, what have I told you about getting in my way when it's my turn to cook?" came Ash's voice.

"It just amuses me how serious you look when you do it." Then a distinct smooching sound. Jeth's heart twisted in his chest. *You've been dead a few days, and it's like you were never here. . . .*

"Go on, get out. Tell Star to get her lazy ass out of bed so we can eat."

"Fine," she groaned in good spirits and headed toward the porch door. Jeth felt an uncontrollable urge to run away before she saw him. He had only made it to the bottom of the third-floor stairs when her throat-rattling gasp halted his step. His limbs became heavy stone as he slowly turned to face her. She stood frozen, wide-eyed, as if she were in the presence of a ghost.

The two were still for such a length of time, Jeth finally had to say something. "An . . ."

The moment her name fell from his lips, she ran across the room and threw her arms around his neck, nearly knocking him over. "Jethril!" she gasped. "Sal be good, you came back!"

He returned her embrace, inhaling her sweet scent only to find it intermingled with Ash's heavy musk. Backing away, he said, "Were you just in bed with Ash?"

"Not since last night. Damn that nose of yours. Hey, you're burnt." Her fingertips gently grazing his face felt like a smack across it.

He winced and pulled away.

Ash came lumbering in from the porch, wiping grease from his hands with a cloth. "You're alive!" His eyes were wide with shock.

"Yeah, imagine that," Jeth said darkly.

"Listen." Ash put his hands out. "We didn't want to leave you back there . . ."

Jeth waved his hand down. "Ah, don't worry about it, Big Fella. I completely understand. A camel and some water would have been nice, but that would have given me a fighting chance at survival, and you wouldn't want that." He gave an exaggerated shrug while glaring intensely into Ash's eyes.

The axe man's jaw tightened as he broke from Jeth's gaze. "Istari's camel could barely hold the two of you, let alone me. The chances of you surviving that temple when Nas'Gavarr went in there were non-existent. Had Star and I tried to warn you, he would have killed all of us."

"How convenient then, that it was only me who went inside that temple?" Jeth's fists clenched as he stepped up to Ash. He looked to Anwarr for a moment then back to Jeth.

"You weren't alone in there," he said.

Anwarr pulled on Jeth's shirt. "Come upstairs, and I can put some ointment on those burns."

He jerked out of her grip. "If it hadn't have been for Vidya, I'd be dead."

"She made it out?" Ash's features softened for a moment.

"Yes, Ash, the warrior woman of your dreams is still alive. You can continue to imagine all the ways you'd like her to 'ride you like a beast of burden' all the while fucking her!" Jeth pointed to Anwarr. "Aren't you a lucky son of a boar?"

Ash cracked his neck before taking Jeth by the scarf and shoving him up against the wall.

"Ashbedael, stop!" Anwarr warned.

He spoke in a calm and intense voice, despite his show of violence. "You need to take a moment and remember who you're talking to, boy. Neither of us wished to leave you behind, but we did what we had t—"

"Horseshit!" Jeth spat. "You never wanted me here, admit it!"

Ash released him, and Jeth straightened up. With nostrils flaring and knuckles cracking, Ash said, "For the first few days, you were an annoyance I would sooner live without, but I've come to think of you as a brother." He straightened Jeth's ruffled collar for him before giving him a light smack on his chest with the back of his hand "Now, cut the shit and tell us how you got out of there for Sag's sake."

Jeth swallowed hard and cast his eyes down to the floor, the shame of his accusations rotting in his gut. A heavy silence enveloped the dining area, remedied only by Istari's footsteps shuffling down the stairs.

"What is going on down here?" she said groggily and stopped at the foot of the stairs. Her jaw dropped. "Jeth . . . ?"

"The Ingle Mage came to challenge Nas'Gavarr and . . . I got away," Jeth said, trying desperately to keep the macabre images from re-entering his mind.

"What Ingle Mage?" Istari asked. "And what happened to your face?"

He touched his cheek, wincing and shaking his head. "It was this light the Mages were using, like fire, but hotter."

"Sunfire. Light and fire magic combined," Istari said. "If I knew how to manipulate fire, I could harness it. It's hot enough to damage the spirit within the body. . . . I can't believe you survived it."

Jeth scoffed. *That was hardly the worst of it,* he wanted to say, but the words never made it to his lips. Just then, the smell of charring meat permeated the room. "Dinner's burning," he muttered.

"Sag damn it!" Ash rushed back out to the porch. The others just stood there, staring at Jeth as if they didn't believe he was truly alive.

Anwarr's eyes were still wide with fear. Jeth didn't know whether to apologize, take her in his arms, or get far away from there. He decided on the latter.

"I need some air," he murmured and made his way to the terrace.

He sat down at one of the empty baths and hung his legs over the edge. It wasn't long before Anwarr was sitting next to him with a jar of some oily substance.

"What's that?"

"It's for your face." She tried to apply some, but he pushed her hand aside. "I'm fine."

"You're not." She put the jar down in exasperation. "What happened? Did you see Nas'Gavarr?"

"Nothing happened," Jeth replied, taking her hand in his and squeezing tight. "Let's go somewhere . . . somewhere far. I've never been to the Odafi coast."

Anwarr fiddled with her hooped earring as her eyelashes fluttered. "The Odafi coast is seven days away, not to mention there's a war going on, in case you forgot."

"Not for much longer, I reckon. Let's go, you and me." He put his arm around her and pulled her closer.

"You need to rest."

"There's no time for rest. A whole world is out there for me to see, isn't that what you said . . . ? Come on," he pleaded, pushing his forehead against hers.

Anwarr gingerly lifted his arm off and braced her palms against his chest. "Jethril, when I said I'd show you the world, that was assuming we'd each be forty thousand gold richer. Plus, Snake Eye is putting me on a reconnaissance job in a week. We can't just leave."

Backing off, Jeth put his head in his hands. "You find out I'm dead and you take another job? How long did you mourn me? A day—an hour?"

"I'm still mourning!" Her voice quavered.

"Really? Is that what you and Ash were doing last night? Mourning together?"

Her breath shortened. "I was heartbroken when you didn't return with the others, but I kept thinking of how close I was to losing all three of you. I'm sorry if my relief in having Ash and Istari alive overshadowed any grief held for you. There was not a moment where I didn't pray to Salotaph to bring you back. And here you are."

Anwarr took him into her embrace, letting his head rest upon her breast. Her soft skin was hot against his sunburnt cheek. His entire body yearned for her, his mind desperately wanted to shut off, but his sense of smell wouldn't allow it. Ash's musk was overpowering. It made his blood boil and his stomach churn at the same time.

Jeth pulled away from her. "An, I can't do this anymore."

"Do what?" Anwarr asked, her voice breaking.

"I don't care how things are done around here or how selfish or pointless it is. I'm tired of sharing you," he blurted.

"You don't know what you're saying," she said, shaking her head.

Jeth half grinned through his heartache. "Three times, I stared death in the face. And each time, all I could think of was not being able to make it back to you. You are all I have to live for in this Deity forsaken world. . . ." His jaw tightened, making it hard to continue. "There is no one else for me, and there never will be. Is there any chance . . ." He scratched at his sideburns and forced the rest of the words out. "I can ever be that for you?"

She put her hand on Jeth's, coaxing him to look at her again. "You only feel this way because I'm the first woman you've been with."

Jeth ripped his hands away, a sudden anger rising into his temples. "Don't talk to me like I'm some idiot child. You don't know what I've seen. . . . I know how I feel about you, and it's not going to go away! Don't you get it?"

"I do, as a matter of fact. I've felt it before, long ago. And I promised myself I would never love that way again."

"Are you talking about Ezrai?"

Anwarr looked down at her hands and nodded. "I was having a hard time making a living as a dancer until I danced for a well-known treasure keeper and his merchant colleagues in Odafi. He told me he could make me very rich, dancing for his connections in wealthy circles and stealing from his enemies. I never imagined I could reach such heights doing what I was good at, and it was all made possible because of Ezrai. I fell in love with him. However, when he earned his seat on the Merchant Council, he changed. He became jealous and controlling. The independence I had fought so hard for was gradually taken from me before I even noticed. My love for him blinded me from what was really happening."

"And then you danced for Snake Eye and got away."

"No, first, I met Ezrai's coin stasher, Istari. She too was trapped by him, and from that, we grew very close. Together we thought of a way to skim off our earnings and hide it so that in time we could make it on our own. Then, Snake Eye caught us stealing from him, and you know the rest. Leaving Ezrai was the hardest thing I ever had to do, but it was opening my heart to other people, like Istari, that freed me. I will not limit my heart to one person ever again."

"Well, I'm not Ezrai," Jeth argued. "I'm not going to take your freedom!"

"You say that now, but you will," she responded in a firm tone.

Those words twisted Jeth's insides. *No one wants you here.*

Shaking his head, he returned to his feet. "I have to go." He took long strides back into the shop.

With a start, Anwarr stood up. "Wait!"

He didn't heed her request as he stormed past Lys and Khiri and out into the stables.

"Where are you going?" Anwarr demanded.

Jeth couldn't bring himself to answer as he hurriedly gathered a saddle and bridle from the tack storage wall. With the saddle and blanket in hand and bridle cast over his shoulder, he turned toward Torrent's stall, but Anwarr stood in his way.

"You just got here, and now you're leaving?" she asked shrilly.

"I don't belong here, and we both know it," Jeth said. "You were all fine before I came, you'll be fine after I'm gone."

Stepping around her, Jeth cast the saddle and blanket over the stall's rail and went to task putting the bridle on his horse. She bobbed her head up and down, making it difficult for him to get the bit into her mouth. "Come on, Tor, I'm in no mood for your shit right now," he griped.

"That couldn't be further from the truth," Anwarr said as she followed him into the stall. "Like it or not, you are part of us now. We're family."

Jeth gave up trying to put on Torrent's bridle in exasperation. "Help me understand this because I've never had a family before, but I'm pretty sure they don't have sex with each other!"

"Some might," she muttered. "But that's not the point."

"If you can't give me a better reason to stay, then there is no point." At last, Jeth was able to get the bridle on before he grabbed the saddle blanket and tossed it over Torrent's back.

"This is ridiculous, do you have any idea where you're going to go?" Anwarr moved to block him from reaching the saddle.

"Move," he warned.

"Not until you tell me what happened at that temple." She clutched the rail harder and widened her stance. "Something has you horribly shaken. Let me help you."

It was then Jeth noticed the shining white gold armlet on her bicep, reminding him of the last time he and she were in the stables together. Jeth floated out of himself, fixated only on the Serpentine charm. A terrible thought came to him. *She was acting so strange in the days before you left . . .*

He motioned to the armlet. "You're still wearing that."

Anwarr glanced at it. "Of course."

"You knew." Jeth took another step toward her.

She remained steadfast, still gripping the wooden railing. "Knew what?"

"You never thought I'd come back, did you?" he said. "Did Snake Eye tell you Nas'Gavarr was going to be there? Was this all a set-up?"

Anwarr began to shake as she released the railing. "I don't know what you're talking about."

"You thought I was going to die, that's why you suddenly wanted to wear it. 'Something to remember me by,' isn't that right?" Jeth's voice had risen beyond his control.

Anwarr started backing away. "Many die traversing the Burning Waste—"

"Did you know Nas'Gavarr was going to be there? How did he know I'd be there?"

"I-I don't know . . ." she stammered. "I think you should lie down."

"Can you be straight with me for one second?" Jeth bellowed.

"Then start making sense!" she yelled back.

"Give me that!" Grabbing her arm, Jeth yanked her toward him, but she pulled back just as hard. He backed her up against the stall railing, knocking the saddle down to the other side.

"Let go!" she cried.

It made Jeth ill to see it around her arm, and all he could think of was getting it off her. He grabbed the clasp of the armlet and tried to remove it forcibly, but a jarring kick to his shin followed by a firm wallop to the side of the head was enough to send him staggering back.

Ears ringing, Jeth shook off Anwarr's blow to find her in a defensive stance, fists balled.

"If you want to leave, go on then, I won't stop you," she said in low, quavering voice. "But touch me like that again, and I will kick your balls into your throat."

At that moment, Khiri came running into the stables. He stared at Anwarr, then Jeth, his eyes wide with worry.

"I want the truth." Jeth reached out to her, and she smacked his arm away.

"Get out!" she screamed, tears wetting her eyes.

Jeth's chest tightened, his head about to explode. Khiri ran to Anwarr, and she hugged him in front of her, both of them staring at him fearfully. *If you don't leave now, there's no telling what you'll do.*

With no time to saddle his horse, Jeth collected his weapons, leaped up onto her back, and kicked her into a trot out of the stables.

Jeth banged his fists upon the dark wooden door in the narrow alley. Yemesh answered, and Jeth gave him no chance to inquire as to his presence.

"Where's Snake Eye?" he demanded as he pushed past the lanky Sunil.

"You can't just barge in here." Yemesh hastily followed him down the stairs.

Jeth stormed past the smoking patrons in the main room where tulwar toting guards attempted to halt him. He ducked between them and reached the hanging curtain closing off the back room, only for a tall Herrani man to stumble out of it, dazed and disoriented. This gave the guards a chance to take him by the shoulders and shove him against the wall.

"You are not welcome here!" the guard barked.

"Sag be good, do we have another immortal in our midst?" a smooth, feminine voice sounded from behind the guard. He moved aside to reveal Snake Eye standing in the doorway with a look of surprise coupled with a sly grin.

"Didn't expect to see me again, did you?" Every smoking patron's attentions focused in on the group. Snake Eye beckoned Jeth and Yemesh into his room absent the guards.

"So you know for the future," he began as they walked through the curtain. "I am not fond of unannounced visitors."

"I don't give much of a shit what you're fond of," Jeth said. "You must have heard the mission you sent us on was a complete failure."

Snake Eye nodded. "Yes, your crew already reported such. What grave misfortune. And yet, here you stand before me. Salotaph is merciful. How did you survive?"

"I wish people would stop asking me that. But, that's not why I'm here. I need the truth. Did you know Nas'Gavarr would be at the temple?" Jeth clenched and unclenched his fists.

Taking a seat on a plush, cushioned bench, Snake Eye spread his arms along the backrest and said, "The Overlord's movements are not easily predicted. It stands to reason that one of his magi might have a spiritual rapport with him and could have given warning. I was hoping you'd be quick enough."

"He and his naja horde made it through the waste mere hours after we did. Someone must have told him we'd be there."

"That is strange, indeed, but what perplexes me more is why he let you go."

"He didn't let me go."

"He would have had to," Snake Eye said, his voice severe and his reptilian pupil narrowing to a thin slit. "People don't just slip through the Immortal Serpent's fingers unless it is his intention."

A shiver ran up Jeth's spine at the sudden change in Snake Eye's demeanor. "I don't know what to tell you. Nas'Gavarr knew who I was. He knew I'd be there at that exact time. Someone in your circle either told him or has a rapport with him. Maybe Yemesh, one of your patrons . . ."

Bringing both hands to his chin, Snake Eye bent forward in contemplation. "My Sunil can never betray his master, and my patrons don't know their heads from their asses while in here. I can't have people blabbing of my healing methods citywide. Those who I trust are few and far between for that reason."

"Then it's you," Jeth guessed. "Is that what you talked to Anwarr about the last time we were here? Was I supposed to be some sort of human sacrifice for your Overlord's death cult?"

Snake Eye patted the silk cushion beside him. "Please sit. You are perfectly safe here."

"I'm fine standing, thanks." Jeth crossed his arms, frustration rising into his temples.

With a sigh, Snake Eye stood up and ambled over to him. "What exactly did Nas'Gavarr say to you?"

"What makes you think he said anything to me?" Jeth wanted to give Snake Eye a word for word transcription, but for all he knew, the ashipu was working for him. "All I can say is he knew who I was before we met, and he knew what I was after, along with everything else about my life."

Snake Eye paused and pressed his tongue to the inside of his cheek. "I don't believe anyone had to tell him about you. Our Overlord has an uncanny propensity to know what the future holds. It comes from his deep connection with the Serpentine Gods, or so his followers claim."

Again, with this destiny rubbish, Jeth thought. "Don't tell me you believe in the Way."

"I am starting to." Snake Eye walked around Jeth, studying him like he was some kind of alien creature. He leaned gracefully against a large glass topped counter across the room and continued, "If what you told me is true, then that can only mean you play a role in Nas'Gavarr's plans. I need to know what that role is if I have any hope of understanding them."

Nas'Gavarr's words instantly came to mind. 'You too have a role in this.'

"What do you think you're going to do to foil his plans?" Jeth said in a hushed voice while looking around nervously. "You might think you're something impressive in these parts, but trust me, you do not want to get in that sorcerer's way."

Snake Eye chuckled under his breath and said in a chilling tone, "Maybe it is he who should not get in my way."

A sinking dread came over Jeth. "B-but you're just an ashipu . . . aren't you?"

With a flick of his hair, Snake Eye smiled. "Do not be fooled by what you see on the surface, my little Gershlon."

Snake Eye sauntered around the table, dragging his fingertips sensually along the surface. His fingers seemed to get daintier, his hips wider, and his drawstring smock tightened around his torso. It took Jeth a few moments to recognize that he was looking at a pair of breasts. He jerked his head upward to find the face of Snake Eye only with much softer features, longer eyelashes, and fuller lips.

"Y-you're a woman!" Jeth rubbed at his eyes, fearing that he was hallucinating. The transformation had been so subtle he wondered if Snake

Eye was a female all along and he just didn't see it.

She giggled at Jeth's reaction. "Are you sure about that?" The woman walked slowly toward him. Before his eyes, her chest deflated, her shoulders broadened, her hips narrowed, and her jaw extended. Soon, there was nothing feminine about who he was looking at.

"You're a Flesh Mage," Jeth murmured. Every instinct was screaming for him to run, that he was in over his head, that some mysteries should not be uncovered. He backed up toward the door, but Yemesh stood in his way.

In a much deeper voice, Snake Eye said, "You have nothing to fear from me. I am not my brother."

"Nas'Gavarr?"

Snake Eye nodded while transforming back into his androgynous self. Jeth was relieved to see it. "I know it's hard to believe. Anyone who ever knew he had a living sibling has been long dead, and he isn't quick to announce it to anyone since. No room for two immortals around here, I suppose."

Feeling his heartbeat start to slow, Jeth asked, "What happened between you two?"

"Quite simply, our goals diverged. He wants to free the world, bring prosperity to our people, but the cost at which he's willing to do so is something I won't pay. I too, want to unite the tribes and stand up to foreign imperialism, but to enact war on every nation perceived as a potential threat is a sure way to get wiped out or enslaved. I think sometimes he forgets that his people, unlike him, can be killed. He will stop at nothing until every nation's power structure has been burned to the ground. Del'Cabria will be the first to fall. Their armies have been decimated and driven back. He is making headway to the Capital as we speak."

A sickening dread poured over Jeth. Del'Cabria can't fall, they're too powerful. He remembered all the stories pertaining to their Confederation Period, and the glorious battles fought and won, now all of it was catching up to them. A part of him felt vindicated on behalf of his own people who had been unwillingly brought into the Kingdom, but then he thought of Olivier, Master Loche, Sir Talbit, and Lady Hanelei. *Sweet Deity, what's going to happen to them?*

"What's it to you anyway?" Jeth asked. "It sounds like your people are going to be living the high life if the Overlord takes the Capitol."

"Not if nations like Credence, Ingleheim, and Rangardia enter the fray, not to mention Del'Cabria will not bow quietly. Too much blood will be shed on both sides, and I know better than anyone what my brother likes to do with blood."

"The Herrani people don't even know you exist, so why do you care what happens to either side? Or do you just want power, like your brother?"

Snake Eye giggled again, but this laugh was more disconcerting than the last. "So, what if I do? It doesn't change the fact that he needs to be stopped. I for one don't want to live the next few centuries in the world Gavarr wants to create. I wish to see a united and free Herran without turning every nation against us. Doesn't that sound better?"

"Sure, it does," Jeth relented, but still uneasy. "Only, I've seen what happened to the last person who challenged him for power. He's now in pieces in the Temple of Sagorath."

"Oh, yes, the handsome Ingle Mage, I heard about that too. Such a shame. Had he succeeded, it would have made my task much easier."

"Listen, I'm going to tell you the same thing I told the harpy. No one is a match for him. Maybe you think you are, but frankly, I don't want to be anywhere near this."

Snake Eye stepped up close to Jeth, stopping mere inches from his face. "Then why did you come to me if not to get right in it?"

"I came here for answers. Just tell me Anwarr is not involved in this, and I'll be on my way."

Snake Eye rolled his eyes and shook his head. "She's an excellent thief and a useful ally, but I could never trust her with something like this. If you truly care for her, I'd suggest keeping this conversation between us, lest she and the rest of the crew play a role in the Overlord's plans alongside you."

Jeth sighed in relief at Snake Eye's denial of Anwarr's involvement followed by waves of guilt for how he had treated her. "Maybe I should get as far away from here as possible," he said with a gulp.

"There's no need to run," replied Snake Eye in a low voice. "Your best chance is to hide in plain sight and continue doing what you've been doing thus far. Be a good little thief and help me collect my artifacts. I've already spoken to Anwarr about one of them. When she finds out where it is, you can all join her here for briefing."

Jeth shook his head. "No, no, I'm out. I won't do any more jobs for you."

"Sagorath knows I won't force you. You can run to the rolling hills of Del'Cabria and wait for your Way to come to fruition. But, I know you're smarter than that. The fact that you survived a confrontation with my brother proves you are more than a forest whelp, far from home. Stay here and do what you do best, and I promise, Nas'Gavarr will no longer be a problem for you or the people you care about."

With a deep breath, Jeth looked to Yemesh, who nodded, then back to Snake Eye. "What of this artifact? Are you sure it can stop him?"

"It will be a damn good start. There is a sarcophagus that holds the remains of Dulsakh. With that piece in my possession, I will be one more step closer to stripping Nas'Gavarr of the naja army he uses to terrorize the world." Snake Eye placed his hand on Jeth's shoulder again. "Be patient for a little longer, my Fae'ren friend, and your Way will soon be yours alone."

Upon leaving Snake Eye's, Jeth took his mare outside the city walls to clear his mind. He raced across the desert plains without an inkling as to where he was going. The wind whipped painfully against his seared face, the world falling into a blur. Soon, he no longer felt the horse beneath him. Her legs were one with his, gliding across the dry emptiness. Closing his eyes, he tried to pretend he was flying off the ground, soaring into non-existence.

Then, the beast halted, skidded along the sand, and sent Jeth flying for real. He opened his eyes just as he landed face first into a large body of water. Splashing to the surface and gasping for air, he was in the Serpentine River. *How did you come this far already?*

Torrent trotted along the bank, neighing after her rider flowing southward with the rapids. Due to his stiff and sore muscles, it took a lot more effort for him to swim to shore than he thought it would. Once he dragged himself onto the bank, he rolled to his back to catch his breath. His mare stood above him, offering shade from the afternoon sun as she nudged him with her snout. "Finally got your revenge, eh, Tor?" he mumbled, letting her nibble on his hair.

Cooled by the wetness, Jeth's paranoia had mostly subsided, but revolting dread still clung to him. "Isn't teaming up with Snake Eye just asking for Nas'Gavarr to find me?" he said aloud. "How am I supposed to go back to normal?" The grinding of dried shrubs in Torrent's mouth was the only response he received.

The barren landscape stretched out endlessly in every direction, but the cloudless blue sky above acted as an impermeable ceiling, holding him down. "I'm stuck," he murmured.

He thought of Del'Cabria, about to be taken. If Nas'Gavarr dismantled the Monarchy, then the price on Jeth's head would be no more. He could go back to Ludesa, try ranching again. . . . *He will still find you.* If Jeth hid in the forest, away from the fairies and the communes, then he could disappear completely. . . . *Being alone wasn't so bad. . . . You can do it again. At least no one else will fall prey to your curse.*

Undecided, Jeth remounted his horse and galloped along the river, not sure if he was ever going to stop.

15

Something More Ominous

Vidya stood at the podium in the Council Chambers, located on the top floor of the Citadel's central building. It was an imposing, oblong room with high ceilings that surrounded the podium in a semi-circular arrangement. At their head was a raised counter with eight seats for each Councilor and several lower seats for lesser officials. Only two people were seated there: The Supreme Commander Ariston, holding the highest position in Credence available to a man, and the secretary with her quill and parchment at the ready. In the other eight seats, looking down at Vidya, were the Councilors, some familiar, others not, having been elected while she was away. She was shocked to find Demeter in her mother's old seat, two down from the Archon's right. Before Vidya left for Herran, Demeter had expressed an interest in running for their mother's Council position, but Vidya laughed it off. *How was she voted in over the countless other qualified candidates?* She pondered. *I suppose pity goes a long way among the Mothers' Assembly these days.*

After the formal greeting was given, Xenith called the meeting to order and turned her attentions to Vidya. "What news do you bring of our enemy?"

"I'm afraid that what I have to report may not be well received by those present."

"You have the floor," urged the Archon.

"I've spent many months in the desert, spying on the Overlord and his followers, consulting with his enemies, studying magic, and still I have yet to learn the full extent of his power. What I have experienced thus far is beyond what we could have imagined. My power alone will not be near enough to stop him."

"O Archon, if I may," Ariston spoke up, stroking his graying beard. Xenith nodded, and the man continued, "To be sure, you are not expected to act alone, O Vidya. You have the full support of our military."

"No disrespect, Commander, but the size of our army pales in comparison to Del'Cabria's, and they have suffered unprecedented losses as of late. Soon, Herran and its naja hordes will overrun their lands."

Ariston replied, "We have Rangardia. Their disproportionately large male population has bloated their military. And, with their recent developments in explosives, they make for a fierce adversary."

"And I'm telling you, it won't be enough." Vidya swallowed hard. "That is part of the dire news I bring. . . . Rangardia may not entirely be on our side."

"Have they allied with Herran?" Ariston asked, incredulous.

"That would be rather foolish of them," said Penelope, the Mistress of Markets. She had gotten much rounder since the last time Vidya had seen her. She wondered if the siren could even fly anymore. "They are still losing women to that horrid disease. Without our Procreation Agreement, they are putting the future of their empire at great risk."

"You know as well as anyone, Councilor," Vidya said. "Credence cannot meet their increasing demand for fertile wombs forever. Herran is bringing the slaving tribes of Ankarr and Tezkhan under its rule. Think what Rangardia can do with thousands of female slaves. They can only benefit from playing both sides as long as they can get away with it."

"Vidya," Xenith cut in. "What evidence do you have to warrant this accusation against our most trusted ally?"

"I found the Overlord's warping gate. The last place he had traveled was to a warp stone mine in Rangardia's Venerra District. It was recently built to keep Nas'Gavarr supplied in warp stone."

A heavy silence permeated through the chambers until the Archon said, "That doesn't prove the entire empire has turned against us. It could be a treasonous operation. The Emperor likely doesn't know of this, and if he did, he would put a stop to it."

Vidya pressed her tongue to the inside of her cheek. *That madman likely doesn't know much of anything going on in his empire . . . or care enough to put a stop to anything he does know*, she thought.

Demeter cleared her throat and spoke in her soft and unobtrusive manner that was in actuality, anything but, "You were married to the Emperor. Do you really believe him capable of betraying us?"

"In my honest opinion," Vidya began, looking right into her sister's bright blue eyes. "I believe he is, if not outright betraying our alliance, ignoring any treasonous thread within his empire."

"Your past grievances continue to cloud your judgment, Vidya," said Xenith. "Though I agree, this warrants investigation."

"The mining officials that I've had contact with act ignorant of any wrongdoing. However, I know Nas'Gavarr has been there. The officials are lying."

"The Overlord could have stolen it without their knowledge," Demeter theorized.

"Someone on the other side has to turn their cranks to complete the pathway. You know that!" Vidya couldn't keep her frustration from coming through in her voice. *How is she one of the eight women running this republic?*

"There is no use speaking more on this matter," said Xenith. "We shall investigate further. Vidya, have you anything else that may help us?"

"I might." She bit her lip.

"Proceed."

"One harpy may not be sufficient to defeat Nas'Gavarr, but if we had more . . ." Vidya paused, not sure she should be bringing this idea to the Council just yet.

"How many more?" Xenith asked with an edge of wariness.

"I propose reinstituting the Harplite."

The chambers filled with gasps and hushed chatter.

Xenith raised her hand to silence the others before she gave her grave reply. "You do realize that the Harplite consisted of nearly five thousand harpies, during a time they could be born. After the sirens ended their vicious rule, Yasharra cast punishment upon them, making it so they could only be created at the behest of Credence's rightful governors. You cannot seriously be suggesting bringing us back to that time."

Vidya recalled the stories her mother had told her, about what the army of harpies could do, how completely they conquered the lands of men, their defeat due only to their own complacency from having been undefeated for so long. Vidya didn't want to conquer. She only needed the harpies to save Credence and leave it to the sirens to maintain.

"Of course not, Archon, but it was you who said that it was time for the Harpy to exact her vengeance against those who threaten our republic. We need to bring back her army. I fear it is the only way to protect us."

The Mistress of Law and Order cleared her throat to speak. "There are about one hundred soldiers currently imprisoned, many of them old by now. If we sacrificed all of them, that would only make thirty-some harpies. The slaughter of so many men, even rapists, and murderers, isn't worth that, surely."

"I agree, Councilor Althea," said Vidya. "However, the Harpy does not require the sacrifices be criminals, just that they be warriors and male."

Ariston jumped in out of turn. "You'd have us send our own soldiers to slaughter as well? Three good men for one of you? Please, O Archon, you must see that this is madn——"

Xenith put up her hand to silence the man and turned to Vidya. "Be very clear about what you are proposing, Vidya, before you give our Supreme Commander a stroke." A hushed giggle came from one of the other seats. Demeter held her hand to her mouth, but she quickly regained composure.

"I would never suggest using our own men, at least none beyond criminals. One thousand harpies would be enough for now."

"That's a third of our entire force!" Ariston blurted.

"Silence, Commander!" Xenith said sternly.

"Apologies, O Archon." He bowed his head.

"As the Supreme Commander said already," continued Vidya. "Rangardia's large male population may prove to be our greatest asset in this war. They could be persuaded to part with some of their more tumultuous ones. If they turn out to have betrayed us, then all the more justified."

This time it was Calisto, the Mistress of Treasures who spoke. She was well into her seventh decade, her wings a glorious golden display, but her body hunched over and frail. There were few coins left in the treasury that were older than her. "My girl, you are asking for the mass slaughter of three thousand men. Besides the sheer amount of blood to be spilled on the Grand Altar, the logistics of getting so many to succumb to such horror . . . is . . . impossible."

"Nothing a siren's song can't manage," replied Vidya.

"There is not a siren in the republic that will consent to influence so many men to their deaths, justified or not," Calisto said, pointing to the table with a bony, quivering finger.

When was the last time you influenced a man to do anything, you old crone? Vidya thought, surprising herself that she would have thought it at all. Instead, she replied, "The sirens who assist in our annual sacrifice to the Harpy, as is their duty."

"Still impossible," the old siren said.

"I know of an artifact in Herran, a dagger made of bloodstone that can absorb the blood of one hundred men. It will make sacrifices quicker and much cleaner. We will only have to enlarge the pool at the Harpy's effigy—"

"I think we've heard all we need," said Xenith, her voice having grown tired in the last few minutes.

"But that is not all—" Vidya went on.

"I say it is!" Xenith's commanding voice echoed sharply off the pillars. "Councilors, you've heard Vidya's report. Is there anyone who'd like to make a motion to go forward with the Harplite?"

A deafening silence fell around them. Vidya cast her eyes down.

"A motion to oppose . . ."

Every siren in the room raised their hand. Even Ariston, who didn't get a vote, raised his hand anyway. The secretary's scrawling upon her parchment was as fingernails scratching the inside of Vidya's skull.

Xenith said, "I pray these last several months you've spent in the desert have not been a complete waste of time. Do you have anything to report on the Overlord's weaknesses, anything at all we can hit him with?"

Vidya remembered the Fae'ren and his resistance to blood magic. *He would probably have been useless,* she thought. Clearing her throat, she said with her eyes cast down, "Not yet."

All eight Councilors stared down at her with their disapproving eyes, making her sweat turn cold.

Xenith stretched her wings. "It appears the Harpy has done little for us. We need to rethink our strategy. Vidya, perhaps you should take some time and come up with a more feasible plan of attack. Otherwise, you may return to your regular combat training." She then turned to her left. "Demeter, you will pay a visit to Rangardia and get to the bottom of this warp stone mine. Urge them to dismantle that gate until we can be sure Nas'Gavarr is not using it. I sincerely hope that this is a misunderstanding. We will need every soldier they have in this coming war."

Demeter's eyes darted around the room as if surprised she would be tasked with any real responsibility so soon. "Um . . . yes, Archon."

". . . And Vidya." Xenith turned to her as she stood. "I had warned that the Harpy's influence is already within you, and now that you are one, your need to see the spilling of blood also increases. Please ensure those urges are directed toward our enemies, not our allies. Do you understand?"

Vidya gave a submissive nod. "I do, Archon, forgive me for ever suggesting such a thing."

"Your mother was a wise Councilor, and her dying wish was to see you elevated in a way fit for the eldest daughter of a siren. Until now, however, there was no high held position a wingless and childless woman like you would be eligible for. I hope you continue to make her proud."

"I will." Vidya nodded again. "Thank you all for your time."

"Then we adjourn."

Everyone else rose from their seats as Vidya turned and walked out of the chambers, her legs gelatinous masses beneath her.

She rushed through the Citadel's lavender gardens on the second-floor terrace, leaped off the marble balustrade, glided between the Harpy and Siren effigies on the Grand Altar, and landed near a circular crevasse carved into the stone. The Citadel was built on a precipice protruding over the western coast, and this crevasse served as the final resting place for Credence's most heinous offenders. They were bled near death at the Harpy's effigy and dropped through the slit in the crag where the ocean waves would drag what was left of their bodies out to sea.

Watching the water foaming upon the jagged rocks below, Vidya felt her mind lifting from a fog. *The Archon is right. In what world could I rationalize the killing of three thousand men!* Before her transformation, the thought of such bloodshed would have made her sick—she was hardly able to stomach the first three sacrifices that made her. Since then, however, the only feeling she could muster was cold indifference toward it, if not a strange satisfaction, and it scared her to the bone. Scarier still was the thought of returning to her old life as a wingless, childless female soldier, to forever be looked down upon for her contributions. Being a soldier was the greatest honor a man could attain, but for a woman, it meant shirking her responsibility to the republic. Provide it with children.

The sinister voice inside her head kept urging her on. *"Nas'Gavarr neither responds to the Siren's influence nor the Harpy's strength. But can he withstand the strength of one thousand harpies?"*

"Rangardia has betrayed us, even if the Emperador is unaware of it. I need to prove it," Vidya muttered. Then to her utter shock, the voice responded. *"There is treachery there. Best to use their men to create harpies loyal to the republic than having to fight against those same men later."*

After a half hour of collecting her thoughts, Vidya decided she needed to speak to Demeter.

She flew around the Citadel in hopes of catching her before she left, but she was long gone. Vidya flew to the estate Demeter had shared with their mother and now had all to herself.

As expected, Demeter was sitting on the cushioned lounging bench of the terrace fountains, braiding the hair of her seven-year-old daughter while her son of five splashed about in the shallow pools with some other boys. Not too far away, two young, bare-chested men were locked in an intense wrestling match. Their muscles glistened with sweat, so much so, one could hardly keep a grip on the other. One had long dark hair cascading down his broad shoulders, his chiseled features clean shaven. Vidya recognized him right away as Camdus, Demeter's breeder. The other was not as well muscled. He had short hair and a cocky demeanor but was younger and spryer than his opponent. Demeter kept glancing up from her task to take stock of the fight. *She has two now?* Vidya supposed it made sense that her sister's advancement would grant her additional perks.

"Demi . . ." Vidya began as she walked up to the bench.

"Look at her wings." Demeter referred to her daughter with a proud grin, caressing the budding tufts of feathers sprouting from the child's back. "They're already coming in. She will be spreading her influence across the island in no time."

"That she will," Vidya said dryly. *Is she using her daughter to rub in the fact I never developed the siren's wings?* Had it not been for Vidya's Rangardian father, perhaps she would have been a siren, as the oldest daughter often was. But it was the youngest of Sarta's daughters that grew the wings instead, courtesy of Sarta's second husband, a well-to-do Crede man she married after her obligation to Vidya's father had run its course.

She nodded toward the wrestling breeders. "What's going on here?"

"I can't choose which one to take to my bed tonight, so I suggested they fight for the honor." Demeter tittered.

"Breeders aren't fighters," Vidya said, shaking her head at their awkward, almost comical combat form.

"Are they not men? Fighting is just as natural for them as any other. I always felt it unhealthy to pamper them too much. It makes them soft, and I prefer them hard."

Vidya crossed her arms and rolled her eyes.

Once Demeter was done braiding her daughter's hair, she sent her off to play in the pool with her brother. "Why do you care how I treat my breeders anyway? You're the one who just tried to get approval for mass murder. Thank you, Vidya, for reminding us why it's the Siren that governs here."

"Never mind that," Vidya grumbled. "When do you plan on leaving?"

"Leaving?" Demeter asked, positioning herself on the bench to better view the grappling men.

"To Rangardia. . . . Were you not present at that meeting?"

"Oh." She waved a dismissive hand. "I'm not going to waste my time. Perhaps you should go. You know Emperador Agustin best. Since you never finished your commitment, perhaps you can try again and actually contribute something to this republic."

Demeter didn't have to finish her sentence for Vidya's blood to boil over. She grabbed her sister's arm and yanked her out of her seat. "I have given everything to this republic, and I intend to give even more than that! It is your job to speak to foreign leaders and maintain alliances, not mine!" she hissed, keeping a firm grip on her skinny arm as her blue-white wings fluttered.

Vidya let go, and Demeter snatched her arm back, holding it close to her chest. "Yasharra's mercy, I can have you flogged in the street like a man for daring to touch a member of the Siren C—"

"Oh, shut up, you silly cow!" Vidya snapped. Demeter gasped, her eyes widened then instantly narrowed in contempt. At the same time, the new breeder flipped Camdus overhead, and he landed on the hard, white stone with a loud smack, followed by a rage-filled bellow.

Trying to ignore all their grunting, Vidya continued in a more controlled tone, "That pain in your arm, multiply it by ten. That was what our mother felt the day she died. That is the strength of our enemy. That enemy has been going back and forth between Herran and Rangardia, and we need to know more."

"I agree," said Demeter, Vidya's handprint beginning to show as a faint bruise on her pale olive skin. "Which is why you should be the one to go. I don't know anything about Rangarders or their customs. You lived there for Yasharra's sake. I just think you'd have better luck with them."

"You have no idea how wrong you are about that," Vidya said. *The moment I see that bastard's face again, I'll kill him,* she thought, her fists clenching at her sides.

Demeter let out an annoyed sigh and said, "Fine. I'll go, but only if you come along."

"Demi!" Vidya griped.

"You can't avoid him forever. He sends message after message . . ."

Just then, a man's yelp attracted the winged women's attention. Camdus had the other breeder in a strangle hold, rendering him helpless and red-faced. The young man slapped the ground with his one free hand, signaling his submission.

With a triumphant exhalation, Camdus rose to his feet, flashing a proud grin on his chiseled face, keen green eyes twinkling with boyish anticipation. "I proved victorious, O Fair Siren. Tonight, your pleasures will be ceaseless."

The man kneeled before her, took her hand, and started caressing it. He kissed it, longing apparent in every movement, his eyes wet with a reverence that made Vidya blush just to be in the presence of it. Watching how Camdus gazed up at Demeter in pure adulation put Vidya's hairs on end, not because she was aroused or envious—not at all, but because of how close his actions actually were to something more ominous. An adoring look could become a malicious glare, a soft touch could transform into a clawing grasp, in all but a few moments. That had always been Vidya's experience.

"Oh, how wonderful, Camdus." Demeter bit the inside of her cheek and looked disappointedly at the other breeder getting up from the ground. "Although, I was hoping to take Rufios to bed tonight."

"Uh . . . but I won the fight." The breeder's jaw trembled with rapidly increasing tension.

"Not to fret, Darling," Demeter cooed. "You will still be rewarded for your efforts. I will simply have to have you both at the same time."

Camdus looked to his defeated opponent's wide grin and back to his mistress. She raised her hand and lightly touched the side of Camdus's sweaty cheek. In a few seconds, the disappointment on his face was replaced with a dashing smile of his own. "As you wish, my Love."

Vidya shook her head in disbelief at how effortlessly Demeter could dampen the man's emotions with nothing more than a grazing touch. The realization gave Vidya an idea. "Alright, we can go to Rangardia together. However, you must arrange to speak to the Palace Administrador. Tell him we wish to discuss terms of the Procreation Agreement or something altogether dull. Make sure it is clear that the Emperador need not attend this meeting and do not mention that I will be accompanying you. I will tell you exactly what to say before we head out. All I need from you is your siren influence. Understood?"

Turning from the kneeling breeder, Demeter nodded to Vidya. "Understood."

With that, Vidya left her sister to her two devoted lovers with only one thought on her mind. *Approval or not, I have to find a way to get those men.*

"We will have our Harplite," added the voice.

16

Swift and Precise

Night had fallen as Jeth rode into the Bazaar. The multicolored lanterns hanging in a zigzag pattern above draped the ever-bustling marketplace in a numbing haze.

Khiri and Lys were sitting out on the front stoop when Jeth approached. The Ankarran boy stood and stared at him as he dismounted. "Khiri, do you want to take Tor back to her stall for me?" he asked in the warmest voice he could muster.

Khiri carefully walked up to the tired mare while eyeing Jeth with suspicion.

Jeth pulled out a short bow and some blunted practice arrows he had purchased in the Bazaar on the way in. "I got you these. Put Tor away, and I'll show you how to shoot later."

The boy didn't hesitate in grabbing the gift before taking the reins and leading Torrent toward the stables. *Hopefully that makes up for something,* Jeth thought.

Not ready to go inside quite yet, he planted himself next to Lys, smoking his pipe. Between puffs, the Crede man said, "Where have you been this whole week?"

"Oh, you know, camping out along the Serpentine, teaching my horse to respond to my whistle and not buck me off every chance she gets. Needless to say, I spent a lot of time chasing her across the desert. So, where is everyone?"

"Out." Another puff. "Except Anwarr. She's sleeping."

Jeth glanced over his shoulder into the shop, but at the moment his backside was glued to the stoop.

"The Lunahalah is almost upon us." Lys drew his attention to the double moons in the darkening sky. The small moon was just touching the large one, and the sight made Jeth snicker.

"What is so amusing?" Lys asked.

"Close together like that they sort of look like a pair of lopsided testi . . ." he trailed off, almost forgetting to whom he was speaking. "Uh . . . two things that aren't that big of a deal." He scratched at his beard as his face reddened.

Lys offered him his pipe. "Not having any gonads doesn't mean I've forgotten what they look like."

Jeth winced as he took a puff. "Sorry, so uh . . . is that all you're missing down there or did you lose the whole works?"

"Thank Sagorath I did not. Full castration is a punishment only reserved for those who rape or abuse women."

"You just hit them," Jeth quipped, taking another puff and handing the pipe back to Lys.

"I hit one," he corrected.

"Do you ever elaborate?"

With a sigh, Lys began, "First, you must understand that in Credence, a man's worth is . . . well, about the same as a woman's worth in Del'Cabria, I suppose. A man lives to serve his country, and if he's lucky enough to get one, he will serve his wife above that. A woman of Credence can only marry one man at a time, but she is free—and often encouraged—to take lovers to maximize the prospects of her offspring." He took off his hat and ran his hand over his receding hair. "However, there is one rule she must follow to keep peace in her marriage. She must bear her husband at least two children before she can dally with anyone else."

"So, yours was a little impatient, I take it."

Lys shook his head thoughtfully. "We tried for years, far longer than other couples do. Eventually, she gave birth to a baby boy. One year later, I come home to find her in bed with a breeder."

"Ouch." Jeth grimaced. "Wait, what's a breeder?"

"Fine male specimens born only to give pleasure and provide any willing woman near perfect offspring. They live pampered lives of luxury for their services. Never work a day." Lys gave a thin-lipped smirk.

"Then you hit her?"

"No. I sat the man down, and we had a civil conversation. I made him look me in the eye and tell me how long he and my wife had been fornicating. He didn't need to say anything. My answer was in his eyes . . . the eyes of my son. I lost control, grabbed the nearest blunt object, and beat in that pretty face of his until it was pretty no more." Lys's jaw tightened after taking one last puff of his pipe and putting it out. "When my wife tried to intervene, I turned my wrath upon her. Of course, I stopped myself before doing too much damage, but that didn't keep her from punishing me under the full extent of the law."

"They took your . . . ?" Jeth felt the urge to close his legs a little tighter.

With a dark chuckle, Lys replied, "My wife said I wouldn't miss them; they didn't work anyway."

Jeth gulped. "I'm sure glad I didn't take that harpy up on her offer."

"What harpy? You met a harpy?" Lys snapped his head around and looked straight at him with wide eyes.

"Yes, I should have mentioned it before. She's apparently the only one of her kind. She offered to take me back to Credence to help her kill Nas'Gavarr. Can you believe it?" he said with a shake of the head.

Lys's normally leather-tanned skin went almost cream white. "They actually made a harpy," he said from a faraway place.

"What do you mean made?"

"Legends say it takes three warrior men to make one harpy. If the Siren Council is willing to bring them back into existence, then they must feel they are under extreme threat."

"Nas'Gavarr is a pretty big threat as far as I'm concerned," Jeth said, willing the lump in his gut to ease up but to no avail.

Lys's light brown eyes held Jeth's gaze. "Harpies are Yasharra's instruments in punishing men. If you come by that woman again, I suggest you run the other way."

"I'll take that under advisement," Jeth said, wiping away the anxious sweat that lined his brow.

"You should go see Anwarr. She's been beside herself since you left." Lys emptied his pipe and put it in his robe pocket.

"Yeah . . ." Jeth rubbed his clammy hands on his pants. "I should . . ."

He didn't even attempt to get up. He only sat there in silence until Lys spoke. "What happened between you two?"

"I . . . uh . . . blamed her for sending me to my death at the hand of Nas'Gavarr." The notion sounded insane now that he was saying it aloud.

"Oh." Lys nodded. "And here I thought it was her denying your request to have her all to yourself."

Jeth snorted. "That too." Lys gave him a pitying look. "I get it. She's a free woman of Herran who belongs to no one while I just want to belong to someone." He wiped his dry nose, unable to meet the Crede man's gaze.

"There is no shame in wanting loyalty in a woman. But you have to make a choice." *'What makes you think you have a choice in anything?'* Nas'Gavarr's voice echoed through Jeth's mind, making him want to bang his own head against the sandstone doorframe. "Maybe you can accept Anwarr for who she is, continue having your fun upstairs—as you all do when you think I don't hear—and stifle that beast deep down that wants to rip the nads off any man who goes near her. But, if you're anything like me, you will only end up hurting her as well as yourself."

"Hah! Only a man with the iron will of a Sunil servant could resist her."

Lys shrugged. "You won't know until you try."

"Easy for you to say." Jeth gestured toward Lys's groin.

"At least I don't have problems with women anymore."

"If that's the secret, sign me up." Jeth took out his khopesh and stuck it vertically upon the stone stoop. "I will lay them out right here and now, and you can take a swing. Promise you will be swift and precise."

The Crede man burst into unfettered laughter, and soon Jeth joined him. He patted him on the shoulder and stood. "Very good, maybe you should sleep on it, though. You look like a camel chewed you up and spat you back out."

Lys put on his hat and offered Jeth an arm for him to pull himself to his feet.

"Doesn't matter anyway," Jeth said. "I know what I have to do. It's time to say goodbye."

"Where will you go?"

"I figured I'd just ride until something stops me."

Lys frowned. "That's too bad. It was nice not being the only foreigner around here for a change."

A few pats on the back and some parting words later, Jeth went up two flights of stairs to the third floor. He stood at Anwarr's doorway for a moment. She was sprawled out on her stomach, one arm off the mattress grazing the floor, her endless piles of clothes and accessories strewn about, overflowing from her wardrobe while garnets and makeup cluttered her vanity table. *I'm sure going to miss this calamity of a room,* he thought with a twinge in his heart.

As he approached her bed, she woke with a start. "Mm Jethril . . . ?" she mumbled while sitting up and rubbing the sleep from her red puffy eyes.

She opened her mouth to speak, but Jeth put his hand out. "Please don't say anything. Just know . . . I'm sorry and—"

"It's all right." She took him by the belt sash and pulled him toward her. "Come to bed. I've missed you."

Why isn't she furious? Shouldn't she be screaming, hitting, telling you to go and never come back?

Jeth's entire body yearned to take her into his arms, undress her, and lose himself in her, but he planted his feet to the floor and didn't budge.

"I can't stay." He shook his head.

"Nonsense." She rose to her feet. "You belong here with us."

"I don't," he replied, steadfast.

"Then why come back?"

"I couldn't leave things the way I did." His breath caught in his throat as he contemplated the words he was about to say. "Something's happening to me that I can't explain. . . . It's not safe to be around me right now."

Anwarr took both his hands in hers. "You mean the Overlord? Do you think you're the first among us to have a powerful adversary out for your blood? It goes with the territory. That's why we have to stick together."

"You don't understand." He slipped out of her hands. "It's not just him."

She took a step back while wiping a tear about to fall from her eye. "You still think I had something to do with what happened to you."

"No, no, I was out of my mind. . . ."

". . . You don't trust me." Anwarr deflated into a seated position on the bed.

"It's me who I don't trust!" Jeth exclaimed. "I keep thinking about how close I came to hurting you on a mere suspicion. It makes me sick to think of what I could have done."

"Again, Jethril, you are not the first man to lose his temper around here."

"You were right," he went on. "I could be your next Ezrai if things go any further. I'm already jealous. Controlling may not be that far off."

Anwarr suddenly put her hand to her mouth and breathlessly laughed through her tears.

"I'm not trying to be funny, An."

Rising from the bed again, she took steps toward him, and he moved backward to maintain distance. "Saying that proves you are nothing like Ezrai. I should never have compared you to him."

Jeth shook his head. "You don't know that. I don't know what I'm capable of so how could you—?"

His back found the wall near the door, allowing Anwarr to close in. She brought her forehead to his and hushed him, quieting his anxious rant. "It's all behind you. All that exists is the here and now."

"It's all going to catch up to us," he whispered back.

Her fingers caressed his face, and a radiating current flowed from the point of contact all the way down to his toes, reminding him how long it had been since he'd felt her.

"Not if we keep moving forward." Anwarr pulled him into her embrace. His heart thudded hard in his chest, and for the first time, he felt hers beating just as violently. He breathed deep and took in her wonderful scent. There was no going back. *Only forward.* He took her around the waist and pressed her against him, his rigid arousal bulging to the point of pain.

"This is supposed to be goodbye, you know," he said, moving her further into the room.

Anwarr yanked him by the beard, looked him straight in the eye, and said, "You don't hear me saying it."

That's when she kissed him. Pleasure sang in his bones and coursed through every tissue. The warmth of her alone sent him into a fevered daze. She softly bit down on his bottom lip, sending his body and mind into a tailspin. He kept oscillating between being with her—the here and now—to reveries of being fused to that temple floor, abandoned by his crew, and trapped under the naja. He was as helpless now as he was then, locked in Anwarr's embrace from where there was no escape.

The voice deep in his mind protested. *You're weak! You can't even stand up to yourself—for yourself. How long do you think you'll be able to pretend this life is for you?* Jeth's raw powerlessness gave way to the ire that he had only felt one other time before—the night he killed Baird and Tobin—like a popping crack in his core that took him out of himself. He forced his racing thoughts from his consciousness and surrendered to something purely instinctual.

With a surge of vigor, he backed Anwarr against the vanity, jostling small bottles. He smacked a box of jewelry off the surface to make space to set her down. She cried out in surprise and wrapped her legs tightly around his waist, inciting him to run his ravenous lips across her neck, shoulders—anywhere he could reach.

He untied the straps of her halter at the base of her neck as she ripped open his shirt. He took her unfettered breasts in hand. Firmly squeezing, he brought his lips to them, licking and sucking her nipples until they hardened against his tongue. She moaned while gripping the mirror behind her. Jeth bit down, turning her moans to pitched cries before he gently caressed them and brought her back to a relaxed state.

Jeth's lips and tongue continued to venture up her chest and neck while his left hand traveled under her sarong hiked up past her thighs, and found the eager wetness between them. He slid his forefingers inside her, making her gasp and her body tighten. As soon as he started caressing her in the way he knew she liked, she closed her eyes and laid her head back, gripping the mirror with one hand and clutching the back of his neck with the other, digging her nails in. The sting only fed his fire, inciting him to go deeper and stroke harder, coaxing her warm fluids into his hand. Anwarr trembled in her pleasure. A couple of her beauty tonics fell and rolled along the floor.

". . . The bed," she gasped.

Jeth swung her onto it as she squealed. He flung off the rest of his shirt and joined her on the bed where she attempted to mount him, but he was in no mood for that this time. It had always been Anwarr telling him what to do, where to put it, and for how long, but not tonight. He snatched her wrists and forced her down beneath him, holding them fast above her head.

Blue frost sizzled in her eyes, her heartbeat was deafening, and her breath, shuddering. *Is she afraid? Should you stop?* Her wicked grin told him otherwise.

While still holding her wrists above her head with one hand, his other stripped away her sarong, exposing her in all her glorious nakedness. The sight of her enticing curvature was enough to provoke his most savage desires. And tonight, Anwarr was finally going to know them.

Releasing her, he said in a gruff voice, "Turn around."

He hastily undid his pants as she dutifully flipped over to her hands and knees, presenting her readiness to him.

Watching her comply excited him more than he expected. He hardly waited for her to get into position before he grabbed her by the hips and plunged into her tight, wet warmth. Her cry of surprise caught in her throat.

Jeth pulled her hips flush against his and penetrated as deep as he could go, and she released another breathless cry. He ran his hand up the length of her Serpentine tattoo then clutched a handful of hair at the nape of her neck. Each subsequent thrust made Anwarr's body more receptive, allowing him to drive harder and faster, her moans becoming louder and more encouraging. He tugged her up to meet him and forcibly held her head back by the hair so he could kiss and bite her neck, the taste of her sweat was intoxicating. Her blood pumped furiously through her jugular, matching the throbbing of his own.

Anwarr gripped the back of his head and gyrated her hips in such a way, the pressure in his loins built up to a near painful level. Jeth lost himself, the warmth of her, how tight she felt around his cock. Made for him alone. This is where you belong. He gripped her around the neck, thrusting harder and deeper while stroking her below with his other hand. Anwarr trembled in his arms, her gasping moans melting away as her climax gushed from her. She rested her head back on his shoulder, succumbing to him. She was completely his in that moment.

Drenched from her pleasure, Jeth let his baser instincts take the lead. He shoved her forward onto the pillows, held her down, and drove into her vigorously. Before long, a radiating inferno erupted from inside him. All his paranoia and anxiety, every ounce of energy drained out of him and into her. Overwhelmed with weakness, he collapsed, his heart pounding against her back. Catching his breath was impossible. *You might just die here,* he thought.

Using his last shred of strength, he flipped onto his back next to her, sweat beading off his face and chest.

Anwarr, glowing and disheveled, let out a sigh of satisfaction as she nestled up under his arm. "That was like making love with Sagorath himself!" She tittered, breathless. "Does this mean you're going to stay?"

Jeth brushed away tangled strands of hair from her face and kissed her on the forehead. "Forgive me," he breathed.

She propped herself up and asked. "For what?"

For all the ways I may hurt you someday, he thought. "For thinking I could ever leave you," he said.

With a radiant smile, Anwarr got on top of him. "You should come with me on my reconnaissance job. We can sail the Ankarran seas, talk to my old pirate contacts, and you will get to see the Odafi coast like you wanted. We leave in two days."

"We?"

"Ashbedael is coming too. He has the most experience fighting the pirates of Ankarr from his Bahazur days, and he's the only person on this crew who knows his way around a ship besides me."

The thought of her spending all that time alone with Ash made him ill, but the thought of going on another job so soon after the last was out of the question.

He sighed. "I need more time."

Anwarr rested her head down on his chest and looked up at him with saddened eyes. "Alright, take all the time you need. Just promise you'll be here when we return?"

Running his hand through her knotted white hair, he chuckled. "I'm not sure I'll be able to leave this bed, let alone Herran."

With an irresistible grin, Anwarr squeezed him tight. "Then for the next two days, we shall make the most of your captivity."

17

A Vicious Voice

"It is an honor to be in your presence, Señora Demeter," said the Palace Administrador Ricardo as a wiry servant poured wine into three crystal chalices at the table. "Sarta was a divine being, and we here, are harrowed by her loss. I am glad to have this opportunity to continue our relationship with her beautiful daughter."

Vidya shifted in her chair, invisible next to her sister at the table. They were enjoying a light meal in the palace, overlooking the exquisite gardens in the courtyard below. Decadent marble statues depicting the female form in all its variations, draped in vines and reflecting the sunlight, were everywhere. Remnants of the empire's period of literal female worship were now expressed as a general female appreciation.

Although Rangardia was as patriarchal as all the other nations, the love and respect they had for their women was admirable even if those women didn't enjoy the same status as men. In recent decades, a horrific disease known as *femena mortum*, suddenly and mysteriously ravaged through much of their female population, making the Procreation Agreement with Credence tantamount in keeping their empire from complete collapse.

"Thank you for having us, Señor," replied Demeter, before taking a sip of her wine. "We are both dedicated to keeping the alliance between our two nations strong in these coming years."

Ricardo sat, cross-legged with one arm casually slung over the back of his chair. He took a modest sip of his wine while eyeing Vidya sitting across from him and to his right. The Administrador looked to have aged considerably since she had seen him last. His face was gaunter, bits of gray peppered his triangular mustache and beard, as well as his black, slicked-back hair that curled behind his ears.

Ricardo put down his chalice. "I must say, it surprises me that you would bring your sister with you, just to revisit the Agreement." Vidya was irked how he addressed her like she wasn't even at the table. He had never acted particularly warm toward her in the past, but he had always treated her with respect. Something wasn't right. She held in her misgivings and allowed Demeter to do the talking.

"I should apologize for setting up this meeting under false pretenses. As you may appreciate, Herran has forced us to do things a little more covertly."

"Then perhaps the Emperador should be in attendance after all?" Ricardo shot another hardened glance at Vidya.

"That won't be necessary," Vidya said, her skin crawling at the notion. "We are only here to ask a few questions of you—nothing worth bothering my husband with."

Demeter cleared her throat softly. "One of those questions is related to a warp stone mine in your Venerra District."

"What about it?" He scratched his mustache.

"We know that a warping gate was built there recently."

"Yes, I approved of its construction myself. Why the interest in this gate?"

Demeter took another sip of wine and set it down on the table. "Nas'Gavarr has built one of his own. We think he has been traveling between his and the one in Venerra, giving him access to all the warp stone he would ever need."

"We don't think. We know," Vidya corrected.

"Is that an accusation?" Ricardo stiffened in his chair.

"We are not accusing you of anything, Señor, but you must understand that both our nations are under great threat. If Nas'Gavarr is robbing your warp stone mines, then it must be shut down."

"Why shut down such a profitable and necessary operation based on mere suspicion? If the Overlord of Herran or any desert follower of his came through that gate, someone would have reported it."

"It is not suspicion, Ricardo," said Vidya, crossing her arms in front of her chest. "I went through the Overlord's gate myself. It led straight to the mine. He had been there at least once."

Biting his cheek, he coldly looked away from Vidya and said to Demeter, "You believe her?"

"Of course, I believe her, why wouldn't I?" Demeter brushed a wavy red strand behind her ear.

"Your sister is a liar."

"Excuse me?" Vidya clenched her fists until her nails dug holes into her palms.

"Let us not digress. . . ." Demeter reached out to touch the Administrador's hand only for him to take his chalice into that hand before she could graze it with her delicate fingers.

Dammit, Vidya cursed inwardly. *She needs to touch him if this meeting is to go as planned.*

Before arriving in Rangardia, the sisters had gone over their strategy. Demeter would use her siren's influence to get Ricardo to confess to treachery. In return for maintaining the Procreation Agreement, Rangardia would have to pay a form of reparations in the amount of three thousand fighters, be them criminals or otherwise. The Harpy's punishment would be much more justified, and the Council would be more likely to accept it if their faith in their long-trusted ally were shaken. If it were revealed that Rangardia didn't betray them, however . . . Vidya didn't want to entertain that eventuality.

Demeter continued, "All we ask is that the stone be removed from the gate until such a time the Herrani threat has lifted. Someone in that mine is allowing Nas'Gavarr to come through it."

"Perhaps one time he did, unexpectedly, like in Credence."

"And if he chooses to return, how will anyone know it is him until it is too late? The mine can remain operational and use galleys to ship to neighboring islands as it has done previously."

Ricardo sighed, smoothing his mustache. "I see your point. I can draw up the order to dismantle the Venerra gate, but for no more than six months."

Demeter gave a warm smile. "Very good, Señor. Your decision will go a long way in protecting our islands."

"Is that all you two came here to talk about?" Ricardo asked, uncrossing and then crossing his leg on the other side.

"Not entirely," said Demeter. "There is another question, one we detest to ask a most trusted ally, but in times like these, we cannot be too careful." Demeter leaned over to touch Ricardo's hand hanging over the back of his chair. He moved it again, and the siren's hand rested upon his clothed arm instead.

"Demeter." His voice took on a severe tone. "I know what you are trying to do, and I ask that you show more respect, as your mother would have."

"I-I'm afraid I don't—" Demeter sputtered.

"Please don't insult me." Ricardo put up a hand to silence her, and her nostrils flared in indignation, something Vidya would find comical under any other circumstance. "The previous Emperador's petulance knew no bounds. Sarta's only means of reasoning with such a stubborn old fool was through her siren charm. When my brothers and I took over, we swore to cultivate true alliances based on mutual respect. She never once needed to use her touch or her voice to ensure her ends, and I remained open and honest with her in return. I hope to continue that relationship with you. Therefore, I ask that you do not touch me—as heavenly as that may be—and I will accommodate you in any way I can, within reason. . . . My own reason."

Demeter swallowed through a tight-lipped smile and removed her hand from Ricardo's arm. "Apologies, Señor. With my mother's sudden death, she did not have the chance to inform me of these matters."

Ricardo grinned warmly. "That is understandable, my dear. Please, ask your difficult question, and I promise to provide you an honest answer."

"If she doesn't touch him, then his word is meaningless," said the voice. Vidya took a deep breath, preparing for nothing short of lies to come pouring from the man's mouth.

"Has Rangardia entered into talks with Herran with regard to an alliance?"

"You ask if we are looking to join them?"

Both Vidya and Demeter nodded.

With his eyes solely on Demeter, Ricardo said, "Rangardia is as loyal to Credence as she ever was. You can be sure we stand beside you against that dreaded serpent."

"So, he hasn't come here to negotiate terms?" Vidya pressed.

Turning a cold eye to Vidya, he replied, "No." He turned back to Demeter. "Does my answer put your worries to rest?"

"That it does. Thank you," she replied with a graceful nod.

Vidya's mind screamed. *He's covering for his tyrant of a brother! There's no way Nas'Gavarr hasn't been to this palace. He probably sat at this very table!*

She decided there was only one thing left to do. "How many fighting men does Rangardia have?" she blurted.

"About, eighty thousand. I would need to consult my brother Jimènez for an exact number. . . ."

"What about in your prisons? They must be bursting. How many of them can fight?"

"I have no idea," Ricardo said.

"Vidya, what are you doing?" Demeter whispered, but Vidya ignored her.

"We need three thousand fighting men, preferably ones you won't be using. We want them sent to Credence as soon as possible."

"I told you that our armies would support you in this war, why do they need to go to Credence?"

"Why should it matter?" Vidya said. "This empire won't miss three thousand unmarried males rotting in their cells or running amok in the streets."

"Do not presume to tell me of what is going on in my empire," Ricardo snapped. *He's certainly taken to thinking the empire is his and not Agustin's. That's a new development since I've been here last,* she thought. "We make good use of our extra men. Some choose castration—we put them to work—enlist them in the military. Shiploads of them had fled to the Tradesmen's Guild on the mainland. A certain number may run amok, as you say, but the Procreation Agreement largely mitigates that. As it stands, our men still give much to this empire and those who do well have been rewarded with Crede wives for two generations now. Even so, men here are disappearing at rates almost comparable to women these days. I do not wish to be responsible for more of that. Rangardia may quickly find itself running out of both sexes if we keep treating our men as disposable."

"Who said anything about disposing of them?" Vidya countered. "We wish for them to serve a higher purpose."

"I'm sure you do." Ricardo nodded toward Vidya's wings. "You intend to sacrifice them to Yasharra. Sarta spoke of such things. Every year, a woman-hating criminal is slaughtered in the name of the Harpy so your republic can keep away misfortune. But, that hasn't been working lately, has it? So, a mass slaughter is needed in order to appease her. Or am I wrong? You wish not to put your own men under the sacrificial blade, so you will use ours, as we have too many as it is."

"Listen to me," Vidya said sternly. "I know Nas'Gavarr has been here, and I know you know about it. Give the order to send three thousand men to Credence, and we won't be forced to rescind the Agreement. Your male-female ratio of ten to one will only widen with every newly infected womb. What will become of your productive male population then?"

Demeter grabbed hold of Vidya's arm and protested, "We didn't come here to make threats." She turned to Ricardo apologetically. "A compromise can be made. If there are men willing to sacrifice themselves to our cause, who are we to stop them?"

At this point, Ricardo gave no consideration to the siren at his table as his dark eyes burned holes into Vidya sitting across it. "How Agustin found it in his heart to forgive you, I will never know. You are more monstrous now than you ever were!"

Vidya's gut wrenched. "Forgive me?"

He said to Demeter, "You come here, accusing me of treachery when treachery's queen sits at your side!"

Demeter cast confused glances between her sister and Ricardo, who continued to rave at Vidya, "You think you can eat at my table, threaten our alliance, and demand the lives of my citizens, after what you did? You deplorable cunt!"

"Señor!" Demeter gasped.

"Does your sister not know?" Ricardo went on. "What did you tell everyone when you left my brother to clean up your mess?"

"Vidya, what is he talking about?"

Demeter's voice was a faint buzz against the sound of Vidya's heart pounding in her ears. Her breath seized as a putrid nausea rose into her throat. *Agustin told him that I did it. . . .*

"Tell her, Vidya. Confess your crimes!" Ricardo demanded, bits of spit flying from his mouth.

Vidya couldn't find the breath to form words. All of her focus was on trying not to lose control.

Ricardo didn't wait for her to respond and answered Demeter on her behalf. "She is a murderer. She slaughtered her own children—my nephews . . . left their little bodies as a parting gift for my brother."

The image of the blood-filled tub flooded Vidya's fractured mind. Don't look! Her rage capsized, and all control of her body was lost. With a violent flap of her wings, she shot across the table, spilling the wine and scattering the dishes across the floor. In half a second, Ricardo's throat was in her grasp.

She dragged him over to the wall and held him against it. "Lies!" she shrieked, lifting him off the ground by the neck.

"Guards!" he yelped before she squeezed his windpipe with both hands and choked off any further cries.

Five guards ran into the dining area from the halls, armed with rifles, all aiming for the harpy with their administrador in her clutches.

"Vidya, stop! Put him down!" Demeter cried.

A shadow formed above Vidya's head, hanging from a chandelier, and spreading its ethereal wings, its fiery yellow eyes blazing into Vidya's soul. A vicious voice came forth. *"It will only take a second. Snap his neck, rip his head off, and present it to his brother. . . ."*

The sound of cocking rifles echoed off the marble pillars, giving Vidya pause. Five rounds would likely kill her, and she wasn't prepared to waste her second life on Señor Ricardo.

"Release him!" one of the guards yelled.

"Listen to them, Vidya," her sister begged.

With a shaking breath, she forced her fingers to let go of Ricardo's neck, and he slid to the ground in a heap, sucking in air in wheezing bursts. The shadow creature was swallowed up into the ceiling as Vidya took slow steps back with her hands up. The guards eased, but they didn't lower their firearms.

Ricardo climbed back to unsteady feet. "And you expect everyone to believe you were the victim. I felt sorry for you once, but I learned who you truly are, even if Agustin can't see it."

"He's lying to you," Vidya hissed.

"All I know is even when he is out of his mind he is still my brother. In Rangardia, there is no stronger bond."

"You're a fool!"

"Leave these islands and don't ever return. May Agustin never learn you were here!"

Demeter spoke at last. "My deepest apologies, Señor. Harpies can be unpredictable. Vidya, make way for the gate this instant."

"You should both go," said Ricardo. "I will honor what has been agreed to already. The Venerra gate will be dismantled until further notice from you. Our nations remain allies, but be sure never to bring that thing here with you again."

Demeter nodded solemnly. "It was good to finally meet you in person, Señor Ricardo. Give my best to the Emperador and the rest of your family." She gathered her dress, curtsied respectfully, and took Vidya by the arm to escort her out.

Vidya yanked her arm away, taking hastened strides past her sister and out of the dining room.

In the carriage heading back to Rangardia's central warping gate, Vidya was overwhelmed with nausea. *He may as well have killed them all over again, the bastard!*

"What was that back there? You could have caused irreparable damage to our alliance!" Demeter's shrill voice broke through her traumatic reveries.

"So now you care about foreign alliances?" Vidya growled, her temples pounding.

"I should have come myself."

"No, you should have touched him so that he would have been compelled to tell the truth about his betrayal. Then he would have agreed to the men and our alliance would be stronger than ever."

"You nearly killed him!" Demeter screeched.

Vidya turned away to face the Rangardian streets out the carriage window rather than the petulant siren beside her. Man after man wandered aimlessly, some bickering amongst themselves and others shoving each other or yelling. Several city blocks passed by without a single woman in sight. Drawing down the shades, Vidya closed her eyes and focused on breathing.

Silence enveloped the carriage until Demeter said in a calm voice, "Please don't take my head off. But what Ricardo said back there . . ."

"You want to know if I murdered my own children," Vidya said through gritted teeth.

"Of course not." Demeter placed a hand to her own chest. "It broke mother's heart when you stopped writing her while you were here, when you refused to see her when she visited, we had no idea what became of you. . . ." *Agustin never let me near the pigeon pens to send a single message, never let me out of the palace. He never even told me when mother came, and the worst part was, I couldn't bear to let her see me in such a pathetic state.* Vidya wanted to confess everything to Demeter, but she held it in with all her might. "Then you come back before the five years was up with no girls for the republic, and no boys left behind, only letters upon letters from Agustin begging you to honor the Agreement. You joined the infantry so you wouldn't have to go back, leaving mother to explain why her own daughter rejected the Emperador of Rangardia. It had always bothered me that you never took an interest in my children, but now I'm beginning to understand."

Vidya kept her eyes glued to the carriage window even though she could see nothing out of it. Her visibly fighting back the tears was enough to give Demeter her answer.

"So, you finished your commitment after all. Did mother know?"

Vidya shook her head.

"Why didn't you tell us?" Demeter asked in a shaking whisper.

Vidya met the tearful blue eyes of her sister. "How could I tell the Mistress of Foreign Relations that the Emperador of Rangardia, our only ally in the fight against Del'Cabrian imperialism, slaughtered my boys in a psychotic rage?"

"She could have done something. We could have had justice for them."

Vidya had wanted so badly to tell someone, especially her mother. But there would have been an investigation, secrets revealed, truths told. Everything that had happened between Agustin and Vidya would be dragged kicking and screaming into the daylight. All the abuse she endured and the tortures she inflicted on him later on. For a woman of Credence to be lowered that way, and the things she had been driven to do to survive those years—it was all so shameful. What would she do if the entire republic found out that after all of that, she let her sons die? *I should have taken them with me. What kind of mother leaves her babies in the care of madman?*

"It's too late," she said. "He's told his whole family that I did it. I figured mother would find out at some point, but Agustin never mentioned it to her."

"He wanted you to finish your five years with him, so it was not in his interest to tell her. He must have told his family that you did it to keep him from facing the consequences."

"So much for winning me back," Vidya muttered.

"Did you . . . see it happen?"

"We're not talking about this anymore."

"I'm sorry I requested that you come . . . I didn't know. . . ." Demeter's voice quavered, her eyes filling up with tears as she stared at Vidya.

"Don't look at me like I'm a wounded animal. I chose to come along because we need those men. We need the Harplite or Yasharra help us."

Demeter turned away and sighed. "We will have to find another way."

Guided by the light of the full moons shining as two overlapping spheres, Vidya landed on her fourth-floor windowsill of the infantry barracks a few miles from the city. Folding up her wings at her back, she opened the shutters and hopped into her one-room abode. She could have spent the night at her family's estate, but she needed the solitude only the minimalistic room could provide. Far from her sister's titters echoing off the high marble arches, the servants shuffling about the halls, and more than any of that, the carefree laughter of her niece and nephew splashing in the fountains right outside her old bedroom window. *I can't handle that anymore.*

After making a fire in her wood-burning stove, a series of knocks sounded at her door. No sooner had she opened it, than a short-statured woman barged in.

"What are you doing back from Rangardia so soon? Guess that means it didn't go too well," said Phrea, planting herself on one of Vidya's chairs and casting a thick leg over the armrest.

Phrea was the first person Vidya had befriended in the infantry. She was a whole lot of woman shoved into a short package, but faster and spryer than many of the male soldiers they sparred with. She, like Vidya, was siren from a Rangardian father through the Agreement, but instead of honoring it when she became of age, she joined the infantry, never showing an interest in marriage or men for that matter. She took on the characteristics of her Rangardian side the most, with a darker olive complexion, brown eyes, and black hair to go along with a fiery temper. The only thing she retained from her mother was hair that grew straight and silky and was the envy of Vidya. Even so, she always kept it in a tight bun.

"What do you know about it? And did I say you could come in?"

"I'm a spy. I know everything." She cackled. "Close the door. You're letting all the heat out."

Vidya was about to do just that, only to find a thin waif of a woman standing in the doorway.

"Why, hello, Daphne. Come on in." She waved her next best friend into the room and closed the door behind her. Daphne was the opposite of Phrea in almost every way. Soft spoken and mousy with light brown hair chopped to short wisps at her ears. She made up for it with adorable doe-like features and large aquamarine eyes that captured many men's attentions, until she opened her mouth to spout boring medical jargon.

Shaking her head at her peculiar mates, Vidya grabbed an iron poker to stoke the flames in the stove. "It's been a while. I haven't seen either of you since I've been back from the desert," she said.

"That's because we've both been out on assignment," said Phrea. "I was sent to keep an eye on the desert coasts to make sure the Herrani fleet wasn't amassing again. Since then, I've been tracking the Overlord through Del'Cabria."

"They have you spying on him now?" Vidya asked in surprise.

"I know." Phrea smirked. "I can hardly believe it either. That was supposed to be your job, wasn't it?"

"The Council wants me to find a different 'strategy,'" she muttered, slamming the door to the stove and dropping the poker on the ground rather than returning it to the holder.

"We heard. So? Did Rangardia betray our alliance?" Phrea asked.

Vidya shook her head and took a seat on the chair across from Phrea while Daphne, with her book bag slung over her shoulder, shuffled over to the bed and sat down. "They proclaim unbending loyalty as always, but I know it's all pigshit."

"Why go there at all?" asked Daphne. "That kind of dreary diplomacy stuff is for sirens."

"It's quite obvious, isn't it, Daph?" Phrea said while picking at her nails that were always filthy. Vidya looked down at her own and found them to be the same. "If Rangardia was revealed to have been consorting with our enemy, a harpy would be there to dole out proper punishment."

Phrea winked at Vidya and returned to her fingernail cleaning. With a curl of her lips, Vidya said, ". . . as only a harpy is expected to do."

"Everyone is talking about the idea you brought forth to the Council—the Harplite," blurted Daphne.

Phrea let her feet down and leaned on her elbows in a masculine fashion with only her exceptionally large bust to allude to her femininity, another attribute Vidya lacked. "Oh, we've been dying to talk to you about that. Were you serious?"

"Read the logs and see for yourself," Vidya said dryly, crossing one leg over the other and leaning back in her armchair.

"I already did," Daphne piped up. "It is a shame the Council didn't support your idea. The War Council has assigned me to Pathogens. I was sent to Fae'ren Province to study that nasty plague making a small resurgence there."

Vidya shook her head. "Daph, I can never follow your thought process. What does my Harplite idea have to do with some foreign plague?"

"Remember to use transitions, Sweetheart," said Phrea, raising her unibrow. Where Vidya tirelessly plucked each hair to maintain two distinct brows, Phrea never bothered. "Here's some context for you: Nas'Gavarr signed some kind of treaty with King Tiberius, and now his armies march for Fae'ren."

"Why Fae'ren?"

"We're still trying to work that out, but that's not the point," said Phrea.

Daphne sat up straight and clasped her hands together with excitement or nervousness, Vidya couldn't tell. "An opportunity presents itself to severely weaken the Herrani warriors. You see, Fae'ren Province is divided into several communal areas and outer villages, all miles apart from each other. This means there is little chance of a pathogen spreading too far. It wasn't until the Del'Cabrian invasion when the disease had means of spreading rampantly through every commune, starting the First Wave. It thinned their population to such a degree those fairy folks stood no chance in defending their lands. Curiously enough, the Del'Cabrians never fell quite as ill, suggesting they already had immunity and therefore, brought the disease with them."

"And the War Council wants to do the same thing, only direct it at the Herrani warriors," Vidya surmised.

Daphne nodded, aqua eyes twinkling. "We hope that most Fae'ren have developed enough immunity from the Second Wave and won't be harmed as gravely as the Herrani invaders who do not. With any luck, some of the survivors will bring the strain back to the desert to cause a widespread contagion that will make femena mortum seem like a mild irritation." The flatness in Daphne's voice made her sound as if she were reciting writings from a medical journal.

Vidya, on the other hand, was anything but calm and collected. She stood with a start. "Those old bats will approve of spreading a deadly disease, possibly killing hundreds of thousands of civilians, but they're opposed to sacrificing worthless criminals?"

"In their defense," said Phrea, cracking her knuckles with her palm. "Those civilians are our enemies too. Thinning the herd lessens the number of soldiers they can draw from that herd. Even the Fae'ren, who aren't hostile now, can be drafted to fight with the Del'Cabrians eventually."

"That's not the point," said Vidya. "This strategy puts us all at risk. The Herrani could bring all kinds of new strains with them when they invade us. I can't believe the Archon would entertain this idea while simultaneously shutting me down."

Daphne nodded, taking out a leather-bound journal from her bag. "I agree. That's why I've been studying harpies lately. Did you know they have a natural resilience to all known pathogens? A harpy army would never have to fear falling ill from foreign diseases. In fact, it is said that thousands of years ago, when harpies ruled Credence, disease was one of the primary ways they defeated their enemies."

"Yes, Daph, I know that. You forget you're speaking to one."

"Don't you see, Vidi?" Phrea said, standing up and casually pacing about the small room. "We're with you on this. Think about what the Harplite could do in regard to tactics alone. They could be our sentinels in the sky, sink every ship that approaches with storm winds, pick off entire contingents from the sky. . . ."

"You don't have to convince me, Phrea," Vidya said. "We would be unstoppable. I went to Rangardia with hopes I would return with enough men to make it happen, but as it stands, they are still our allies."

"If the Overlord of Herran can walk into a major mining operation and make off with warp stone, surely nobody would notice a few scrappy men disappearing. My father runs a military installation on the northernmost island. It's tiny, has no warping gate, but easy to fly to. I owe him a visit. Perhaps I can take a look around, see who the best candidates might be. It's a whole lot easier than breaking into a prison."

"Whoa, Phrea." Vidya put her arms out to brace her. "Three thousand soldiers disappearing will not go unnoticed."

"I'm not talking about three thousand." Phrea snorted. "Just six. Three for each of us." Phrea pointed to herself and Daphne whose eager doe eyes lit up.

"You want to be harpies too?"

"Of course!" Phrea exclaimed. "We watched your transformation, and we know it won't be pleasant, but—"

"Why you, Daphne? You don't fight."

"The pathogens," she said, standing up as well. "I can do much more with the disease as a harpy, be it infecting the right targets and finding a cure for the current strain. And . . . playing with wind could be fun."

Vidya chuckled. Fun was not something she associated with Daphne, given her idea of such was collecting cadavers and examining what was found in them.

"Three harpies are stronger than one," continued Phrea. "We snatch Herrani warriors from the air, sacrifice them, and gradually increase our numbers. The Siren Council will have no reason to object at that point."

Daphne cleared her throat and pointed to a page in her book. "Actually, Phrea, the ritual deals in flesh magic, meaning the bloodlines of the sacrifices must be similar to one another for the transmogrification to take place. The first ones were Crede men so the rest should be as well. Rangardians should do fine since our bloodlines have been mixing throughout history, but Herrani are too far removed to create a harpy."

"Then we can make do with six Rangarders."

Vidya put up her hand. "How do you propose we smuggle these lucky fellows to the Citadel without anybody noticing? It won't be like sneaking in to watch my transformation ritual. How did you two childless soldiers get past the guards by the way?"

"Maramus got us in. He was with the Infantry Commander that night," Daphne replied then stuck her finger in the air. "Valerian."

"There's no Commander Valerian." Vidya scrunched her face in confusion.

"No, the sedative . . . for smuggling the Rangarders out."

"Oh." Vidya nodded.

"Good thinking, Daph," said Phrea. "We can invite some boys out for drinks and a few drops of valerian later, they'll be out for the night. We'll just need a plan to deal with the Citadel guards while we're using the altar."

"And we'll need a way to get the sacrifices there, be it by warping gate or boat," Daphne added.

Vidya bit the inside of her cheek. The only way she could see such a thing being pulled off was with the help of a siren. *Demeter may now pity me enough to agree to this,* she thought.

"Leave that one to me. I think I have an idea."

"Fantastic!" Phrea clapped. "So, you're with us then? We get to be your harpy sisters?"

A bubbling anticipation rose from within. *Finally, women who recognize what must be done.* Vidya said, "Phrea, write your father, tell him you're coming for a visit, and ask him if it's all right we tag along."

18
Forgiveness

(A Month and a Half Later)

A ship with a single mast sailed into an unregulated port off the Odafi coast. Men and women balanced crates of goods on their heads and shoulders, weaving between one another with the fluidity of opposing streams, their bright clothes blending into a rainbow sea against skin shining dark umber in the early morning sun. Standing at the waterfront among the flock of traders and merchants, Jeth and Istari eagerly waited for the small sloop to dock.

"This is the one. I can see Ash's cobra grin from here," said Jeth.

Istari gushed with relief, "Thank the Serpentine Gods!"

"I know Ankarr is a dangerous region, but Ash wouldn't let anything happen," Jeth asserted, more for his own reassurance than Istari's. Anwarr had been gone a couple weeks longer than anticipated, making both Jeth and Istari nervous wrecks until the day they received word via pigeon that they were coming home and with a surprise. *Perhaps she freed another slave boy to keep Khiri company,* he thought.

"I had no doubt they'd make it back," Istari said. "I was more afraid they'd miss the Lunahalah. It will be Ana's first time celebrating it."

"Really? I know it only comes around every three years, but I figured she would've celebrated it at least once considering she talks about it all the time."

"It was disallowed by the harem. Then, when it came around again, she was with Ezrai. He kept a tight leash on her, especially in that week."

"I never knew. . . ."

As the two waited for the docking ramp to be put down, Istari continued, "Yes, a week of pure self-indulgence where every experience is new and consequences are non-existent. That often manifests in sexual exploits, but it doesn't have to."

"Everything goes, I hear."

"Not entirely." She turned to look at Jeth. "There are two unwritten rules of the Lunahalah: Every new encounter must be consensual, and it must all be forgotten when the sun rises."

"I imagine we'll be witnessing some pretty wild things tomorrow night. I can hardly wait." Jeth rubbed his hands together.

Istari chuckled. "You have no idea. One year, my camel went missing. He was returned to me on the third night . . . and he was never the same."

"Let's hope whatever happened to him was consensual." Jeth snorted. "Speaking of new experiences, what sort will you be looking for tomorrow night?"

Istari bit the inside of her cheek in contemplation. "I haven't thought much about it, to be honest. Who knows? Maybe I'll take a man to bed."

Jeth perked up while Istari scrunched her nose and shook her head in disgust. "Don't reject the idea so quickly, Star. You just haven't met the right one yet. . . ." He raised his eyebrows and grinned.

She eyed him up and down. "I doubt that."

"You can just forget about it afterward."

"Or we can forget about it now." She gave him a push while chortling through her nose.

Of course, Jeth wasn't seriously looking to sleep with Istari. But he was glad to get a laugh out of the Light Mage at any rate. With Ash and Anwarr being absent, living with Istari had been like living with a ghost. She came and went at all hours of the day and night, most of her time spent stashing the shop's excess gold reserves in caches she had hidden all over the city. When she was around, she and he had little to say to one another.

The lull in their conversation allowed Jeth look about the pier. A tall man in black and white robes approached from the corner of his eye. He whipped his head around, but the mysterious figure had vanished. Jeth took a few steps forward and scanned the crowd, but there was no one. About to give up, the figure appeared in his periphery but from the other side. Jeth turned ever so slightly and saw him. The tattooed face and naja teeth strung around his neck. His chest heaved as he shut his eyes tight. *Not again. This isn't real!*

He inhaled a long and slow breath until his lungs were near bursting, and opened his eyes. The phantom in the Overlord's form was gone. *It's been well over a month, and you still see him everywhere!*

"Oh, they're disembarking." Istari pulled on Jeth's sleeve and led him through the droves. He nearly tripped on two shirtless boys running underfoot.

Anwarr scuttled down the ramp and into Istari's outstretched arms. She seemed paler than usual, dark circles under her tired eyes, but her smile beamed through it all. She wore a colorful, form-fitting sarong and a backless top, showcasing her Serpentine tattoo in all of its shimmering splendor. Her hair was partially braided, tied off to the side, and over her shoulder, held in place by a red bandana. Anwarr and Istari kissed passionately while Ash and Jeth gripped fingers and pulled each other in for a quick pat on the back.

Once Anwarr's lips parted from Istari's, Jeth took steps toward her, only to be blocked by a group of pirates carrying a large, rectangular, shrouded object.

"Whoa, what's this?" he asked in surprise.

Pressing her cheek against Istari's, Anwarr cheered, "Guess!"

"The sarcophagus," Istari gasped, leaving her embrace and lifting the shroud to get a look. "You found it!"

"I suppose the job is done," Jeth said, disappointed that he wasn't able to help retrieve it. All the odd thieving jobs he went on in their absence weren't enough to keep his mind off the horrors that followed him, and he hoped a big one with the whole crew would remedy that somehow.

Anwarr slapped Istari's hand, making her drop the covering. "Don't let anyone see it. There are others besides us looking for this thing."

The pirates plunked the heavy stone coffin on the dock, all wiping their brows and breathing hard. "Where do you want it?" one of them asked gruffly.

"Uh . . . I have a storage site nearby where I can hide this thing with a cloaking spell," Istari suggested.

"I know the place," Ash said. "Come on, boys."

He joined the pirates in lifting the sarcophagus while Istari pointed them to where the mounts were tied.

At last, Jeth was able to approach Anwarr. Before he could take her in his arms, she braced him with one hand and doubled over, groaning, like he had punched her in the stomach.

"You all right?" he asked.

She clasped her hand over her mouth and ran for the edge of the dock to throw up into the sea.

Jeth stood there stunned. "It hasn't been that long since I've last bathed."

Istari left the others and went to tend to the vomiting thief. "Ana, what's wrong?"

After completing her final retch, she splashed some water on her face. "Residual sea sickness. . . ."

Istari took her under her arm. "Come and rest up. Wouldn't want you missing tomorrow night. The Odafi coast is the best place to be on the Lunahalah."

"Yes, I could use some sleep," Anwarr said.

"Hey, An, want me to come with?" Jeth placed his hand on her lower back as they walked along the dock.

"Jeth, you should rent a cart to take our bounty to my storage site. I'll handle our girl," Istari said and continued ushering Anwarr away.

"Sure thing," he muttered, looking after them. His guts twisted in knots. *A few hours of sleep and she'll be fine,* he assured himself.

By the next night, the Odafi beaches were alive with music and dancing.

The crew was at an outdoor inn of sorts. Ash and Jeth filled four cups from an elaborate fountain, spurting red wine. On their way to find the women, Jeth asked, "Do you know what's going on with Anwarr by chance?"

"Ankarran food doesn't agree with everyone," he replied. "But you saw her. She's doing better now."

"Not that. I mean, is she upset at me about something?"

"Not that I'm aware. Why don't you talk to her?"

"I tried this morning, but Star stopped me. She said An didn't want anyone to see her looking . . . well . . . less than perfect."

"Sounds like horseshit to me," Ash said.

"That's what I thought. Did she say anything to you . . . on the ship?" he pressed.

A man wearing a taxidermied antelope head in place of his own and nothing below, charged toward a similarly attired fellow. Jeth winced at the jarring conk of the two men clashing horns, the force knocking them both onto their backs where they groaned in pain and laughed hysterically at the same time. Ash guffawed at the antelope-headed fools, almost spilling his freshly poured wine.

Ash presented the pristine beach with his arm. "Look where we are, Fairy Boy. Odafi is home to the most beautiful women in the world, and you are lucky enough to be here on the Lunahalah. Do yourself a favor and don't waste it worrying about one woman's fluctuating moods."

Women wearing revealing sarongs of bright, clashing colors merrily frolicked from one place to another.

"I'll take that under advisement." He nodded while pondering whether Ash and Anwarr had grown closer during their mission and this advice was his way of convincing Jeth to go elsewhere.

They finally found the women on two plush benches under a technicolor canopy. Upon a round, glass table between them was a brass water bowl with floating blue lilies.

Anwarr, looking rejuvenated, waved the men over while in the middle of a story. "I finally had him good and drunk, and he was this close to confessing everything he knew." She made a squeezing motion with her thumb and forefinger.

"Who?" Jeth went to hand a cup to her only for Ash to inadvertently beat him to it. He instead put the cup in Istari's hand in one smooth motion. Ash sat down next to Anwarr, leaving no room for Jeth and forcing him to sit beside Istari on the couch perpendicular to theirs.

"The pirate captain," Anwarr replied. "And wouldn't you believe it?" She playfully tugged on Ash's hair tail. "This one here breaks down the door and embeds his axe into the poor man's spine. I was so livid."

Setting his axe down underneath the couch, Ash said, "I was listening outside the captain's quarters like she asked me to. But, those damn Ankarrans speak like they have a mouth full of rocks. I mistook the man saying 'Come closer so I can tell you' for 'Come closer so I can kill you.' Didn't make a whole lot of sense, but I had to act."

"Hah, maybe I should have come with you two. I wouldn't have made that mistake," Jeth said, pointing to his ear.

Ash guffawed. "Don't forget who the novice is here. Ana told me about that horse diversion with the Tezkhan."

Jeth chuckled along but thought with bitterness, *that's the only real job you've completed since you've been on this crew and you weren't even a part of it yet.* He took a giant swig of his wine, the taste of it souring in his throat.

"So . . ." said Istari. "How did you find out where the sarcophagus was?"

Anwarr grinned. "Ashbedael had to fend off a few disgruntled pirates after he killed their captain for no good reason, but eventually, the rest of the crew submitted to him." Anwarr rubbed his shoulder. "Thankfully, one of the crew members left alive knew enough of the captain's secrets and told us which of the tiny islands in the Naja Archipelago it might be on."

"The northernmost one," Ash finished. "Pirates are in fierce competition with each other to locate the sarcophagus. By presenting it to the Overlord, they'd hoped to gain his favor. Only two crews besides mine knew which island it was on, and one of them happened to have found it."

Anwarr held her cup close to her mouth, but would not take a sip. "As luck would have it, we came across their ship on the way back. With the help of Ash's new pirate crew, we were able to take it. I'm hoping Snake Eye will increase our reward for early delivery."

"Here's to early deliveries!" Istari lifted her cup up for the crew to clink, which they did with gusto.

A woman's angry screech diverted the group's attentions toward the wine fountain. Two drunk men were sidling too close to a woman filling her cup. She splashed one of them with the deep red contents. When the man raised a hand in retaliation, Ash stood, only to find another man of comparable size, march over to intervene. He wore two crisscrossing leather straps over his bare torso and a pole axe at his tattooed back. He wore a knee-length skirt over leggings, leather boots, and a bronze helm on his head. An older man of identical dress, but with a plaited blonde beard, approached the fountain to assist in keeping the peace.

Jeth asked, "Who are those fellas?"

"They're Bahazur," replied Ash, sitting back down and trying not to make eye contact with them. "They get paid to police the Lunahalah to make sure everyone follows the first rule."

Istari reached over Jeth to pat the big axe man on the knee. "Relax. It's not like they want you back or anything."

"There is certainly little chance of that," a deep and eloquent voice sounded from behind them.

They all snapped their heads around to find a tall, ebony-skinned man in colorful, embroidered robes and a high cylindrical hat that Jeth had seen on many a well-to-do merchant in Odafi. Jeth had sensed someone behind them since Ash sat back down, but he didn't think anything of it. Whoever he was, he had the whole crew's heartrates increasing at the same time.

"What are you doing here, Ezrai?" Istari asked.

So, this is the treasure keeper that stole An's heart? Jeth thought with a huff from his nostrils. He was much older than he'd expected.

"I should be the one asking what brings you all to my establishment?"

"You own this place?"

Ezrai grinned, thin-lipped and close-mouthed, yet his pale blue eyes did not smile with him. "I own most of this strip, but don't let that make you feel unwelcome. Enjoy yourselves, drink the wine, gamble, whatever you like. It is nice to see you all again." His insipid gaze locked onto Anwarr. "You have formed quite the crew."

"So you've heard of us," said Anwarr, her usual melodic voice cold as the frost in her eyes.

Ezrai pulled up a chair and sat down in front of the group. "You're known across all the tribes. The thieves that stole from the fearsome Tezkhan raiders . . . even dared to rob the Overlord himself." He turned to Jeth. "And you must be the Desert War Traitor, presumed dead, but now alive by Salotaph's mercy. Or was it Nas'Gavarr's?"

How many people know about that? Jeth scratched the prickles at the back of his neck. "I'm a fast runner," was his only response.

Ezrai narrowed his gaze, studying him in the way everyone else had when confronted with his survival—like they didn't believe him.

"Is there something you want, Ezrai?" Anwarr said.

The treasure keeper put his hands up. "I understand that I'm not the person you were hoping to run into tonight of all nights."

"That's putting it rather mildly," Anwarr replied. "The last time I heard from you, you had sent the Bahazur after me and Istari."

Ezrai exhaled subtly from his wide nostrils. "Yes, well, when you two ran away with over twenty thousand gold from my coffers, I may have overreacted. But, it all turned out well for you. That man is sitting beside you now as your loyal beast. If you wanted, you could send him after me."

Anwarr raised an eyebrow. "Not a bad idea."

"Of course," Ash cut in, putting a hand of warning on Anwarr's thigh. "All the Bahazur on this beach would come to your aid, and I'd be outnumbered."

Jeth instinctively looked around the beach and counted at least four helmed men with tabars wandering through the crowds and one sitting at the bar inside the gambling hut several feet north of where they sat. Standing under the upper floor rooms of the inn was an imposing figure dressed in dark robes, his face and hair obscured beneath a shroud, and looking right at them. Jeth's spine tingled. His imagination was getting the better of him again, and he closed his eyes, hoping the others would not notice the sweat forming on his brow. But when he opened them again the man was still there with his empty stare. He was real this time but too large to be Nas'Gavarr.

Pointing over his shoulder, Jeth said, "What about that big goon over there? He one of yours too?"

Ezrai looked to where he indicated and nodded. "Yes, that's my bodyguard. A man of my position can't be without a certain level of protection." He adjusted his robes, jostling a gold pendant worn around his neck on a long chain that reached his abdomen. The cobra insignia caught Jeth's eye. So those spies were his!

Istari said, "If you want your coin, you'll have to come back later. We don't have it on us at the moment."

"That was a long time ago. I haven't attempted to collect from you since the last time, and I don't intend to now."

"Bullshit," Jeth said. "We caught your spies following us twice now."

"I have no reason to spy on any of you. Ashbedael, tell them what happened the day you returned from your last assignment?"

Ash scrunched his brow in confusion.

Ezrai began, "This man returned to my treasury, tossed a bloody tooth at my feet, and said . . ."

"I said I was not going to rough up young women for you, and I no longer cared how much gold you threw my way."

"And what did I say after you told me to whom the tooth belonged?"

Nobody answered.

Ezrai continued, "'If my Anwarr can sweeten a member of the Bahazur, after losing a tooth, she probably should try to make it on her own.' Then I paid you, even though you didn't finish the job." Ezrai looked at Anwarr. "You have nothing to fear from me, Anwarr. I was wrong to send the Bahazur after you, and you were right to leave. I can see you've done quite well for yourself. You should be proud."

Her eyelashes fluttered, and her mouth twitched. "Just tell me what you want."

"Your forgiveness," he replied without pause.

"I have long forgotten our time together. But, if that is what you need to move on, then you may have it. Now, is that all?"

Ezrai's jaw tightened as he made a quiet huff. "Yes, thank you. Enjoy your Lunahalah." He nodded to each of them cordially before getting up and heading to the bar, his gigantic bodyguard still watching from afar.

Everyone else breathed in deep and then let out long exhalations.

"So, you did knock An's tooth out," Jeth said to Ash. "I thought that was just a running jest between you two."

"It is now." He chuckled. "All I wanted was for these two to give me the gold. Star got in my face, so I manhandled her a bit, nothing too rough. But then Ana came at me from behind with a sword and cut me right here." Ash showed Jeth the underside of his bicep. The scar was barely noticeable next to the black snake winding up his arm. "I punched her out, and that tooth went flying."

Jeth's eyes widened as Anwarr continued, "Then he picked up my tooth, which I thought he was going to give back, but then he ran away with it."

"Not my proudest moment," Ash said. "But, I made it up to her. I came back a week later and showed her how to wield a sword properly."

The group laughed over the story, but Jeth couldn't find it in himself to join. Guilt still gnawed at him for how violent he nearly got with Anwarr back in the stable.

He took a sip of his wine as Ash nudged him hard enough to cause him to choke on it. "Hey, isn't this where you usually add a witty remark?"

Clearing his throat, Jeth said, "Being the only one on this crew who has yet to hit a lady, I'm not one to comment." He took down the rest of his wine and placed it on the glass table.

"I get no satisfaction in hitting anyone weaker than me, be they man or woman," said Ash.

Istari added, "We aren't the delicate flowers you Del'Cabrians like to think we are. There's no reason to treat us any differently."

"I'm not a Del'Cabrian," Jeth corrected Istari. "I only think that being equal doesn't necessarily make us the same."

An awkward silence fell over the crew, remedied by Anwarr setting her still full cup on the table. "Enough sitting around, I need to dance."

She eyed a group of gyrating dancers, draped in sheer fabrics, atop one of the larger tables, and causing quite the stir amongst those watching. "Anyone care to join me?"

"I'm going to get another drink, then I'm off to the gambling hut," Istari said, grabbing her empty cup and rising to her feet. As Istari left, Jeth noticed two young women on the adjacent lounge. They were giggling to themselves, shooting occasional glances their way and shyly hiding their grins with their wine cups.

"What are you boys going to do?" Anwarr asked.

Ash flagged down a shirtless young man in a silk loincloth, his skin covered head to toe in gold paint. He held a basket of water pipes and various substances to smoke in them. "Something I haven't tried before." The young man took one of the pipes and lit the oil flame in the bowl for Ash. "The poppy seed, please, my boy."

"Jethril?" She turned her hip out and wrapped one of her braids around her finger.

Now she acknowledges your existence?

"I'm good here," he said.

Anwarr let out weak grin while glancing at the two other women for a moment. "Are you sure?"

Jeth felt as if he were about to rip in two with one half following Anwarr and the other remaining planted in his seat. *Enough with her games. She gets to seek out other pleasures, but you can't?*

"Go knock yourself out . . . but don't lose any more teeth," he quipped.

Anwarr shifted her weight and brushed her hair from her shoulder. "Hmm, well, enjoy your poppy seed. They don't call it the *Flower of Joy* for nothing." She waved to the two men on the couch and scuttled off toward the dancers.

After a long exhalation, Jeth looked to his right. The woman closest to him was beyond stunning, with smooth, chocolaty brown skin and masses of white curls so tight they grew straight out instead of down, bouncing weightlessly off her shoulders. A bright green and yellow dress wrapped around her body becomingly, where only one sharp breeze need come along and blow it off. Her friend had Anwarr's skin tone. Rosy cheeks and wicked tawny eyes accentuated by dark eyeliner, her form was short and curvaceous under silk robes, her hair hidden beneath a blue hood with a headdress of what looked like bronze coins. Jeth tried not to look too intently at them, but they wouldn't stop staring at him.

While he was pondering whether to offer to refill their cups, the darker one spoke. "Forgive us for eavesdropping, but are you really the Desert War Traitor?"

Jolted by the question, Jeth scratched at his chin and sputtered a reply. "W-where did you hear that term?"

"Just in passing from Del'Cabrian soldiers around these parts, before they were driven out, finally." She rolled her eyes.

"Oh." He perked up. "Did you meet any archers? One with red hair and mustache, perhaps?"

The girls shrugged and shook their heads. The big-haired woman said, "I don't remember what they looked like. One pale-faced, pointed-ear man looks like the next. However, you are quite different."

"Did you actually face the Overlord?" the other woman asked, her voice more girlish than her appearance indicated.

Jeth touched the small scar on his cheek where Nas'Gavarr had cut him with the dagger. He wasn't sure what he should tell them.

"Uh . . . yeah, that'd be me," he said.

Both women shuffled from their couch and over to Jeth's. The one with the big hair said, "I'm Sahadina, and this is Lela."

Lela planted herself on Jeth's other side, cutting him off from Ash who was sitting under a smoky haze.

After Jeth introducing himself, Sahadina continued, "How did you get away?"

"You know . . ." He shot paranoid glances all around him. His gaze fell to Ash only that wasn't who was sitting beside him. Serpent eyes and a skeletal face stared back at him. *'Like a champion!'*

Jeth shuddered and blinked, revealing only Ash laying back against the headrest, lost in an opium induced stupor.

"Tell us!" Lela shook Jeth's attention back to them.

"I-I really shouldn't be talking about it. It's not every day a lowly thief like me escapes the Overlord. I made him furious, and he is still hunting me." Although he was trying to use the element of danger to appear more attractive to the ladies, he was breaking into a cold sweat.

Lela was wide-eyed. "Really?"

Sahadina smacked him playfully on the arm. "If he were hunting you, I think he'd have found you already."

Jeth gulped. He scanned the crowds through his periphery, praying not to find skeletal magi faces among them. The enormous black-clad goon of Ezrai's stood in the same spot. Ezrai himself was speaking to someone at the bar and eyeing Anwarr, subtly grinning while he sipped his wine. Jeth's fear of Nas'Gavarr had now shifted to fear for Anwarr's safety. She and another woman were engaged in a seductive dance with each other. Her breathy laughter beckoned to him, and he began to regret his decision to stay where he was. *You should go over there,* he thought. No, she knows what she's doing. It's not your job to protect her, remember?

With a dry cough, he turned back to the two women next to him. "Well . . . given that I'm still in one piece talking to you beautiful ladies, that's simply not the case."

"You might be full of shit, but I like you," Sahadina said, resting her elbow on the couch's backrest.

"Perhaps it is best not to talk about it. I hear Nas'Gavarr has spies everywhere," said Lela.

"That's ridiculous. He has no need for spies, he can just use spirit magic and read all of our minds whenever he wants."

Jeth's heart leaped into his throat.

Lela giggled. "Dina, it doesn't work that way. Besides, he's too busy invading the kingdom of those dreaded imperialists." She then put her hand to her mouth. "Oh, sorry, that's your homeland."

"Not anymore." Jeth spread his arms over the back of the couch as the girls nestled in closer. Sahadina's perfume was intoxicating, whereas Lela's was a far too strong, but if he scaled back his sense of smell enough, he could tolerate it.

"Poor boy, you must be under constant strain, always looking over your shoulder," said Sahadina.

"All part of being a thief and a traitor," Jeth said.

Sahadina reached for the water bowl on the table and took out one of the blue lilies from it. "Cael petals are just what you need." She ripped three of them off and handed one to her friend.

"Those aren't decorative?"

"Not at all." Sahadina giggled. "You place one of these on your tongue, and you'll be a changed man."

"Are you girls getting bored with me already?"

Lela rejoined, "On the contrary. You might be the least boring one here tonight." Jeth flushed as Lela moved in closer, her fingers gingerly stroking his hair. "Ooh, soft."

Sahadina snuggled up to Jeth as well and told him to open wide. He knew that these women were only interested in him because he was foreign, something never before experienced, to be discarded in the morning, but he didn't care. He'd do anything to escape his jealous, anxiety-ridden thoughts. *It's the Lunahalah for Mother's sake!*

Jeth put his head back and opened up, letting Sahadina place the soft petal to his tongue, and they took theirs right afterward. He had only sucked on it for a few minutes before a soft haze fell over everything, like being in a dream. His hyper senses dampened, all except his sense of touch. Soon, he felt every breeze, the moist vapors from the ocean waves yards away, and the smoke of Ash's water pipe cradling him. He became all too aware of the couch beneath him, the clothing constricting him, the urge to remove them was overwhelming. He closed his eyes, taking in the hypnotizing drone of someone plucking at an oud to the beat of a drum.

Sahadina's fingertips gently grazed Jeth's face, his skin sizzling at her touch, sending an electric current flowing through his veins, and leaving behind a pleasurable warmth. Lela took his earlobe into her mouth, and he wanted to cry out at the sensation.

"Wow, this stuff is more potent than Fae'ren grass," he muttered. He touched Sahadina's shoulder, becoming irreversibly aroused the moment he made contact. The next thing he knew, he was kissing her, then Lela, then the two women were kissing each other.

The three of them carried on for what felt like hours. Before Jeth knew it, they were off the couch and out on the beach. Fire Mages blew flames from their mouths, creating a swirling technicolor blaze so hot, the trio recoiled from the heat sizzling against their oversensitive skin. It brought back images of the sunfire in the temple, and Jeth's breath seized.

That memory was quickly cast aside by the tumblers flipping overhead and swinging from ropes strung between wooden posts. Jeth was so enraptured by their acrobatics he hadn't noticed the girls running into the ocean without him. They splashed about, laughing breathlessly from the salty liquid on their skin. He ran to join them but was distracted by the softness of the sand beneath him. He took to his hands and knees, sifting the cool particulates through his fingers. He remained there, utterly fascinated until the ladies, with their garments soaked through, dragged him to his feet.

"Come, Desert War Traitor, there is more fun to be had. Rooms are free on the Lunahalah," Lela cooed.

"If one is lucky enough to find any available," added Sahadina.

Jeth didn't object to their plan. With the two of them under each arm, they ventured back toward the inn. They ducked under the awning, and a sharp odor attacked his nostrils. *You've smelled that before,* he thought, honing his sense of smell a little further.

Images of the Tezkhan Tribe Lands flooded his mind; jarring and familiar. Jeth's adrenaline pushed through the glorious cael petal haze, and hardened reality forced its way back.

There was no mistaking that stench. *Khat leaf!*

Jeth pulled back his sense of smell to block it out.

There's nothing to worry about. Plenty of people chew khat leaf, he figured. Odafi was the trading center of the desert after all, but a nagging recollection kept surfacing. *'It only grows in the most desolate plains of the Tezkhan.'*

"This way," Sahadina sang, pulling him farther away from the scent.

Jeth slipped out of the two women's grasps and looked around. The partygoers had increased substantially, and he couldn't spot Anwarr anywhere among them . . . nor Ezrai or his goon. *You have to warn her!*

"Hey!" Lela gave him a playful pat on the face. "Don't fade on us now."

Her touch had nowhere near the same effect that it did a second ago. He was somehow instantly and completely unaffected by the cael petal.

"Sorry, ladies, I have to go check something."

"What?" Sahadina whined.

"I'll be right back, don't go anywhere."

They threw their arms up as Jeth dashed into the drunken crowd. He scanned every moving body, listened for any familiar voices. Not finding Anwarr among them, he went to the gambling hut in search of Istari.

She was standing in a circle of men and women carrying on. Half of them shouted obscenities while the other half cheered, spilling their drinks on one another in the process.

Istari yelled, "Come on, fight, you damn useless bug!"

Two scorpions were dueling within a tiny manmade ring encased by the circle of gamblers.

"Star." Jeth pulled her out of the group. "Have you seen An?"

"A little while ago, why?" She took a clumsy gulp of wine and wiped a few spilled drops from her chin.

"I need to talk to her about something important. Where did you see her last?"

Istari looked around the hut, unsteady on her feet. "She was dancing, then she . . ." She trailed off with a few slow blinks.

"Then she what?"

Shaking off her stupor, Istari replied. "Oh right, she was going to get some gold . . . somewhere." She made a weak attempt to look around, then returned to her drink.

"What would she need that for? Everything's free," said Jeth, his guts twisting.

"Maybe she wants to gamble or pay someone to stick a python up their ass, who knows? She can do whatever she wants. It's the Lunahalah!"

"I think the Tezkhan Chief is here."

Istari threw her head back and laughed, nearly spilling her wine all down her arm. "What have you been smoking tonight? No Tezkhan would dare show his face around here, not with all these Bahazur walking about. For Sag's sake, Jeth, you know Ana can take care of herself so stop obsessing over her. . . ."

"Dammit, Star, I'm not obsessing!" he snapped.

Istari placed a hand on his shoulder and leaned in, the smell of all kinds of booze coming off her breath. "We both know that you want her all to yourself, but in Herran, sticking your prick inside a woman doesn't make her yours, so let . . . it . . . go."

"What is your problem? You'd think I was the one who had my way with your camel!"

"I wish that were the case, I honestly do. Because at least a camel can't be impregnated by a man's seed." She threw back the rest of her drink and tossed the cup away.

"What in Sag's name are you talking about?" Jeth's throat started to close.

Istari tapped his forehead with her pointer finger. "You heard me, Fae'ren. Our girl is with child."

19
Remind Me

Istari's revelation hit Jeth like a firm wallop to the side of the head, nearly knocking him to the floor.

The group beside them erupted in cheers and bellows. She turned from him and joined in. "Yes, that's what I'm talking about, right in the underbelly!"

Jeth grabbed her by the elbow and pulled her back to face him. "Anwarr's pregnant?"

Yanking out of his grip, Istari said, "She didn't want me to say anything, but it makes me furious that she'd be this careless. When I find out which one of you two morons did this to her, I'm going to—"

Jeth stormed off before Istari could finish. His sweat had turned cold. *You absolutely need to find her now!*

Ash was right where Jeth had left him on the couch, eyes glazed over with a dopey grin on his face. *Never mind him. Find her yourself. So much for looking out for one another.*

He raced back to the inn where Sahadina and Lela stepped out in front of him.

"There you are," Lela sang as she linked her arm around his and started leading him away again.

The khat leaf stench still lingered in the air. He smoothly spun out of the girls' grasp.

"Sorry, ladies, I have to go."

"Are you not attracted to us or something?" Sahadina accused.

"Maybe he's not attracted to women at all." Lela pouted.

"Oh, I am, and any other night I would prove that to you, but something's come up," he said as he backed away.

"Fine, maybe we'll see if your big muscular friend is busy," Sahadina huffed.

"Yeah, you know what? He'd like that. Go find him."

Sag damn it, An, that baby better be mine! Jeth begrudgingly left the two gorgeous women standing there in disbelief, yet again.

He followed the sharp scent. The farther he walked, the stronger it became until his nostrils stung. He found the dried green substance on the ground where someone had spit some out. Remnants of the stench led Jeth through a quieter indoor area of the inn. He winded around stages where contortionists, showcasing tattoos on every part of their exposed skin, bent their limbs and spine in unnatural ways. He soon came upon a long hallway. Bright red wallpaper with convoluted designs above the wooden paneling dizzied his vision.

Two Bahazur were guarding a door at the end of the hall. Whoever he was tracking had to be beyond it, but there was no way past the guards without drawing attention. He turned back and circled around the building from the outside, finding what he believed to be the room's window. The thick wooden shutters were locked tight, but through them, Jeth heard muffled voices along with the scraping of gold bricks being stacked, a familiar sound since he entered the thieving life.

Pressing himself against the wall next to the window—more to keep passersby from noticing him than to hear better—he honed in on what was being said.

It was Anwarr who spoke, and his heart sank. "It's all there. Now you have your gold, and we are done."

"I told you, I don't want your gold. All is forgiven," said Ezrai.

"Even so, I don't want it hanging over my head anymore."

"Be honest for once in your life. We both know you hold no qualm in taking what is not yours. You certainly weren't quick to pay me back before, even after the thrashing Ashbedael gave you."

"Things change," she said, stiffly.

Ezrai chuckled. "You were always so good at pretending—right up until the very end of our time together. You know just the strings to pull to get exactly what you want out of everyone you meet. But that won't work on me anymore."

"You think I was pulling your strings?" said Anwarr, aghast. "You controlled every aspect of my life, told me who I could dance for, who to talk to, even when to piss and shit!"

"Someone had to keep an eye on you," he shot back. "Left to your own devices you would fuck anything with legs, never thinking about how your behavior reflected on me and my position."

Anwarr released a sardonic laugh. "Yes, I can see how I've marred your flawless repute."

"I've learned a great lesson since then." Ezrai brushed by her comment. "Never trust a harem slut."

A white-hot anger rose up from within Jeth. It was all he could do not to break through the shutters and sock Ezrai in the teeth, but he took a few deep breaths instead. *Trust in her abilities,* Jeth reminded himself.

Anwarr replied in a low voice, "You sicken me."

Then get out of there! Jeth's mind shouted.

He heard the shuffle of a chair as Ezrai got up and moved across the room. Jeth gripped his khopesh, waiting for the sound of Anwarr's distress, but it didn't come.

"If I disgust you so much, then why did you come here by yourself? Is your Mage lover hiding in the corner somewhere, ready to strike me down and steal from me again? Or are you looking to rekindle a flame long snuffed out?"

"Guess again."

"Sagorath knows how much I missed you, how many nights I lay awake, wondering where you were . . . who you were with. It was so hard to let you go and seeing you now . . . it will be harder still." Ezrai's impassive voice was now hushed with a hint of desperation.

"Lay one fingernail on me, and I will slice off your entire hand," she hissed.

Deep, snorting laughter came forth. "I wouldn't dream of it. You're not mine to touch anymore. Alas, you belong to another."

"I belong to no one," she said in a shaking voice. Her heart began to race in Jeth's enhanced ear.

"That's not what I heard. You swore before the Equestrian Gods to submit to your husband." Ezrai's tone was chilling.

Jeth's heart now picked up pace while Anwarr's strangely lessened.

"Tezkhan raids have increased in severity at the Ankarran border recently," he continued. "A wayward chief was looking for something stolen from him. He described the thief as a woman with a double serpent tattoo on her back who claimed to be Saf'Raisha. I knew exactly who he was referring to."

Floorboards creaked from an adjacent room.

Ezrai went on, "You haven't changed a bit. Still throwing yourself at unsuspecting targets and robbing them blind. It's too predictable. One thing I hadn't predicted, though, was you coming to me first. I was planning on getting you alone at some point tonight so thank you for making this easier."

He called out, "She's yours, Chief!" then said more quietly to Anwarr, "Now, we are done here."

A door swung open, and heavy-set footsteps trudged into the room.

Jeth didn't think twice in jamming his sword between the shutters.

"Ezrai, you piece of shit!" Anwarr bellowed.

"As I said before, you never needed to pay me back. The good Chief has already offered what is left of his treasures as a finder's fee for the greatest treasure of them all."

Jeth heard Anwarr run for the door and throw it open, but the Bahazur were still waiting on the other side. "Let me go!"

Bracing his foot against the outside wall, Jeth tried with all his might to pry the locked shutters apart.

"You already have the real Raisha!" she screamed.

"After what you did to me, I was shamed by my people. Nas'Gavarr rescinded our alliance. Without the emerald you stole, he will leave us all in the dust. If I cannot reclaim it, I will never be a true Tezkhan Chief."

"Too bad for you. The emerald's been sold!"

"Then you will take me to the one you sold it to, and I will take you back where you belong!"

"I'd sooner drown myself in the Serpentine River than return with you as your wife!" she spat.

"Wife? Oh, no," Ukhuna said darkly. "A woman as treacherous as you would be the lowest of concubines to the most brutal of my brothers. However, that is not the fate in store for you. Your punishment lies in the hands of your so-called father."

Jeth finally busted the lock on the shutters, and he fell on his backside. He jumped up to his feet and bashed through the now unlocked window. He landed on an office desk as Ezrai backed up against the wall. Two Bahazur were holding onto each of Anwarr's arms while Ukhuna grabbed her by the hair with one hand while wielding a lariat pole with the other.

Not having the space nor time to switch to his bow, Jeth leaped off the desk and onto Ukhuna's wide back, driving his sword through this shoulder. A jarring clank reverberated through his arm. *You should know by now that armor can be worn under robes!* He thought.

Before Jeth could change tactics, Ukhuna threw his back against the wall, squeezing Jeth between his massive frame and a bookshelf. Both men grunted as stacks of papers and heavy brass bookends toppled from the upper shelves, one nailing Jeth in the shoulder. The Chief moved away, and Jeth hit the floor. He sprang back up and charged into him. Without the room for a proper running start, his shoulder buckled by the force, and Ukhuna did not budge an inch.

"Baird? You shouldn't be here." Ukhuna punched Jeth in the face, knocking him back into a large vase in the corner and shattering it.

"Jethril!" Anwarr cried.

"Take her outside!" yelled Ezrai.

Jeth shook off the sound blow as well as the soil from the broken vase. "An . . ." he rasped.

The Bahazur spun their struggling captive away from the scene, but she ran up the wall on diagonal and flipped out of both of their grasps. She didn't hesitate in grabbing one of their upward curving knives and thrusting it deep into his lower back. She tried to kick away the other one, but he caught her leg in mid-air and shoved her back hard, sending her wheeling over the desk and onto the floor behind it. The blade clattered to the floor beside her.

Jeth tried to run to her aid, but Ukhuna, with his lariat pole, caught him around the neck. With a violent tug, Jeth hit the ground on his back. The Chief dragged him across the floor, then twisted the thin rope around his neck another few times, cutting off his airways completely. Jeth struggled to release himself from the cutting fibers, but it only constricted further, splitting his neck's flesh.

A Bahazur had come up behind Anwarr as she recovered from her tumble, and put her in a stranglehold. She kicked wildly, biting the large man's bare arm and drawing blood as Jeth helplessly watched, the cartilage of his own neck cracking by Ukhuna's might.

"An . . ." he mouthed, his voice severed. Flashes of light danced in his vision as his body weakened, Anwarr's struggle fading from his sight.

Then, just like outside the Temple of Sagorath and again with the cael petals, Jeth's focus returned with a sudden fury as if he were honing all his senses at once. He found a broken vase shard on the ground and jammed it into Ukhuna's face. The Chief shrieked in agony and released his grip on the lariat pole.

Jeth unwound the rope, then turned over on his hands and knees to choke back air. Ukhuna roared. The shard was lodged into his right eyeball with blood pouring down his cheek and saliva flying out of his mouth through gnashing teeth. Enraged, the Chief got on one knee and took out his tulwar, about to slice.

Another flood of adrenaline mixed with a familiar spark ignited within him. The Chief's tulwar slowly cut through the air. *It's happening again, like in the snake pit!*

Jeth took his own sword in hand and leaped out of the way. Ukhuna's blade cut through his pant leg just as he kicked off the wall and flipped overhead. The Chief hadn't even completed his swing by the time Jeth made it to the other side, catching his throat in the crescent of his blade, and pulling back hard. Time sped up as he sliced open Ukhuna's throat, spraying arterial blood all over the wall where Jeth had just been a fraction of a second prior.

The Chief's head slung backward against his shoulders. His one remaining eye rolled back, and his mouth gaped in a macabre expression. The giant Tezkhan fell to his side, blood spurting and leaking in between the floorboards.

At this point, Anwarr managed to flip the last Bahazur over her head and onto the desk lengthways with his head hanging over the edge. As she dove for her weapon on the floor, Jeth brought his khopesh down hard over the man's neck and decapitated him in a much cleaner fashion than he did Ukhuna.

Ezrai, his eyes wide, snatched the sack of gold bricks and ran for the exit. Anwarr vaulted over the headless corpse on the desk to get in front of him and pointed her blood-stained knife at his face.

Nostrils flaring, Ezrai said, "Think. You don't want the murder of a Merchant Councilman on your hands. You will never be allowed in Odafi again if you can even escape with your life."

Anwarr was breathing hard, her knife-wielding arm shaking, and her face contorted with fury. "Take your gold and get out of my sight. And if I ever see your face again, I will gut you!"

"You dare threaten me, bitch?" Ezrai snarled.

"A Bahazur taught her how to wield that weapon she's holding, and she just used it to kill one of them, so you might want to do what she says," Jeth said.

She raised an eyebrow, daring Ezrai to make a move. He clutched the bag closer to his chest then looked at Jeth. "You're a fool to follow her. This woman poisons everything she touches."

Anwarr backed away, offering a wide berth for Ezrai to go through the door. He didn't hesitate to do just that.

Jeth nocked an arrow and aimed it at the brightly dressed treasure keeper scurrying down the long hallway. "That's our hard-earned gold he's making off with. I can pick him off from here, just say the word."

"Don't." Anwarr touched Jeth's drawing arm. "The Merchant

Council oversees the entire Odafi marketplace. They essentially rule the tribe. If you kill him, you'll have all the Bahazur hunting you down for the rest of your days."

With a sigh, Jeth brought his bow down as Ezrai slipped around the corner and out of sight. "I have almost every power-hungry leader in the world after me already, what's one more?"

"Why did you follow me here?" Anwarr asked, her tone accusing.

After putting away his weapons, he replied curtly, "Look, I know it's not my job to protect you, but dammit, An. As long as I'm still a part of this crew, I'm going to look out for you, whether you want me to or not!"

Anwarr collapsed into a chair near the desk, tears suddenly welling up in her eyes. "You came for me." She sniffed. "Nobody else did . . . just you. . . ."

"I was the one who could smell Ukhuna. When I couldn't find you—An, what were you thinking meeting him by yourself?" He wanted to grill her about her pregnancy, but he wanted to hear it from her first.

She wouldn't meet Jeth's eye as she scratched at her bruised arm. "I wanted to see if he had really changed. If I came here with someone, he'd continue with his façade."

"And if he had, then what? You'd go back to him?"

"I never go back!" Anwarr snapped.

"Then why?"

She shook her head and sighed. "I had to make sure he was never going to weasel his way back into my life. I had no idea he'd pull something like this."

"You're always talking about knowing your target's weaknesses, but when are you going to recognize your own?" Jeth asked, taking steps toward her. He winced at the sting of his thigh brushing up against his pants.

Anwarr looked to his leg. "You're bleeding."

The ripped fabric was stained red due to a horizontal gash just above his knee. "He must have nicked me."

Anwarr went over to Ukhuna's body. She picked up the fallen tulwar that had been her wedding gift to him. She looked back at Jeth, her brow furrowed.

"I saw you wash it in the river before giving it to him. There can't still be venom on it . . . can there?" he said while wrapping his wound with a ripped piece of his belt sash.

"Water can't cleanse a blade of naja saliva, but over time, it does wear off."

"How much time?"

She swallowed hard. "Depending on how little the sword has been used . . . as long as a year."

Jeth's stomach flopped. "Right. Where can we find some naja blood at this hour?"

Anwarr sheathed the tulwar and strapped it to her back. "I think I know of an Apothecary House somewhere around here."

They left the inn and walked amongst the obnoxious celebrators. A giant snake puppet being carried by a line of people with sticks beneath it blocked their path. With his adrenaline waning, searing pain shot up and down Jeth's entire leg, granting him increasing awareness of every bruise doled out by Ukhuna. *How did Loche take this pain for as long as he did? And his gash was way larger than yours.*

Once the snake puppet passed by, Anwarr took Jeth under the arm, and they walked through the coastal marketplace. Even when they reached a closed thoroughfare far from the raucous crowds, Jeth's head was pounding. He concentrated on the double moons acting as a single beacon in the night sky to guide them. The light fell on the beach as a thin haze, and he realized the effects of the cael petals was returning, hence the unusual pain sensitivity.

The Apothecary House was easy enough to break into. They went to a back room where they set down their weapons. Jeth plunked himself upon a small bed while Anwarr searched through the shelves carrying various jars of powder and vials of liquid.

"Found it." She grabbed a bottle filled with a brown substance then said, "I'll get some water."

The throbbing of his leg counted each second Anwarr was gone. She returned a few minutes later with a water dish, some cloth, and wraps. She knelt down, wet the cloth, wrung it out, and started cleaning the wound, making Jeth grind his teeth in pain.

Clearly sensing his discomfort, Anwarr said in a reassuring voice. "Naja blood has numbing properties. . . . Helps with the pain."

"Good," he murmured.

Anwarr dumped a rather large dollop right into his gash. The substance bubbled and foamed as Jeth cried out every curse he could think of.

"But it does sting at first," she said, biting back a cheeky grin.

She was right. The pain subsided almost as quickly as it came.

"It's good that we're here," Anwarr said as she continued to clean and dress his leg. "The antidote's reaction to your blood confirms there were traces of saliva. You'll be all right now." She took out the tulwar and applied the rest of the antidote to the blade. The liquid bubbled again before she wiped it off.

Without the incessant pain hogging all his focus, Jeth's mind could return to the matter at hand. "Istari told me," he blurted.

"Told you what?"

"Don't act like you don't know."

Anwarr's eyes drifted down as she finished tying the medical bindings around his thigh. "Damn you, Stari."

"Were you ever going to tell us?"

"I wanted to wait until I could confirm it," she said.

A slight relief washed over him. "Oh, so you might not be pregnant after all."

"I haven't bled for well over a month. And if that isn't enough of an indication, earlier today, Istari shone a light up inside me, and she could tell from the color—"

"Oh, that's hardly a reliable test," Jeth dismissed. "Have you tried pissing on barley and wheat?"

"What do you mean?"

"It's what the midwives tell the women to do in Fae'ren. Midwifery is a pretty big deal there."

"Oh? Tell me how it works." Anwarr said with piqued interest.

He scratched the back of his neck. "Uh . . . well, you piss on it, and . . . it tells you if you're pregnant—I don't know. I'm not a midwife."

Anwarr let out an annoyed sigh. "When we get back to Herran, I'll get an ashipu to perform a more reliable test, but I know my body, so I'm going to go ahead and assume I'm with child."

"Alright, alright, that's fine," Jeth conceded, putting his hands out. He then wiped the sweat from his palms on his pants while Anwarr set aside the water bowl and bloody rags.

"So . . . you think it's mine?"

Anwarr froze. She then slowly looked up at him and nodded.

"B-But it could be Ash's."

"I haven't been with him since the day you returned from the waste."

"R-Really? But you were with him the night before that day."

"I drank Rangardian tea right after like I always do. It must be ingested within two days of every encounter. The night you returned a week later, however . . . with everything that was happening, I . . . forgot."

Jeth nodded in recognition. They had spent nearly all their time in bed together in the days before she left for Ankarr, he never did recall her making tea at any point.

His gut wrenched. "I've been such a horse's arse."

Anwarr, still on the floor, put both hands on Jeth's knees. "No, I should have told you as soon as I got back, but I was scared of how you'd react."

"I can't be a father." Jeth was suddenly finding it hard to breathe.

"If you don't want this child then just say so," she said. Jeth could hear her heart rate pounding faster than his. "I can get rid of it."

Jeth clutched her hand on his knee. "Hey, no, I don't want you to get rid of it!"

"You don't?"

"Do you?"

She shook her head. "Any other time, maybe, but, no, I don't want to get rid of it."

"I didn't mean to make you think that I didn't want—it's just wars are erupting all over the world, Nas'Gavarr tried to kill me this year and still might, not to mention your vengeful ex-lover has it out for you now. But, we can figure something out," he said with a nervous chortle, his head spinning so fast he could hardly hear his own words pouring from his mouth.

Anwarr's hand slipped out of his as she used it to stifle a sudden cry. "Oh, Jethril, I don't deserve you."

Despite his stomach flopping about, he almost laughed at her words. "Have you met me? I'm cursed. Maybe you haven't heard."

"Ezrai was right. I am poison. I've tricked more men than I can count and enjoyed every minute of it. And now I'm going to mother a child? If Ukhuna had taken me . . ."

Jeth took Anwarr by the hands and pulled her up onto her knees before him. "But he didn't. Because I was there."

"Ukhuna almost killed you!" she said in a shaking voice.

"He didn't. Neither did Baird, and neither did Nas'Gavarr." He brushed aside her hair from her shoulders. "I can be faster, see farther, and hear better than anyone. Nothing will touch us. My bow and my swords are all I have to offer, and they're yours for as long as you need them," Jeth spoke with a sudden intensity that surprised even him. Beneath it all, however, a painful lump was forming in his gut.

Anwarr nestled between his legs and touched his face. "Let's leave. It doesn't matter where, as long we're together."

He blinked in confusion. "You don't really mean that."

"I can be yours and no one else's," she went on. "I will love and honor you or whatever wives are supposed to do. We can be an actual family. Please . . . let's just go."

"Are you sure that's what you want?" He was now hearing the words he only dreamed he would hear from her, but not under these particular circumstances. It didn't bring him the bliss he had hoped it would, but his heart knew no other course.

Choking back tears, she nodded. "Always forward, right?"

Jeth nodded as well. "Never back."

As he said those words, his airways started to seize up, and his heart continued to race along with his thoughts. *If you stop thieving, will you have enough coin to live off of? You know nothing of being a father. You can't avoid Nas'Gavarr forever. Nowhere is safe!*

His chest tightened even more. He was on the verge of complete panic until Anwarr pressed her lips to his, slow and deliberate, and his panicked thoughts melted away.

Distant whoops and hollers sounded amidst the pops and whistles of fireworks back on the beach.

When their kiss ended, Jeth whispered, "We should head back to the festivities, see what the others are up to."

"Or we could not," she said softly, pulling at his shirt.

"But this is your first Lunahalah."

She wrapped her arms around his neck and burrowed her fingers into his locks. "I will celebrate it however I please, and I choose to spend it right here."

Tilting her head up, Anwarr kissed him again. He sputtered, "What if you forget all about this when the run rises?"

"Then you'll have to remind me," she whispered between kisses. "And keep reminding me every sunrise to come."

With the help of Snake Eye's guards, the crew struggled to carry the massive coffin down the narrow staircase and into the back room.

His reptilian eye, exposed by his hair being braided off his face, glinted with eagerness. He clapped his hands together and sang, "Hello Dulsakh, I've been looking so forward to meeting you!"

With a groaning effort, the six men carrying the heavy stone coffin plunked it down against the wall. Four of them left the room and drew the curtains closed behind them, leaving the crew alone with the ashipu and his Sunil.

"It's gorgeous." Snake Eye gasped in awe while running his delicate fingers across the sculpted lid, dislodging the caked dirt and sand from the likeness of a fierce reptilian beast. "I do hope none of you opened this at any point."

Ash shook his head. "Nope, it's all yours. May I ask what you're planning on doing with it?"

"I'm not paying you enough to worry about it, my Tattooed Titan," Snake Eye replied without pause.

"Fair enough," Ash said with a shrug.

Not taking his attentions away from the sarcophagus, Snake Eye said, "Yemesh, please draw up the notes for eighty thousand gold, split five ways."

The Sunil bowed and went to task. Once done, Yemesh handed Istari the gold notes, and she said, "I'll get these changed right away, but first, I could use a drink."

"I second that," Ash joined and headed for the door.

"We'll be there in a minute," said Anwarr.

Snake Eye finally pried his eyes from the sarcophagus long enough to see the two individuals left in the room with him. "Doll, you look a little ragged. Was it some nasty pirates that roughed you up or the Lunahalah." He winked.

Anwarr started fussing with her hair, tied in a messy bun at the top of her head. "What? I don't . . ." She turned to Jeth. "Do I look that bad?"

Putting his arm around her, Jeth immediately and repeatedly shook his head.

She cleared her throat. "Actually, there is something we need to discuss with you."

"Can it wait?"

"I reckon you'll want to hear this now," said Jeth.

"Well, now you have me worried." Snake Eye finally gave them his undivided attention.

Anwarr paused before sheepishly saying, "I'm with child."

For a moment, his wary expression didn't change then all the sudden his face lit up. "Oh, that's wonderful!" He rushed to take her hands in his. "I take it all back. You look fantastic. How exciting for you . . . at least I hope it's exciting. Are you here because you wish to terminate? I should inform you that I'm not that kind of ashipu."

"I'm keeping the baby," Anwarr said.

"Oh, praise Salotaph. So, who's the naughty culprit?" He moved his eyebrows up and down.

Anwarr didn't answer, only looked to Jeth. "Oh." He kept one brow raised while swathing his eyes over Jeth with a lopsided grin.

"Yeah, so . . ." Jeth scratched his head. "We wish to leave the thieving life and are wondering if you have any jobs you absolutely need us to do before we call it quits?" He hoped that Snake Eye would understand the jobs he was referring to involved the artifacts required to defeat Nas'Gavarr.

Snake Eye looked directly at Jeth. "I may have a job . . . a dangerous one that I was going to send someone more expendable to do, but come to think of it, you might be able to complete it in half the time."

"Go on," Anwarr said.

"I had scouts infiltrating the Herrani warriors laying siege to Ingleheim. They were supposed to gain access to the impassible mountain ranges to perform reconnaissance on some items I aim to get my hands on. However, only one of them managed to return to me alive, thanks to the heroic efforts of a rebel group there."

"Wait a minute, why does Nas'Gavarr want to take Ingleheim after just taking Del'Cabria?" Jeth asked.

Snake Eye shrugged. "The reasons for him invading Ingleheim do not concern me at the moment, only the opportunity it presents."

"So, you want us to go there and steal something before Nas'Gavarr gets his hands on it," Jeth guessed. "Last time we tried something like that, it didn't turn out so well—especially for me."

Snake Eye gave an appreciative nod. "I promise that this time, Nas'Gavarr will be nowhere near you—only Saf'Ryeem—but I'll assign you to a contingent far from him. Even so, what I want you to steal is of no interest to either of them. If anything, you'll be safer out there given that Nas'Gavarr will be returning to the desert, leaving the siege to his son and his generals."

With a sigh, Jeth nodded apprehensively. "Alright then, what is it you want us to retrieve?"

"Do you know what Steinkamp Magitech is?" Snake Eye asked.

"The weapons they use to kill their targets in various horrible ways?" posed Jeth.

"More or less. They are devices enchanted by Essence Mages to be used by ordinary, non-magic users. Steinkamp soldiers have weapons enchanted by every essence except life force. Weapons like that would be very useful to me."

"Why?" said Anwarr. "You don't ask for weapons, at least ones that don't serve a decorative purpose. What are you up to?"

"That is not for you to worry about, Bright Eyes," Snake Eye dismissed.

"Sorry, but I am going to worry about it. I won't have you sending the father of my child off to the land of Steinkamp soldiers without good reason. To face them is death assured."

Snake Eye walked around Anwarr, placed his hands on her bare shoulders, and started rubbing them. "Not to worry. They'll have no reason to come after him." Snake Eye put a hand on Jeth's shoulder as well. "Try not to engage them, and you'll be fine."

"There must be something else he can do," Anwarr pressed.

"An, it's all right," said Jeth, taking her hand in his and rubbing his thumb over the top of it. "I've survived worse. How much more dangerous can a Steinkamp be compared to Nas'Gavarr? The stories about them are probably exaggerated to frighten those who challenge them. If they were actually that deadly, Ingleheim would have conquered every square inch of this world by now."

"That's the spirit," Snake Eye gave his shoulder a pat.

"This is serious." Anwarr brushed Snake Eye's hand off Jeth's shoulder. "I will decide whether he goes or not."

Both Jeth and Snake Eye exchanged glances. Snake Eye rubbed Anwarr's arms affectionately. "Pretty Doll, you should eat something, you are almost as pale as he is." He motioned to Jeth with his head. "You and I can discuss this further at a later date, for now, I wish to speak with Jeth alone."

Anwarr jerked out of Snake Eye's grasp. "Jethril, let's go."

Jeth met her frosted glare with a shrug, not intending to budge an inch, and not able to explain to her why. She huffed dramatically and stormed out of the room.

"I'm going to pay for that later, aren't I?" he commented after she was gone.

Snake Eye chuckled. "My Anwarr is a fiery one, and you just put a baby in her. Good luck with that."

He took a seat on his ground pillows and lit up his water pipe. Jeth sat down across from him. "So, what do you need these weapons for?"

"I have a number of Herrani warriors loyal to me. If my plan to defeat Gavarr is to work, I will need them thoroughly armed." With a puff of smoke from his lips, he continued, "Dulsakh's emerald and bones will take care of the naja. The Bloodstone Dagger was supposed to take care of the human warriors. Magitech, however, will allow my warriors to fight both if my plan is to go awry."

"And what will take care of the Overlord himself?"

With a sideways blink, Snake Eye said, "Why me, of course."

"How do you know so much about this stuff? Have you been to Ingleheim?" Jeth wondered.

"No, but desert tribes used to trade with them a little, before their leader, or the Führer as they call him, murdered all his rivals and used his golems to further isolate his people."

Snake Eye snapped his fingers for Yemesh.

"Yes, Master?" He bowed.

"Hand me my flesh whip, if you please."

The Sunil went to a chest across the room, pulled out a brown leather lash and put it in Snake Eye's outstretched hand.

"The ancient leather that this lash is made from was one of the things we used to trade. My brother and I crafted these by flesh magic back in the day." Without warning, Snake Eye cracked the whip at Jeth. He put his arm up in a flash, the thick leather wrapping around his forearm. To Jeth's amazement, the leather instantly transformed to the color of his skin and fused to it. "What's happening?"

No sooner had he sputtered his question, did Snake Eye squeeze the whip's handle, returning the lash to brown leather, which fell from Jeth's arm.

Snake Eye began, "I've heard they found a way to combine earth magic with this leather so that it can mold to rock and metal as well as skin. They have wind-guided blades that can cut through the toughest of hides, devices that blot out all light in a room. These are just a few of the many trinkets I'd like to add to my arsenal."

"I do this job, then that's it? You'll have everything you need to take on your brother?" Jeth asked.

"You and your new family will be safe and very rich," Snake Eye replied with another puff of smoke.

"When do you want us to head out?"

Snake Eye gave the lash back to Yemesh to put away before replying, "Hopefully, no later than a month from now. I can get you in with the Herrani warriors for the duration. From what my scout reported, there is no easy way into Ingleheim. The one and only pass is guarded by several giant golems and its cliffs are impossible to climb. Saf'Ryeem and his naja will find a way in sooner or later. When he does, that will be your chance."

"But that could take months," Jeth said.

"Yes, it could. You will have to be extra resourceful. If Saf'Ryeem fails, you may have to resort to shooting the golems down with an arrow to the eye like the Great Gershlon before you." Snake Eye winked. "What I can do, is let my General Nadila know you're coming. She has contact with some rebel soldiers in Ingleheim that may be able to help, but I cannot guarantee they will be much use. Improvisation is key."

"Where will I be stationed?"

"In Fae'ren Province. The lands that border the cliffs of Ingleheim. The ones they call the Barrier of Kriegle."

A lump of anxiety formed in Jeth's gut at the very mention of his old homeland. He imagined thousands of naja traversing the forested paths, all the people fleeing in terror. How did Saf'Ryeem plan on feeding all his beasts while camped out there for months on end? He tried not to think about it. He didn't consider himself Fae'ren anymore, and yet his dread about the whole situation clamped down hard on his heart.

"Right," Jeth murmured. He rose to his feet and turned to leave the Flesh Mage to his new artifact. "I should find Anwarr. Enjoy your Najahai bones."

Before he made it out the door, Snake Eye said, "Jeth, I was wondering. Whatever happened to Gershlon after the Golem Wars? The tales don't speak of his feats afterward."

With a dark chuckle, he replied, "Yeah, there's a reason for that."

"Do tell."

"Del'Cabria had agreed to give Fae'ren back their independence as a reward for Gershlon winning them the war. That obviously didn't happen, so he reformed what were known as the Fae'ren fighters to force independence. He lost. His fighters were disbanded or killed, and he was hanged."

"Oh my, that's a shame." Snake Eye broke eye contact.

"Yeah, it is. Anyway. . . ." Jeth sighed. "See you in a couple weeks."

Pushing through the curtains, Jeth shook off a chill as he walked through the water pipe haze toward the exit. *At least this way, Anwarr will have access to a Fae'ren midwife, and they'll have to accept her, even if they won't accept you.* It didn't matter what he wanted anymore.

One way or another, it was decided. To keep Anwarr and his child safe in the long term, Jeth had to finish this one last job, even if it meant facing Steinkamp soldiers, a naja horde, or Nas'Gavarr himself.

Even if it meant that he'd have to go home.

So much for never going back.

20

The Harpy's Punishment

With two semi-conscious Rangarders under each arm, Vidya glided across a narrow strait. The double full moons shining as one guided her way to the Venerra District warp stone mine. They were the last two of the six men she had carried over from the island military outpost. Having already taken care of the night guards, she landed before the entrance to the warp stone crushing facility without incident.

Everything had gone according to plan.

Phrea's father allowed his daughter to spar with the trainees so she could determine their combat skill level while Daphne checked their medical records to ensure none of the candidates carried the female killing disease. The shadow voice in Vidya's head helped her distinguish which of them had hurt women in the past to narrow down their selection. It had been easier than she thought. She'd expected a nation of men deprived of women to treat what few they had left like queens. However, it seemed that as the women disappeared, so did the men's respect for them. The status of women in Rangardia was far worse than Vidya could have imagined. *I will enjoy killing these bastards.*

Phrea came out of the building to help Vidya take the two stumbling Rangarders to where Daphne was waiting with the other four.

Their hands were bound behind their backs, and most were drooling on themselves. One of the bigger ones was passed out cold, lying next to a pile of his own vomit. "Daphne, are you sure you didn't give them too much? They need to be conscious for the ritual."

"It would be easier if they weren't," commented Phrea as she worked on tying up the final two men.

"The Harpy requires they suffer, at least a little," replied Daphne. "Not to worry, though. I brought something to counteract the valerian's effects when needed."

"Let's just hope their cries of agony don't alert the guards at the Citadel," said Phrea after getting up and leaving the last two men to tip over on their sides.

"Provided Demeter hypnotizes them with her song, they will hear nothing," said Vidya.

It hadn't been easy, but Vidya was able to convince her sister to agree to the plan as long as they agreed only to transform Phrea and Daphne for now.

"I hope you're right," Phrea said in a wary tone.

"She'll do it," Vidya reassured her. "She's the only one who can work the gate on the other side, so unless she wants to leave us stranded here . . ." She trailed off, not wanting to tempt fate by saying anything further. The plan had been going smoothly so far. Almost too smoothly, Vidya thought.

"You are doing Yasharra's bidding. These men must be punished," came the snarling voice. She found the winged shadow with its glowing yellow eyes, perched upon a conveyor several feet away from the group.

"I'm going to activate the gate," Vidya said.

"I'll go check on the guards upstairs," Phrea offered, turning and heading up the metallic staircase leading to the offices above.

Vidya nodded and walked to the warping gate on the west side of the room. Taking hold of the protruding handle from the ring just above the crankshaft, she pushed the heavy granite around in a circle until the dais was pointing in a southeast direction. She took out her bag with the warp stone stolen from Nas'Gavarr and placed it in the empty cubicle at the machine's base. With everything in place, she turned the crankshaft until the stone started to hum. It took only a few minutes for the clear liquid energy to splash into existence. *Thank Yasharra you came through, Sister.*

Phrea was returning from the offices when the big man, vomit still smeared on his face, jumped to his feet and sprinted for freedom.

"Hey! Come back here!" Phrea yelled as she rushed down the remainder of the steps and bolted after him.

Daphne stepped to halt him, but the thin medic was knocked on her backside with little effort from the runaway soldier speeding for the exit.

Vidya spread her wings and jumped off the gate platform. She used an air gust to propel herself forward, quickly gaining on the man, flying over his head, and landing right in front of him.

He yelped and skidded to a stop. "You're a siren!"

Vidya smirked. "If only, for your sake." She lunged to grab hold of his arm, but he pivoted out of the way and laid a bracing punch across her face. *Pretty hard hit for someone dosed with three drops of valerian nectar,* she thought. She didn't move an inch from the doorway, only rubbed her aching jaw and searched for blood or broken teeth with her tongue. The Rangarder's eyes widened in shock at how well Vidya took the hit as if having expected her to fly out the door.

"Wow, with a right hook like that, how do the prostitutes you rough up even feel it?"

"Punish him. . . ."

His fist came at Vidya's face again, but this time she caught it in one hand and struck him on the side of the head with her other, intending to knock the thick-skulled man unconscious. Instead, she heard a sickening crack, blood flecked out from the man's eye, and he crumpled to the floor with hardly a grunt. He lay there, motionless, his blood pooling in his caved eye socket.

A throaty titter emanated from the shadow on the conveyer, a guttural mocking for Vidya alone to hear. *"Oops, you killed him."*

"Dammit!" Vidya growled, pulling at her hair.

Phrea ran up to the scene. "Is he dead?" After inspecting the body for herself, she snapped, "Great, where are we going to get a sixth man this late? I knew we should have taken a seventh just in case. This means one of us won't be turned into a harpy tonight!"

"He probably wasn't worthy anyway. Like a coward, he tried to abandon his friends here," Vidya said through the shadow's irritating laughter. "Some soldier you picked out."

"Oh, don't put this on me," Phrea griped. "You don't know your own harpy strength."

It was true. She hadn't been able to fully test her new strength on actual human beings. She was used to sparring with men twice her size and putting all her weight behind every strike. It was not an easy habit to break.

"It doesn't matter now." Vidya sighed and turned back to the other prisoners. "Maybe we can use one of the guards we have tied up."

Phrea scoffed. "They can't fight worth a damn, and we don't have time to test their blood."

"Then we will have to make one harpy tonight and find someone else later," Vidya said.

"It should be me. It's not fair that I get punished for both your mistakes?" Phrea pointed to Vidya and Daphne.

"My mistake?" Daphne's round eyes grew even rounder.

"Yes, you gave him too high of a dose, causing him to throw most of it up. It wore off too fast."

"I measured the dose exactly for his body size. He must have induced regurgitation and played possum so he could maneuver out of the bindings when our backs were turned." Daphne picked up the untied straps. "Maybe if you tied better knots, he wouldn't have slipped out so easily."

"My knots are fine!" Phrea spat.

"Shut up, both of you!" Vidya barked. "It doesn't matter who gets to be a harpy first. The wings take a month to form fully, and it takes many more to learn how to use them. Whether you transform tonight or tomorrow night, it won't make a difference. Just decide between the two of you, and let's get moving!"

Phrea growled and stormed off.

Just then, a red-headed siren emerged through the gate with pursed lips and hands on her hips. "Are you ladies ready yet?"

Demeter looked over to the body near the doorway and glared down at Vidya from the gate platform. "Vidya, what did you do?"

"Why are you assuming it was me?"

Demeter cocked her head.

Vidya glanced at both her friends then back at her sister. "Alright, it was me, but—"

"Yasharra, help us." Demeter put her palm to her forehead. "We will have to make do. Get the sacrifices through the gate while my hypnosis on the Citadel guards is still effective. We have a short window of opportunity here."

The other three women nodded in agreement as Demeter descended the steps of the platform. "Now, where are all the guards I need to touch?"

"Upstairs." Vidya indicated toward the far staircase with her head.

Another important part of the plan was for Demeter to influence the guards to lie about everything that happened that night as well as return the gate to its original position and remove the warp stone after she went back through.

Demeter started making way toward the second floor while everyone else dragged the sedated men through the gate and into Credence. Once everyone was on the other side, Daphne turned the crank several more times to keep the energy going for Demeter.

Vidya spouted off her orders, "You two, dump the body in the sacrificial crevasse then chain three of these men to the effigy. Demeter should have the water and everything else ready. I'll get the feathers."

With that, she leaped off the bridge connecting the gate to the Citadel's second floor. She circled down underneath it, past the gardens, and into the mausoleum below. Only one torch was lit on the wall when she reached the bottom of the stairs. She grabbed it to light her way through the long crypts. Sarta's vault was on the first level. The polished marble plaque looked like it had been placed there only yesterday.

Swallowing the lump in her throat, Vidya placed her torch in an empty holder and grabbed the edges of the vault. With a violent tug, she pulled it out from the wall, then carefully set it down as not to chip the marble flooring. Preparing herself for the stench of decay, Vidya held her nose. The pungent aroma of death floated about the tomb, but she realized, like back in the Temple of Sagorath, it didn't bother her so much. How the corpse looked, however, was a whole other matter. Sarta's beautiful face was now a sunken, peeling rind of what it once was. Grubs wriggled about in her sockets. Her hair fell as dark waves, chunks of it having fallen out from her shrunken scalp and now rested upon her skeletal frame. *Should I not be horrified?*

Vidya wondered. Had her harpy transformation numbed her to the sight of her own decaying mother?

Sarta's cream feathers were all that remained of her magnificence. They had yellowed slightly, but unlike the rest of her, were still intact. "I'm sorry to defile your wings a second time, Mother. But, I do this for Credence," Vidya whispered.

"For the Harplite," said the hunched over creature in the dark corner of the crypt.

Shivers ran up and down Vidya's spine as she took her now empty sack and started filling it with the dried plumage. None of them required an ounce of effort to pluck as most had already detached from the shriveled flesh of her wings.

When Vidya was done, the sound of roaring men and Phrea screaming obscenities echoed down into the chamber.

The guards!

Vidya's heart jumped into her throat as she lifted up her mother's resting place and shoved it back into the wall with an echoing boom. With the bag of feathers around her shoulder, Vidya flew full speed toward the altar.

To her surprise, it wasn't the Citadel guards that had caught them, but a group of ten men with swords and spears in hand, seemingly defending the Harpy and Siren effigies. Vidya was confused as she took flight overhead, but when she got a closer look at the statues, she noticed sticks of dynamite fastened to their bases.

They're here to destroy the effigies!

"Don't let them!"

Demeter's hypnosis worked too well. In allowing the women to perform the ritual without detection, it also allowed traitors passage to the sacred place.

Phrea threw herself into combat mode, punching and kicking soldiers in every direction. She disarmed and brought down two. These men are infantry! Vidya recognized some of the younger ones from training.

One of the men, carrying a torch above his head, shouted at Phrea and Daphne, "Leave this place and put your victims back where you found them, or I will light this fuse."

"Do you think we're going to let you get away with violating Yasharra's daughters?" Phrea roared back.

"We don't follow Yasharra anymore. The Immortal Serpent has shown us the way. He will free us from siren tyranny!"

Phrea came in for the attack, and the man lit the fuse for the Harpy statue before she could reach him. She tackled him to the ground, but he wrestled her into a choke hold. Vidya collected a maelstrom of wind behind her as she nose-dived toward the altar. Every man was knocked violently aside, and all other torches were blown out before the Siren's statue fuse could be lit. Phrea wriggled out of her opponent's grip, grabbed his sword, and severed the fuse before it reached the Harpy's base.

The man screamed and dove for her, but Vidya landed between them, grabbed him by the scruff, and threw him off the altar. The nine remaining Crede men came at her with their swords drawn. Not having her arm blades with her, she couldn't block their strikes, so she relied on her command of the winds to push them away or her wings to deflect their attacks. One of the swords slashed across her left wing, drawing blood and loosing feathers.

Vidya growled and pushed off into the air. She circled around in flight and dove back into the fray, tripping up one man after another. She broke shins, smashed ribcages, and snapped arm bones in half. A few seconds later, all nine men were groaning upon the altar, holding onto their broken limbs, and helplessly dragging themselves across the marble to get away. Phrea had captured the first torch-wielding man from where he had been tossed off the altar, and she threw him down with the others.

Vidya recognized him as Maramus, a young recruit who had trained with her often. Never would she have pegged him as a traitor. A rotten feeling festered in her gut.

"Look at him! He's strong, and the only one left more or less intact . . . Give him to me. . . ."

"Not him," Vidya whispered, shaking her head. "I know him."

"He's an enemy of Credence now. He must die!"

Clenching her fists, Vidya approached Maramus. He gazed up at her, trembling. "Vidya, please believe me. We do not wish to see the status of women lowered like those in Del'Cabria. We should be equals like we would be if we were in Herran."

Vidya crouched down before him and said, "We've sparred many times, Maramus."

"Yes, and I've never held back with you because I respected you as a soldier." He started to crawl backward to get away, but she grabbed his ankle and sharply yanked him toward her.

"And I thank you for that. Were it not for you, I wouldn't be the soldier that I am today . . . well, you and the three who died to grant me these wings. Now, you will be one of three who grant them theirs." She bobbed her head back to Phrea and Daphne standing behind her. "You were at the ritual before. You remember how it works."

Maramus shuddered, cold sweat glistening in the moonlight. "No, no you don't have the authority!"

"I'm sorry, Maramus, but you chose this." Despite the pit of dread growing inside her, she needed this like the air in her lungs.

Vidya dragged him by the ankle, kicking and screaming toward the Harpy's effigy.

"Phrea," she ordered. "Unchain one of these Rangarders."

"Wait! You can't!" cried Maramus as Phrea solemnly went to task.

After Vidya clamped the manacles down on the man's wrists, Demeter emerged from the staircase.

"What is going on?" She gasped. "What are all these soldiers doing here? Vidya!"

"You're just in time, Demi," Vidya said. "These men are traitors. They tried to destroy the effigies in the name of Nas'Gavarr."

"If that is the case, then they must stand trial!" Demeter protested.

"I can't take the chance that the Council will disapprove of using them to create more harpies. Plus, how will I explain all of this to them?" She presented the captured Rangarder soldiers to her sister. "Give these men a chance to testify in their own defense and the Council will learn what we tried to do behind their back. If we are going to do this, we need to do it now, and the Council can never find out."

Demeter looked around at the wounded Crede men, and the quivering Rangarders, then at Phrea and Daphne's pleading expressions. "But, what about the rest of them? Are you going to sacrifice them too?"

"Unless we can hide them until we find another woman willing to be transformed, we will have to send them off the crevasse. At least for now, they can bear witness to the ritual."

"This is monstrous, Vidya, don't do this. Phrea, Daphne, please!" Maramus begged while the men suspended in chains beside him looked on in dazed confusion. "It is our Yasharra-given right that we stand trial before the Mistress of Law and Order!"

"Give him the Harpy's Punishment," said the shadow, perched on the effigy's base in the same position as the statue, looming over the sacrifice's heads.

"But you've denounced Yasharra," Vidya said darkly. "Therefore, it is the Harpy's Punishment you will receive now." She extended her hand to Daphne who placed the sacrificial knife within it. There was no going back.

Vidya moved toward the sacrifices, taking her first steps toward creating her Harplite. "One to love, and one to fear."

21

Cursed

(One Month Later)

A ten-day ride across the vast fields of Del'Cabria and two more days traversing the woodland terrain of Fae'ren Province had brought Jeth and Anwarr to Fairieshome. It was the largest commune in the province. People would come from all over the expansive forest lands to barter their goods, meet friendly faces, and return home ever richer for the experience. Jeth could only imagine what that might be like. To him, Fairieshome was a muddy hovel of a town, modeled after other Del'Cabrian villages. It had been the hardest hit by historical injustices in the region, but it was there they could at least find a warm meal and a semi-comfortable bed.

The two thieves were eager to stop for the night. The farther from the desert heat they had gotten, the more Anwarr complained. It hadn't taken Jeth too long to climatize, but it happened to be the rainy season, and Anwarr did not appreciate the constant cold and wetness.

Wrapped head to toe in a woolen cloak, Anwarr squirmed in her saddle. Jeth didn't require the layers that she did, but he still wore a cloak and hood over his fairy locks and desert attire for the purposes of not being recognized as either Herrani or Fae'ren.

When they approached the commune, they found it barricaded.

"This is new." A pit of dread developed in Jeth's stomach as the two rode up to the man at the gate. Torrent shook her head back and forth, resisting his commands to get closer to the entrance. "I'm right there with you, girl," he muttered.

"From where do you come, travelers?" the burly man asked with the familiar Fae'ren dialect. It surprised Jeth to hear it, as the man had shaved off his locks and no longer appeared Fae'ren at all. This only added to Jeth's reservations.

"Herran," Anwarr replied. There was no point in lying as her dark skin, blue eyes, and white lashes could still be seen under her hood. In addition, Snake Eye had informed them the Herrani had free rein of the Del'Cabrian provinces as part of the treaty, free rein now used by thousands of Herrani warriors to get to Ingleheim's border.

"What is your business in Fairieshome?"

Jeth motioned to Anwarr. "She requires a midwife. Last I checked, any pregnant woman, provided she be on Fae'ren soil, is entitled to one until her child is born."

The big Fae'ren nodded. "Dismount and approach." After they did so, he said, "Please open your mouths."

"Why?" Anwarr looked to Jeth with concern.

"I have to check you for sores before I let you in. As of now, this commune is free of the plague, and we aim to keep it that way this time."

"Plague? Again?" Jeth said with surprise. "You've got to be kidding me!"

"Open your mouths or continue on elsewhere." The man was curt.

Jeth was the first to comply. Once both his and Anwarr's mouths were inspected to the gatekeeper's satisfaction, he told a Fae man to open the tall wooden doors.

"How far has it spread?" Jeth asked.

The gatekeeper shrugged. "From what I've heard, it's been isolated in one of the southernmost communes, same place it started last time."

Jeth took the man's word for it, as he appeared old enough to remember the Second Wave. The Fae gatekeeper didn't allow them to ask any more questions. He ushered them through the gate and swiftly closed it behind them.

Neither Jeth nor Anwarr felt any safer behind the barricade. The commune was more crowded than Jeth had ever seen in his adolescence. It was overrun with Fae'ren, likely having fled the southern areas to get ahead of the outbreak. They mingled with Herrani warriors on their way to the siege. The thoroughfare was a giant mud pit in the center, grime coating the bottoms of men's pant legs and women's skirts as they splashed through it. Livestock was bogged down, pens full of sheep, their wool having turned a sickly brown. Various pungent aromas, some familiar, others altogether new, conglomerated inside Jeth's nostrils and nauseated him.

"And I'm home," he murmured with a sigh.

"I'm cold, and my thighs are killing me. Can we find a place to sleep already?" Anwarr griped.

Without argument, Jeth led their mounts to one of the inns that he recalled had beds free of fleas, or at least they were several years ago. Jeth flicked the stable boy a gold coin, much to his delight, and headed inside.

The plump woman at the front desk with a mountain of fairy locks bundled atop her head, hardly paid them mind as they approached. Then suddenly her eyes lit up. "Oh, how do you do? I haven't seen you in these parts."

"Huh?" One of Jeth's own locks had come loose and was hanging outside his hood.

"What's your family name, lad?" the woman inquired jovially.

Without answering her, he plunked a few gold coins onto the counter. "Do you accept these?"

Looking down at the Herrani gold, she replied, "That will fetch you a room with a fireplace on the top floor. You both look like you could use it." She pushed the coins back toward him with a warm smile. "But not to worry, dear. I just need your family name, and you can go right on up."

Jeth pushed the coins back toward the innkeeper. "Top floor then. Please and thanks." The woman's expression soured as she took the coins, saying nothing as they continued past her and up the creaking staircase.

When they found an empty room to their liking, Anwarr immediately tore off her damp cloak while Jeth set down their bags, along with his weapons, then went to light a fire in the hearth.

"Great," Anwarr huffed. "You agree to this dangerous job in volcanic mountain ranges while leaving me to rot in this disease-ridden shithole."

"Are you daft? I'm not leaving you here," Jeth said. "It's just for tonight. I wasn't counting on the plague making a comeback. We'll have to go to Lanore, farther east. It's close to the Deep Wood and more isolated. It was one of the few places that had been spared the Second Wave."

"But didn't you say Fairieshome has the best midwives in the world? Now I have to spend the next few months in the middle of nowhere with an inferior one?"

"You can see the worst midwife in Fae'ren, and she would still be ten times more competent than anyone you'd find back home. I promise you'll be in good hands." Jeth struggled to keep his tone controlled. *She's carrying your baby, she's carrying your baby,* he reminded himself repeatedly as he stoked the flames. She had been nothing short of impossible for nearly the entire trip, and she wasn't even that far along yet.

Anwarr sighed heavily and plopped herself onto the bed. "I'm sorry. We've been riding for too long. I'm exhausted and freezing. And why is everything wet? It's just strange being this far from the desert. I'm not used to being such a . . ." She paused to hold her head, her face scrunching in pain.

Jeth attempted to finish for her, "Such a——"

"Don't say it," she warned.

"Outsider?" Turning from the fireplace, Jeth started taking off his own clammy clothes. Anwarr met his eyes and nodded thoughtfully.

"Welcome to my world." He made a sweeping motion with his arms.

Anwarr giggled and put her feet up on the bed. "You lived in this town?"

Sitting on the bed next to her, he took both her legs and placed them over his lap so he could start rubbing them down. "For a little while, until too many people figured out I was cursed."

Anwarr closed her eyes and moaned as he massaged her calves.

"I don't understand," she said. "The innkeeper treated you like family returning from a long absence, and yet you dismissed her. What was all that about?"

"It's hard to explain," he began as he worked his way to her thighs. "At first, people here will assume you're like them and will treat you accordingly. Then they always end up asking that question I don't have an answer for."

"Your family name."

He nodded. "I haven't been able to find out what it was. So many people died back then. It wouldn't have mattered who my parents were. Their name is forever cursed and therefore so am I."

"Couldn't you have made one up? People in Herran do it all the time." Anwarr winced when Jeth reached her inner thighs.

Jeth chuckled. "Oh, I tried all sorts of things. Sooner or later, you get found out. People gossip, fake names get around, or you make the mistake of revealing your borrowed family name to someone from that family. Without any skills to offer or goods to barter, there was no point in staying."

"It doesn't make any sense," said Anwarr. "They have the nerve to send you away to find fame and fortune in faraway lands while the rest of them sit here in muck and misery. They have no idea what they threw away."

Anwarr's previously frosted gaze warmed considerably, and Jeth found himself reddening at her kind words, a rarity in the last week. "What can I expect from my people? They don't know any different."

"That's no excuse." She entwined her hands in his, stopping the massage. "If your people spent less time shunning their own and more time standing up to their real enemies, they wouldn't have to worry about cursed orphans in the first place."

"The Fae'ren have fought back once before. Most of them were killed. Now all that is left are those too weak or too afraid to do anything about it."

"Do you miss this place?"

"Doesn't matter." Jeth shook his head. "Tomorrow, we'll find you a midwife, then I'll head over to the Barrier of Kriegle, and return richer than we've ever been. Soon, we can settle anywhere we want."

Anwarr pulled Jeth's face toward her and kissed him. They maneuvered under the old woolen blanket and lay on their sides, facing each other.

"I have a terrible feeling, Jethril. I don't get why Snake Eye wants this Magitech, and I feel like you aren't telling me everything."

"It's really not as dangerous as he made it seem." He brushed a few strands of her hair, curled by the humidity, behind her ear. "It'll be fine. No Steinkamp is going to get me. They'd have to catch me first."

"You won't even see them coming, that's how they eliminate their targets. It doesn't matter how fast you are."

"I've spent all of last month learning to activate my focus and speed. It's just like honing any of my other senses," he reminded. "Granted, my speed is a little unpredictable, but I can count on it when it really matters."

"That's all well and good, but what if something happens to the baby while you're gone? What if something happens to both of us and our child becomes an orphan in a place that hates them?" Anwarr's voice was shaking.

Jeth didn't let his mind go there. No one spoke of what happened to parentless newborns in Fae'ren. It was rumored that they were given back to the forest, but only if the parents' deaths could be confirmed. Even in cases where the parents were believed dead, many midwives didn't have the courage to dispose of the child in the off chance someone could return to claim it. To harm a child not actually cursed brought even greater misfortune on the perpetrator than the cursed child would have. Such were the complications inherent in Fae'ren superstitions, and they made less and less sense to Jeth every day.

"Will you stop? Nothing is going to happen to us or our baby. The chances of you dying in childbirth here are so slim that it's not even worth worrying about. I'll be back well before the birth, I promise," Jeth said, kissing her forehead.

"Don't go," Anwarr whispered. "Forget the job, let's just take the gold we have. We can make it work."

Jeth's gut wrenched. *If I don't finish this job, Nas'Gavarr will find us, and he will finish what he started in the temple, he wanted to confess,* but instead, he said, "You know I have to. Trust me. We'll be better off this way."

Releasing a quivering sigh, Anwarr nodded and cuddled in closer to him. While holding her, his twisting guts refused to unwind. He hated seeing Anwarr so scared and wondered what happened to the fearless thief he had fallen for. The last time she worried this much about him leaving, he went on the job that had almost killed him. *Just get to Ingleheim, grab that Magitech, and return it to Snake Eye. Then that'll be it.*

Anwarr's heartbeat eventually slowed as she fell into slumber. Jeth, on the other hand, was far from asleep. Rain pelting on the roof sounded like thousands of rocks falling from above, burying him alive. When the rains finally stopped, he tried to tune out everything else but to no avail. The constant hacking coughs of patrons below or in homes nearby brought the fear of an outbreak back to the forefront of his mind. Every laughing howl of one drunken lout or another was like a stab through the eardrum, shocking him back to full alertness each time. *When did this place become so damn loud?*

One voice, in particular, stood out above the others because of his familiar dialect. "I know it was you, Fae bitch!" a Herrani man menaced.

"You have me confused with someone else," said a woman whose dialect indicated she was Fairieshome born.

"Yesterday, I received your services, which I thoroughly enjoyed, and paid you what you were due, but when I left, ten additional coins were gone."

"That wasn't me!" she insisted.

At that, Jeth was out of bed and heading toward the window. He opened the shutters a crack, rainwater dripping down on the sill.

A tall man with a shaven head, wearing the black brigandine armor and tan pants of a Herrani warrior, was following a short-statured Fae woman down the muddy streets, across from the inn. Two other men ambled behind him, seemingly to back him up.

"You take me for a fool, whore?" he growled, catching up to her and grabbing her arm. "Either give me back the coins or services of the same value. Your choice!"

"I have no coins . . . someone help!"

A shorter Herrani leaned against a support post of a nearby building. "Should have thought about that before you swiped his gold."

A burning rage bubbled up inside Jeth. Everywhere was the same. Everyone was the same, there was no getting away from it. *I'm getting awfully tired of this shit.* Jeth looked over to his bow and quiver resting against the wall near the hearth. One arrow could frighten the men enough for them to move on, but could also alert them to his and Anwarr's location for possible retaliation.

"Let me go!" the Fae woman hissed, struggling to get out of the Herrani's grip while everyone else passed by, pretending not to notice.

"I've had enough of you thieving whores back home," he snarled. "You think I'm going to take this from a Fae?" The woman clawed at his face, and he reacted with a bracing backhand slap, casting her hard into the mud as the other two men snickered. *That's it!*

Jeth threw on his smock and took only one of his khopeshes before quietly exiting the room. He stormed out into the moist, night air.

"Please, don't hurt me," the woman cried. "I have a young son. I'm all he has, by the Mother Oak, please!"

She tried to crawl away, but he bent down and grabbed her roughly by the arm. "Not my problem!"

"Hey, Baldy!" Jeth barked.

With the Fae woman's arm still within his grip, he and his friends turned to Jeth.

"Mind your own business, little man," said the scrawny Odafi man with a nasal voice.

"You've got the wrong girl, the one you're thinking of is in that new brothel around the corner where those stables are," Jeth pointed east. "She swiped eight gold from me last week."

The bald one looked to where Jeth pointed, then down to the woman. "Oh . . . really?" He carelessly tossed her back into the mud. "It's so hard to tell. You all kind of look the same. Can you show me to this new brothel?"

"I'd be delighted." Jeth clenched his fists as he approached him. "It's right this way."

He cracked his fist against Baldy's face and followed up with a few more before the other two warriors intervened. Scrawny swung at him, but Jeth caught his wrist, pivoted around him, and twisted the arm behind his back before using the momentum to fling him into the mud. Shorty charged at Jeth, bashing him into the post. Rainwater from the eavestroughs splashed over their heads. He slid down the post, out of the man's grip, then kicked his legs out from under him before elbowing him hard in the head once the man was on the ground. The woman clambered to her feet to run away, but Baldy grabbed her and forced her back into the mud. Jeth was on his feet running for Baldy when Scrawny, from the ground, threw a knife at him.

A spark of adrenaline ignited and the knife slowed in mid-flight. Jeth snatched it out of the air with ease, spun around and tossed it into Scrawny's right shoulder. Through the man's screams of pain, Jeth dove for Baldy and took him down. Baldy grabbed a handful of Jeth's loose locks and met his face with a headbutt. For a split second, everything went white, and he could feel blood running down his nose. With a roar, he activated his focus, blocked the Herrani's next strike, and punched him in the throat, sending him right back down into the mud. Jeth's fists came in hard and fast on the man's face until bones crunched beneath his welted flesh. He didn't stop until his fists were numb and the man beneath him moved no more.

While pushing himself off the unconscious Herrani, Jeth's heart pounded in his throat. Shorty sat near the post in a daze while Scrawny crawled, moaning through the mud to get away or get help.

The Fae woman rose to her feet, her eyes red and raw, mud caked to the ends of her locks kept under a white bonnet.

"You all right?" Jeth asked her, out of breath.

"You're a—why are you dressed like them?" she sputtered.

Looking down at his Herrani attire, he shrugged.

She eyed the sickle shaped scimitar hanging from his belt. "You're here for the siege. You're helping them."

"Not exactly. . . ." He stepped toward her, and she took more steps back. "I won't hurt you," Jeth reassured her.

"You're cursed," she said in a shaking voice.

A small group of onlookers began to gather around the scene, some Herrani, others Fae'ren, all of them staring at him and whispering to each other.

"Who is he?"

". . . 'bout time someone took care of this Herrani menace."

". . . *cursed.*"

Jeth's heart sank, having forgotten how alienating it was to be back in his home province. "Just get home safe, alright?" he muttered as he turned to walk away.

"I'm cursed too," she blurted.

Jeth turned back around to see a much warmer expression on the Fae woman's face. She looked around at the onlookers, hugging her arms and sinking into herself.

"Do you need me to walk you home?" Jeth offered.

She met eyes with him and nodded, and the two of them walked side by side around the corner and out of sight of the curious crowd.

Jeth wiped the blood from his nose and said, "I've, uh . . . never met another cursed before."

"We are hard to find. I'm Henna," she said.

"Jeth."

"I take it you left at a pretty young age. May I guess to Herran?" Henna probed, continuing to hug herself as they trudged down the muddy road.

"Ludesa first, Herran more recently. I'm not really fighting with them. I'm just—"

"You don't have to explain," she said. "Why not fight for the Herrani? It's not like any of our people would fight for us. They were happy to assume that I was a cursed prostitute thief like those men thought. I don't know why you helped me, but I am grateful you did. It's so rare to see one of us fight so well. Those men didn't know what hit them."

Jeth became more aware of the blood caked between his knuckles. He wasn't sure if he should tell her that he did it primarily to release all of his pent-up anger and relieve his anxiety more than to help her. It frightened him to know how good it felt.

"Why haven't you left?" Jeth asked, putting his bloodied hands into his pockets.

Henna brushed a loose lock behind her pointed ear. "I don't know. We've learned how to get along here for the most part, and I can't imagine living anywhere else."

"We? You and your son?"

"Yes, Ellion. He's half Del'Cabrian, so he didn't inherit the locks. When he's older, he may pass for an urling and make a place for himself."

"Then what about his father, won't he help you?" Henna's lips formed a thin line and her jaw tightened. *What would a Del'Cabrian want with a Fae bastard, you idiot?* He thought.

"I don't know where he is," was her only reply.

Jeth didn't know what else to say until Henna stopped at a ramshackle storage shed beside a barn.

"You live here?" Jeth said aghast. He too had lived in a shed outside a barn at Talbit's ranch, but it was a palace next to what he was looking at now.

"It's not much, but it's been abandoned so there's no one to chase us out.

Would you like to come in? I was going to cook a warm broth. You look like you could use some."

The thought of anything warm flowing down his gullet was beyond tempting, but he worried about Anwarr waking up and finding him gone. "I'd love to, but, I should be heading back."

"Are you sure? At least come in and wash up," she urged as she unlocked her rickety wooden door and shoved it open. The movements of at least two other people knocked about inside the tiny abode.

"Momma!" A small boy ran out the door.

"Yes, Little Pumpkin, I'm back." She scooped up the toddler into her arms and kissed his chubby cheeks.

A strange tingling sensation flowed over Jeth's chest as he watched the little boy clinging to his mother's locks.

Henna turned back to Jeth. "There must be something I can do to repay you."

"Well . . . I'm about to have a child of my own soon. Maybe you can give me some advice, given that I have no idea what I've got myself into," he said with a nervous chuckle.

"I'm not the best one to be giving out parenting advice, but I remember something my own father said before he died. 'A father's duty is to provide for his children what he never could for himself, and through that, he ensures each generation is stronger than the last.' The plague robbed my father from doing that for us, as it did for so many others. My only wish is that I can do it for Ellion, that he may be stronger than me, and his children stronger still."

Jeth nodded and started ambling away from her door. "I'll keep that in mind. Thanks, Henna. Take care of yourself, aye?"

"Same to you, Jeth." She smiled and with her son in her arms, disappeared behind the rickety door.

It began to rain again as Jeth jogged back to the inn. Avoiding the road where he had caused the scene, he returned to the room to find Anwarr still sleeping peacefully.

He found the basin in the corner and turned the water within it brownish red after washing the dried blood off his fists and mud from his locks. Exhaustion finally took hold as he came down from the rush of the fight. Stripping out of his filthy smock and pants, he climbed back under the warmth of the covers.

Anwarr turned over in the bed, away from Jeth as he settled in behind her. "Where did you go?" she mumbled groggily.

"Just taking a piss." He wrapped his arms around her and pulled her warm body up against his. Henna's words only served to make him more anxious. *'Provide for his children what he never could for himself.' Where do you, a man who has virtually nothing, even start?* One thing was for certain; running away, no matter how tempting Anwarr made it seem, was not going to work anymore. *That's all our child will ever know. I can't let that happen. . . . I won't.*

22

A Harpy's Hands Are Never Clean

Vidya floated outside her body as she walked toward the Council chambers. The Archon had called an emergency meeting and demanded Vidya be there specifically. It had been almost a month since the ritual that turned her two best friends into harpies, and now suddenly the Council wanted to see her after all this time.

She and Demeter had been meticulous in covering up any evidence, and the rainstorm caused by the ritual had washed away the fresh blood. Even if they had left some trace behind, it would be attributed to the annual sacrifice that took place a few days before theirs. They had thrown the traitors down the crevasse, their remains having long been washed out to sea, and Phrea and Daphne had been undergoing the rest of their transformation in Vidya's dorm room where nobody but herself ever went. As far as their commanders knew, Phrea, along with Daphne were still on hiatus in Rangardia visiting Phrea's father.

They can't know . . . unless Demeter didn't fully hypnotize the guards and one of them reported the incident, but why now?

Pushing her worries from her mind, Vidya opened the double doors to the Council chambers and walked across the floor, her boots echoing off the tile. She took a seat next to the secretary at the lower table to the sirens' left.

"Thank you, Vidya, for meeting us on such short notice," Xenith said.

"It is no trouble." She tried her best to keep her voice from betraying her uneasiness.

"I'll get right to it then," Xenith began. "Our spies on the mainland are reporting that Nas'Gavarr has passed over Del'Cabria and is laying siege to Ingleheim."

Vidya nodded, relief washing over her.

Xenith continued, "As you may be aware, Ingleheim is historically impossible to invade, and yet Nas'Gavarr believes he can. From what you've seen of him already, can you provide any insight into why he would do this?"

"I don't know," Vidya stated.

The Archon sighed, casting a gray strand of hair from her shoulder. "We must make use of your wings once again."

"How can I be of service?" Vidya was now confident Xenith held no knowledge of the ritual.

"We need you to fly to the siege, find out why the Herrani are there and what their Overlord wants with the Ingles."

"May I ask why? Wouldn't it be better to have his sights set on them instead of us for the time being?"

"That's exactly why I want you out there," Xenith declared. "He started a war with Del'Cabria, effectively won that war, then just leaves them alone. Even going as far as signing a treaty. What does Herran get out of such an arrangement other than peace they would have had anyway had he not antagonized them in the first place. None of this makes any strategic sense, even for a man who revels in war for the sake of it."

"I've watched him for months. He is on a plane that we may never understand. There is no use in identifying his motivations at this point. We just need to destroy him and be done with it," said Vidya.

"That's all well and good," joined Althea. "But unless we gather insight into what he wants from Ingleheim we may never find out what he wants from us."

"Why not send regular spies to collect this information?" Vidya asked with frustration.

Xenith replied, "Because we don't just want you to collect information from the Herrani, but the Ingles as well. The spies we did send have not been successful in gaining access to their mountain ranges. You can fly right over them, seek an audience with their leader, and formulate an alliance."

"So now you will join with the mainlanders?" Vidya said. "The Ingles treat their women almost as badly as the Del'Cabrians."

"We will work with who we must to protect this republic. Ingleheim has a history of isolationism. They are not likely to interfere with our ways, but could prove to be a powerful ally against our common enemy and Del'Cabria, if they ever try to expand again."

Vidya bit the inside of her cheek and nodded. Xenith was right to at least try joining with Ingleheim, if temporarily, but the snarling voice beside her didn't agree. *The Führer is a man most monstrous. He can never be trusted.* The hairs on the back of her neck stood on end at how the creature could assess a man's character without Vidya herself knowing anything about him.

With a nod, she settled, "You make a fair point, Archon. Is that all?"

"For now. Report to the Supreme Commander for more details."

Vidya rose from her seat and bowed. "As you wish, Archon, Council."

As Vidya turned around to leave, Xenith cleared her throat. "Vidya, before you go . . ."

She turned back around but didn't sit. Her fingers twitched at her side as she waited for Xenith to continue. "I trust that you are prepared to follow orders this time."

"I-I've always followed the Council's orders. . . ."

"We know what happened in Rangardia," Xenith's stern voice echoed off the pillars.

Vidya's throat seized. All she could do was glare at her sister who refused to make eye contact. "You told them?"

Demeter opened her mouth to reply, but Xenith spoke first. "She didn't have to. Señor Ricardo sent a message to me personally. You had no business being there in any diplomatic capacity. I know Demeter requested you go with her, and she has been reprimanded for that oversight." Xenith gave a disapproving look over to Demeter before returning her harsh gaze to Vidya. "But your disrespectful and violent treatment of our most trusted ally, especially after the warning we gave you from our last meeting, makes me wonder if you are truly fit to serve Credence at all. Consider this mission to Ingleheim a second and final chance to prove that making you was not a mistake."

"My deepest apologies to the Council. I lost control that day, but it will not happen again—"

"Be sure it doesn't." Xenith's tone was now as cold as her steel gray stare. "Harpies are made . . . and they can be unmade."

"The Harpy shall never rule Credence again." The creature tittered sinisterly in Vidya's mind. For a moment, she thought about telling Xenith about the voice, about what it knew. Maybe she would understand—maybe she could make it go away. But Vidya didn't attempt to open her mouth. The shadow harpy was a part of her, and she could never betray it. Yet she was terrified of it.

Vidya bowed to the Council, muttered another empty apology, and left the chambers.

Vidya flew back to her apartments to check on her harpy sisters in transition.

When she climbed through the window, Phrea flew up in a fright and backed herself into the upper right corner of the room, while Daphne remained motionless in her cot along the opposite wall.

"Shit, Vidi, can't you use a door like a normal person?" Phrea spat.

"I'm not entirely a person anymore, and neither are you." Vidya closed the shutters and drew the curtains. "Come down here, let's see how you're coming along."

Phrea slid back down the wall, then lay on her stomach upon her cot.

One-third of her soft gray down had given way to elongated feathers as jet black as the hair on her head.

"In another week, you should be able to sustain flight," Vidya said.

"Thank Yasharra," Phrea replied. "Being cooped up in here has not been easy."

"Must be easier than the first week though." When Vidya had undergone her transformation, her wing exit wounds wept for weeks, staining countless linens with blood and suppurate. And the pain had been ceaseless.

"I've been holed up in this room with a medic who has stashes of opium. I do all right." Phrea chuckled.

"I wasn't so fortunate," Vidya said, looking to Daphne still sleeping, her light brown wings wrapped around herself, moving up and down with every breath.

Phrea waved her hand as she rolled up to a seated position. "Daphne took most of it. I wanted to feel as much pain as I could stand. It reminded me of my new purpose. Seeing to the suffering of the enemies of Credence means little if you haven't been made to suffer yourself."

"I felt the same way when I was going through this," Vidya said, taking a seat on her own bed across from Phrea's cot. "I thought it would be strange to not be the only one anymore, but I'm excited to finally share this with someone."

"I can't imagine having to do this alone," Phrea condoled.

The two women sat in comfortable silence for a time, but Vidya could no longer wait to ask the question that had been on her mind for weeks. "Have you started hearing . . . the voice yet?"

"Voice? What voice?"

Vidya inhaled a shaky breath. She had hoped her friends would have told her about it on their own, but perhaps they were scared, as Vidya had been. She was disheartened that her shadow companion was still something unique to her.

Changing the subject, she said, "Never mind. I came here to tell you that I've been ordered to return to the mainland. I'll have to find a way to take you both with me. There, you can learn to fly and command the winds without Crede witnesses. Then we will formulate a plan to gradually make more of us."

Phrea snorted. "That will take a while. With any luck, Nas'Gavarr will die of old age before then."

Vidya released a knowing chuckle.

A light rapping on the window shutters made both Phrea and Vidya jump. Vidya opened them to find Demeter, of all beings, perched on her windowsill, the afternoon sunlight bouncing off her brilliant blue-white feathers.

"Demi?"

The siren hastily ducked into the room and closed the shutters behind her.

"How is everything going?"

"You shouldn't be here. It looks suspicious for a Siren Councilor to be hanging around a military dorm," said Vidya.

"Oh, relax," Demeter dismissed. "No one saw me, and who are they to question? Can't a siren once in a while pay a visit to her harpy sister?"

Vidya crossed her arms. "Why are you here?"

"We need to talk."

"For the last time, Demi. There's nothing to talk about. We got away with it," Vidya said.

"It's the male uprising that has started to worry me. It's what Nas'Gavarr was trying to incite the day he killed Mother. It has got me thinking . . ."

"Oh, that is not for you, Red," Phrea quipped from her cot.

Demeter cast the new harpy a snooty glare and continued, "I was thinking, that all our commanders were in that chamber and heard what he said. What if one of them took it to heart and has been passing the message on to his men? The ones we killed that night were infantry."

"You may have a point there," Daphne piped in with a stretch and a yawn. *When did she wake up?* Vidya wondered.

Daphne smoothed her short hair, sticking straight up, and continued, "That pathetic attack on the altar may go all the way to the Infantry Commander, perhaps the Supreme Commander."

"Do you really think our own military could turn against the republic?" Vidya asked. "The commanders have been charmed by every siren they've come in contact with. They can never act against the Council."

"That's what I thought at first," said Demeter. "But I don't recall seeing any of them being touched lately. You know the influence wears off after a time. Ever since Ricardo, I'm beginning to wonder how many other men around us have been artfully avoiding the siren's hand."

"Well, you know what to do, Red. Get out there and start touching those bastards," said Phrea.

"I'm not sure it will be that easy anymore," Demeter replied, worry lining her forehead. "We need to warn the Council."

"And what are you going to tell them? How we witnessed an attack on the Grand Altar in the middle of the night when none of the guards can corroborate, then we waited almost a month to mention it for some reason that we cannot say?"

"Surely, we can come up with some reason for us being there. If we ignore this for any longer, we are putting the republic in even greater peril. Do you want the only female-ruled nation in the world to fall?"

"Of course not." Vidya unfolded her arms and paced around the room. "I just never thought you to be one to care so much."

"Why else do you think I ran for Council? For the entertainment?" Demeter spat. "This is my Credence too. And it will be my children's after me. I won't have it ruled by men, and I refuse to see my daughter answering to them as they do on the mainland!"

"I promise, it won't come to that," Vidya said in the most calming voice she could muster. "But we can't tell the Council without implicating ourselves and halting our progress thus far."

"Well, we can't do nothing! What if there is another attack? You can't make more harpies if the effigy gets blown up. Worse still, next time there may be innocent casualties!" Demeter said with a fortitude Vidya had never seen from her.

Maybe she had underestimated her sister. *Does she care about the people of Credence or fear for her own charmed life? It's not like this is the first instance men have tried to take control, and it certainly won't be the last.*

The harpy's shadow took form in Vidya's periphery. It leaned against the doorframe of the lavatory, mostly hiding itself behind it. *"Men will always misbehave . . . a harpy's hands are never clean."*

"We don't tell anyone," Vidya said. "We will see how this plays out."

"You can't be serious!" Demeter said, incensed.

"Let the men rebel. That only means more sacrifices, which means more harpies."

Demeter kept shaking her head in disbelief.

Vidya said, "Phrea, Daphne, I change my mind. You're not coming with me to the mainland after all. You're going to look out for the next male uprising, and you're going to make sure it happens."

"What?" Demeter's feathers puffed as if hit with a cold wind.

"And what are you going to do out there?" Daphne asked.

She was supposed to make friends with the leader of Ingleheim, but what she really needed was a weapon that would allow her to store the blood of the traitorous sacrifices until she needed it.

"I've got a Bloodstone Dagger to retrieve."

23

A Place Where You Truly Belong

(Three and a half months later)

The first rays of sunlight Jeth had seen in days peeked through the impenetrable ash clouds of the Ingle skies as he drove his cart filled with Magitech toward Fae'ren Province.

While Jeth exited the dark tunnel, carved through the Barrier of Kriegle, the hard granite stone beneath the horse's hooves gave way to an impacted dirt path lined with war-trampled foliage.

He turned to the sorceress riding beside him and said, "Should be able to find my way from here. Thank you."

Jenn smiled at him warmly. Tired after a long journey, her thin physique slouched over her reins, and dark circles lined her small rat-like eyes.

"No. Thank you," she said in her rigid Ingle dialect.

Jeth halted the cart. He didn't realize how hard it would be to leave the land of golems and the friend accompanying him whom he'd come to know quite well the last few weeks.

"You could have taken your Magitech and made for home days ago. But you chose to stay," she went on. "We are in your debt."

"You make it sound like I did all the work." Jeth blushed. "I only shot down a few golems and took out a couple naja."

"And Steinkamp," she added, flicking her short dark hair off her face.

"Right"—Jeth nodded—"I actually killed Steinkamp soldiers. I can't wait to tell Anwarr. She was sure I would get my arse eliminated by one of them." *What a way to end your thieving career*, he thought, relieved it was finally over. "At any rate," he resumed. "I'm glad to have helped the little that I did, but you're the ones who'll have to clean up the mess."

"Siegfried can handle it, Verishten be willing." A reference to her volcano god.

"If anyone can do it, it's him," Jeth said. "He's one impressive fella, I'd say. A great fighter and so . . . statuesque." He paused when he noticed Jenn starting at him. "So, I'm a bit infatuated. There's no shame in that."

"Perhaps you should be getting back to your woman." Jenn snickered.

"You're not wrong." The last few weeks helping Siegfried and Jenn was the only time he hadn't been thinking about Anwarr every second. For the months spent waiting in the Herrani warrior camps, he constantly worried about how she and the baby were faring—what name he would give it if it were a boy or a girl. In all that time, he hadn't been able to think of a single one.

"Where will the two of you live?" Jenn asked.

"I don't know yet, but somewhere far from the thieving life would be a start."

"Well, Siegfried's offer still stands," Jenn reminded. "You are welcome back here anytime. No one would ever find you in Ingleheim."

"I'll have to run it by the lady first. She hates the rain, and I reckon she'd hate volcanic ash falling from the sky even more."

"There is more to these ranges than what you've seen so far. If you do decide to come back, we'll help you out. Siegfried would probably love to have you in his personal guard."

"That's a tempting offer, but complete and utter seclusion sounds more preferable, at the moment," he said, although not entirely sure his words were true. *You've lived in relative seclusion before, but Anwarr hasn't.* "What are you going to do now?" he asked.

"Help clean up the mess, I suppose . . ." She stared out into the vast forested terrain. ". . . But then there's the naja. I should . . . do something."

"You're just one witch, and there are thousands of naja," said Jeth.

"Someone has to try. . . ." She pursed her thin lips and started turning her horse around.

"If there are more good-hearted Spirit Mages like you out there, you might have shot."

Jenn's pale face turned a bright pink, and she didn't respond. Her talent with both essence and spirit made her a force to be reckoned with, and now that Melikheil was dead she might be the most powerful Mage in Ingleheim.

"I wish you luck at any rate," he added.

"And to you, Jeth. Thanks again." Jenn gave him a nod and kicked her steed into a canter back into the tunnel.

Jeth continued his way through the ravaged lands of north Fae'ren. Many of the Herrani encampments had disappeared, leaving rocks overturned, forests clear-cut, and paths trampled to oblivion. The full damage to the province wasn't as apparent when Jeth had been living in those camps himself, but seeing the aftermath upon his return made that hard lump in his gut start to churn. *You shouldn't care about this place. It never cared about you.* Even so, he knew the Fae'ren people didn't deserve this. Nobody did.

Luckily, the camp where Jeth was supposed to make the drop was still there. In fact, many of the warriors from the other camps had retreated to that point, still not ready to give up the siege even after their crushing defeat beyond the Barrier. Jeth gave the cart of Magitech to General Nadila, and she provided him with a pre-signed note for ninety thousand gold.

"I'm pleased you survived," said the middle-aged general with light blonde hair braided in four sets. "When I received word of a Steinkamp soldier tearing up your camp, I thought you'd been slaughtered for sure."

He shrugged. "Surviving is what I do best."

"Well, you're free to go. Keep the armor, and take the Steinkamp steed with you." Nadila motioned to the horse being unstrapped from the cart.

"I will. But I think I'll rest here first," Jeth decided.

He went to wash the dirt and ash off himself and lay down to sleep. By the next morning, he was on the road to Lanore, clean and refreshed.

The black Steinkamp gelding was so responsive and agreeable it made Jeth miss Torrent all the more. He couldn't wait to take his feisty mare out on the Ludesan plains and bring her to top speed. Not being battle tested, Jeth hadn't been allowed to take her to the siege, and it had been a good thing, too, since he would have been separated from her with little chance of tracking her down.

Another day's ride saw Jeth to Lanore. Nerves fluttered about in his stomach as he rode up to the communal stables. He handed the reins of the Steinkamp steed to the stable boy and went to see how his own was doing. Both Torrent and Anwarr's buckskin were side by side in their box stalls munching on hay.

Jeth didn't waste a moment in rubbing Torrent's head as she nickered away. The stable boy said, "I tried to take her out a few times, but she kept bucking me off. We had a bitch of a time getting her back in here."

Jeth guffawed. "Sounds like my girl."

After feeding her some carrots the stable boy had given him, Jeth thanked him and made his way to the cottage where the midwife had set Anwarr up for the duration of her pregnancy. Nestled behind a cluster of trees and well-trimmed hedges, the old mudstone cottage appeared smaller than it actually was. Besides the tavern, it was the largest structure in the commune, which allowed it to house at least six other pregnant women and their children. When he had left this place three and a half months ago, it was bustling with activity, but not today. Only one pregnant woman, a dish under her arm, was outside throwing feed to the hens as Jeth passed.

Upon noticing him heading for the front door, the Fae woman—Jeth couldn't remember her name—put down the feed and rushed up to him. "Are you here for Anwarr?"

"Yes, can I go in?"

"She's not here." The woman's top lip quivered as she spoke.

"Well . . . when will she be back?" A pit of dread began to form in Jeth's stomach.

"Did she not send word?"

"No word could reach me. Is she all right? Where did she go?"

The woman stood there tight-lipped and wouldn't answer him.

Without another thought, Jeth let himself into the cottage and strode right for the back room that he knew belonged to Anwarr.

"Wait, you can't go in there," the woman protested, but Jeth's heart pounding in his temples deafened him.

He swung the door open, hoping that Anwarr would be in her bed, right where he had left her, but instead, he found a startled ginger woman with a newborn suckling at her breast.

"O-oh . . . sorry. . . ." He quickly closed the door and turned to the Fae woman behind him. "Isn't this Anwarr's room?"

"That was her room," said an older woman, coming out of another room a few doors down. Jeth recognized her as Twilla, the head midwife. "She left a little over a month ago."

Jeth's head spun, and he had to lean on the doorframe to keep from falling over. "What do you mean she left?" His whole mouth turned to dry wool. "She's almost six months pregnant. She wouldn't—did something happen to the baby?"

The midwife put her arms out to brace him, clay beads around her neck clacking together as she approached. "The child was fine the day Anwarr left." Pulling aside her long gray locks from her shoulder, she shuffled over to a small table in the hall and pulled a rolled-up parchment from the drawer. "She asked that I give you this if you returned."

Jeth took it in a shaking hand and unrolled the note. Falling out from the parchment and into his palm, was the white gold armlet. The weight of it was overwhelming. He quickly put it in his pocket and tried to focus on the Herrani characters scrawled on the page. It appeared to be Anwarr's handwriting, but he couldn't be sure.

"I can't read this—she knows I can't . . ." he murmured, looking down at the chicken scratch ink marks. The only words he recognized, like 'waiting' and 'safe,' provided no real meaning. *Maybe she's waiting for you somewhere safe?* Jeth thought, but the return of the armlet suggested otherwise.

He crushed the note in his trembling fist, his chest tightening even more. He became all too aware of his heart straining to beat.

Twilla said, "I'm sorry for the confusion, but I must attend to my duties."

"I'm not going anywhere until you tell me why you let a pregnant woman walk out of here all by herself," Jeth demanded through clenched teeth.

"She was not by herself. Three men came for her. I advised her not to travel in her condition, but she was dead-set on going. I figured they were men she trusted."

Jeth's heart was now racing. "What did they look like? This is important. She could be in danger."

Twilla bit the inside of her cheek in contemplation. "They were different than other Herrani I've seen in these parts. They wore strange hats with serpent broaches festooned to them."

"Were two of them wearing red tunics, and was the other one big and armored?" Jeth finished.

Twilla nodded. "Good. So you know them."

How did Ezrai's spies find her all the way out here? Jeth ran a sweaty hand over his hair. "Did she tell you where they were going to take her?"

The midwife shook her head, her earrings, made of some type of bird talons, knocking together. "All she said was that they were taking her home. They were very respectful, and she went with them willingly, although she seemed distraught about having to leave."

Jeth looked down at the crinkled note in his hand. "Twilla, is there any chance you can read Herrani script?"

"I'm afraid not. Again, I'm deeply sorry, but I have a woman who has just gone into labor," she said, "I'm sure you and Anwarr will be reunited soon."

Jeth stormed out of the cottage in a mad daze, the world spinning in dizzying circles around him. He paced back and forth along the chicken coop to try and get his thoughts straight. *She wouldn't go back to Ezrai. She doesn't go back! Where does she think she's going with your child?* His rage finally broke the surface, and he lashed out at the nearest object. He smashed open a large clay pot with his khopesh, spilling chicken feed all over the grass. The hens squawked and fluttered about in their pen. She can't do this! The Fae woman ran out to investigate, bringing Jeth out of his enraged stupor for a moment.

"Sorry about the pot," Jeth grumbled and stepped past the woman.

"It's a boy," she said.

"What?" He turned around.

"Anwarr told me. The barley sprouted, which means you're going to have a boy . . . if that's any consolation."

Swallowing a hard lump in his throat, he nodded. "Thank you."

He returned to the stables and saddled Torrent in bemusement. He was prepared to ride out of there when the stable boy called out, "Hey, don't you want your other horses?" Jeth looked back at Anwarr's Tezkhan bred steed she had left behind.

"Keep them or sell them. They'll fetch you a good price."

With nothing more to say, Jeth kicked his dapple-gray into a canter.

With Torrent galloping at full speed, Jeth reached Fairieshome by dusk. The moons hung full and large, the smaller one finally having pried itself from the larger to form two shining, distinct spheres to light his way.

Once he was within the commune barricade, Jeth was further disheartened to find not a single Herrani among the throngs of Fae'ren walking about. *Great, now that you need one, they're nowhere to be found.* He overheard various conversations about the siege and how it displaced at least four northern communes, but rumors of Herrani retreat, courtesy of the Ingles, gave them hope that they could return and rebuild.

By nightfall, Jeth came to Clive's Tavern, a place he had been thrown out of numerous times as a young lad, but hoped that tonight he would find a Herrani or two. After tying up his horse at a post, Jeth headed inside. He scanned the patrons, not finding a single dark-skinned face or white head of hair that didn't belong to an aging Fae'ren.

Exhausted and utterly frustrated, Jeth approached the big, burly man behind the bar. "I need a pint."

The man, his locks short and wiry, hardly looked at Jeth as he grabbed a tin mug. Before filling it with the dark brown brew, he asked gruffly, "Family name?"

Jeth plunked a gold coin down on the counter. "I'm a paying customer."

The bartender eyed the coin then Jeth before saying, "We don't serve the cursed in here. There's a proper Del'Cabrian tavern down the road. They'll take your coin."

Jeth slammed another one down. "I'm not having a very good day, so just pour the Mother forsaken ale." Some of the patrons sitting closest to the bar started shuffling out, having overheard that a cursed one was in their midst.

"Best you be on your way, lad."

"Best you give the man his damn ale!" said a woman in a firm voice. Jeth turned with a start to find, Vidya, wearing her brown leather attire and shoulder cape. He wasn't sure if this surprise would make this day better or worse.

"And what are you going to do about it, lady?" the barkeep sneered.

"I can have the rest of your patrons running for the door in one second flat." She shifted her cape aside to reveal the pistol in her holster, and right away the bartender paled. With a low grumble, he filled the mug and slid it over to Jeth.

Vidya didn't take her intense gaze from the man. "There are two coins on the table. Make another."

"I don't want any trouble," he said as he filled another tin mug.

"I don't anticipate there being any, do you?" Vidya took the second mug in hand. The barkeep shook his head and turned away while Jeth and Vidya sat down at one of the recently vacated tables in the corner.

"I never expected to see you again," said Jeth. "What business does a harpy have in Fairieshome?"

"I've been tracking Nas'Gavarr as he wages war on yet another nation."

"He's been back in Herran for months now." Jeth took down a mouthful of the refreshing, foamy liquid. *There is nothing quite like Fae'ren ale,* a nostalgic thought.

Vidya shook her head. "Oh, he's here . . . or at least he was—I keep losing him in. Spying overhead is virtually impossible. with all these damn trees."

"I don't know what to tell you. He left the siege in the hands of his son who probably won't be here much longer himself," Jeth said.

"Why, what have you heard?"

"The Ingle armies and their golems cleaned them right out. Those that survived are falling back." Jeth took another gulp.

"How do you know this? Don't tell me you're fighting for the Herrani now?" Vidya pointed to the armor he still wore while taking a swig of her ale.

"Something like that."

"Credence wants to ally with Ingleheim against Herran, but their Führer is even harder to peg down than the Overlord. Sounds like they don't need any help," said Vidya.

"I'll say. They'll have the Herrani high-tailing it out of here in a couple of weeks, at most." Jeth chuckled and gulped down the rest of his pint, which was already doing wonders to take his mind off Anwarr.

"The Council is not going to like that." Vidya made eye contact with the bartender and signaled for two more. He personally brought the mugs over and roughly plunked them down on the table, brew spilling over the tops. He stood there, waiting for payment, but Vidya looked up at him with a closed mouth smile. "Surely, these are on the house?"

Scowling, the man cleared away the previous mugs and stomped off.

"You don't have to do that, I can afford to pay the man," Jeth said.

"Are you not a thief?"

"I only steal for hire and survival."

"I've come to know how things are done around here, in particular with you orphans. They denied you your whole life because your parents happened to die when you were a child. The man owes you. They all do." She laid back in her seat against the corner wall, putting both feet up on a nearby chair, and gulping down her second ale.

"Why are you being so . . . nice? After how we ended things the last time, I assumed you'd want nothing to do with me."

"Whatever gave you that impression?"

"You called me, and I quote, a 'small-minded, weak-willed man.'"

"So? Doesn't mean the two of us can't enjoy a good pint." Jeth shrugged, and Vidya went on, "So what's next for you then? Return to your crew?"

His reply caught in his throat. He took Anwarr's note out of his pocket. "Don't know. . . ."

"What's that?" Vidya pointed to the parchment as he fiddled with it.

"It's a letter, but I can't read it."

"Don't you want to know what it says?"

"Of course, I want to know what it says. I can't read it because . . . I can't read."

"How do you not know how to read?" Vidya's mouth curled in an expression of pity or disgust. Jeth couldn't tell.

"Where would I have learned?" he said. "Not that it matters because it's Herrani script anyway."

"I read Herrani," said Vidya.

"You do?"

She nodded. "My mother taught me how to write in nearly every type of script. Give it here."

Jeth was hesitant. Now that he had the chance to know what Anwarr wrote him, he was unable to give it up.

With a grunt of impatience, she snatched the letter out of Jeth's hands. He instinctively tried to grab it back, but she held it out of his reach.

"Just let me read it to you," she griped.

"Fine. Get on with it." Jeth sat back in his chair and took a long gulp of his ale before plunking it down and wiping his mouth.

As Vidya looked over the parchment, Jeth sat helplessly across from her in a cold sweat, his second mug of ale already empty. "What are you waiting for?"

"In a second. I'm making sure I understand these characters before spouting them off."

In the meantime, Jeth called a waitress over, put two coins in her apron pouch, and told her to hurry with two more pints.

"Oh dear," Vidya said. "You're not going to like this."

"Just read it," he said, tapping his fingers on the table while waiting for his fresh mug to arrive so he could drown himself in it.

Vidya cleared her throat. *"Jethril."* She glanced up at him. "Your name is actually *Jethril?*"

"Woman, are you going to make fun of my name or read the Deity forsaken letter?" he snapped.

She rolled her eyes and continued, "Jethril. By now you've returned to find that I am gone. I can only hope you found a Herrani to read this for you because I couldn't trust this message told from someone else's memory."

Finally, the two pints were set in front of them. Jeth took a long-awaited sip, letting the mind-numbing effects take hold.

"After two months of waiting for you, I realized that we don't belong in each other's worlds. I have been living a lie, and I refuse to do it any longer. I am sorry to have hurt you this way, but you will be better off without us, though you don't know it yet. Please do not try to find us. There is no need to worry. We are safe. I hope you find a place where you truly belong. I will think fondly of you, always. Love, Anwarr."

Jeth held his head in his hands through the entirety of the letter. Each breath he took required more effort than the last. Ash's words kept repeating in his mind. '*She will never belong to you.*'

Vidya slid the note across the table. "That was bracing. Who's us?"

"She's carrying my son," Jeth rasped then finished his third pint.

"That is cold-hearted." Vidya winced. "And I'm saying that as a harpy whose sole purpose is to punish men. Barkeep!" She made a wheel-like motion with her hand. "Keep them coming."

A minute later, two more mugs were brought to the table, and Jeth didn't hesitate in starting on his fourth. While he drank it down, his skin flushed, and his head started to whirl.

He exhaled and wiped the foam from his beard. "What about you? I don't want to be the only drunk at the table."

"I have the constitution of three men. It will take a lot more than a few pints to get the better of me," she said.

"Then you require three times the brew." Jeth turned around in his chair. "Barkeep. The lady needs three more."

He came over again with three tin cups. "This is it for you both. You'll drink me right out of business."

"You know what, Clive, is it? I feel your pain. Take these and see that you don't stop refilling our cups until this woman is drooling on herself and I'm passed out on my arse." He took a handful of coins and tried to put them in the man's hand only to have them spill out all over the place. "Sorry." He chortled.

The barkeep grumbled and started picking them up while Vidya snorted back a laugh of her own. "To Clive's Tavern," she said, raising her mug.

"Hear, hear." Jeth clinked his mug to hers and took its contents down his gullet.

If anyone had told Vidya she'd be getting inebriated with the irritating Fae'ren from the Temple of Sagorath she would have laughed that person out of the room.

Having spent considerable time in Fae'ren Province, witnessing the ravages of the outbreak in the south, and knowing her people were in the process of spreading it further made her feel somewhat complicit. *If I had been able to defeat Nas'Gavarr months ago, it wouldn't have to come to this,* she had thought. Then, upon walking into this tavern to find that Jeth was one of the cursed, she felt guiltier still. It was why she had gotten him the ale and why she continued to listen to his heartbroken ramblings now. It also didn't hurt to silence the shadow harpy in her head with copious amounts of alcohol.

"And you know what really burns me?" Jeth pointed a finger at Vidya. "I was so close to leaving that woman before all this happened. But she convinced me not to. And she's the one who told me she'd honor me and that. She said we'd be an 'actual family.' Everything I ever did—it was all for her. Never did I get a 'thank you, Jeth,' or 'I love you, Jeth.' No, only *'I hope you find a place where you truly belong,'*" he said in a mocking feminine voice, complete with the Herrani dialect. "It's like I'm the butt of some joke that I don't even get. And I'm the one who makes the jokes!"

Vidya sipped her eleventh pint. "The Siren Council are the same way. All I've ever done was serve Credence from the moment I came of age. I gave up my entire future to become a harpy, and they give me a few months to defeat the most powerful Mage in the known world all by myself! I tell them it's not enough and they dismiss me, treat me like they've always treated me: a childless, wingless girl. I may as well be a man."

After bunching her curls in her hand, she took down the rest of her beverage and began on the twelfth, the entire tavern spinning in circles around her.

"What a bunch of ignorant twats," Jeth said. "You know what you should do? You should tell them, 'hey, I'm a harpy, you're not . . . so you have to do what I say.' You know, make them listen."

"That might be the smartest thing you've ever said," Vidya said, awestruck.

Jeth shook his head in a drunken daze. "No, winged lady, I say smart things all of the time. Even so, Anwarr would still rather make it on her own than give me a chance. Do-do you think she thinks I'll be a bad father because I never had one?"

Vidya scoffed. "I never knew my father, and I'm no worse off for it."

Sarta had taken Vidya back to Credence after five years when no second child came to be. Vidya hadn't had the chance to visit him after because he was killed in a riot. Demeter's father was the closest thing Vidya had to one of her own, but they never shared much of a bond. In fact, she was pretty certain the man held no love for her at all.

"Oh, so you're saying my son will be fine without me. Great. What am I worried about then?"

"That's not what I meant," Vidya relented. "Anwarr's taking a huge risk in raising a child on her own. Even in Credence, children fare better with a father to provide resources. I was fine because of my mother's high position."

"She won't stay on her own for long, believe me. If she's even alone right now," he said bitterly.

"From what I've gathered so far, I'm guessing this Anwarr was too beautiful for you and would have left you no matter what you did."

"Should I be insulted or comforted by that?" Jeth huffed.

"You were blinded by her physical attractiveness and gave no thought to the person beneath. And she likely knew that and used it to her advantage. I see this sort of thing all the time."

Jeth scowled, gripping his tin cup tightly. "You're wrong."

"If you knew her beyond a pretty face, then you'd see this coming a mile away." Vidya took another gulp. "Trust me, you're better off without a woman like that. She reminds me of my sister. Men are toys to her." She toys with them, but you kill them, Vidya suddenly thought. She was unsure if that thought came from her own mind or the shadow. She couldn't see it anywhere, but decided to drink a little more just in case.

"She sounds just like my type. When can I meet her?" Jeth chortled darkly.

Vidya decided to change the subject and leaned in close. Putting her hand to her mouth, she whispered. "Hey, do you want to hear a secret?"

Jeth shrugged and nodded, one of his eyelids drooping.

"I'm building an army of harpies."

He gasped. "Don't you have to kill a lot of fellas for that?"

She brushed by her astonishment that he would even know such a thing and continued, "I'm not making a very big army, for that reason. You can be sure though, that it will be big enough to challenge Nas'Gavarr."

"Good luck with that. To harpy armies." Jeth raised his cup and Vidya didn't hesitate in clinking it and taking down the rest of her brew.

"I wish Nas'Gavarr were still out here. It would be nice to get my hands on that magic dagger of his."

Jeth slapped the table. "I'm not going to revisit that day, but I suppose you can afford to die."

"I'll be ready for him this time," she said.

"What's your plan?"

"I've thought of so many ways I could take it from him, but honestly, it all comes down to swooping in and swiping it." Vidya made the motion of her arm flying in and snatching an imaginary blade.

"Ah, the ol' swoop and swipe. A classic," Jeth quipped, following with a belch.

Vidya grimaced, but then an idea hit her. "Better yet, you're fast. You can do it, easy."

Jeth guffawed.

"No, no, I mean it," Vidya insisted, wobbling in her chair. "I can distract him with a wind storm. Then, you just sneak up and take it. He won't even see you, it's the perfect plan."

"By the Crannabeatha, you're one mad git, you know that?" Jeth said.

"Come on, let's do it," urged Vidya. "There's a reason why we ran into each other again. Yasharra is telling us that we should take the dagger. Without it, Nas'Gavarr can't sacrifice you to the Serpentine Gods, and I can use it to make my army. Then my harpies will take care of him, and poof, both of our problems are gone."

During her spiel, Jeth kept looking at two urlings marching into the tavern, wearing blue buttoned military tailcoats and tricorn hats.

"I wish that were my only problem," he muttered as they marched in stiff fashion toward the barkeep.

She couldn't hear what was being said over the other drunken oafs, but Jeth was fixated on them. The barkeep nodded over to the two sitting in the corner. Afterwards, the soldiers walked toward them, but turned last second and took a seat at the empty table right behind Jeth. His body tensed as he turned his head slightly to glance at them from his periphery, then snapped his head back around.

"What's got into you? I get Del'Cabrian soldiers aren't exactly welcome around here, but—"

"Quiet." Jeth put his hand out to silence her.

He tilted his head and darted his hazel eyes about nervously, as if listening in on something, but the men behind them weren't saying a word. Jeth cursed quietly to himself.

"What is it?" Vidya whispered.

In a low voice that Vidya could barely hear, Jeth said, "These men are here to make me nervous so that I will leave and walk right into their trap. Clever bastards."

"What trap?"

Jeth looked straight at Vidya and said in a quiet and controlled tone, "The six men waiting outside to arrest me for treason—*that* trap."

24

A Living Coward or a Dead Hero

The tavern stopped spinning, and Jeth's focus pushed through his depressed drunken haze. He listened to the whispers of several men near the entrance outside who waited for him to emerge. There were a few at the back door as well.

"You're a traitor?" slurred Vidya.

"Keep your voice down," Jeth hushed. "I'm trying to think of what to do."

"There's only one thing to do," Vidya whispered. "You said there are men outside waiting for you to leave. I say we don't leave." She pointed at her head and nodded proudly.

He groaned at her useless intoxicated input and surveyed the tavern. Thinking only of finding a means of escape. Though, his intentions to run must have been more obvious than he hoped because the chairs behind him scraped the floor and the soldiers rose to their feet.

They approached the table, and a lanky mustached urling cleared his throat to speak. "Forgive the intrusion, miss." He bowed, stiffly.

Vidya snorted her reply, "What can we do for you, officers?"

With a hand resting on the grip of his sword, the soldier turned to Jeth and said, "We have confirmation that you are the one they call the Desert War Traitor,"

"The Desert War Traitor?" Vidya raised an eyebrow. "That's general. Were there no other traitors in the Desert War who can share that title or . . .?"

The two soldiers exchanged glances and shrugged. "There is only one of note," said the stouter, human soldier.

"Listen, officers," Jeth began. "You all seem to think every person with fairy locks looks the same. I don't know how you got your information, but you have the wrong man."

"Someone who knows you confirmed your identity before we came in here," said the urling soldier in a typical stuffy fashion.

"Not to mention you are wearing Herrani armor," the human one added. "Now, will you cooperate or will we have to use force?"

"Is there any chance we can do this another time? I've had a cunt of a day." At those words, the soldiers drew their swords. "Force it is then."

The human soldier grabbed his arm and yanked him up from his chair while the urling took the other, pressed it to his back, and began reciting, "By order of the King, you are hereby under arrest for the murders of Sirs Baird and Tobin of Del'Cabria Proper, and for assisting the enemy during times of war."

Jeth prepared to flip the urling over his head and break free, but Vidya put up her hand. "Hold on!"

To Jeth's surprise, the soldiers stopped what they were doing and watched the harpy, still with her hand up, drink back the rest of her ale.

Finishing, she released a satisfied exhalation before cracking the human one over the head with her empty mug, making a distinctive dong sound against his skull. Jeth wriggled out of the urling's grip while Vidya grabbed the soldier by his buttoned lapels and tossed him over the bar. The patrons who were left in the tavern clambered for the exits.

"This is why I don't serve the cursed!" the barkeep complained as he helplessly watched his customers disappear.

"I think we overstayed our welcome." Jeth grabbed Vidya's arm and pulled her toward the door.

"We were never welcome."

The rest of the soldiers piled into the tavern through the line of escaping patrons. Seven men took position all around them—swords out and shields raised.

"Don't move, Jeth!" barked an eighth man leading the company of swordsmen. "We have you surrounded. There is no escaping this time." He stepped forward, and stood regal, his sword hand at the ready.

"Major?"

"The colonel made you my responsibility. I am not permitted to return home until I bring you in. After tonight, I may finally get to see my family again," said Faron.

". . . And Loche?"

"He lives, but don't think that excuses you from what you did! Now, on your knees and hands on your head."

Jeth did what he was told while thinking of how he was going to maneuver through Faron's men without getting sliced to bits. *If your speed activates then it won't be a problem, but if it doesn't . . .*

Faron turned to Vidya. "Madam, for your own safety, you should leave here at once."

"Why of course, good sir," Vidya mocked the major's uptight way of speaking while curtsying drunkenly. "But not until I remove you first."

"Vidya. I can handle this, just get out of here," Jeth urged.

His words fell on deaf ears. Vidya picked up an entire table, and every soldier in the room hollered and backed away. She stumbled around with it for a moment before tossing it straight at Faron and two other men standing nearest to him, knocking them over, and trapping them under the heavy oak.

The entire tavern erupted in battle cries as the remaining five men moved to attack Jeth and Vidya both. Now Jeth's adrenaline kicked in, and the battle around him slowed to a crawl. He dodged the multiple sword tips that came at him. Grabbing the arm of one young soldier, he spun him around, yanked the sword out of his grasp, and kicked him against the wall. Before the soldier could react, Jeth stuck the sword through his coat tails and into the wood paneled wall so he couldn't get back up. Another soldier threw a knife at Jeth's leg, but he caught it in midair, spun around, and jammed it through the boot of another coming up behind him.

Vidya, despite being inebriated, was holding her own rather well. She smacked one man across the room with a backhand slap, broke a bar stool over another's back, and flipped the last one into the tables and chairs. Cups went flying, spilling their liquid contents all over the soldier's fine uniform. Now, all eight men were groaning on the floor, some bleeding, others unconscious, but each one alive.

"Let's go!" Jeth called.

As they headed for the door, the table Vidya had thrown was pushed over, and Faron was up on his feet. The major's heart was beating furiously, but his hardened expression remained the same as always.

"Halt!"

Vidya stepped in front of Jeth. "You can't take him."

"Step aside, miss," he ordered. Two of his men rose to their feet behind him.

"Out the back," Jeth said. They turned to run, and Faron threw his knife. It embedded itself in the side of Vidya's left thigh. She released a screeching growl, tore off her cloak, and extended her wings. Jeth was knocked to the ground by the force, and he watched her shoot across the room, bowling over the two men on her way to grab Faron and fly out the front door with him.

Jeth clambered to his feet and ran outside. "Vidya!"

She halted in mid-air, clutched the major's collar with one hand, and jammed her pistol to his jugular with the other. Faron dangled impotently in the harpy's grasp. For the first time ever, Jeth witnessed emotion in the man's eyes, and that emotion was pure terror.

"You should be more careful where you throw sharp objects, Major," Vidya hissed.

"Vidya, stop," Jeth shouted. "If he dies, you will be declaring war on Del'Cabria on behalf of Credence!"

She pushed the pistol's barrel harder underneath the major's chin, choking out his cries. A chilling hatred was in her eyes. A sick need emanated from them, convincing Jeth that she would fire the round straight up through the man's skull.

"Please, put him down!"

She slowly descended, still clutching Faron. Hovering a couple feet over the ground, she dropped him in the dirt. "Take your men and leave this place. You are welcome to arrest your traitor after I'm done with him."

Faron rubbed his neck and backed away, not taking his eyes from the wrathful harpy. With a grunt, she pulled the knife from her leg and tossed it to Faron who placed it back in his scabbard with a shaking hand.

"Don't think you've evaded justice, traitor!" he spat. "I will personally ensure that you hang."

With that, Faron ran back into the tavern to check on his men. When Vidya returned to the ground, she collapsed to her backside, blood spurting from her leg wound.

"Everything is spinning." She swayed in a clockwise motion. "We should probably get out of here."

"You think?"

The soldiers were already limping out of the tavern. He took Vidya under her arm and helped her onto his horse. A swift kick sent Torrent galloping through the thoroughfare and into a forested area within the barricade. Once satisfied that they were far enough away from the soldiers and wouldn't be found, he stopped. Vidya fell forward off the horse's rump and landed on her back with a grunt.

Jeth pulled extra material from his saddlebag and wrapped it around her leg with haste. She laid there partially groaning in pain and giggling hysterically.

"What was that back there?" Jeth griped. "Had you let me get away clean, you wouldn't be a bleeding, drunken mess right now. As if they didn't have enough reason to arrest me!"

"What are they going to do? Hang you twice?" She snorted, then followed up with a grimace.

Blood from Vidya's leg leaked through the tan colored fabric until it was entirely red. "We'll need something to help close this wound. I'll be right back."

"I heal fast—not Nas'Gavarr fast, but faster than any human," she said.

"Keep pressure on it." Jeth ran into the bush in search of vera leaves. Thankfully, they were common in Fairieshome, and he didn't have to hone his sense of smell too far to locate the plant's unpleasantly strong odor amongst the foliage.

"Hey, what are you doing over there?" Vidya called.

Jeth didn't answer, only ripped off a few leaves and returned to her, still on the ground. He squeezed out the yellow gel and lifted the fabric to apply it to the open gash.

Vidya shoved his hand away. "Get that away from me! It stinks."

"It's going to close your wound, relax." He shook his head and exhaled through his teeth.

Vidya turned her head to the side and clenched her jaw as Jeth put the gel over her wound. "There," he said when he was done.

At that point, he caught Vidya's inebriated stare. Accusatory and enthralled at the same time. "Oh. I see you've finally noticed my rugged good looks. Sorry, but I'm not ready to move on just yet," he quipped with a twinge of discomfort.

"You drank almost as much as I did," she said. "Why are you tending to me with herbal remedies instead of vomiting all over yourself?"

"Feel free to pass out now."

She narrowed her gaze at him. "Wait a minute, are you actually sober?"

Jeth nodded.

Once he finished rewrapping her makeshift bandage around the vera treated wound, she roughly grabbed his arm. "Is that how you did it?"

"Did what?"

Her eyes widened. "That's how you got away—that's your secret."

Jeth jerked out of her grasp and stood up. "What are you talking about?"

"The blood magic." She pulled herself to her feet using a tree branch and rested against the trunk. "No one can brush off that level of intoxication in only one second. Whatever is making you sober now is the reason you were able to escape Nas'Gavarr."

"That's a bit of a stretch, isn't it?" Jeth scratched his head.

"Just be straight with me! We both know you are no ordinary man any more than I'm an ordinary woman. We are the only ones who faced the Overlord and survived. Together, we can take the Bloodstone Dagger from him."

"For the last time, Vidya, forget the Overlord!" Jeth barked.

"Don't you get it?" she shot back. "I was created specifically to defeat him. I have to do it even if it kills me! Do you think his temporary defeat in Ingleheim will put his ambitions to rest? He has lifetimes to get to where he's going, and we're a part of it! What will it take for you to fight back? Does he have to murder someone you love? Does he have to threaten your people? Or do you care about anything other than your own hide?"

"Don't presume to know what I do or don't care about." He stuffed his hands into his pockets and clenched the armlet in his left.

"You might be the only one who can come close to hurting him," she protested.

"You're drunk!"

"What do you have to lose?" Vidya swayed against the tree. "Your woman wants nothing to do with you. You have no crew. It's only a matter of time before you'll be hanged by the neck until dead. You may as well go out fighting the most powerful Mage in the world. You can become a legend, or you can run and hide in the woods like a frightened doe. Either way, I need that dagger."

"I do have something to lose. A son," said Jeth.

"Then decide how you want him to think of you. As a living coward or a dead hero." The coldness in Vidya's voice washed Jeth in an uncomfortable dread.

"Is a living hero not an option?"

"You will have to join me to find out," she said.

Jeth's jaw tightened as he gazed down the forest road. All he could think of to do was what he had always been doing. Running—forever moving forward, and never looking back, but the love of his life wouldn't do that with him anymore. You're still stuck, he thought, utter hopelessness setting in. *Maybe the harpy's right. Maybe your survival wasn't just blind luck.* However, that in no way meant Jeth was capable of facing Nas'Gavarr again. He wanted to let Snake Eye take care of him as promised.

"You should rest up, let that leg heal. I need to figure some things out," Jeth muttered.

"Figure what things out?"

"I'll consider your offer, alright? Can you fly?"

Vidya nodded. "Not in a straight line, but I can get back to town quick enough. I'm staying at an inn across from Clive's Tavern. If you decide to help, you can find me there. But once my leg has healed, I am going to find Nas'Gavarr with or without you."

Jeth nodded as Vidya limped back to the path and faced toward the town. "Thanks for the patch job," she said, half under her breath.

With a flap of her wings, she cast herself into the air and flew until she was but a winged silhouette against the moon of Sagorath. Jeth took to his mount and bolted down the forest path until he reached the eastern barricade exit. Once the gateman let him out, he galloped full speed in an eastward direction.

As conflicted as he felt in that moment, one thing was for certain; he needed to get to the bottom of his abilities, and his first step was finding one of the only other beings that shared them.

After tying Torrent's lead to a low hanging branch in a clearing, Jeth trudged through the underbrush of the Deep Wood. He wouldn't dare damage the deer paths with a horse's hooves.

This forest was sacred.

It was the home of the Mother Oak and also the fairies. He didn't expect to find any for a while, given that they rarely showed themselves to humans unless those humans overstayed their welcome. He could only hope that one of them might recognize him and appear.

Pushing his way through the lush greenery brought him back to the many days of his childhood running effortlessly through it, chasing fairies up and around the great hollow oak trees. Spring had only begun, and already the mosses covered everything in sight. Oak branches grew out in all directions like fairy locks, unmanageable, but beautiful in their disorder. Many believed the matted strands of the fairies helped them camouflage with the mossed branches and roots. Jeth would have no clue if they were there had he not known their scent. His nose told him he was alone.

Eventually, he reached the Grove of the Crannabeatha. The massive and ancient oak loomed over him. Gentle streams encircled the great trunk, surrounding it in elegant waterfalls glistening by the rising sun, peeking through the endless network of branches and illuminating the floating pollens.

Jeth came to a cluster of roots at the tree's base that formed a large, natural cradle in the earth. It was the place where fairies were birthed from the Crannabeatha's roots, and it was also where Serra had found him when he was a baby, wailing at the top of his lungs. She used to take him back here to visit. He would find a comfortable nook to sit in while the giant oak whispered to the fairies, whispers he could never hear, but he used to imagine he would be able to someday.

He gazed up into the complex web of branches overhead, the familiar whistles and chirps of wildlife he used to fall asleep to every night sang in his ears. *How can you feel so at home and yet so lost at the same time?* He pondered, his heart heavy.

Closing his eyes and inhaling the cool refreshing scents of nearby flower patches, Jeth whispered to the great tree, "Crannabeatha, if you can hear me, tell me . . . do I belong here?"

The great tree's response was nothing more than the breeze rushing through its abundance of leaves and the branch's creaks and groans.

"Of course, you won't talk to me. I'm not quite fairy enough to hear you," he muttered.

Sun beams raining down through the space between each branch warmed him, but also made his head ache. The effects of the previous night's ale was finally taking its toll, and all he wanted was to collapse into the deep nest of roots and pass out.

He did just that; causing a group of sparrows to flutter off as he plunked himself down and laid back against a mossy root acting as a headrest. He was out before he could formulate his next thought.

A sharp jab in Jeth's side broke him from his slumber, but he wasn't about to move from his resting place.

"So, you're breathing, and you can move, that must mean you're still alive," tittered a young female voice at his right.

He grumbled. Then came another poke. Slapping away whatever was bothering him, he turned away from the source of the irritation, without being aware of what it even was. Then came a tickling sensation on his nose. He scratched it, only for it to return with a vengeance.

With great effort, Jeth forced his eyes open and found a pollen dancing around his forehead. He swatted it away only for it to bounce about his entire face. With a frustrated groan, he was wide awake. He hardly had a chance to recall where he was before he spotted a pair of legs positioned just behind his head.

"What the . . . ?" He snapped to a seated position to find a small young woman sitting on the largest root. She wore garments fashioned by fibrous leaves, slender vines entwining up each leg and her torso, then running through her long-twisted strands of matted hair, indistinguishable from the mosses she sat on. It fell in thin chaotic clumps over her shoulders, obscuring much of her form.

"You were much smaller the last time I found you here . . . and pudgier," she said, tilting her head to the side.

"Serra?" Jeth shielded his eyes from the sun poking through the leaves to the west, his head still pounding. "How long was I out?"

"You look different." Serra leaned forward and sniffed him. "And you smell different, too, and not great." She scrunched her face and held her nose.

"Hey . . ." Jeth lifted one arm and took a whiff of himself then recoiled. "Right. Maybe I'll jump in the stream before I go."

"Go? You came all this way to take a nap?" Serra said, shifting her head to the other side.

Jeth climbed out of the giant cradle of roots. "No, I came here for answers."

"What sort of answers?"

"For starters, I need to know who I am and what my purpose is here."

Serra bounced down from the roots and walked over to Jeth with her hands held behind her back. Her brown and green, iridescent wings stretched open before folding down at her back. They were extraordinary in how they resembled a root system, sprouting from her shoulders, ribcage, and lower back as if she were part tree.

She replied, "You're Jethril, and I can't possibly know your purpose here if you won't tell me."

"Do you have to be so damn literal all the time?" he griped.

Serra's lips pursed as she looked up at him apologetically with her oversized green eyes under long dark lashes. "It's been quite a few years since you've seen me, so how do you know I'm literal all the time?"

"Just listen." Jeth sighed with frustration. "I've discovered that I can do things that other humans can't . . . things that only fairies can do."

Serra was taken aback. "Like what?"

"Like—I can see, hear, and smell things other humans shouldn't be able to. And I'm fast. Very fast. As fast as you."

Serra laughed at him, a juddering cackle. "Nobody can move as fast as a fairy."

She demonstrated by zipping around Jeth to get the jump on him. As she did, Jeth just as rapidly took a few steps back so she couldn't get behind him.

"Hey! You can't . . . but . . ." she huffed, donning a startled expression. Something not often seen among her kind.

"I can also do something else that I don't quite understand. It's like I can bring myself into focus despite what is happening to my body. It lasts as long as I need it, but the longer I go, the more exhausted it makes me."

Serra put her finger to her chin. "Hmm, sounds like our fairy spark."

"You mean like the sparkling energy you use to catapult yourself through the air? Because I can't do that, at least not that I know of. . . ."

"Not quite." Serra paced around the grove. "It's the spark inside of fairies. It gives us a boost of temporary stamina beyond what our physical bodies are capable of. For forest pixies like myself, that energy can also be transferred into the vegetation to help it grow and live longer."

Serra crouched at a small flower patch and cupped her hands around a single stem that had yet to bloom. As Jeth had seen Serra do many times, the flower glowed a brilliant green within her palm, and the stem sprouted higher out of the earth. The bud slowly formed and the soft violet petals unfurled. "It is life force; an essence that fairies have been able to utilize since the beginning."

"But how does it work?" Jeth asked.

"It exists in every living thing. We can transfer it from any lifeform into plants because it is all connected. Sometimes, the forest needs our help to maintain itself, so usually, we take the life force from ourselves rather than from something else. We have a lot of it as you can imagine." Serra rose to her feet to face Jeth. "For you, a human, to be able to manipulate life force at all, without being a Mage . . . doesn't make sense."

"I can't grow plants or shoot fairy sparks out of my arse, but everything else I told you is true. I don't know why I can do these things when other Fae'ren can't. I was hoping you could tell me what it all means."

"I don't know." Serra shook her head and shrugged.

"Great, so coming here was a waste of time." He trilled his lips in a huff. "I should get going. I'm not exactly welcome here, am I?"

"I wouldn't say that," replied Serra with a couple blinks.

"Don't you remember what you said to me the last time I was here? 'Leave, or we will make you?'" A bitter discomfort stirred within his core as old feelings of rejection slowly resurfaced. *You should not have come here.*

"You know we had to say that. Humans can never live in the Deep Wood," Serra stated, matter-of-fact.

"Yeah, you made that perfectly clear," Jeth snapped. "Except for one thing. Why?"

"I've told you this before." Serra fluttered up to take a seat upon a low, lumbering branch. "Thousands of years ago, when humans came upon this land, they marred it. Many fairies lost their lives defending it. We managed to save what we now call the Deep Wood, and we swore never to allow humans to step foot in it again unless they come to pray to the Crannabeatha. Your people, having fairy blood within them, understand this and have done well in keeping that promise."

"I don't want a history lesson right now!" he blared. "I know why humans can't live here, so why allow me to live at all? Why didn't you just let me die like all the other unwanted, parentless whelps brought here? Out of all of those children, why did you save me?"

Serra's expression remained empty, unable to feel the impact of Jeth's frustrations directed at her. "The Crannabeatha answered your mother's prayers and requested that the fairies of this Dominance ensure your survival into adulthood."

"You're not answering me," Jeth said. "Why were my mother's prayers answered at all? Countless babies just like me died by the plague, why did I matter?"

Floating down from the tree, Serra put her head down and replied quietly, "I wish I had answers for you, Jeth. You know our Mother keeps her plans from us. She only informs us of what she deems necessary. But, if you want my opinion, I believe you were spared because your life holds great meaning to this world."

"And you didn't think to ask her why you had to raise a human child for the first time in history?" Jeth asked.

"It is not a fairy's place to question our Mother's wishes," she said. "Although, I wonder if you might be a throwback to the first generation of Fae who had limited fairy abilities. Either that or your seclusion in here, living among us, allowed the fairy within you to come forth. One thing is for sure—you are very special."

"If I'm so damn special, then why force me out?" Jeth asked. "I tried to live with the other humans, like you told me to do, but they shunned me! It would appear as if I am more fairy than man. Therefore, if I don't belong here with you, then I don't belong anywhere! What is the point?"

"The Crannabeatha knew you were meant for something more than what can be gained here alone. I'm sorry your people shunned you, Jeth, but they are still your people. We are not."

"But to me you were! You were all that I knew!" Jeth could feel himself breaking down, his lungs ready to burst from his chest. "I can understand why the rest of them gave me the boot, but not you, Ser. I thought you were different than the others. You seemed so . . . different. . . ."

"I did what was requested—"

Jeth let out an exasperated groan, cutting off Serra's reply. "Never mind. I keep forgetting who I'm talking to. In what reality does a fairy with no capacity for human emotion understand the connection between a mother and son?"

Serra frowned and blinked, creating a sinking feeling in Jeth's chest that was almost as debilitating as when Vidya read Anwarr's letter to him. *She will never be what you need her to be. . . .*

"Forget it." Jeth waved a dismissive arm. "I'll be on my way, and your sacred forest can once again be free of a human presence."

"Don't go," Serra called after him.

"Now you want me to stay?" He turned back around with reluctance.

Serra's large green eyes seemed saddened, at least for a moment. "I always wanted you to stay."

"Really didn't seem like it."

Walking toward him, she said, "I've been a pixie of this forest for one thousand and fifteen years. I've been a mother to you for only that fifteen. None of us knew the first thing about raising a mortal. And you're right, we don't feel things the same way humans do, but that is not to say we feel nothing at all. We cannot perform our sacred duty if we are devoid of all emotion. We know the pain of loss, we know love, even if we don't express it as you would. I love this forest, I love my brothers and sisters, and believe it or not, Jeth, I love you, too."

The wind completely knocked out of him, and he took a few steps back. Of all the people to ever say those words to him, it was Serra, the one he had believed incapable of anything close to it, the one he carried so much resentment toward for all of this time because of it. "I-I don't understand. . . ."

"Over one thousand years I've taken care of this forest, but never have I learned the extent of a fairy's love until I started taking care of you. Had I known how important it was for you to know that growing up, I would have told you sooner. We fairies never need to express such things because it already . . . is. But, as much as I love you, Jeth, I cannot disregard our Mother's wishes. You leaving here was for the best, despite what any of us wanted."

"I wish I could believe you." Jeth gulped back a lump in his throat. "Everything is falling apart. I-I don't know what to do . . ." His eyes lifted to Serra's. Suddenly all his strength left him, and he was that child again, grasping for the only mother he knew before she flew away in a burst of green sparks.

Words began to spill uncontrollably from his throat. He told Serra everything. From the act of treason to the horrific run in with Nas'Gavarr, and the most recent event of Anwarr running off with his child. "Who am I? Not a soldier. I'm no thief. I'm not a father . . . anymore. I'm nothing but a curse. That's all I ever was. No matter how far I run or who I try to be, it follows me. Now you say you love me? How can you? How can anyone?"

When Jeth ran out of breath, the entire forest fell silent. Not even the birds were chirping. He could hardly remember a word he had just uttered. He was too busy steadying his breathing, trying to keep himself from fleeing into the woods and becoming lost forever.

Serra shuffled up close to him and to his utter shock, put her arms around him in an awkward embrace. "It's going to be all right, Jeth," she said.

"W-what are you doing, Ser?"

Without letting go, she replied, "I've since witnessed humans doing this when they are upset. I think it's supposed to help. Is it working?"

Jeth suddenly couldn't stop snickering, and he hugged her right back only to have her push against him to get away. "Ah, mind the wings."

"Sorry." He let her go. "As great of a gesture as that was, it doesn't exactly help me make a decision."

"What is your heart telling you to do?" said Serra with a stretch of her wings.

"To run my arse off and go live with the ogres." He chuckled while simultaneously choking back a sob.

Serra giggled in her reply, "Your head is telling you to do that, silly human. That's where your fears reside. Your heart is beneath it all." She placed a hand on his armored chest. "It is not about what you want to do or even what you should do. It is about what you need to do. Find your sacred duty."

With a long-drawn-out sigh, he said, "I have to find Anwarr."

"The mother of your child?"

He nodded solemnly. "I may be able to accept that she never wants to see me again, but I need to make sure my son is safe at least."

"You don't trust her to keep him safe?"

With a dark chuckle, Jeth said, "I don't trust her in general, to tell you the truth. One thing I do know though, is she does not go backward. If there is the slightest chance that she needs my help, for the good of our son, I have to find out. I mean . . . that's my duty, right?"

Patting him firmly on the chest, Serra said, "It's a good start. I guess I raised you right after all."

Another deep silence enveloped the space between them. Jeth cleared his throat. "I suppose I should be on my way."

"Will you ever come back?" she asked with a few more blinks.

"Will I be welcome back?"

"Of course, how else will I get to see my grandson? I'm curious to know what a Fae'ren Herrani baby might look like."

"Heh, well, here's hoping there will be a day we can both find out."

Serra touched his armored shoulder. "Be careful."

"I will."

Serra embraced him again and wouldn't let him go.

After a moment or two, she said, "I've also seen people do this during goodbyes, sometimes for a long time. I don't know—when should we stop?"

"We can stop now."

"Good." She stepped back with her hands behind her back.

"Thank you, Ser."

"For what?"

"For . . ." Jeth's words nearly caught in his throat. "For saving me."

Back in Fairieshome, Jeth found Vidya on her way out of the inn across from Clive's. She was walking with a slight limp, and her eyes were lined with dark circles, but otherwise, she appeared as good as new.

Jeth stepped in front of her in the street, halting her stride. "I'm coming with you. But on two conditions."

"You don't get to make conditions," she said. "You still owe me, remember?"

"I already returned the favor by mending that leg of yours." Jeth pointed down to the fresh bindings around her thigh.

"Only because I stayed to help you."

"Help that I didn't need. In fact, you may have increased the price on my head with the stunt you pulled with the major."

"Fine," she relented with a roll of her eyes. "What are these conditions?"

"We will go to Herran, and there you will help me track down Anwarr."

"You've got to be kidding me." Vidya threw up her arms. "Do you need me to reread that letter to you?"

"I'm not about to risk my life without making sure my son will be taken care of. He's still my responsibility regardless of what Anwarr thinks," Jeth said with fortitude.

Crossing her arms over her chest, Vidya nodded. "I suppose that's rather admirable of you. Okay, what else?"

"We run our plan by Snake Eye first."

Vidya shook her head. "No way, she just wants the dagger for herself."

"Wait. She?" Jeth cocked his head in question.

"Isn't . . . she?"

"I don't know. I'm asking you."

"Well, I don't know."

"Never mind." Jeth shook his head. "Snake Eye has a plan to stop Nas'Gavarr, and the Bloodstone Dagger is key in doing that. If we're able to retrieve it, he will probably let you borrow it to make your army if it helps him take down the Overlord."

"Alright, but I get to decide how much of my plans I want to let her in on. Got it?"

"Understood."

"You know," Vidya began. "I've been using Snake Eye for information for months, and she never told me she was out for Nas'Gavarr. How do you know so much?"

Jeth shrugged. "I'm special, I guess. Do we have a deal?" He put out his hand.

Vidya bit her lip in contemplation before taking Jeth's hand in hers and giving it a firm shake.

25

Trick of the Light

Night had fallen when Jeth arrived at the spice shop after his twelve-day journey from Fae'ren. Lys was sitting out on the front stoop smoking his pipe.

As soon as Jeth was in his sights, he stood up to greet him. "And the Fae'ren returns once again. Anwarr is not with you . . . ?"

"That's why I'm here," said Jeth. "Are the others inside?"

A gust of wind blustered by them as Vidya made an abrupt landing. Lys jumped back, tripped over the stoop, and fell on his backside. A few passersby yelped and ran into the nighttime Bazaar crowds. Without a word in greeting, Vidya unwrapped her cape from around her waist and refastened it over her shoulders to cover her folded wings.

Lys paled at the sight of her. "A-a harpy . . ."

"Oh, so you've heard of them," said Vidya.

"L-let me get the others." He opened the door to the shop, but Vidya ran up the steps and shut it on him.

"Not so fast. You're Crede."

"You are mistaken." Lys trembled.

"You've abused a woman before." Her brown eyes once again oozed with a wrathful hunger.

"You told her that?" Lys snapped at Jeth.

"I told her nothing about you, I swear," Jeth reassured. "Leave him alone, Vidya, you don't know what he's done."

"A harpy can sense these things," she said, not taking her attentions from the frightened Crede man.

Beyond antsy, Jeth dismounted and placed a hand on her shoulder. "Hey, can you bring down the scary a bit? He made one mistake, and he's paid dearly for it."

"I won't go back to Credence." Lys's quivering hand turned white gripping the door's handle.

Vidya moved aside. "Not that either of you could stop that from happening, but Credence doesn't want the likes of you back anyway. You can relax." She released the door.

With an audible gulp, Lys rushed inside the shop.

"So, you can sense the bad deeds of men? What do you find when you look at me?" Jeth asked as they led Torrent in the stables.

She eyed him up and down before saying, "You can be a bit of an ass, but nothing that warrants punishment . . . yet."

"Your harpy senses really tell you I'm an arse?" Jeth scoffed.

She gave him a wry glare. "No. My own senses do."

After putting Torrent away, they came in through the back door. Light footsteps could be heard coming down the staircase. Jeth turned toward them in hopes they might belong—by some miracle—to Anwarr, ready to throw herself into his arms like all the events leading to this point were just some colossal misunderstanding.

His heart sank at the sight of Istari. As soon as she looked upon Jeth standing at the foot of the stairs, her lips pursed. "You dare show your face here after how you two left us high and dry? Where's Ana?"

Jeth broke eye contact. "I was hoping she'd end up here somehow." He turned and walked the rest of the way into the shop.

"What is this I'm hearing?" Ash came stomping in from the baths, wearing nothing more than a towel wrapped around his bottom half and tracking in water behind him.

"Have any of you seen Anwarr?" Jeth asked.

"You're joking, right?" said Istari. "No, we haven't seen her. Is she still pregnant?"

"Last anyone checked."

Ash cracked his knuckles within clenched fists before shoving Jeth up against the wall. "What did you do?"

"Hey!" Jeth pushed back against Ash's scorpion chest, moving him just enough to give himself space. "When I came back from my last job, she was gone."

Ash took Jeth's scarf into his fists. "If anything happened to that woman or that baby, I will crush your skull with my bare hands!"

"I appreciate your concern for my baby, but—"

"It's just as likely mine as it is yours and you know that! Isn't that why you took her all the way to Fae'ren with you?" Ash bellowed, bashing him against the wall again.

Jeth pinched the sensitive flesh under Ash's bicep, and he released him. Ash's fist came at Jeth's face fast, but he ducked it, and Ash struck a jar of spices instead. Dried green powder billowed through the shop as Lys groaned and Istari coughed and moved out of the way.

Ash swung again, but Jeth avoided it effortlessly then socked him hard in the gut and again in the face, forcing him into a spice shelf. A few jars jostled, but Ash steadied them before they could topple over. Lys sighed with relief.

"Will you stop and listen to me for a second, you meathead?" Jeth snapped.

"You little shit!" Ash raised his fist one more time. Vidya appeared behind him and caught his bulky wrist in one hand. He struggled against her grip, veins bulging by the strain. She twisted his arm behind his back and bent him over one of the spice counters.

Holding his head in place, she said, "This is getting boring so allow me to explain. Anwarr ran off with a baby inside her and may be in danger, so ease off the messenger, will you?"

Jeth couldn't help but snicker to himself watching Vidya handle such a large man with ease. *Harpies can come in handy for some things.*

"Okay, okay, let go!" Ash pleaded. Vidya did so, allowing him to recompose himself, flushing with embarrassment. "Sorry, Vidya, I didn't see you there. Sag damn it, you're a strong one . . . h-how have you been?"

"Your towel's unraveling," Vidya said dryly.

Ash caught it before it fell off entirely. He smiled and turned even redder. "T-thanks."

Vidya rolled her eyes.

"So, you're with her now? Is she the reason Ana left you?" Istari accused.

"What? No, she's helping me."

Vidya pointed to Jeth with her thumb. "Do you really think I'd go for him?"

"Yeah, Star, don't be ridiculous." Ash scoffed.

"You want to know why she left? Here." Jeth shoved Anwarr's letter into Istari's hand and turned away to avoid watching her reaction while she read it.

Istari finished but kept her eyes on the paper. "I don't understand."

"She went with those spies from outside of Snake Eye's hideout," Jeth said. "The midwife told me they were taking her home. You knew her better than any of us. Where did Anwarr grow up? What was she running away from for all these years?"

"She never told me." Istari's bottom lip quivered as she handed the note back to Jeth. "Are you sure it was those men who took her?"

"That's how the midwife described them." Jeth folded the letter and shoved it back in his pocket. "Ezrai has a pendant that matches the sigil they wore."

"I saw it too," she said in near whisper. "Dammit, Ana." She spun around and ran her hands down her face.

Jeth calmly said, "If Ezrai has her then she needs our help."

"Do you think she would actually go back to that merchant slime?" Ash joined, clutching his fists in his hands and cracking each knuckle.

"She doesn't go back," Jeth insisted. "He could have threatened her—

threatened our child, to coerce her back with him. We need to find her."

Istari began, "But her letter says not to follow—"

"I don't give a shit what the letter says! We don't even know if those are her words," Jeth countered, the sting of them still fresh.

"Jeth's got a point," Ash said. "If Ezrai's involved, then I vote we err on the side of it not being Ana's choice. She's not part of our crew anymore, but she's still a part of us. We need to make sure our girl's all right. If she is, then I suppose we have to let her go."

"That's all I'm asking," Jeth agreed.

"I'll have Khiri set up your mounts for the journey to Odafi," offered Lys.

"Odafi? That will take days," Vidya grumbled.

"We might not have to go far." Istari's eyes lit up. "It's auction season here in the city. For as long as I've worked for Ezrai, he's never missed it."

"Convenient for us," Jeth said, anxious anticipation bubbling within him.

"Not that it matters," said Ash. "We won't be permitted access to the selling grounds without significant wares to pedal."

Lys cleared his throat from behind the counter. "Ashbedael, we're standing in a spice shop, and you can't think of anything we could sell?"

Ash immediately rolled his eyes at himself. "Right." He glanced at Vidya for a second, but she paid him no mind.

"Good thinking, Lys." Jeth turned to the rest of the group. "How many of you are up for a little shopping tomorrow?"

The next morning, the crew closed up shop for the day to attend the annual Herrani auction at the central arena. Brightly colored canopies filled the selling grounds. Everything from high-quality silks, rugs, and artworks to livestock were up on the blocks. Auctioneers blared from one end of the arena to the other, giving Jeth an awful earache as he strode through the crowds.

Hundreds of vendors from all across the desert were setting up their kiosks along the outskirts of the event, hoping to take advantage of the barrage of new buyers from more distant tribes. Lys and Khiri went to put up their spice kiosk while the rest of the crew searched the grounds for anything that could lead them to Ezrai.

Ash and Vidya walked well behind Jeth and Istari. "So . . . Vidya," Ash said in a low voice, likely not realizing Jeth could hear him. "Perhaps when all this is over we could . . . uh . . . finish what we started in the shop."

"You mean where I was about to beat you senseless?"

"Well . . . yeah."

Vidya groaned in disgust. "Don't ever speak to me again in your life." She lengthened her stride and left Ash to himself.

"We don't need to speak," he muttered, and Jeth snickered.

Amongst the auction blocks, there were private pavilions where rich merchants rested throughout the day. They brought large covered carts filled with gold, all of them heavily guarded by hired security forces.

"There's a big tent over that way." Ash pointed to a fairly obtrusive yellow pavilion on the south end. "Bahazur are guarding it. I think we found our man."

"Could be any of the fifty Merchant Council members though," Istari surmised.

"I'll make sure." Jeth dashed ahead of the group and ducked behind a line of camels waiting to be sold. He then honed his hearing to capture conversations within the large yellow tent.

The deep voice of Ezrai finally emerged through the barrage of other voices. "He's here," Jeth announced to the others behind him. "But not in the yellow one. He's in the red one farther down."

Istari gave Jeth a pat on the shoulder. "Great, let's go in. Everyone stay close to me."

With that suggestion, Istari placed a cloaking spell over Ash, Jeth, and Vidya as they casually approached the large red tent and edged past the Bahazur guarding it. The three thieves and a harpy slipped through the tent flaps and into the luxurious temporary abode of the Merchant Council's Treasure Keeper. He sat at a desk beside a stack of gold bricks, discussing business with another Odafi colleague of advanced age, his long sandy blonde beard, contrasted with charcoal skin.

Ezrai dismissed the older man, who took a few bricks and walked straight past the group and out of the tent. Istari slowly approached Ezrai's desk and unshrouded only herself.

The merchant jumped in his chair and yelped at the sudden sight of Istari standing before him. He drew a deep breath, exhaling with a throaty growl. "Istari, what a surprise. Are you here about Anwarr?"

"Where do you have her?" she asked, clutching her staff at her side.

"Have her? Whatever do you mean?"

"Cut the shit, Ezrai," Istari hissed. "I don't know how you figured out she was at that Fae'ren commune, but you are going to tell me where she is and what in Sag's name you're up to."

Ezrai stood up from his chair and circled around his desk. Istari involuntarily took a few steps back to accommodate his looming physique. "I have no idea what happened to that deceitful whore, so I will ask that you leave my sight . . . or in your case, leave here physically."

"You're lying!" Istari gripped her staff even tighter.

"Guards!" Ezrai called.

A second later, four Bahazur rushed into the tent to apprehend the Mage. The invisible Ash and Vidya knocked them all out in a few short moves.

Ezrai took out a knife of his own, only for Istari to knock it from his grasp with her staff. At that moment, the cloaking spell was removed from everyone in the tent, revealing Ash and Vidya restraining the guards and Jeth stepping up next to Istari.

"Just tell us where she is. Either you took her, or you know who did," he said.

"Oh, now I see." Ezrai smirked. "She finally abandoned you. Did I not warn you? It's what she does."

Jeth took another step forward but stopped himself from pummeling the man before he could get the truth.

Ezrai continued, "Personal validations aside, I don't know where she went, and I don't care. All I can do is offer you three some advice. Consider yourselves fortunate to have her out of your lives. In searching for her, you will only cause yourselves greater pain. Trust me, I know."

"That's not an option," Jeth objected. "She's with child!"

Ezrai's pale blue eyes lit up at the notion. "Now there's a twist. Which one of you . . . ?" He pointed to Jeth and Ash, then dismissed them with the wave of his hand. "Never mind. It's clear now where she must be."

"Where?" Jeth asked.

"She went to seek an ashipu to terminate her pregnancy. I can't see her wanting to carry either of your offspring to term."

Without warning, Jeth lunged at the treasure keeper, grabbed him by the collar of his robes, and bent him backward over his desk.

"Ah, so it's you," he rasped. "I had my coin on Ashbedael."

Jeth grabbed the pendent from the folds of Ezrai's robes and held it right up to his face. "The men who took her were wearing this sigil. You know something!"

He let Ezrai go so he could sit back up. "These were given to all Merchant Council members to grant us access to certain properties belonging to the Overlord. They represent the good will between our tribes."

"The Overlord," Jeth echoed, the hairs at the back of his neck standing on end.

"I can't imagine why someone wearing one of these would have followed her all the way out to the forests of Del'Cabria, but it wasn't me."

"They were also wearing red tunics," said Istari.

A glimmer of recognition flashed in Ezrai's eyes. "Did they seem younger than they were?"

"I-I guess. Except for the big one with the tulwar."

"Interesting . . ."

"What do you know?" Istari became rigid.

"The men you seek are eunuchs . . . from the harem."

"What would harem men want with Anwarr? She hasn't worked for them for over five years," said Ash.

Ezrai rubbed his chin and began pacing about the pavilion. "I assume you all know how she came about that tattoo on her back."

They all exchanged glances and nodded, everyone except Vidya who was lounging on a cushioned bench and picking at her fingernails.

Ezrai went on, "I had always wondered how she was able to convince one of the few Serpentine tattoo artists to mark her—a harem attendant—as a daughter of Nas'Gavarr. Seems to me anyone willing to do such a thing would be inviting grave misfortune on themselves. Although, I've seen her charm many a man to act against his self-interest numerous times, so I had dismissed her story as truth. But it never added up to me. She is too beautiful to be a mere attendant. A concubine, sure, but wives and concubines are not marked with the Serpentine. It serves to prevent the Overlord from mistakenly taking one his own daughters to bed."

"You think she might actually be one of his daughters?" Every tissue in Jeth's body recoiled at the thought. *It can't be. Nas'Gavarr would have found her long ago. He'd have a rapport with her . . . unless he does, and that's how he knew so much about you!* Jeth shook his head at his own frantic thoughts, imagining everything he had said to Anwarr—everything he had done with her and to her—that Nas'Gavarr could be aware of it all. His gut tied itself in knots, and it took all of his concentration not to throw up at Ezrai's sandaled feet.

"Those eunuchs are taking her home," Istari's voice shook. "Back to Herrani Palace where she was never supposed to leave."

Ezrai explained, "When the daughters come of age, they are allowed to leave the palace as long as they are under guard. When they marry or turn twenty-five, whichever comes first, they are as free as any other. Knowing Anwarr, she probably grew impatient. Now pregnant, she yearns for the luxuries she left behind."

Jeth was still shaking his head. "It doesn't make sense. She never goes back. . . ."

"Priorities can shift drastically for a pregnant woman," Vidya piped up from the bench. "Her body isn't totally hers anymore. It can be a rather frightening realization."

Everyone stood in silence, unsure what to make of Vidya's uncharacteristic input.

"Great, well"—Ezrai clapped and rubbed his hands together—"I've told you what you need to know. Now please leave. All of you. I am going to miss the camel auction."

"We're not done yet," said Jeth. "You said that pendant gets you into Overlord properties. Is one of those properties the palace?"

Ezrai nodded and narrowed his gaze at Jeth.

"You're going to help us get in."

"Are you insane?" Ezrai spat, "I'm not using my access to let a bunch of thieves run amok in one of the Overlord's most private places."

"Vidya," Jeth called. "Do you sense anything about this man right here?" He motioned toward Ezrai as the harpy rose from her seat and ambled over to him.

Looking him up and down, Vidya said, "This one reeks of violence toward women. He thinks they are tools whose only purpose is to satisfy his need, whether they want to or not."

"You have a lot of nerve to speak to me that way, woman."

Without another word, Vidya grabbed the treasure keeper around his neck and lifted him clear off the ground with one arm. Even shorter than him, she was still able to lift him high enough above her to cause his legs to dangle helplessly.

"What—how—what are you?" Ezrai wheezed.

Jeth said, "I forgot to introduce you to Vidya. She's a harpy . . . from Credence."

"Do you know what we do to men like you where I am from?" Vidya said with her usual sinister expression, only this time her wrath was replaced with what could be construed as delight.

Jeth cupped one hand around his mouth and whispered loudly, "They cut off your balls."

"Okay, okay!" Ezrai choked. "I'll help you. Put me down."

Vidya dropped him, and he took gasping breaths. Ash and Istari exchanged nervous glances of their own.

"Can I at least attend the auction first?" Ezrai croaked while massaging his throat.

Vidya answered his request with a thin-lipped scowl.

"Never mind," he said. "But I can't get you into the palace looking like a bunch of lowly thieves. You will need uniforms to blend in."

"I'm sure with your connections you can find enough for all of us," said Istari with an insincere grin.

"It may take a few days, and it will cost."

"How about you use that twenty thousand gold Anwarr and I let you keep. That, and I won't let the harpy play around with your insides," Jeth said. Vidya's face lit up at the mention of such a violent act, which did little to ease Jeth's discomfort in teaming up with her.

Ezrai looked straight at Jeth. "Anwarr has done nothing but lie to you for as long as you've known her. Her child may not even be yours. Why not just leave her where she is?"

Because she may know what Nas'Gavarr wants with me . . . and I still love her. He could barely stand to think those words let alone say them aloud.

Instead, he clenched the armlet tight in his palm before turning to leave. "Someone keep an eye on him. I'm taking a walk."

It didn't take much longer than a day for Ezrai to track down uniforms for the crew. Two red tunics for Jeth and Lys, armor and a tulwar for Ash, and blue, wraparound garments with a sheer head covering for Istari. Vidya had opted out due to the fact that her wings would be impossible to hide under the female attendant uniform. Instead, she agreed to wait outside the palace with everyone's clothing and weaponry.

As Ezrai lead the team to the service entrance, he turned to address them. "I can get you into the main atrium. You should be able to avoid suspicion while wearing those uniforms." He pointed to Jeth. "You may attract more attention with your complexion. I still think you should let the others go in for you."

Jeth had considered waiting with Vidya for that reason, but he knew he had to be the one to speak to Anwarr himself. "Don't worry, I can be unnoticeable when required."

"Very well. The harem is off limits to anyone with fully intact man parts. I hope you boys strapped yours away properly. Periodic checks are not uncommon, I hear. You wouldn't be the first men to sneak into this place to peek at the Overlord's treasures."

Ash and Jeth nodded uncomfortably. Jeth tried with all his might not to constantly readjust himself down there. *The faster we find Anwarr the better,* he thought.

Ezrai led them to the doorman where he showed his pendant and briefly explained that he was delivering new harem staff. They didn't question him too much and allowed everyone passage. Inside, the service halls opened up into a breathtaking atrium. Jeth gaped at the high dome ceilings, carved with depictions of cobras, naja, Salotaph, and Sagorath, all among dizzying, technicolor swirls.

They ventured down a great hall where at the end stood bronze gates to an outdoor terrace. The laughter of women and children could be heard beyond. Ezrai stopped. "The harem is through those gates. Wait for another eunuch to use his keys to enter and go in after him. Once inside, I cannot vouch for you any further. If you get caught, you're no longer my problem."

"Then we are done here. Hopefully, we never cross paths again," said Istari.

"I hope you're right." Ezrai gathered his robes and walked away.

The group ambled nonchalantly toward the gate. A eunuch, dressed in the same attire as Jeth and Lys, eventually came through the gate from the other side. Acting as if they were on their way in, the crew stepped through, nodding to the eunuch on his way out. The gate closed and locked with a clank behind them as they calmly walked by the guards standing like statues in the hallway leading to the courtyard. Beads of sweat formed under Jeth's tightly wrapped headwear, feeling their eyes on him as they passed.

They hadn't quite made it out of the hallway before a firm hand clamped down on Jeth's shoulder.

"You don't look like you belong here," a guard said while pulling him over to the right.

"Sure, I do," he protested.

Ash tried to come to Jeth's aid. "It's fine, he's new here."

"And who are you? Who is your charge?"

Ash hesitated in his reply. The guard ordered both Jeth and Ash to stand against the wall. Lys and Istari took the opportunity to continue past.

The guard called over another, and the two ordered them to spread their legs out so they could feel around for genitalia.

"Is this really necessary?" Jeth complained.

"I get no more joy out of this than you. Now hold still."

Jeth held his breath as the guard felt around between his legs. *Everything is going to be fine,* he told himself, *this is why you had to tuck it away.*

He closed his eyes, and one of the guards said, "You're free to continue."

With a sigh of relief, he looked up to find the guard waving Ash along. Jeth started after him, but the other guard pulled him back. "Not you, pull down your pants."

His heart jumped into his throat. "Pull down my what?"

The guard didn't bother repeating himself. He snatched Jeth's pants and pulled them down forcefully. Jeth's entire body flushed in mortification that only amplified when he spotted Istari standing, unseen, against the wall, eyes directed below his waist.

"Oh, my apologies, I—uh . . . didn't realize you lost all of it," the guard said.

"Huh?" Jeth looked down but couldn't figure out what the man meant. He quickly pulled his pants back up as the guards stepped aside and let him by.

He met up with Istari. "I don't understand what just happened."

"A trick of the light," she replied. "And you're welcome."

"Oh, thank Sagorath." He exhaled in relief. "I hope you didn't drain all of your light aura pulling that one off."

"I should have enough left to get me through the day," she said dryly.

Ash appeared beside them. "You got lucky there, Fairy Boy."

"Who's really the boy here, Ash?" Jeth retorted. "They searched you pretty thoroughly down there as well, but it was me they had to inspect."

"Because you didn't tuck it away properly."

"Maybe it's not so easy to simply tuck mine away."

Ash chortled. "They didn't have a problem letting you in here. I guess they didn't see much."

"But Istari—"

Lys interrupted with a curt whisper, "Can you buffoons argue about the size of your pricks after you get out of earshot of actual eunuchs!"

"Sorry, Lys," Ash and Jeth droned in unison.

"I'm sure you are."

The whole fiasco had been so distracting, Jeth hadn't noticed they'd walked to the center of the beautiful courtyard. Lush greenery lined the walls, trees sprouted from smooth stone tiles that reflected the sunlight beaming down through the open roof. Fountains with reptile likenesses filled sky-blue pools where children splashed about. A few of them almost collided with Jeth's legs as they ran by squealing.

Past the pool area, there were several arched alcoves where women lounged about on plush pillows and bedding, chatting, eating, or playing games. They were so striking, Jeth thought he must have died and gone to some paradise of the afterlife. *Anwarr could actually get lost here*, he thought.

"It's not quite fair, is it?" Ash said, his eyes darting from one beauty to another.

"That one man can possess so many women and still choose to live in a temple filled with corpses? What's the point?" said Jeth.

"These women don't want for anything, their children are taken care of, and the Overlord gets to make as many Mages as possible to put in his army," Istari replied.

"We should disperse to cover more ground," Lys suggested. "Ask around for any pregnant women brought here in the last few months."

Istari nodded. "Good idea. I'll go with Ash. Lys, you go with Jeth. Whoever finds Anwarr first, brings her back to this spot and waits for the others. Then, I can use a cloaking spell to get her out."

"If she even wants to get out," Ash commented, still gazing at the opulence at every turn.

Two giggling women scampered past, both topless, skin wet from having just left the pool, and breasts bouncing. Jeth, Ash, and Istari all stopped dead.

Lys sighed. "Keep your eyes in your heads. You're supposed to be eunuchs, remember?"

"I'm not," Istari said without taking her eyes from the women.

"Istari," Lys chastised.

She let out a groaning sigh. "Fine, we're here for Ana."

"For Ana," the men repeated in unison.

At that, the crew split in two and went down two separate hallways toward the indoor area. Jeth honed his sense of smell in hopes of picking up Anwarr's scent. Various perfumes wafted past him, making it near impossible to distinguish between them. Jeth and Lys peeked into several lounging areas where women sprawled about on pillows, half naked, smoking water pipes or sleeping, some of them even pleasuring one another. It was all Jeth could do not to become distracted. He spotted a few pregnant women among them, but none were Anwarr.

Upon emerging in another outdoor area, an overpowering flowery scent smacked him in the face. It brought with it instant memories of the Lunahalah—the ocean, the sand, and a slight arousal, though the scent was unpleasant. *You know that perfume.*

Jeth veered off to the left, surprising Lys. "Where are you going?"

"Not sure, but something's not right."

His nose led him to a small, private pond nestled in a circle of thin trees. Wading ankle deep was a woman holding her bejeweled sarong up to her knees and wearing a strapless top, partially covering her back tattoo. She was shorter than Anwarr and her figure more compact. "Excuse me?" Jeth asked as he approached the lone woman.

She turned around and right away Jeth recognized her sizzling tawny eyes.

"Lela?"

"That's not my . . ." Her words were caught in her throat. "Wait—you can't be in here."

She looked around frantically before opening her mouth to scream. Jeth dashed for her, took hold of her arm, and clasped his hand around her mouth before a sound could escape.

"It's all right. I'm not here to hurt you."

Lela screamed in his palm just as Lys appeared. "What are you doing, Jeth?"

"I'm looking for someone, and I think you know who," he said to Lela.

Her heartbeat lessened pace as she quieted down. She nodded.

"Now, I'm going to let go of you and ask you questions, but if you scream, I'll have no choice but to smother you until you lose consciousness. Got it?"

She nodded again, only quicker. Jeth released her, and she backed away but made no move to run.

"What do you want to know?" she asked breathlessly.

"If you're a daughter of Nas'Gavarr, what were you doing in Odafi on the Lunahalah?"

"Is that relevant right now?" Lys asked.

Jeth continued, "I'm guessing you and your friend were looking for more than a good time with me."

"Sahadina was a friend I met in Odafi. She was looking for a good time. I was supposed to lure you away while my betrothed took Anwarr. We were going to deliver you both back to my father. I didn't ask why he wanted you. I had to do it so my marriage could go forward."

"Your betrothed? Chief Ukhuna? You're Saf'Raisha!" Jeth said, flabbergasted.

"Yes. But you killed him, and now I have to wait until another beneficial marriage comes around. Thanks for that."

"Trust me, I did you a favor. Now tell me where to find Anwarr. I only want to make sure that she and her child are safe. Then I'll go."

Raisha's eyes widened. "You're the baby's father." She turned away and muttered more to herself. "That's why he took her away yesterday."

Jeth took hold of her arms. "Who? Where?"

"Father," she said in near whisper. "He's taking her to his Temple of Sagorath."

"Why?"

"To punish her, I imagine. She ran away and became impregnated with another man's seed. It is at the temple where the child will likely be terminated, and she will be sentenced to serve those repulsive magi. That is what they say happens to women who dishonor the Overlord."

Releasing her, Jeth recoiled in horror. "No . . . h-he wouldn't do that to his own daughter."

"You misunderstand," Raisha said. "Anwarr is not his daughter. She's his *wife.*"

26

I Blame You

Jeth kept shaking his head, unable to make sense of the words coming from Saf'Raisha's mouth. "No, no, that can't be true. She has a tattoo on her back like yours."

Raisha crossed her arms and said, "Oh, I'm aware. Clever how she came by it too. To be a new wife of the harem can be thrilling at first, but becomes tiresome after a while. As daughters, we get to go to market, talk to outsiders, but the wives and concubines . . . they're basically prisoners."

"So how did she end up with it?" Jeth asked.

"An artist came to mark those of us who had come of age. One of my sisters had fallen ill that day, and Anwarr had offered to let him know she wouldn't be able to make it. Then all of the sudden, Anwarr was sporting the tattoo. My sister had to wait another year before the artist would return. No one wanted to say anything as there was no telling how many would be punished for her little ruse. We all stayed quiet and let her roam about as a daughter instead of a wife. It seemed to work since my father never took her to bed again."

Jeth's guts twisted in painful knots at the mere thought of that murderous Mage taking her to his bed even once.

Since Jeth was unable to form words, Lys went on for him, "It would also allow her to leave the palace."

Raisha nodded. "She didn't stick around for much longer. She went to market, ditched her bodyguard, and was never seen again. That was until the Tezkhan reported that his Herrani bride and her Sunil servant made off with his most precious possession." She shook her head and huffed, "Bitch had some nerve posing as me."

"Don't I know it," Jeth muttered, nausea creeping up into his throat.

"I have nothing more to say on the matter." Raisha took steps out of the pool. "I'm sorry you had to hear it all from me, but you're too late. She is probably through the Burning Waste by now."

Jeth said nothing as he watched Raisha disappear behind the line of trees. He shoved his hand in his pocket and clutched the armlet until its tiny rubies cut into his palm. His body was stiff and unmovable.

Lys's hand on his shoulder jolted him out of his silent rage. "Come. We need to meet up with the others."

Jeth jerked away from him and marched back out of the water. "And then what? Tell them they've been harboring a runaway wife of the Overlord for the past several years? Sag damn it, what we do, Lys? Go after her? Leave her? I . . ." He doubled over, struggling not to vomit. He tried to breathe, but each inhalation made him gag.

"Anwarr is a liar and always has been . . ." Lys began.

"Look, I get it!" Jeth snapped, pushing himself to an upright position. "Lying is what she does. I have no one but myself to blame for falling for her. So why then, should any of this surprise me, right?"

"What I mean is"—Lys stepped closer to Jeth—"we were all deceived by her in one form or another, but she had her reasons. It's how she survived in this brutal world. I spend a lot of my time observing you all from behind my counter. I've seen how she interacts with the others and how she is when she thinks she's alone. . . . I can't tell you what's the right thing to do. What I can tell you is, that if anything about Anwarr is true, it is how much she loves her crew, and you most of all, I think."

"In her letter, she said that she was living a lie. She was talking about being Nas'Gavarr's wife. They have a connection, whether it's a rapport or something else. Either way, she must be the reason he knew I'd be at the temple that day."

Lys sighed heavily, shaking his head. "Such a thing we may never know for sure."

Later that day, the crew had returned to the shop and were sitting cross legged around the dinner table. Lys had prepared a nice meal of spiced lamb in an attempt to lift everyone's spirits, but nobody could get past the first few bites. Even Khiri, who usually inhaled his food, sat somberly on the end, closest to the third-floor stairs, not touching a morsel on his plate. Even the man who prepared the meal didn't partake, likely to avoid possible conversation with a harpy.

Ash dropped a piece of bread he was about to bite down on to ask, "Are you sure Saf'Raisha was telling the truth? Anwarr can't be a wife of Nas'Gavarr."

"You saw the harem," replied Jeth. "Practically one-third of Herran's female population is held up in that place. I say the chances are pretty damn good that she is."

Istari's expression was deadpan. "All these years, she would never talk about her home, nothing from her past. She knew everything about me, and I hardly knew her. She must have been terrified all the time."

"Not terrified enough." Ash puffed through his nostrils. "She stole an emerald and a sarcophagus right from under her husband's nose."

"Maybe her way of getting back at him somehow," Jeth surmised, giving up on his meal and sitting back against the wall.

"She told us she didn't recognize those eunuchs. Why didn't she trust me? I could have helped her. . . ." Istari's bright blue eyes began to well up with tears.

"There was nothing you could have done, Star. You shouldn't blame yourself," Jeth said.

"I don't." Her eyes met Jeth's and turned to ice. "I blame you."

"Me?"

"I knew from the start taking you into this crew was a mistake," she said in a low, quavering voice that made Jeth's stomach lurch.

"I get that you're angry right now, but she lied to us all. How was I supposed to know any of this would happen?"

Istari steadily began to raise her voice. "You couldn't just let her be, could you? She just had to be your possession!"

"Hey, it was her choice to quit the thieving life!"

Istari scoffed, tears flowing down her cheeks. "You put a baby in her and all the sudden she wants to run away with you, back to your forest, as if she couldn't find a good midwife here. What did you think would happen? You'd be a happy little family? We were her family, and you took her from us!"

Jeth sat across the table, stunned, his heart beyond heavy. He knew he had never been Istari's favorite crew member, but never did he think she held this much animosity toward him. *Maybe it would have been better if you'd just left that night.*

"I love her too, Star." His voice cracked at the words.

"That doesn't make this any less your fault!" she screeched. In a flash, she threw her wine glass straight at Jeth's head. He dodged it, and it smashed against the wall behind him, making Khiri yelp in his chair.

"Star, calm down!" Ash barked.

"Don't take his side now!" she blared at Ash sitting beside her. "Where is all your talk about crushing his skull if anything happened to our girl?"

Ash's gaze darted between Istari and Jeth. ". . . Yes, but—"

"Well, something happened, and he's right here!"

"I'm not going to kill him!"

Vidya, sitting unobtrusively at the far end of the table, opposite of Khiri, cleared her throat. "Umm, you all better not. I need him for later."

Istari pointed to Vidya while screaming at Jeth. "Why is she still here? Are you two fucking or something?"

"I don't know why you keep suggesting we're—"

Istari cut Vidya off, "Why did Ana really leave you, Jeth?"

"She didn't. Those harem men came and took her." He could feel a fire rise to his face.

"You expect me to believe that? Even in her vulnerable state, if she didn't want to go with them, she wouldn't have."

Bringing his head down, he gritted his teeth. He had hoped Anwarr had been taken against her will, but if she had, why leave the armlet and a note with the sole purpose of breaking his heart?

Istari went on, "What could have possessed her to go against her serpent's philosophy and potentially put her own child at risk?"

"Enough, Star," Ash warned.

"I think I know what happened," she theorized. "You finally had her all to yourself, but you knew you wouldn't be able to keep her happy, so you tried to control her. That's why she willingly went with those men. . . . To get away from you!"

"That's crazy!" Jeth protested.

"May I interject?" said Vidya. "As a harpy, I can tell if a man has mistreated women in the past and Jeth is not one of those men."

"I didn't ask for your input, harpy bitch!" Istari hissed.

Vidya narrowed her gaze at Istari. "You might want to watch your mouth, little girl!"

At that moment, a high-pitched shriek ripped across the table. Everyone clutched their ears to muffle the painful wailing of Khiri. Once attentions were firmly directed at him, the boy buried his head into his arms upon the table and wept.

"Khiri . . . ." Istari peeped as she placed a comforting hand on his shoulder. He shook her off and bolted up the stairs.

Jeth continued in a controlled tone, "What do you want from me? To get on my knees and beg forgiveness for taking Anwarr away? Because I won't. I did want her all to myself, I'll admit that, but for you to say that I would do anything to hurt her just proves you took zero time to get to know me."

"You're right." Istari wiped away her tears. "I didn't get to know you—I didn't want to. You're just another entitled Del'Cabrian prick."

"But had you, you'd realize that I'm not!"

"Maybe you didn't mean to hurt her, but it changes nothing. Anwarr's gone because of you. I want you to remember that."

Istari's words were like a blunt blade being lodged into Jeth's sternum, making it painful to breathe. She stood and was about to storm off to the kitchen patio, when Vidya called out, "For crying out loud, the woman's not dead . . . at least not yet."

Istari stopped, her shoulders slumped in defeat. "She might as well be."

"Vidya's right," Jeth said. "He won't kill her. He's waiting for me to finish the ritual."

"The what now?" Ash scratched his bald head.

"I know what I have to do." Jeth rose to his feet and walked around the table.

Ash scoffed. "Don't tell me you're going to try rescuing her. You barely survived the last run in with Nas'Gavarr."

"Except I did," Jeth reminded.

He went to collect his weapons at the foot of the stairs as Vidya rose to do the same.

"I may hate you right now, but that doesn't mean I want you to commit suicide over this." Istari couldn't even look him in the eye as she spoke.

Stepping up to her, Jeth said, "If you love Anwarr so much, prove it. Help me bring her home."

"Don't be stupid." Istari shook her head. "This isn't a standard job. You're talking about stealing Nas'Gavarr's wife right in front of him. We'll all die, and Ana wouldn't want that."

"Star's right," Ash stood to join them. "Do you even have a plan?"

"Not really, but any plan we come up with, no matter how clever, will likely fail. There is only one way to get Anwarr back and protect my son. I have to give Nas'Gavarr what he wants. And what he wants is me. Don't ask me to explain how I know that, it's a long story." Jeth belted his bow and quiver to his back and placed his swords in their scabbards.

"And if the baby's not yours?" Ash posed.

"She told me it was mine, Ash," said Jeth. "I have no reason to trust her at this point, but I have to believe she wouldn't lie about that."

Ash bit the inside of his cheek. "I suppose it doesn't matter who the father is. She still chose you."

Jeth swallowed the uncomfortable lump in his throat. "Does that mean you're not coming with me?"

Both Ash and Istari kept their eyes down. It was Khiri, pitter-pattering down the stairs, who approached Jeth with bow and knife in hand.

Jeth crouched down and took him by the skinny shoulders. "You're a brave kid, Khir. I'll be sure to let An know you wanted to come for her, but it's too dangerous." Khiri stomped his feet and voiced a grunt of dismay. He wiped the tears still welling up in his raw, red eyes. "I promise I'll bring her back in one piece, alright?"

With another growl of frustration, he dashed back up the stairs. Jeth felt a twinge of guilt for not being able to take the boy with him, but more so because he made a promise he wasn't sure he could keep.

"Anyone else?" Again, nobody made a sound. Only Vidya stepped beside Jeth, as he expected.

"Guess it's just you and me again." He turned and drilled his gaze into the two thieves. "Think of it as my final initiation."

Ash's fists clenched, but he wouldn't make eye contact.

With a nod to Vidya, Jeth walked out onto the kitchen balcony, and she followed close behind.

"You'll die if you go back there," Istari called after him.

"We'll see," he replied.

Vidya took off her cape, tied it around her waist, and spread her wings. Jeth put his arms out so she could wrap hers around his chest. A push off the balcony launched the two of them into the sky.

"Salotaph's mercy, not her. . . ." Snake Eye lamented.

Vidya and Jeth had stopped by to inform him, in case he could assist. They, Snake Eye, and Yemesh now stood somberly in the private back room.

"Did you know she was married to him?" Jeth asked.

Snake Eye shook his head. "To be honest, I thought she might have been his daughter. When I caught her trying to steal from me the first time we met, there was no telling what I would have done had I not noticed her tattoo. I decided to take pity on her, believing her to be my niece."

"Would have been nice if you told me this a long time ago," said Jeth as he crossed his arms.

With a wave of the hand, Snake Eye said, "She denied it, of course, and I was content not to pry further. Oftentimes, our lies serve more as a method of protecting ourselves than as a tool of destruction."

Vidya spoke up, "Let's get into it. Jeth tells me you are building an arsenal."

"Yes, and I assume you are here because you want me to use it to save Anwarr," Snake Eye surmised. "I regret to say I am not ready."

"What more do you need?" Jeth pressed.

"A Spirit Mage would be a start. And more time."

"We don't have time. Tell me what you are planning to do with the artifacts."

Snake Eye sighed. "I can't. . . ."

"Have I ever given you any reason not to trust me?" Jeth asked.

"You still won't tell me what Gavarr tried to do to you in that temple or how you escaped," the ashipu said, crossing his arms.

"I escaped by sheer luck," Jeth replied. "But I can tell you what Nas'Gavarr was about to do to me."

Snake Eye's eyes widened. "So, you were hiding something."

"Guess I was protecting myself."

With a bite of his lip, Snake Eye relented, "I'm working on a resurrection spell. A big one."

"Dulsakh," whispered Jeth.

"I can use his remains to resurrect the body with flesh magic, but I need a powerful Spirit Mage to extract his spirit from the emerald. Without the spirit of Dulsakh, I fear I will have no means of bringing the naja army under my control."

"How would it work?" Vidya asked.

"Dulsakh created all the other Najahai. And they transformed themselves into naja to fight the hybrids, leaving five true Najahai to rule. A warrior Mage, knowing the Najahai were near immortals, used powerful spirit magic to exercise Dulsakh's soul out of his living body by extreme tortures. The Mage absorbed all Dulsakh's life force into himself and buried the rotting corpse in the Archipelago. He became the Immortal One as a result and went on to eliminate the rest of the naja. Realizing they had lost, the final four Najahai went into a permanent slumber on various islands, awaiting the day their progenitor is made whole again. A spirit always prefers its own essence and flesh. I bring the body back, release the spirit from the emerald, and Dulsakh is made whole."

"But you don't have his essence? Or do you?" Vidya asked.

"The Immortal One passed down Dulsakh's life force to his descendants . . ."

"You're one of those descendants," Jeth guessed.

Snake Eye nodded. "Which is why I have to be the one to awaken Dulsakh. My brother cannot be trusted with that power."

"Won't that awaken the other four Najahai?" Jeth asked.

"I will only use Dulsakh to turn the naja against Gavarr then put him right back where I found him," said Snake Eye.

"I met a Spirit Mage in Ingleheim," said Jeth. "She discovered a way to free the naja's minds, undoing the hold that Saf'Ryeem has over them—"

Snake Eye put a hand up to stop him. "I will send for this sorceress. However, her process would be far too slow. Through Dulsakh's spirit, I can free them in an instant."

This all sounds insane, Jeth thought. Ancient naja progenitors and harpy armies were way over his head. None of it was going to get Anwarr to safety any time soon, if at all.

Jeth said, "Nas'Gavarr took Anwarr to the temple yesterday. He could have already sucked my son's life force out of her womb. I have to go now."

"You have yet to tell me your secret," said Snake Eye.

"He tried to sacrifice me to the Serpentine Gods using the Bloodstone Dagger."

Taking a step back, Snake Eye grimaced at Jeth's words. "Whatever for? Such practices were eliminated after he wiped out the Death tribes. Are you sure that's what he intended?"

Jeth nodded, the helplessness he felt so many months ago still fresh. "He said I can help him free humanity or something."

"He has truly lost his mind, or he knows something I don't," Snake Eye mumbled to himself as he continued to pace about the room. "He was never the same after he returned from Elmifel."

"Elmifel Province?" Vidya piped up. "Where the ashray live?"

"Their society is extremely closed off from humans, even urlings. Only the Royal Family of Del'Cabria has access to their Holy City. Gavarr was one of the few humans allowed tutelage there. The ashray are near immortal themselves and were interested in how he was able to live for so long. He studied in a monastery in the Holy City of Thessalin for thirty years while I struggled to keep the Herrani tribes together. When he returned, he was different . . . more fanatical. He wouldn't tell me what happened in that monastery."

"Is that when he started believing in the Way?" Jeth wondered aloud.

"Yes, as a matter of fact," Snake Eye said. "He put the Death tribes to flame, repurposed their gods, unified the desert people, and established freedom and equality for all. Except, instead of sitting back and ruling the freed tribes, he allows them to fall into this crime-ridden anarchy while he continues to wage war. I fear we will fall back into our old death worshiping, slave trading ways if we continue down this path."

"I'm sorry, I wish I could help more, but if the Way is real, and his and mine are connected as he said. Then I have to face it," said Jeth.

Snake Eye placed a hand on his shoulder and gave it a hearty pat, not the squeeze and rub-down he usually did. "I'm sure going to miss you, Little Gershlon. If you manage to get Anwarr out, I promise to treat her child as if he were of my own blood."

"I've seen how you treat your own blood," Jeth said with a raised eyebrow.

"You know what I mean."

"I do . . . and thanks." Jeth touched Snake Eye's hand upon his shoulder.

With a heavy sigh, Snake Eye turned to Vidya. "And I suppose you're still going with him?"

"I don't have much of a choice either, I'm afraid," she said.

"Still looking for that warping gate?"

Vidya opened her mouth and hesitated to speak. "Yes. We will use it to escape with Anwarr. I need a way to destroy it from the other side though."

He stuck his finger into the air. "Ah! I may have just the thing."

Snake Eye asked Yemesh to unlock one of the large drawers in his bureau and bring him a small pistol shaped apparatus and a pair of black leather gloves. Jeth recognized it from the Steinkamp Magitech he had acquired.

"Is that blast gel?" he asked.

Handing the gloves to Vidya, Snake Eye nodded. "That it is. You will need to put on those gloves to activate the fire essence imbedded in this gel."

"How does it work?" Vidya's lips curled in a curious smile as she put the man-sized gloves on her much smaller hands.

"Allow me to demonstrate." Snake Eye ever so slightly pulled the trigger mechanism on the dispenser and pushed out the tiniest amount of clear gelatin in one of his clay bowls on his desk; it appeared as nothing more than a drop of water. "A little goes a long way, so use sparingly." He motioned for everyone to stand back. "Now squeeze your left hand into a fist to ignite the fire essence."

Vidya did, and a loud pop noise rippled through the room, shattering the clay. Everyone shielded their faces.

"Rangardia would love to get their hands on some of this," Vidya said as she shoved the blast gel dispenser in her pocket.

The wooden desk caught fire in the tiny explosion. "Oops. I have just the thing for that. The ice powder, please, Yemesh."

The Sunil brought out another Magitech item in a small white sack. Snake Eye poured a bit of the grayish powder in his palm and turned to Vidya. "Squeeze your fist when I tell you."

Snake Eye sprinkled the powder on the fire like a chef finishing his signature dish with a dash of spice. "Now!"

Vidya balled her gloved fists again. A spray of frost spread along the corner of the desk, putting out the fire and turning the wood to ice. With a hard tap from Snake Eye, the corner of his desk broke off. "It works on anything that is not living tissue, though it will still cause some damage."

Vidya gasped again. "Amazing! Can I have some of that too?"

"I would love to give you all the Magitech you can carry, my winged warrior, but it won't do any good against an Essence Mage as powerful as Gavarr."

She frowned as Snake Eye handed the packet of powder back to Yemesh to put away.

"I guess this settles it then," said Jeth. "We swoop, we swipe, and we blow up the gate."

After their final goodbyes, Yemesh escorted Vidya and Jeth out of the building. When the Sunil went back inside, Jeth said, "Why didn't you mention you were coming along for the dagger?"

She pursed her lips. "I thought about it, but you didn't trust her enough to tell her how you really escaped, so how can I trust her with my plans? She intends to resurrect the Najahai. Do you know how brutal they were? And people think my Harplite idea is ill-advised." Vidya walked past Jeth and out of the narrow alleyway. "Now come on, we're wasting time."

Jeth gulped. Vidya had a point. For all they knew, resurrecting the Najahai could very well be worse than leaving Nas'Gavarr alive . . . but so could the Harplite. *If either of them are successful at defeating the Overlord, what then?*

A shiver ran through him.

27

One Honest Thing

Soaring toward the Temple of Sagorath, Jeth spotted two camels tied up near the entrance.

"They're here," he called up at the harpy carrying him. She veered over the temple's roof and dove through the skylight, bringing them safely to the ground on the side of the statue with Salotaph's likeness.

Once Vidya released him, Jeth stretched his sore arms. The stench of decay still hung in the air, bringing gory images of Melikheil flayed alive to the forefront of his mind. He honed all his senses to ensure they were alone in the atrium.

"We're clear," he said.

"I'm going to find the gate and see if it's operational while you look for Anwarr," Vidya said.

"Are you sure you remember the way?"

"I think so. I'll come find you after I've activated it. Remember, the first one of us presented with the opportunity to swipe the dagger should do so."

"My first priority is getting Anwarr to safety," Jeth reminded her.

"And the dagger is mine," she replied.

"Alright."

"Just . . ." Vidya bit her lip.

"What?"

"Try not to die."

"Thanks." Jeth smirked. "But if I do, can I count on you to get Anwarr out of here for me?"

Vidya sighed heavily. "Sure."

Her response didn't inspire a lot of confidence. "I'll try not to die then," he muttered.

Vidya spun on her heels and headed toward the staircase to the basement labyrinth.

Once she was out of sight, Jeth nocked an arrow. He stepped out around the giant statue, keeping his arrow aimed and ready to release. The temple atrium was empty. Even the corpses in the cages had mostly rotted away. Dried brown flecks of blood still lined the walls where Melikheil had been ripped apart. Jeth fought back his urge to vomit as he continued around the statue and up the staircase on the other side of the room.

Honing his hearing as far as he could, the only sounds coming to him were the bleating of the camels outside. *It's too quiet in here.*

Jeth edged around corridors on the second floor overlooking the atrium. He expected a magus or two to jump out at him, but there was none.

At the end of the hallway was another flight of stairs. He climbed to the third floor, and the smell of death lessened to where he could distinguish other scents like dust, sand, and the burning oil in the wall sconces. Sharpening his senses further, Jeth finally picked up faint fragments of Anwarr's enticing aroma. He quickened his pace through the corridors—his heart pounding harder as the scent grew stronger. Reveries of him touching and kissing her rushed through his mind like an unstoppable river. *One waft of her and all is forgotten?* He tried to keep his mind clear as he approached a stone door and pushed it aside.

He spotted a modest bed and an old chest around the corner. To his left, sitting on a chair made of bones, and staring vacantly out the arched window, was Anwarr.

Bringing his bow down, Jeth stood, frozen. She looked different than he had expected, having filled out a bit in the face and breasts. Her hair, partially covered by a sheer scarf, was tied back and fell as twisted bundles over her shoulder. She wore a two-piece pantsuit of gold embroidered white silk, her protruding belly exposed.

Jeth opened his mouth to say her name, but nothing came out. Even after all this time and all that had happened, Anwarr was still the most beautiful thing he'd ever been in the presence of, and he hated himself for not knowing what to do. His bow fell from his weakened grip and clattered to the floor.

Anwarr gasped and turned to face him. Her gaze was sorrowful, eyes like melting icicles of grief. She didn't say anything, only turned back to the window.

"An." Jeth slowly stepped toward her, his knees aching by the weight of his own legs. "Are you all right?"

She shook her head, still not facing him. "How did you find me?"

He swallowed hard, fists clenching and unclenching. "Where is he?"

"I haven't seen him in hours," she whispered, still not looking at him.

"Good, then let's get out of here."

Anwarr didn't move a muscle other than to keep shaking her head back and forth. "You shouldn't have come here."

"It's too late now, so come on." He went to grab her arm, but she pulled away. "You need to leave."

"Not without you."

At last, she looked straight at him. "I mean it, Jethril. We are fine here, just forget about us!"

Jeth dropped to one knee before her. "You're an idiot if you think that's ever going to happen." He grabbed her hand, and she winced and tugged it from his grasp. Her right hand was bandaged with a round red blood stain at her palm. "Your hand—"

"Jethril, please," she cried. "If you don't get out of here now, he's going to kill you!"

"He can try," Jeth said with fervor.

"Do you think it was easy for me to write that letter? I did it so that you wouldn't follow me here. Why do you always do this?"

Jeth placed his hand on her stomach. "You should know by now I'm not keen on following orders."

Anwarr bit her quivering lip, looking as if she would snap at him again. Instead, a breathless, shaking laugh escaped her. At that moment, the baby kicked against Jeth's hand. He gasped and put his ear up to it and heard a new world of noises, including a tiny rapid heartbeat distinctive from Anwarr's and his own.

She sighed as she ran her hands through his hair. While still listening to his baby, Jeth whispered, "You didn't have to go with those eunuch's, An."

"But I did," Anwarr replied. "Just weeks after you left, Herrani men arrived in droves. The so-called isolated commune was swarming with them for months."

Jeth lifted his head off her. "Why? There were no warrior camps anywhere near Lanore."

"They were mostly laborers and some stonemasons from the Tradesmen's Guild. They were building something nearby. I'm not sure what. Soon after they arrived, Saf'Ryeem came to the commune, and the eunuchs showed up a few weeks later. Saf'Ryeem somehow knew I was there and sent a mind message back to his father."

"Then why not write me that?"

"Because then you'd come for me, which is why they took me back with them in the first place. I left you that note so there would be a chance you might stay away. I'd find a way to survive, like I always have, but you . . ." Anwarr closed her mouth to choke back more tears before turning from him.

Jeth shot up to his feet. "So, you did know Nas'Gavarr was using you to get me back here."

"Yes, he told me," said Anwarr.

"Did he tell you before or after you wrote this note to keep me away?" He snatched it out of his pocket and flung it onto her lap.

She clutched it in her hands and sputtered, "I . . . I figured . . ."

"You knew the whole time, didn't you?" Jeth's tone lowered as he retreated inside himself.

She wouldn't respond—wouldn't even look at him. His anger finally erupted. "Look at me! Tell me you didn't know what Nas'Gavarr wanted with me this entire time!"

Finally meeting his eyes, she stated, "I didn't!" then continued more quietly, "I didn't know what he wanted exactly. . . ."

"Do you have a rapport with him?" Jeth blared.

"No. There would need to be a strong emotional bond between him and me, and there is no such thing, I assure you."

"Then how did he come to be here that day?"

Putting her head down, her tears started falling upon the parchment she twisted within her hands. "Remember when I told you those eunuchs waited for me outside of Snake Eye's place? They weren't gone by the next morning. The bodyguard got the jump on me, intent on taking me back to the harem. But they made me an offer instead. . . . My freedom in return for delivering you to the Overlord."

Jeth sank to his haunches, put his head in his hands, and tugged at his locks. But no matter how hard he clung to them, the Crannabeatha's peace eluded him. "I'm not hearing this."

Anwarr kept going, "I asked them why they wanted you, but even they didn't know. I couldn't tell them where the shop was, so I ended up telling them you'd be at the temple a few days later. I suggested to Ash that he let you go in alone as an initiation. I didn't think I had a choice."

"Sweet Mother . . ." he rasped, floating outside of himself.

"When you never returned, I couldn't forgive myself. Then you did, and I was so relieved—"

"Horseshit!" Jeth straightened up. "You had the chance to come clean, but chose not to. I thought I was a danger to you when all this time I should have been running from you!"

"It was unforgivable. I know that," Anwarr cried. "But I never expected to fall for you."

"I should have left when I had the chance." The lump in his gut started to consume him from the inside out.

"What's in the past no longer exists—"

"No, An! There are some things that you can't run from, things that can never be erased," Jeth bellowed. "You let me go to my death, and you're doing it all over again! All to keep from having to go back to a life of luxury in a palace. Is that existence so awful for you that you'd sacrifice my life?"

Jeth was instantly brought back to the night when Anwarr asked him a similar question. *'Is your navigator's life worth your freedom?'* It was staring him in the face the whole time, Anwarr's true nature obscured behind that luminous smile and frosted gaze. *You're such a fool!*

"I didn't know if he'd kill you!" Anwarr spat back. "And what about my life? My mother was ill, the harem needed new concubines, and my father thought, 'I have too many daughters as it is, I'll sell one to the harem, and our problems will vanish.' I was apparently so pleasing to the eye the Overlord decided I'd be better used to breed with than to solely receive pleasure from. The man who fought for the freedom of every man, woman, and child in Herran, keeps slaves for himself. All because I'm the object of desire for some greedy immortal Mage, I don't get the same freedoms as everyone else? How is that fair?"

Jeth's anger dampened momentarily after listening to Anwarr's lament, but it wasn't enough to quell it completely. "I'm sorry that happened to you, An, I really am. It's not any fairer than being born parentless in a place that shuns orphans, but that's the nature of things. It doesn't excuse you from what you did. I would have done anything to protect you, probably even volunteered to face the Overlord for you, knowing how much of an idiot I was back then."

"I'm so sorry, Jethril. I wish I could take it all back. That's why I wanted you to stay away this time."

"And what would happen to you if I didn't show?"

"Nas'Gavarr may be a murderous warmonger, but he is a man of his word. He promised I'd be safe if I came to him willingly and never attempted escape. He even promised to allow our son to grow up with the harem like one of his own. This was the best way I could ensure all our survival."

A heartbreaking silence enclosed the space between the two of them. Jeth felt like he was sinking deeper into the floor as if an Earth Mage were liquefying the stone under his feet.

"I'm sorry. . . ." she whispered again.

"Yeah, you said that already." Jeth grabbed her by the arm and lifted her from the chair. She had gotten so much heavier.

"Wait," she pleaded. "If we go, he'll kill us both!"

Jeth bent down and grabbed his bow from the floor. "No, he won't. I'm taking you to Vidya. She'll get you out of here, and I'll be staying behind." He roughly tugged Anwarr along with him and out of the room.

"Who's Vidya?" she sharply pulled back her arm, but Jeth's grip didn't wane.

"Stop struggling." He yanked harder, making her cry out as he practically dragged the pregnant woman down the hallway. She began to cooperate as they made their way back to the atrium.

They circled around the statue and headed toward the downward staircase. Anwarr suddenly gasped. Her arm tore out of his grasp as she collapsed to her knees. She began to wheeze, her complexion paling.

"An!"

Jeth sensed movement from within the empty pool—a shirtless man with skeletal sapphire-laced tattoos. His heart sank and accelerated all at once.

"I'm glad you came, but I wish you would not leave so soon," said Nas'Gavarr in a calm voice. *How did you not see him there . . . ? A cloaking spell?*

"Jeth . . ." Anwarr moaned breathlessly, clutching her stomach.

"Stop whatever you're doing to her, you sick bastard!" he growled.

"Drop your weapons, remove your armor, and step away from my wife."

"Alright, alright." He dropped his bow and quiver first, then unsheathed and threw down his blades. He took steps away from Anwarr while working to undo the bindings holding his armor in place.

As soon as the dusty brigandine hit the floor, Anwarr could breathe normally again, and color returned to her extremities. It was all Jeth could do not to run to her, but he remained still.

"I thought the first time you came here would have been the end of it. Know that I didn't want it to come to this, but such is the Way. It had to be today, and it had to be for them." Nas'Gavarr pointed to Anwarr, still resting on her hands and knees and holding her stomach.

"How can I be sure you'll let them go after you're finished with me?"

Taking the green and red-speckled dagger out from his scabbard, Nas'Gavarr gazed upon it. "I only need enough of your blood to turn this entire blade red. You may survive."

"Then what? You'll just let me go with your wife and my unborn child?"

"She can live out her days in my palace where she belongs in return for your cooperation."

"Let them go first. Then we can get started," Jeth countered.

Nas'Gavarr nodded. "Anwarr, you may go. Ride to the Burning Waste and wait for me."

"I don't understand," she said. "What are you going to do with him?"

"An, do as he says," Jeth said firmly, not taking his eyes from the Overlord.

"Tell me what you're going to do with him!" she shouted.

Nas'Gavarr looked to Jeth. "If there is anything you wish to say to her, I suggest you do so now."

Jeth swallowed the permanent lump in his throat. "An?"

"Yes?" she said with defeat in her voice.

"I need to hear you say one honest thing."

Anwarr pushed the crumpled, tear-stained parchment along the floor toward Jeth. "Everything I wrote in this letter is true. We do not belong in each other's worlds."

Jeth let out a shaking exhalation as he stared at the parchment on the ground, unable to pick it up.

"But that is not to suggest that I don't love you. I do . . . with all my heart . . . as deficient as it is."

He nodded, despite his own heart twisting in his chest. "Thank you," was all he could say in return. He still wasn't sure if he believed her even now, but he would have to take it.

"Come to me, Jethril," Nas'Gavarr beckoned.

Jeth slowly took steps toward the empty pool, thinking, *I could really use a harpy's distraction right about now.*

"Wait!" Anwarr pushed herself up to her feet and ran to him. She pulled him back to her and joined her lips to his. He lacked the energy to react. He neither kissed her back nor turned away.

The kiss ended, and she pressed her forehead to his. "Survive this," she breathed, sniffing back the tears running down her cheeks, "and we can still be a family someday."

Jeth's heart broke at those words. They felt empty, even though she likely meant each one. He shook her off. "Get out of here!"

Anwarr wiped the tears with her sleeve, gazing at him sorrowfully before turning and running for the exit. She pushed the doors open, the sun stinging Jeth's eyes and obscuring her face as she turned to look at him one last time. The heavy stone doors closed, cutting her silhouette off from view.

Jeth continued his walk of doom down the steps and into the empty pool, bringing him face to face with the Overlord.

"Know that I can affect Anwarr's blood from miles away. Only after the ritual is complete will she and your child be safe. Understood?" Nas'Gavarr said.

Dammit, if you make a move now, he can still kill Anwarr, he thought with a gulp.

"Understood." Jeth put out his arms, presenting his body. "So, how are we doing this?"

Nas'Gavarr didn't move toward Jeth, only paced around him, spinning the dagger about in his hand. "You are a very special human being."

"You know, I've been told that a lot lately. I'm so glad you noticed."

"There is a delicate balance in this world of ours. For thousands of years, it was the ancient ones that maintained that balance on behalf of the gods that created them."

"Ancient ones?"

The Overlord nodded. "Fairies, naja, sirens and harpies, golems, and the ashray. Their dominion of this realm is coming to a close. It is time for humanity to decide our own Way, to put an end to the gods that have enslaved us for so long. With your blood, I intend to cast the first stone."

"And what is so special about my blood that it can do that?"

"You have the blood a champion," replied Nas'Gavarr with fervor. "The Champion of the Crannabeatha more specifically. Her life-fostering power is all that can overcome the cycle of death that is the Serpentine."

"So, you just spill my blood before this statue and that does what exactly?" Jeth backed away.

Nas'Gavarr regained the distance, holding up the dagger for Jeth to see. "This multiplies the blood contained within it. It can hold one hundred times the amount in your entire body, enough to fill this pool and bring forth Sagorath and Salotaph. And you will destroy them for me."

Sudden, uncontrolled laughter escaped Jeth. "Oh, sweet Deity, what am I doing here? You're one hundred percent, beyond the pale, batshit insane! Surely the Crannabeatha didn't keep me alive to die for this!"

Nas'Gavarr smirked. "As it is, we are all born to die. Sometimes, it's the meaning of our death that gives meaning to our life." He stepped up closer, his green and red-speckled eyes blinking sideways, almost gleeful. "I wish to enter your mind and bring it into the plane between the corporeal world and the spirit realm beyond."

"You mean the Spirit Chamber?" Jeth asked.

"Yes. It is there where you will face the Serpentine Gods in essence and spirit."

Jeth repeatedly shook his head in disbelief. He thought he'd be more terrified than he was, but there was something comforting in knowing, despite the absurdity of the moment, he was where he was meant to be. That he could at least provide one thing for his son that he couldn't for himself. A chance to live.

"Do what you will," he said with his arms out again. "Just promise me one more thing. Let Anwarr and my child go free. Don't force them to live with your harem."

Nas'Gavarr raised his chin as he contemplated Jeth's request. "Very well," he said, placing his hand on top of Jeth's head and gripping tight. "You have my word."

At that moment, the Overlord's skull-like features blurred. And everything went dark.

28

Destructive Overgrowth

Jeth opened his eyes to utter darkness. Only a hazy moonlight seeped in from the skylight. *Is it night already?*

He was alone. Nothing to hear or smell.

It was the Temple of Sagorath—but altered somehow.

When Jeth realized he could move his limbs, he ran for the front doors, only to find they weren't there. *You're trapped!*

He headed left first, tracing his hand along the stone wall in the darkness in hopes of finding a way out elsewhere. As he neared the corner where Melikheil had been killed, Jeth tripped and fell, his feet clanging against a large metal object on the ground.

A massive chain scraped along the stone floor as it shifted about. Jeth's gaze followed the chain to a giant iron ball at one end. Shackled to the other end was a large black creature, indiscernible in the darkness, hunched over in the corner and breathing laboriously. Cautiously rising to his feet, he attempted to step over the chain.

"SQUAWK!"

The black creature sprang at him, snapping its enormous black beak and nearly taking his head off as he jumped behind the iron ball. He scurried out of the bird's reach, not taking his eyes off it. Powerful wing beats blew dust about, making Jeth hack. *It's a giant raven!*

Soon, a fiery glow expanded in the darkness. The raven recoiled into the corner until it faded into the shadows.

A sharp, rumbling hiss cut through the stale air. Spinning around, Jeth came head to head with an enormous green and red marbled cobra. Its body coiled in a ring around him, his heart thumping at a humming pace.

"What do you want?" Jeth shouted.

The snake spoke with Nas'Gavarr's voice, "You are in a part of my mind. Here, my spiritual form is all you can see. Through me, you will be granted access to the Spirit Chamber."

"What do I do when I get there?" Jeth asked warily.

"Your blood will guide you," hissed Nas'Gavarr with a flick of his massive forked tongue.

A sharp pain twisted in Jeth's gut. He clutched his side. Warm blood trickled between his fingers.

"W-what's happening?" His legs wobbled, and he collapsed to his knees. The stone floor below him was wet and warm. The coppery smell overwhelmed his senses. Dark red seeped up from the cracks in the stone, flooding over his hands. He yelped and sat up straight, and the blood formed a puddle around him, rising higher until it was up to his thighs.

"Stop this!" he blared at the grinning serpent. It too was rising higher above him. It took Jeth a moment to recognize that the blood wasn't rising at all. He was sinking.

It was now up to his waist. The more he struggled, the deeper he sank.

Diving forward into the blood, Jeth tried to swim out of it, but the edge kept moving out of reach, the pool growing wider—endless in every direction.

Nas'Gavarr slithered outward to avoid the expanding crimson lake Jeth was powerlessly trapped within. He took a deep breath and held it just before his head was submerged. At that moment, he was no longer sinking . . . he was falling.

Vidya found the warping gate with little trouble. *Strange. There's not a single magus down here.* Her wary thoughts didn't keep her from her task, however. To her relief, a warp stone was nestled in the cubbyhole. *So, he found some more, meaning this gate has been used since the last time we were here.* She was about to start turning the gate toward her destination when she noticed the dais was not pointed to the Venerra gate in the southwest or any other Rangardian gate for that matter. This time, it pointed in the opposite direction, to the northeast.

"Where would he have gone in the northeast?" Vidya muttered to herself.

She wondered if Nas'Gavarr had pointed the gate to a random direction to sever a previously used pathway. To satisfy her curiosity, Vidya turned the crank. To her surprise, the yellow rock started to glow and pulsate upon sensing another in that direction. She spun the crank even faster until the stone was humming. Then, the liquid energy splashed within the confines of the ring, proving there was someone else on the other side to complete the pathway.

With a few more crank twists for good measure, Vidya walked out in front of the energy field. There was nothing but blue beyond. She hesitated. *Will I end up under water somewhere?*

To be safe, she took a deep breath and held it before stepping through. She emerged in a glistening blue cavern where she exhaled. She walked to the edge of the base. It was in a natural alcove overlooking a network of underground rivers flowing through tunnels of brilliant blue quartz. Distant waterfalls created a humid mist throughout the cavern, causing Vidya's already wiry locks to frizz within the short time she had been standing there. At the crank, there stood a robed magus staring at her in shock. "W-who are you? How did you find this gate?"

"What is this place?" she asked.

"You best turn around now or I will have no choice, but to flood these tunnels," the magus hissed.

Vidya remembered these priests specialized in either water or fire magic; him making good on that threat was a definite possibility.

I don't have time for this, she thought. Knowing she may need to return later, she decided to ease the magus's suspicions as best she could.

"Apologies," Vidya said with a bow. "My gate in Credence must be turned in the wrong direction. This will not happen again. Good day."

She walked calmly through the energy field, then turned the ring around to sever the pathway. Bringing to mind maps of each nation, she tried to judge where she had just been. Elmifel Province was in the northeast and was the primary source of water in both Del'Cabria and the desert. *Could that have been the Holy City of Thessalin? Or somewhere close to it?* Vidya wondered. Nas'Gavarr did study there. She decided not to dwell on yet another secret gate as she pushed this one to the direction of Rangardia. A few minutes of spinning the crank once again resulted in the new pathway. She stepped through and into the building that housed Rangardia's central gate.

Vidya approached the operator. "On behalf of Credence, I request that you leave this pathway open for as long as possible. Do you understand?"

The young man gave an obedient nod. "Yes, Señora."

With that, she walked back to the temple, flew out of the room, then retraced her steps through the labyrinth.

She returned to the atrium to find rain pouring through the skylight, into the urn in Salotaph's arms and overflowing into the pool surrounding the base. *There is no way it can be raining here without Mage intervention, she thought with a start.* She dashed behind a pillar ahead of the staircase and peeked around it.

"Shit," Vidya silently mouthed. On the Sagorath side of the statue, Nas'Gavarr was kneeling at the edge of the rapidly filling pool . . . only it was not filling with just water, but blood—pouring endlessly from the knife he held out over it.

Don't look! Her mind screamed, bringing her back to the bathtub from her nightmares. Turning away, she took a few deep breaths and forced herself to keep watching.

Vidya clasped her hand over her mouth to keep from crying out. There was Jeth, floating in the pool of blood, unconscious and bleeding from a gash in his side. *All that blood can't be from him!* It was then that the harpy's shadow materialized upon the sandstone arm of Sagorath, peering down at the grotesque ritual below. She pointed a clawed finger to the Bloodstone Dagger.

Adrenaline raced through Vidya and yet she stood frozen behind the pillar. *I can't*—she hesitated—*I'm not fast enough.* Nas'Gavarr's eyes were closed, appearing to be in some kind of trance. This might be my only chance. She felt a twinge of guilt for what was happening to Jeth, but she pushed it down, summoned the winds from outside, and gathered them around her. It was now or never.

Spreading her wings, she pushed off the ground with all her might and sped toward the entranced Mage. Before she knew it, the bloody dagger was in her grasp, and she was flying full speed toward the temple doors. I have it. I did it! A childlike glee came over her as she burst through the heavy stone doors and flew out into the desert downpour.

Both camels were still there, one of them was untied, but it had hardly ventured far from the other. A Herrani woman was beside it, drenched to the bone from the rain, and clutching her pregnant womb. Anwarr!

Vidya could still remember the agony in her own womb when she had lain screaming on the lavatory floor, birthing her first child, five months too early. All because of one vicious kick to the midsection from her husband in a jealous rage. Vidya hovered over Anwarr for a moment. "Are you all right?"

She stared up at the harpy in shock before her face contorted in pain, she groaned breathlessly, "The baby . . . ." She doubled over.

"Come on, I'll get you out of here," Vidya offered as she landed in front of her.

"It's not going to make it. I need Jethril!" She collapsed to the sand with a guttural moan.

An enraged roar alerted both women to Nas'Gavarr marching out into the rain.

"What did you do to him? Tell me he still lives!" Anwarr shrieked.

"At the moment," Nas'Gavarr replied in an eerily calm voice and turned to Vidya. "Return the dagger to me."

Gripping it tightly in her hand, she glanced over at Anwarr, a wet, weeping mass upon the sand. She's a lost cause, she thought. They can be together in death.

Vidya cast herself into the air, pushing with all her might to gain distance from Nas'Gavarr. Wet sand shot up from the ground, forming a giant human hand and wrapping large, granular fingers around her entire body. She was plucked from the sky like a fly in a man's fist and sent hurtling back down to the ground.

Gasping for air, she clambered out of the heavy hill of sand to find

Nas'Gavarr standing right above her. She reflexively drew her pistol and fired at his head. Chunks of flesh and bone sprayed from the Overlord's face. His head reeled back, then returned with his left eye and half of his cheek missing, revealing part of his actual skull next to the one tattooed on his face.

She fluttered her wings, struggling to take flight, but the damp sand was lodged between her feathers, making it difficult to steady herself in the air. She attempted to use a gale of wind to assist, but a wave of the Overlord's hand canceled it out, and she dropped back down to the ground. His regenerating skin climbed up and over his skull, and a new eye formed in the blown-out socket, even the 'U' shaped marking on his forehead returned.

Before he could completely recover, Vidya attacked full tilt with her arm blades, slashing across his midsection, then again across his chest. Sparks came off her blades as she scraped them against his bronze neck brace. She backed him toward the camels. They screamed and dispersed. Anwarr was gone. *Perhaps she ran off to give birth somewhere safer than here.*

That one distracted thought was all Nas'Gavarr needed to grab hold of one of Vidya's arm blades on her next attack. It cut into his palm before the steel liquefied and fell away by his touch. He then grabbed her arm and swung her around him. It ripped from the socket, pain shooting through her shoulder and up into her neck. With an incredible momentum, he hurled her against the outer wall of the temple, the force of the impact cracking a protruding window's support column down the center. Vidya crumpled to the ground, her arm limp and useless, both wings shattered in various places, and the wind taken right out of her.

The Harpy's voice was screaming as the Overlord took calm steps toward her. *"Get up! Punish him! What are you good for?"*

"Shut up!" she snapped at the voice.

"Hand over the dagger, and I won't take your second life," said Nas'Gavarr. Before Vidya could respond, the earth beneath them started to violently quake.

"It's happening. He's doing it!" Nas'Gavarr said with dark jubilation.

There was a deafening crack from above Vidya. The protruding windowsill separated from the temple wall. She willed her limbs to run, but it was no use. Another crack and the structure came down upon her in a mountain of heavy sandstone.

Jeth landed hard on the ridge of a dune and proceeded to roll down it uncontrollably. Blood rained from the sky. Wet sand clung to him as he continued to somersault, stopping only when he reached the valley below. Spitting out crimson granules, he dragged himself to his feet.

Where are you now? There was nothing but a desolate landscape in every direction, not a single cactus or a patch of dried-up foliage to be seen. There were only sun-bleached bones, half buried in the sand, arranged in a circular pattern around him.

"Hello?" Jeth called, his throat raw, the putrid taste of blood ever-present on his tongue. He realized it was his own. Fat red droplets from the sky pelted down harder, splattering upon the white skeletal remains. The sun sank in the horizon as the dread in the pit of his stomach was rising.

Vibrations—sand moving beneath his feet, the bones subtly shifting. They were not separate pieces, but part of an elongated whole, a never-ending ribcage slithering in and out of the sand dune. Two enormous skeletal snakes coiled around him, trapping him in the middle.

"I've had enough of these games, Nas'Gavarr. Show yourself already!" Jeth yelled.

The rain of blood stopped just before something burst from the sand below Jeth's feet. He screamed and fell to his hands and knees upon a hard, white surface. Two electrical bolts zapped on either side of him, causing him to leap backward and off the rising platform. He slid down a long series of vertebrae and landed right back into the bloody sand. A giant snake skull with two crackling eyes of lightning reared its anterior. Another skull rose from the sand to meet it, its eyes two balls of flame burning within massive sockets.

Jeth, paralyzed on the ground, gazed up in awe of the gigantic skeletal cobras. The one with the fire eyes brought its head down to him. He frantically backed away, but was halted by a ribcage behind him.

"Who dares challenge the Serpentine?" a foreboding male voice boomed from the fiery skull.

"I-I have no quarrel with you!"

The lightning-eyed skull lowered its head next to the other. "Only a Conduit can stand before another. You possess the essence of one"—its voice a sinister feminine whisper. They're Sagorath and Salotaph, Jeth realized, his head reeling.

"Conduit?" he repeated.

"Which do you represent, human?" demanded Sagorath.

He recalled Nas'Gavarr's speech from earlier. "Uh . . . the Crannabeatha?"

At those words, the two cobras reared back, taking what appeared to be defensive positions.

Salotaph hissed, "What are your demands?"

"Demands?" Jeth said, puzzled. "I just want to get out of here."

"You are here to destroy us!" boomed Sagorath.

"That's what Nas'Gavarr wants, but I don't," Jeth said while looking around for an escape route.

Salotaph said, "If you are here as Crannabeatha's Champion, then you do not have a choice!"

An electrical blast shot out from Salotaph's eyes. Jeth barely jumped away in time. He landed on his stomach, pain burning in his side. The flame in Sagorath's eyes flew at him. He rolled up to his feet and ran with a burst of speed. Unbearable heat blazed at his back as he slipped between two rib bones. He managed to escape the snakes' coil, and the flames didn't reach him. All he could see beyond was the endless desert with nowhere to hide. But that didn't stop him from running as fast as his fairy speed would allow. He left the skeletal snake gods behind only to eventually find himself running full speed toward them.

Jeth skidded to a stop. *It's one big loop. There's no escape!*

Both giant snake skeletons spun around. Another lightning burst cracked from Salotaph's eyes and at the same time, Jeth ignited his spark within. The bolt struck him dead on. Immense pain coursed through his body, yet he didn't go down. In fact, Jeth felt grounded. Living vines entwined up his legs and torso, wrapping around his arms and up to his neck, tethering him to the earth.

Sagorath's fire blew toward him again just as a cluster of thick roots sprang up from the sand and formed a protective barrier around him. The roots burnt away, but Jeth remained unscathed.

The surviving vines and roots wrapped around him, becoming extensions of his limbs. He pushed them out in every direction, creating enormous oak roots that lifted him off the ground, suspending him like a heart attached to veins and arteries. More vines, thicker and larger than what came before, spread along the sand, entwining up the serpents' vertebrae and winding around their ribcages. Sagorath and Salotaph shrieked as their bones snapped and popped by the force of the unstoppable growth of foliage. The roots expanded inside of them, forming into tree trunks, and bursting between each bone. Branches stretched through their ribcages and up into their skulls.

Salotaph's skull broke in half, followed by Sagorath's severing from his neck and falling into the newly made forest floor below, the fire and lightning from their eye sockets extinguished. Soon, both snake skeletons were replaced by two massive oak trees that continued to grow. Sagorath and Salotaph had disappeared completely into the undergrowth.

The foliage, now out of Jeth's control, was rapidly overtaking him. He couldn't move a muscle as the vines tightened, making it harder to breathe. But he wasn't afraid. He was home. This was where he belonged. It didn't matter that it was all in the Spirit Chamber.

Then, came a tug on his shoulders, and he felt himself lifting out of the cradle of vines. He fought against it, never wanting to leave the comfort of the budding forest of which he was at the heart.

One firm heave and Jeth was ripped from the foliage. He screamed, falling upwards into the desert sky.

With heavy rain pelting on his face, Jeth was yanked from a pool of blood. A frantic woman's grunt in his ear brought his awareness back to him. He sank into the blood and flailed in panic. *You're still drowning in Nas'Gavarr's mind!* He yelped and kicked, somehow managing, with the assistance of someone, to climb back to the stone surface. He hadn't realized until he lay flat on his back that the entire temple was crumbling and shaking violently.

Anwarr, hair soaked and eyes red, appeared above him. "You're alive! Oh, thank Sal, you're alive!"

"Is this real?" he asked dazedly.

Anwarr nodded and wiped the blood from his face with her shawl. "I know you're hurt, but you have to get up."

As Jeth did so, a burning pain in his side took the wind out of him. He was still bleeding profusely from an open gash. *If this is real, does that mean everything else was too?*

"We have to get out of here," Anwarr urged.

An earsplitting crack of stone shook the air. Sagorath and Salotaph split straight down the middle as a massive tree's trunk burst up through it. Both Jeth and Anwarr gasped as the Sagorath half fell forward, about to crush them. Jeth's adrenaline kicked in, and the pain in his side no longer hampered him. He took Anwarr by the arms and leaped over to the side. The statue crashed to the floor as Jeth held Anwarr against the wall. The pool of blood and the floor beneath gave way. It and what was left of the statue fell to the labyrinth below, causing an ear-shattering crash of breaking rocks and splashing water.

"I thought you left," Jeth murmured in Anwarr's ear once the noise died down.

"I won't bring our son into this world without you by my side." She grabbed her belly and groaned in pain. ". . . and the time is now."

"But . . . it's far too early for that," he sputtered, noticing blood leaking through her white pants. A frantic dread came over him. She cried out and slid down the wall.

Jeth held her up and took her under his arm. "Hold on!"

Vines rapidly climbed up the walls and across the ceilings, breaking balustrades from the second floor, pieces raining down. They ran for the center of the atrium. Hanging cages broke from their chains and crashed into the ground, blocking the most obvious path to the exit. Where's a harpy when you need one?

Roots and trees erupted from below, creating rippling cracks in the stone as they ran.

Jeth spotted another path around the fissures. While still holding onto

Anwarr, he sped for the exit, dodging falling rocks and violent, twisting tree branches sprouting out from every imaginable place. Another iron cage detached from its chain. Jeth heard it just in time, allowing him to skid to a stop as the cage crashed down right in front of them.

Anwarr screeched. The cage split the rock and a thick root, relieved by the fissure, shot up through it.

The ground crumbled beneath their feet. "Jump!" Jeth yelled.

Holding firmly onto Anwarr's bicep, he made a running leap and grabbed hold of the bars of the cage in front of them just as the entire floor collapsed. He swung Anwarr forward, hoping she'd be able to grab the bars as well, and they could then edge around the cage and continue on. But, the small ledge beneath Anwarr's feet crumbled away as well.

"Jeth!" Still holding onto her arm, Jeth kept her from falling to her death.

"I got you," he grunted.

She dangled over a high drop. Below was the warping gate, spared the temple's destruction for the time being. It was activated, but Vidya was nowhere in sight.

Anwarr was too heavy for Jeth to lift her up with one arm, and the blood coating his skin made it difficult to keep a good grip. His hand slipped from her bicep to just below her elbow.

She screamed. Jeth gritted his teeth with the effort, but the tighter he gripped her, the more she slid. She tried to grab hold of Jeth's arm with her other hand while he fought the urge to let go of the cage's bars to free his other hand.

"Grab my arm!" he shouted.

Her one arm slipped out of his grasp, and his heart flopped in his chest, but she grabbed hold with her other hand just in time.

Temporary relief washed over him. Then, another piece of the floor under the cage fell away. It shuddered and groaned, tipping further toward the drop. Anwarr slipped once again. "No!" Jeth cried. He clutched her wrist, her fingers turning blue from his tight grip. The ground beneath his feet was crumbling by the weight of the cage and the two people hanging from it.

Anwarr's hand started to slide through Jeth's fingers ever so slowly. The panic in her eyes was replaced with a profound sorrow like she knew this was the end.

"I won't let go! I won't let go!" he kept repeating as their bloody, sweaty hands failed to keep their grip.

One moment he had half of her hand in his and a second later, there was nothing. Jeth's adrenaline pulsed through him, forcing everything into slow motion. He hung there helplessly, watching every muscle in her face contort in terror and hearing her long, drawn-out screams tear through his ears. Reaching as far as he could, he willed for roots to shoot out from somewhere—anywhere and catch her. He kept visualizing vines wrapping around her and lifting her back to him, over and over again as she fell farther out of reach. His cries lodged in his throat, unable to join with hers.

There was nothing Jeth could do, but hang there and watch Anwarr's agonizingly slow descent into the destructive overgrowth.

29

Let's Go Back

Jeth hung there, paralyzed and numb as the woman he loved vanished into a sea of green.

The cage shook and Jeth was jolted back into action. Now able to use both hands, he climbed up the bars to reach the top of the cage as it tipped. He made a desperate leap to secure ground just as the cage plummeted to the basement floor below.

He wasn't given a chance to process what had happened or what to do next before time sped up again. More trees took root and crashed through the ceiling. Rain pelted down like a waterfall, washing the blood from his skin. Another tree broke through the floor, right in front of him, and it gave way. He yelped, falling along with broken rocks and debris, grasping for anything in sight to slow his descent. He grabbed a cluster of vines, swung around the new tree trunk, and smacked hard against the basement's north wall. Pain reverberated through his left shoulder, and his grip waned. Small branches snapped off the vine as he slid down it.

Jeth hit the ground hard, the shooting pain in his ankle returned full force, but the mossy earth softened his landing enough not to break it.

The temple continued to quake, and more sandstone blocks rained down. He knew he should take cover, but he kept thinking of Anwarr alone, possibly having survived the fall, now vulnerable to being crushed by the temple itself. You have to get to her.

He staggered to his feet and started running through the dust and debris, dashing around falling rocks and archways until a giant root burst from the ground and hurled him against the fallen cage. He opened his mouth to cry out, but no sound came.

Too exhausted to get back up, Jeth crawled into the broken cage, hoping it would serve as cover from the remaining debris crashing down all around him. For a moment, he watched the rapid vegetative growth climbing toward the sky until the quaking lessened, and he could regain his bearings.

He limped out into the open of what used to be the warping gate room, now resembling the overgrown ruins in the ogre-infested woods of Fae'ren. The only thing still intact was the gate itself, alight with clear energy. *Where's Vidya?*

He pushed that worry out of his mind and focused only on Anwarr. His legs buckled with every step, his vision hazy. The pain in his side burned, weakening him. He tripped and fell into a puddle of water—still with remnants of his own blood within it. Nausea crept up into his throat as he held his bleeding gash. Forcing his vomit down, Jeth found his spark again to help him back to his feet and maintain focus despite his loss of blood. One of his khopeshes was sticking out from a broken pillar, now covered in vines. He pulled it out, sheathed it, and continued on.

His heart turned to ice in his chest when he spotted something white in the bushes beyond. He sped toward it, finding only Anwarr's headscarf, stained with blood. *She can't be far.* He frantically looked around. From behind a tree, a few feet from where he stood, a bloody arm lay on the ground.

Holding his breath, Jeth limped around the trunk, dreading what he would find. Half her face was buried in the dirt, the other half covered by hair. Her white garments were soaked through from rain and made pink from blood. Jeth's spirit felt like it had left his body as he rushed to her side. Turning her over to her back, he found a gaping head wound. Blood covered the entire left side of her face and hair. One of her legs was bent in an impossible position, but Jeth dared not move it.

"An?" He sensed the faintest of heartbeats, her breathing shallow and labored. "Please wake up, please . . ." he begged, shaking her.

One of her eyelids opened to a slit, the other sealed shut by the swelling. "That's it, look at me. You're going to be all right."

"Jeth . . ." Her voice was so faint he had to keep his hearing honed to make out her words.

He took her head in his quivering hands. "I'm going to get you out of here. Just through that warping gate over there."

Anwarr's one frost-blue eye was fully open now. Jeth was right above her, but she was not looking directly at him. "I can't see you."

"I'm right here."

Tears streamed down her face as she continued to stare blankly in Jeth's direction. "I can't feel the baby."

He instantly put his ear to her womb and kept his head there for a painfully long time, hoping to hear just one little heartbeat—one subtle movement. There was only a void of silence inside her. Tears of his own pushed their way down his face and onto Anwarr's bare stomach.

"Is he okay . . . ? Please, Jeth . . . Jethril?" Anwarr cried.

Jeth lifted his head and placed Anwarr's on his lap. "He's fine. He's going to be fine. . . ." His voice cracked in his struggle to hold back sobs.

Anwarr raised one weak arm to ever so lightly touch Jeth's face. "I want to go back . . . please can we go back?" Jeth kept nodding, unable to reply as he choked back tears.

"Let's go back . . . let's go . . . ." Her arm dropped limply to her side as her eye rolled back into her head.

"An? An!" Jeth cried, shaking her. A final wheezing breath escaped her as the weedy thudding of her heart ceased. "No . . . no. . . . Crannabeatha please . . . ."

He held her body until it grew cold in his arms, and her beautiful honey brown skin paled to the hue of sandstone. His arms started to ache, and he was forced to lay her down. He fell over her in a crumpled, trembling heap. Twigs snapped beneath the feet of someone walking through the underbrush toward him. The footsteps ended a few feet away, but Jeth didn't have the energy to lift himself off Anwarr to see who it was.

"It's breathtaking, isn't it?" came the voice of Nas'Gavarr. "The landscape has forever changed because of the sacrifice you made here today. The desert tribes are now free of their old gods. Thank you."

Jeth slowly sat up and turned his heavy head to Nas'Gavarr. In a low voice, he said, "You're thanking me? You should have killed me."

Nas'Gavarr looked upon the dagger in his hand, the red specks upon the green stone having grown to large red splotches. "By all rights, you should be dead, not her. I gave her freedom, but she chose to die for you instead."

A boiling rage erupted inside Jeth. With a determined roar, he rose to his feet and charged for the sorcerer with his one and only sword, not thinking about where or how he was going to hurt him with it. Nas'Gavarr grabbed Jeth's sword-wielding hand mid-swing and shoved him all the way back to Anwarr's body. The khopesh went flying out of Jeth's grip and embedded itself in the tree's soft trunk. He rolled back to his feet and ran for his blade, but an overwhelming weakness took him back to the ground.

"If you'd like me to kill you, I will oblige," Nas'Gavarr said, holding a hand out to Jeth. "I still have plenty of your blood held within this dagger."

Every muscle in Jeth's body weighed a hundred pounds—every inhalation was in vain. A part of him wanted to succumb to the blood magic, but the amount of hate he felt in his heart, the adrenaline in his veins, all fueled his need to see Nas'Gavarr go down with him.

"That's nice," Jeth rasped. "Won't do you any good, though."

With what little spark he had left, Jeth pushed through his body's need for blood and regained control of his limbs. He sped over to the tree, yanked out his sword, and raced for Nas'Gavarr. The Mage hardly had time to react before Jeth shoved the end of his khopesh through his midsection. With all his might, he ripped the blade out of the Overlord's side. Viscera tumbled out from the gash he made, followed by a crimson flood. Nas'Gavarr's throat rattled as he clutched his hemorrhaging torso. He stumbled back and collapsed to one knee.

The Mage tried to gather his innards back into his body before the wound could heal. Jeth swung his sword a second time, and Nas'Gavarr fired a burst of lightning from his hand, hitting him square in the chest. He flew through the air, rolled through the foliage, and stopped in a puddle of water.

Unlike the Spirit Chamber where he had taken Salotaph's bolt, no vegetation came to his aid. The pain was unbearable, every muscle fiber burned and spasmed.

The Overlord limped toward Jeth while still holding his split midsection together. "Somehow, you manage to move even when your blood is stopped in your veins. No matter, I don't require magic to end your life."

Jeth sparked once more, his heart pounding to the point of pain, but he was able to move his arms and push himself to his knees. His legs, however, were two trembling masses that could no longer support his weight.

Nas'Gavarr kneeled before him, took hold of his neck, and forced him back down into the puddle. Jeth groaned in exhaustion and pain as his body continued to shudder.

"There is no need to fear," said Nas'Gavarr. "Your purpose has been fulfilled. Allow yourself the peace that only death can bring."

Jeth now knew what peace was. He had felt it, cradled in the roots of the Crannabeatha. What the Overlord offered was not even close to that.

He pressed his hands against the Overlord's impassive face, but he was powerless against the superior strength that strangled him.

Vidya came to, half-buried under rubble and tree roots. What in Yasharra's name?

While pulling herself out, she realized her arm was no longer broken, and her wings were more or less moveable. *If I healed this fast, then that can only mean I died and came back to life,* she thought with a gulp. She only had one life left.

On her feet, Vidya patted herself down to find the Bloodstone Dagger gone, meaning Nas'Gavarr had dug her partially out to get it back. *He could have decapitated me while I was dead,* she thought. *Why didn't he?*

Vidya surveyed her surroundings. The temple and the barren canyon beyond had transformed. A lush forest had overcome the entire place. She had a strange feeling the Fae'ren had something to do with it.

She dove into the temple turned old growth forest, hoping the warping gate was still active. After dipping under branches and weaving around hanging vines, she found the gate and Nas'Gavarr kneeling a few feet from it, suffering a serious gash to his abdomen in the process of closing. She landed and took a crouched position behind some bushes. Jeth was pinned to the ground, struggling against the Overlord's hold.

"That is one resilient bastard," Vidya murmured in disbelief.

She picked up on Nas'Gavarr saying something to him. ". . . Allow yourself the peace that only death can bring."

"Speak for yourself, you skull-faced lunatic," she growled.

With a powerful beat of her wings, she catapulted across the room, the wind flattening the foliage as she went. She bashed against the Overlord, took him under the arms, and carried him on an upward curving trajectory toward the active warping gate. They both went hurtling through the energy field and into Rangardia beyond. Fearing for her third and final life, Vidya pushed him away with all her strength, sending him further down the building hallway before halting in midair. She pushed herself backward through the gate with a burst of air and landed in a skidding crouch on the other side. She clambered to the cubbyhole and tore out the warp stone, extinguishing the energy. Nas'Gavarr wouldn't be coming back that way for a long while.

Vidya remained on her hands and knees for a moment, chest heaving. A quiet scuffing came from behind her. It was Jeth, dragging himself toward the dead body of his love, letting out gurgling breaths with each movement until he collapsed at her side.

After placing the warp stone in her bag, Vidya went to check Jeth's vitals. His pulse was frighteningly weak. The stab wound was still hemorrhaging.

"How are you alive?" she murmured. Kneeling next to him, she sliced off a piece of her cloak and attempted to wrap it around his torso. "You didn't happen to bring any of that smelly wound closing goop with you? That stuff actually did wonders for my leg," Vidya said, keeping pressure on the gash.

"I know," Jeth croaked, his eyelids drooping. "Just take us . . . to Snake Eye."

Vidya finished wrapping Jeth's wound as he lost consciousness. She stood and reflected on her options.

I had that dagger in my hands. She clenched her fists. She'd be on her way back home right now had it not been for Anwarr's early labor distracting her. As she looked at the dead pregnant woman beside Jeth, an immense guilt tugged at her insides. She thought of the baby she herself had miscarried and nearly crumpled to her knees. What if she had given birth to it and it had been a girl? How different her life could have been. *Now I have caused that same pain to Jeth.*

Why is it that when I'm the one who deserves to be punished, the shadow harpy is silent? Vidya wondered.

Sniffing back tears now starting to form, she put Anwarr and Jeth under each arm and took to the sky.

30

Another Must Suffer

The sandstone ceiling of the shop's third floor was the first thing that came into view when Jeth lifted his heavy eyelids. He was in the comfort of his own bed with no memory of how he got there. Reaching an arm out to his left, he expected to feel the warm body of Anwarr beside him, only to find the sheets bare. His body was so stiff and sore he could barely move his head to the side to see if he was, in fact, alone.

Reveries of being embraced by roots repeatedly cajoled him back into unconsciousness, but a skeletal arm kept yanking him out of it. He couldn't bring himself to face it. Only death was at the end of that arm.

It wasn't until Jeth spotted a winged woman perched on a chair in the corner of the room that he came to full and sudden awareness.

He groaned as he attempted to sit up his on elbows, only to have his weak arms give way.

"You're finally awake," the harpy said as she rose from the chair and walked over to the bed.

"How long have I been out?" he croaked. His throat felt like he had swallowed a quart of sand. There was a bowl of water on his bedside table, and he tried to reach for it, but his arms were too heavy. Vidya was already there scooping water into a clay ladle and putting it to his lips. He took down the warm liquid in one audible gulp.

"A couple of days," she said before giving him a second ladleful.

After his last sip, he wiped his mouth, and rasped, "And you've been watching me this whole time?"

"No." She returned to her chair. "I had to get Snake Eye to come heal your stab wound before you bled to death. She's recuperating in the next room over." She pointed across the hall . . . *Anwarr's room.* Jeth's guts twisted in knots, making him want to throw up all the water he had drunk.

"What do you mean recuperating?"

"That's not important right now," said Vidya. "We need to talk about what happened in that temple."

"I-I don't recall a whole lot."

"What's the last thing you do remember?"

'Let's go back. . . .'

Without responding, Jeth struggled to sit up. He automatically grabbed at his side, only to find the pain was gone. He moved the sheets aside and saw no evidence of a stab wound, yet the rest of his body was on fire.

"Listen," Vidya went on. "I know what you went through was . . . traumatic. . . ."

"You don't say?" He let out a dark chuckle, resting his head back against the headboard.

"Nas'Gavarr's plans go far beyond what we could have ever guessed. The entire temple and all the way to the Burning Waste has transformed into a forested oasis in a matter of hours. The game has changed."

"I'm not playing the game," he said weakly.

Vidya crossed her arms and pursed her lips. "Be that as it may, I need details of the spell he performed with you. Did he stab you with the Bloodstone Dagger? Where did the rest of the blood come from? It couldn't all have come from you. What caused the trees to grow like that?"

Jeth grunted. "And here I thought you were just worried about me. Where's Anwarr?"

"Shrouded in the stables. The others are preparing her for her funeral pyre."

"They're going to burn her?" Jeth said with a start.

Vidya shrugged. "Istari mentioned something about . . . 'only through fire or water can she be ushered into the afterlife.' They say Anwarr would prefer to go out by Sagorath's flame."

"Sagorath is dead. I need to find Snake Eye." Jeth attempted to get out of bed. Without the strength to stand on two legs, he collapsed to his hands and knees.

Vidya bent down to assist. "Your wound may be healed, but your body is still recovering from that lightning blast."

"I don't need your help." Jeth brushed her off.

Ignoring him, Vidya wrapped one of her arms around his waist and hoisted him up anyway.

"I need to get Anwarr back, so don't try to stop me!"

"I'm taking you to Snake Eye."

Jeth sighed. "Oh. Right, then."

Putting nearly all his weight against the harpy, he hobbled across the hall and into Anwarr's old room. Jeth hardly recognized it all cleaned up—as if she had never been there—except her aroma, which broke his heart all the more. Snake Eye was sitting cross-legged on the bed, stripped of sheets. His eyes were closed and his body motionless.

Vidya plopped Jeth down on a cushioned bench, and Snake Eye opened his eyes, his expression listless.

"I'm glad to see you are well," he said to Jeth.

"If you call this well," Jeth retorted. "But . . . I suppose I have you to thank for being alive."

"You are always welcome. I simply couldn't bear both you and Anwarr being torn from this world."

"What are you doing?" Jeth inquired.

"You've undoubtedly witnessed my brother heal himself in mere moments. He combines the magic of flesh and life force to do so. Being a Flesh Mage only, I must resort to meditation. My brother and I can both use our physical mastery to stave off the aging process, which builds up our life force, but only he has the power to manipulate his." Snake Eye lifted his shirt, revealing bandages wrapped around his torso. He peeked under them and said, "It's closing rather nicely. In another hour or so, it should be completely healed."

"How did you get stabbed?"

"Oh, you see, Flesh Mages can repair themselves easily enough, but to do so for others, there must be a sacrifice. For me to heal you, another must suffer a similar injury."

"Is that why you don't want your methods to be known because someone else has to be hurt?"

Snake Eye replied, "If the sacrifice is someone of a similar bloodline to the patient, even someone of the same ethnicity, I wouldn't have to injure them as much to fix a wound of greater severity. Being that you are short on relatives in these parts, I inflicted a wound equal to yours on myself, as I can heal on my own."

Jeth rubbed the back of his sore neck. "I know how much that must have hurt. I-I don't know what to say. . . ."

The Flesh Mage shrugged and nodded. "Think nothing of it."

Jeth hesitated before asking his next question. "So . . . would it be too much to ask you to bring Anwarr back as well?"

Snake Eye's lips formed a thin line as he gave Jeth a pitying look. "Healing spells cannot bring people back to life, Jethril."

"Why not? You're trying to bring back a Najahai that's been dead for thousands of years, but you can't bring back one woman and her unborn child? I know, I don't have the right to expect this of you, but . . ." Jeth ran out of breath before he could finish.

"You must understand. I cannot resurrect that which has no spirit. I can reanimate her corpse, but it will not be her."

Jeth's heart tore in his chest, unable to accept what Snake Eye was saying. "I get that, but there has to be some way to—"

"Had anyone the foresight to trap her spirit in an emerald before it dispersed into the Spirit Realm, maybe, but even then, I don't have the ability to reignite her life force to heal her body. She would continue to rot, requiring constant healing and countless flesh sacrifices to maintain her state of being. Resurrection is a harrowing process that often leads to the recently revived wishing they'd remained dead."

Putting his head down in shame, Jeth clenched his jaw.

"I'm sorry, Jethril," Snake Eye said softly, "but our Anwarr is gone."

The ashipu shut his eyes again, leaving Jeth and Vidya with nothing else to do but return to Jeth's room. The sickening rage inside him built to an unbearable level.

He pushed weakly against Vidya and collapsed back on his bed. He clutched the sheets in white knuckled fists, doing all he could to keep from weeping uncontrollably. He screamed and pounded his fists into the bed over and over until exhaustion overtook him.

She's never coming back. You'll never hear that laugh again, never smell her scent . . . never look upon your son's face. They're gone because of you . . . because of your Way . . . your curse.

"There was nothing you could have done," Vidya peeped.

Jeth ran his hands through his loose locks. "I should have stayed away. . . ."

Vidya sat down on the bed next to him, not looking his way. "Nas'Gavarr did this, and he will pay. For your loss as well as mine."

Bringing his head up from his hands, he clenched his fists, thinking of all the ways he would hurt him, but he knew he never could. That Mage probably can't even feel pain.

"He killed my child. It was because of his blood magic Anwarr went into labor," Jeth said. "There is not one terrible act I don't yearn to inflict on him, but . . ." His words caught in his throat. You're powerless. The thought made another stream of tears run down his cheek that he quickly wiped away. "Why are you still here?" he asked Vidya.

"I've lost children too," she blurted.

"What?" Jeth was so flabbergasted he became distracted from his darkened thoughts for a moment.

"One to miscarriage . . . and two small boys, Alonz and Spyros." Vidya's bottom lip quivered as she bit into it.

"I-I'm sorry. I had no idea."

"It was my husband. Our marriage agreement had ended, and I was supposed to return to Credence. He didn't want me to take them back with me. He told me he'd see them dead before he let that happen." Tears dripped down Vidya's face, but she held her jaw taut, and her eyes fixated on the doorframe. "The truth was, he never wanted children because he knew that after two, I would be required to leave him. He wanted me to stay for as long as possible. All I wanted was to get home. So, I left my boys and headed for the warping gate. As I arrived there, I had this terrible feeling in my heart that something was wrong. I ran back to . . . ." She swallowed hard and forced out the words, ". . . They were dead."

"By the Crannabeatha," Jeth said. "What did you do . . . to your husband?"

Vidya's chest heaved, and she struggled to wipe her tears coming out in steady streams. "He's the Emperador of Rangardia . . . the one man I can't punish." Jeth carefully rubbed his hand along Vidya's back, and she jumped up to her feet. "What are you doing?"

"I—nothing."

"Don't think because you saw a few tears I'll just succumb to your filthy desires." The sadness in her brown eyes had all but gone and was now replaced with a blazing fury.

Jeth was so taken aback by her sudden rage he recoiled. "Desires? What desires?"

Vidya shook her head. "Forget it, just forget everything I told you!"

With that, she leaped out the window and disappeared into the morning sky.

A few hours of rest later, Jeth was strong enough to walk on his own and join the others in paying their respects to the dead.

In a desolate area a few miles outside the city, Anwarr's body was laid to rest upon a pyre. Everyone stood in a circle around it, wearing drab smocks and head coverings. Vidya hadn't returned, which was all right with Jeth after their interaction earlier that morning.

Herrani funeral rites dictated that those who knew the deceased the longest were typically the first to pay their respects. Istari approached the pyre.

The Mage's eyes flooded with tears as she touched Anwarr's hair. Her features wavered between hard and soft, lips quivering until broken sobs escaped. Jeth scaled back his hearing so that the words tumbling off Istari's trembling lips were muffled and indistinguishable from the rest of her cries.

Snake Eye followed Istari. He fixed bits of Anwarr's clothing and hair before placing his hands over hers and giving a melancholy smile. Jeth didn't make out what he said to her either. The guilt that already gnawed at his bones was painful enough; he couldn't bear to witness the grief of the others at the same time.

Ash was the third to approach. He tautened every inch of his face as he struggled to hold back his tears. Caressing Anwarr's cheek, he said, "I should have tried . . ." He stayed planted there for a moment before storming away.

Lys stepped up to the pyre, stood still with his hands behind his back, and looked down at Anwarr with a fatherly countenance. A few moments later, he nodded then left without saying a word. Khiri followed close behind Lys.

He placed in her hands, folded over her stomach, a bundle of white lilies he had snatched from a vendor in town. Tears streamed down his face as he repeatedly choked them back.

As Jeth slowly came up behind Khiri for his turn, the boy glared back at him and ran to bury his face in Istari's arms. Now, it was only Jeth at the pyre. His own tears had all run dry at this point, but the pain was as fresh as it was the moment she slipped from his grasp.

He took out the white-gold armlet he had brought with him. "This is all I have to remember you by," he whispered. "This belongs to you."

Jeth caressed her cheek with his fingertips and bent over to kiss her cold forehead, trying to keep his sense of smell as weak as possible. Despite the strong perfumes, Jeth's nose could all too readily pick out the rot, and that was not the smell of Anwarr he wanted to remember.

He placed his hand over her still womb. A tremor ran through him as he swallowed the hard lump in his throat. "I know I haven't named you, but I promise you . . . I will spend the rest of my life being the father you need me to be. I will provide for you what I could not for myself, even if you're not alive to know it." He rested his forehead on Anwarr's stomach, let the last few of his tears drop upon it before taking steps back to the where the others were waiting.

Istari and Ash lit the oil-doused torches and set the pyre aflame. Jeth took this moment to approach Khiri and offer some kind of comfort. Khiri glared up at him again, his lips quivering and fists clenching.

"Hey, kid . . ." Jeth was interrupted by a well-aimed spittle on his cheek from Khiri's mouth.

The boy ran to Lys, leaving Jeth to wipe his face. Istari, having returned from the pyre, witnessed the whole altercation.

"Heh," Jeth chuckled in an attempt to hide the sting of an eleven-year-old's wrath. "I guess that's what I get for breaking my promise."

"Her death is going to be harder on him than any of us," said Istari.

"I tried to bring her back, Star, I really did," he began.

"Vidya told us what happened," Istari said. "Anwarr chose not to leave you behind. I guess she loved you after all."

Jeth shook his head while watching the flames climb up the driftwood, the kindling around Anwarr's body starting to catch. "You were right. I should have resisted her from the start. Little did I know, she was marked for death the moment I agreed to come with her on that first job."

Istari sighed and stepped a little closer to him, but kept her eyes on the burning pyre. "I shouldn't have said those things to you. The truth is, I've been in love with Ana since the moment we met. I had hoped for so long she'd leave Ezrai for me, and she did, but she wouldn't commit to one person after him. I settled for a piece of her. I thought it was better than having nothing at all."

"I know what you mean." Jeth kicked up sand with his foot.

Istari continued, "From the day you showed up, I had always sensed something between you two, but I kept telling myself it was temporary. The moment I knew I had lost her was the day she decided to keep your baby." A tear fell down Istari's face, and she wiped it away. "It was the one thing I couldn't give her."

"If she'd have chosen you, she'd still be alive," said Jeth.

Istari shrugged and nodded. "Either way, I can't hate you even though I want to. The fact is, you risked your life and faced the Overlord when the rest of us, except little Khiri, were not brave enough to try. Don't beat yourself up too much." She gave him a pat on the shoulder before walking away.

The flames were now blazing full force, hugging Anwarr's body in smoke. Red fingers twisted around her head, singeing off her hair and melting her beautiful face. Jeth couldn't bear to look at her anymore and swiftly turned away.

Ash put a hand to Jeth's shoulder. "Hold on."

"Can you wait to crush my skull until after this is over?" Jeth asked, only half-joking.

"Crushing your puny skull will give me no satisfaction on such a mournful day. I just want you to know, you'll always have a place on this crew . . . if you want it."

Patting Ash's muscular shoulder, Jeth said, "I appreciate that, Big Fella. But, I've come to realize I don't belong here. And that's all right."

"Where do you belong, if not with us?"

"I'll let you know when I find out."

Soaring toward the setting sun, Vidya flew over the burning pyre and spotted Jeth sitting by himself at the top of a sand dune. She circled above him before coming in for a landing, then sat down cross-legged beside him.

She whipped out a clay bottle from her bag and uncorked it, the strong liquor smell shooting straight up her nostrils and making her eyes water. After taking a gulp, her entire mouth burned, including her chest, which she'd expect a fine whisky to do, but it immediately left a putrid aftertaste that made her want to gag.

"What do you have there?" Jeth asked.

Vidya scowled. "Probably the worst whisky I've ever tasted. Bought it off a merchant caravan heading into the city. Here." She handed the bottle to Jeth, and he didn't hesitate in taking a hearty gulp of the contents.

He coughed and beat his chest with his fist. "It's no Fairieshome ale, but it'll do."

Jeth offered her a second sip, but she put her hand out. "Keep it."

They sat in silence for a while, and Vidya finally started to relax. She wanted to forget ever telling Jeth her horrible secret, and she was glad he wasn't bringing it up or her embarrassing behavior afterward.

"What's your plan now? Track down Nas'Gavarr and try for that pesky dagger again?" Jeth asked, taking another swig and grimacing.

"I need to find out what that dagger can do, and how he used it to create an oasis in the middle of the desert," she said.

After another moment of silence between them, Jeth quietly confessed, "It takes the blood of one man and multiplies it, meaning all the blood you saw belonged to me."

Right beside Vidya, the shadow harpy materialized. Despite the sunset giving the sand a golden hue, she was as ethereal as ever. She whispered into her ear, *"Three men means one hundred of us; three hundred means ten thousand—the Harplite will rise again."*

This news changed everything. The dagger did not hold the blood of one hundred separate men, but a hundred times the blood of one man. *When will I have the opportunity to nab it again?* She thought with a twinge in her gut.

Looking Vidya straight in the eye, Jeth continued, "He used his spirit magic to take me to the place between the Spirit Realm and ours. I met the Serpentine Gods and . . . I killed them."

"The forest really *was* you," Vidya gasped.

With a nod, Jeth said, "Nas'Gavarr knew what would happen. He knows what I'm capable of. And I need to know what he knows."

"How do you find that out if even his own sister is in the dark?" Vidya wondered aloud.

"I don't know, but I refuse to believe my *Way* was to destroy the gods of the desert while inadvertently abolishing everything I cared about in the process." Jeth glanced over to Snake Eye, still standing before the blazing pyre. "I'm done running, Vidya. It's about time I stop waiting for others to act. If Nas'Gavarr thinks he knows who I *really* am, then I'm going to find out who *he* is . . . find out what he wants more than anything in this world . . . and I'm going to take it from him. He will come to know my *curse.*" He finished off the whiskey and tossed the bottle down the dune.

Vidya's spine tingled at Jeth's words, arousing the harpy's violence within her. "We warp to Rangardia and get the dagger. Then, my Harplite will—"

"Forget harpy armies!" Jeth snapped. "Don't you see? That's what he's after—the entire world up in flames. Until we find out the reason why, we can't give it to him!"

"So, what are you suggesting? We try to kill him ourselves, just the two of us?" She scoffed.

Jeth nodded, an intensity behind his hazel eyes she'd never seen in him before.

"The man has no weakness we alone can exploit," Vidya argued. "I don't have another life to give. It's the Harplite or nothing!"

"Maybe you haven't found any weaknesses because you haven't been looking in the right places. You can try stealing the dagger from him again if you want, I sure as shit won't stop you, but you said it yourself. The game has changed."

"But you won't play it," she reminded him.

"No, I won't," Jeth agreed, rising to his feet. "Because I'm making my own game. First rule: know your target's weaknesses as well as your own capabilities."

"And how do we go about doing that with the *Immortal Serpent?*" Vidya asked warily.

"By going to where it all started for him."

"The Elmifelian monastery." Vidya rose to her feet alongside him.

"Only we won't be allowed entry to the Holy City," Jeth said. "You'll have to fly us in and hope we don't get spotted."

Vidya crossed her arms and said, "I may know of a better way."

3 1

Creation's Mystery

There was nothing left of the Burning Waste when Jeth and Vidya glided over it on the way back to the temple warping gate. Black pillars of smoke were replaced by towering trees, charred sand transformed to lush greenery, and pools of burning oil became clear lakes and streams. Groups of people were already exploring the once deadly landscape, praising the Serpentine Gods for such a miracle. It made Jeth confused and uncomfortable to witness how happy people were as a result of his horrific loss. *Are you doing the right thing in trying to stop Nas'Gavarr?* Jeth wondered. Hopefully, he'd find his answer at the Holy City of Thessalin.

Snake Eye had agreed to meet them at the warping gate after gathering some warriors. Jeth and Vidya didn't know how long they'd be gone and required someone to let them back through the gate and watch for any magi in the meantime.

It didn't take long for them to find the gate within the ruins. As soon as they landed, Jeth walked absently to the spot where he had held Anwarr in his arms. The foliage was still flattened in the shape of her body. Her weak voice still echoed through his mind. *'Let's go back. . . .'*

He remained frozen in that spot, until Vidya called, "Jeth, come here and turn this crank, will you?" She nodded up to it while placing the warp stone back in its cubicle.

Shaking off his grief, he joined her on the gate's base and took hold of the crank. "I was just thinking," he said, hesitating to spin it. "What's stopping Nas'Gavarr from coming back here after we're gone and making short work of Snake Eye and his men?"

"As long as we complete the pathway to Elmifel before Nas'Gavarr can complete one from Rangardia, he won't be able to get through until our energy runs out," Vidya said. "Hopefully, Snake Eye gets here in time to keep the energy going. She can handle her brother at any rate. Or so she claims."

"What if Nas'Gavarr uses the Elmifel gate to escape Rangardia, and we walk right into him when we get there?"

"It's a risk, I'll admit, but it's better than flying," Vidya said while pushing the gate around to face northeast. "At least this way, if we run into trouble, we can turn right back around and remove the stone again."

Once the gate was in place, Jeth turned the crank, and in a few minutes, the pathway was established. Vidya went on through, and Jeth hesitated, realizing he'd never stepped through one before. Suddenly, Vidya's arm shot out from the energy, grabbed him by the shoulder, and pulled him in forcefully.

Vidya and Jeth were now standing in glistening blue caverns. *Good, this place isn't flooded,* she thought with relief.

"Whoa." Jeth gaped at the shining quartz in the cave walls.

Vidya looked to the magus at the crank. "Hello again."

"You came back, and you brought someone new," he said with a sigh of disappointment.

"Expecting someone else?" Vidya asked.

The magus stepped in front of the pair. "I cannot allow you to go any farther."

"Relax. We only came for the sights." Vidya pushed the magus off the platform.

Jeth pointed down to the dais at their feet. "This gate is pointed in a southwest direction, but not west enough to be the Herrani gate."

"And not south enough to be Credence," Vidya added.

"Rangardia then?"

Vidya bit her lip in concentration. "I don't think so, that's farther west. This gate is pointing to somewhere *between* Rangardia and Credence."

"Which is?"

"Ocean," she concluded.

"Hey, Magus," Jeth called to the priest, brushing dirt from his robes a few feet below them. "You wouldn't happen to know why your master needs a gate in the middle of the ocean, do you?"

"My master's plans are known to him and him alone. Now leave here or be drowned."

At the magus's words, the river below sloshed back and forth within the channel and started to rise. An echoing rumble of rushing water soon followed.

"We can deal with this later." Vidya grabbed Jeth under the arms, dove off the edge, and swooped into the tunnels. The river gathered behind them, forming a wave intent on pulling them beneath the rapids. A wall of water rose up in front of them, and they were seconds from smashing against it. Vidya sensed light illuminating the caverns above. *A way out!*

"Up!" Jeth yelled. With a determined grunt, Vidya flapped her wings furiously, doing all she could to gain height and clear the giant waves coming at them from either side.

"Damn Water Mages!" she growled as she struggled to lift both of them through the vertical tunnel. The opposing surges crashed together, the force of which shook the caverns. With one last heave for the light, they shot up into the skies above the Holy City of Thessalin.

It was a breathtaking sight. The city was built on a naturally fortified glacier spring where towering cathedrals and other stone structures stood upon six separate islands, linked together by elegant arch bridges. Roaring falls stretching from south to west put the ancient civilization on a liquid blue pedestal, feeding into the massive Elmifel Deltas of Del'Cabria and the Serpentine River in the desert. To the north and east, jutting snow tipped peaks formed a protective barrier from Ingleheim expansion.

Only the ashray were allowed to live in this city while urlings and some humans were permitted to settle in the vineyards beyond the falls. What Jeth and Vidya were gazing upon hadn't been seen by a human for over one hundred years.

"Look out for anything that resembles a monastery," Vidya said.

"Every building looks like a monastery."

They circled above the city for several minutes until Jeth shouted up at her, "Down there!"

He pointed with his foot to a building on one of the smaller islands, built in an upside down 'U' shape, much like the symbol tattooed on Nas'Gavarr's forehead.

"Hold on." Vidya veered on a downward angle, dropping Jeth safely on a flat surface of the roof while she landed a few feet beyond.

They searched the roof for an entrance but found none. There was, at the roof's center, a massive domed skylight over a magnificent library. Books and scrolls sat on shelves reaching all the way to the glass ceiling. Monks, dressed in light blue hooded robes passed by on bridges and steep stairways, connected by stone balconies which allowed them access to the various stacks. Polished stone ducts carried glacier water down each level to fill indoor pools encircling the entire bottom floor.

"I say we start our search for information here," suggested Vidya.

"Great idea . . . except I won't be much help. Can't read, remember?" Jeth said.

"Just keep your eyes and ears peeled for any monks."

"*That* I can do."

Vidya found a window pane and forced it open easily.

Jeth said, "I see only three monks down there. It's odd. I can't hear them."

"Maybe you need to be closer."

When the coast appeared clear, the two glided down to the highest level and quickly ducked behind some stacks.

They explored the vast library for a reference list that could lead them to any book or scroll the Overlord of Herran might have been interested in.

Jeth weaved nimbly through the stacks, peering around shelves for approaching monks, and nodding to Vidya when it was safe to continue. They eventually found a wall of square cubbyholes stuffed with scrolls in alphabetized fashion. They waited for a monk to move on from the area before approaching it.

Vidya unrolled a few of the scrolls under various letters. Each of them listed book titles and their locations.

After reading a few, Vidya sighed. "These only tell us what books are on this floor. We have a long day ahead of us."

"Maybe we should make a monk tell us what we need to know."

"Sounds good to me," she agreed, stuffing the scroll back into its slot. "That's more my style anyway."

They continued through the stacks but made less effort to be stealthy. Now that they were looking for one, there was not a monk to be found.

"Maybe if we wander around the bottom floor, someone will spot us," Vidya said.

Once there, they came upon a large swiveling globe made of dark red quartz, suspended above an upward curving base. From afar it resembled a volcano where the base was the mountain, and the sphere was billowing ash clouds erupting from it. Various depictions, painted in vibrant colors, were intricately carved into the stone.

"Ooh, pictures. I like pictures," Jeth quipped as he carefully turned the globe on its axis.

"Wonder what they mean?" Vidya said, studying the strange images with decorative symbols etched into the stone around them.

The bottom of the sphere was painted a fiery red, like lava spurting out from a volcano's base, then it faded into blue oceans with fish swimming around the sphere. At the center, on one side was an elaborate tree and on the other, a gale of wind, aiding a ferocious winged creature in flight. At the transition points between the middle layers were human faces, male on one side and female on the opposite. The top layer was yellow, illustrating desert sand where a long skeletal snake wrapped around the sphere with a skull at each end. Jeth halted the spinning sphere and pointed up at the skeletal image.

"I know what it means," he began. "I think each of these pictures represents a god."

"Are you sure?"

Jeth nodded. "That up there is what I fought in the Spirit Chamber. This tree in the middle has to be the Crannabeatha . . . and the bottom here, that's Verishten, the volcano god the Ingles worship."

"You're right," said Vidya. "This bird represents Yasharra, and the ocean and fish below must be the Spirit of Elmifel."

"Strange that the monks who worship only Elmifel would give credence to all the other gods in their artwork."

Upon further inspection of the artistic squiggles around the sphere, Vidya gasped. "These inscriptions aren't merely designs," she pointed out. "It's ancient urling script."

"Can you read it?"

"It's been a while but . . ." she trailed off as she concentrated on the words etched beneath each picture.

Starting from the bottom, she read, *"Earth gives rise to all things; the source of life gives way to progress; there is no progress without suffering; suffering brings death."*

"Uh huh." Jeth scratched his head.

Vidya pointed to the pictures that corresponded to each phrase she had read. "Look, *earth gives rise to all things*—that's referring to the volcano, then the water is the source of life, the tree is progress, and the bird brings . . ." She paused.

". . . Suffering," finished Jeth.

Vidya huffed, "Right . . . and the Serpentine must be death."

"The Death tribes had it right all along," said Jeth. "But what does it mean?"

"I think this is showing us how the gods work together. It's the story of creation."

Vidya spun the globe around. "There's more." She pointed to etchings around the sphere's circumference. *"Ruins are overgrown, pain is washed away, pestilence devours the living, and the rivers run dry. The foundation collapses, and all fall with it."*

"What do you think the faces represent?" Jeth asked.

"Creation's greatest mystery," a melodious voice echoed through the stacks.

Both Vidya and Jeth spun around to find not one ashray monk before them, but eight, all identical in height, approaching from the edge of the indoor river surrounding them. They stopped and brought their blue hoods down at the same time, revealing identical hairless heads with the familiar 'U' shaped marking and pointed ears so long they would put most urlings to shame. Vidya was surprised by how unnatural they appeared. Their skin was near translucent, showing the intricate network of blue veins set alight by the shining blue blood within them. Large oval eyes, absent lashes, took up considerable space on their faces, set far apart to accommodate wide nasal ridges. Small lips and a long thin neck combined with a lithe, yet broad physique gave each monk a genderless appearance. Vidya wondered if she was seeing the same being eight times over rather than eight separate beings.

"Aye, just the ones we're looking for," said Jeth.

"This place is forbidden to humans," the central ashray said.

Vidya stepped out to address the line of monks. "We want information on a student of yours from a hundred years ago. Maybe you remember him. I'll give you a hint: he's not an ashray."

The first monk cast his large violet eyes down before responding, "Gavarr."

"That's the one," sang Jeth. "Care to tell us why he left this monastery to become an all-powerful god killer?"

"The knowledge held here must be protected at all costs. If you do not leave, we will be forced to remove you," the monk stated plainly.

Jeth put out his hands in a non-threatening fashion. "We aren't here to steal your precious knowledge. We just want to know what Nas'Gavarr may have learned here that sent him on his warpath." All the ashrays tilted their heads in question while more began to file into the library. It was as if they had all heard some silent alarm bell. "I take it you don't know what he's been up to for the last hundred years," Jeth concluded.

"He was banished. We no longer intervene in mortal affairs," a third monk said.

"Why banish him?" Vidya asked.

The first ashray spoke again, "It was a mistake to give a naja-human hybrid access to the secrets of creation. Del'Cabria was looking to bring the desert tribes under their rule. The Royal Family decreed that the Immortal sorcerer who had been uniting the tribes should study at this monastery. It was hoped his time here would turn him away from the Death cults and toward a Del'Cabrian belief system. It seemed to have worked . . . at first. Over the course of thirty years, he abandoned his old gods but replaced them with something much darker. The worship of man . . . of himself. He believed humanity's salvation would only come if all ancient beings were annihilated."

"Surely, he learned *something* that provoked this change," Vidya said.

"What he learned, we cannot share. Such knowledge is for the ashray alone," yet another monk said.

"And how is keeping the world's knowledge out of human hands working for you so far?" Jeth asked heatedly. "I hate to break it to you all, but Nas'Gavarr already used that knowledge to destroy the Serpentine, and Elmifel could be next."

Every ashray in the room gasped in uncanny unison.

Vidya continued, "And we're guessing he learned how to do that here, making you all partly responsible. So, either you're going to give us the answers we need or get out of our way while we search for them ourselves."

At that ultimatum, all but one of the monks left the library. "Are you certain Sagorath and Salotaph are gone from this world?" the remaining ashray asked once they were alone.

Jeth nodded. "I was a witness to it. Now, is there a name we can call you?"

"The ashray are of one mind; individual names are unnecessary, but since your human minds can better communicate on an individual basis, you may refer to this body as Garwin."

"Alright." Jeth proceeded to relay to Garwin how the Burning Waste transformed into an oasis but left out exact details of his part in it. "Have you any idea what he's trying to do?"

Garwin approached the globe and slowly spun it around. "There are five of what humanity worships as gods, but that is not what they are. They are Conduits, channels through which the Unnamed siphon their infinite essence and spirit into our world. Through these Conduits, they can influence this primitive realm through a force known as the *Way*."

"Wait a minute." Vidya shook her head. "Are you talking about the Deities That Cannot Be Named?"

The ashray monk nodded once.

"So, you're saying the Goddess Yasharra is nothing more than a conduit to the Deities those woman-hating imperialists worship?" she asked shrilly. The thought of such a thing being true made her sick to her stomach.

Garwin blinked at her choice of phrase, but he replied with another nod. "In a sense, yes. Yasharra is just one facet of the Deities that reside in the Spirit Realm, providing all the spirits that exist in every sentient life form on this plane."

"That's a load of pigshit!" Vidya snapped.

"Then killing one is not a good thing, I take it?" Jeth said while Vidya paced around the room to get her head straight.

"Conduits cannot be destroyed as they do not have a physical body in this realm. What was defeated was only the Conduit's influence in this world. No new naja can ever come into being again. Any power they derive from the Serpentine cannot be wielded, and the Deity associated with death and decay no longer has a connection to this realm. Fortunately, the Serpentine has not been too active in the last few centuries, and its absence will not likely be felt worldwide. However, if all the Conduits were to be closed . . ."

"That's what Nas'Gavarr wants to do," Jeth said, meeting eyes with Vidya before turning back to Garwin. "He wants to shut them all down. How will that be good for humanity?"

"It won't." Garwin frowned. "Without Conduits through which the Deities can provide our world with essence and spirit, what is left here will be all there is. Spirits of the dead will disperse into the Spirit Realm without new ones to replace them. This will lead to the gradual extinction of all sentient beings, including humans."

"Nas'Gavarr must know this," Vidya surmised. "That *can't* be his plan."

"It may have to do with his obsession with Creation's Mystery," Garwin said.

He turned the sphere and touched the depiction of the man's face. "Humanity . . ." Jeth murmured. "We're the mystery."

"No, we're not," Vidya dismissed, giving the globe a good spin and blurring the pictures together. "Yasharra created us. Well . . . she created the island we live on, but then she . . ." She looked to the ceiling, trying to remember the old lore she was taught as a child. "Wait, no, she gave birth to the Harpy and the Siren first who created men to fight and women to take care of them . . . although some interpretations state that humans were already there."

Jeth joined in with his people's story, "Humans came upon the forest, and the fairies defended it against them. Some fairies rebelled and joined the invaders, interbred with them, and the first Fae were born. That ultimately ended the struggle as the Fae learned to respect the forest and the Mother Oak where the first humans did not."

Then, Garwin began to relay the ashray's run in with the first humans, "They came upon the Sacred Spring of Elmifel thousands of years ago. At first, their presence fascinated us. They lived such short and meaningless existences, limited to their base, animalistic natures, and separate individuality. It was their ability to procreate with their own bodies that captivated us most of all. We have always been as one consciousness with additional bodies born from the Sacred Spring every century. At that time, we found a way to implant our seed of life into their females' wombs, creating what you know as urlings today. We had hoped our influence would give them more unity of mind and thus ability to move forward from their primitive ways. It became apparent that their mortal minds and bodies were incapable of fully realizing our way of being. Our influence taught them to live in larger societies and advance their civilization, but they could not be persuaded to stop brutalizing one another. So, we left them to their own fate."

Jeth and Vidya exchanged horrified glances, before turning back to Garwin.

"You abandoned your creations like some failed experiment?" Vidya exclaimed.

"Ancient ones throughout the ages have done similar things when dealing with the plague of humanity. Golems embraced them with disastrous consequences. Naja and harpies enslaved them with much of the same result. Ashray and fairies do what is most merciful; keep humans away from what is sacred and let the Deities do with them what they will."

Jeth burst out laughing, causing Vidya to raise an eyebrow. "All the times I've heard urlings bragging about their ashray blood, I never thought it was what *actually* contributed to their superiority complex! I know humanity isn't perfect, but a plague? It was because of your meddling we have this divide between those with round ears and pointed!"

"We assure you," Garwin stated, "that divide has and will always exist in humanity. It is your nature that leads you to destruction, not the ashray's."

"No wonder Nas'Gavarr was obsessed with this so-called human mystery," Jeth huffed. "He wants to make things right in his own twisted way because none of you are willing to fix your mistakes!"

"Don't tell me you sympathize with him now," Vidya said.

"I may be starting to understand him, but that doesn't make what he's doing all right. We need to find out which god—I mean Conduit he plans on hitting next." Jeth's hands fiddled with his sword's grip. Similar anxiety gnawed at Vidya's insides. Whichever one he'd destroy next would cause a natural disruption of similar proportion to what occurred in Herran, only she was willing to bet those landscapes would not turn into oases.

Gazing up at the globe, a thought came to her. "Creation started from the bottom up, but Nas'Gavarr started at the top."

Garwin added, "This globe depicts the order in which each Conduit came into existence during Creation. It stands to reason they would be destroyed in the reverse order."

"Which means one of ours is next . . ." said Jeth with a gulp.

"Yes, it is believed the Crannabeatha and Yasharra came into existence at the same time. As life progresses, suffering occurs in tandem with it. Without pain or anguish, there can be no reason for life to continue moving forward," said Garwin.

"But Nas'Gavarr will need someone to sacrifice," Vidya said.

"Sacrifice? So you are familiar with the Champions?" Garwin asked.

Jeth came clean about how it was his blood Nas'Gavarr used to shut down the Serpentine.

"Then you must be Crannabeatha's Champion," Garwin said.

"What does that mean?"

"Champions are called upon throughout the ages whenever a Conduit's domain is under threat. They are typically endowed with aspects of ancient abilities. They have always been mortal, as they can incite fellowship with other mortals and lay down their lives if need be."

"That's why Nas'Gavarr has been waging war all over the place. He's trying to awaken champions, like Siegfried of Ingleheim," said Jeth.

". . . And me," Vidya murmured. "He threatened my home, not to take it over, but to incite fear in the Siren Council so they'd make a harpy to protect them."

"Then how did I get called? He never threatened Fae'ren, at least not directly. Although, Fae'ren is always under some sort of threat. I could have been called from the moment I was abandoned in the Deep Wood."

Vidya's eyes drifted back to the globe. "Our next step should be finding out who these other champions are and get to them before Nas'Gavarr does," she said.

"No one champion can be used to close any Conduit," said Garwin.

"Right," Jeth recalled. "Nas'Gavarr did say I was the only one who could defeat the Serpentine."

"The answers you seek are on the globe," said Garwin, spinning it around again and pointing to the gloomy message Vidya had read out earlier.

"Pain is washed away; pestilence devours the living," she repeated. "Jeth, I'm pestilence, which is meant to destroy what nurtures life . . . your Mother Oak."

"Why do you assume that?"

Because my people are about to spread disease throughout your homeland, Vidya almost blurted, but instead replied, "Birds are known to carry such things, and harpies harbor a resistance to all known pathogens. The Champion of Elmifel is the water that washes pain away, the pain being Yasharra."

"Garwin, you must know who the Champion of Elmifel is," Jeth said to the monk.

"Thessalin hasn't been under significant threat for thousands of years, even with all the wars Del'Cabria has fought. We are not aware of any champion having been called."

Vidya said, "I'm willing to bet Nas'Gavarr already knows who it is. And don't think that this place isn't under threat, Garwin. He managed to build a warping gate under your Holy City without your hive mind being aware of it."

The ashray gasped and said in a low register, "Take us to it."

Vidya offered to carry Garwin along with Jeth back to the caverns. They landed in front of the gate. Unfortunately, the energy had run out, but the magus was still there. Once he caught sight of the monk, he didn't hesitate in hurling himself off the edge and into the cold rapids below.

"We must search for secret tunnels Gavarr may have used to access this place. We will ensure they are never used again. Thank you for bringing this to our attention," said Garwin with a subtle bow of the head.

"And thank you for all the information," Vidya replied.

"The Sacred Spring of Elmifel will be one of the last Conduits Gavarr comes after. We will not allow him to get near it."

"Hopefully, your champion can help with that when the time comes," Jeth added.

"Make sure to remove the stone from this gate after we step through it," said Vidya.

Garwin nodded and went to start his secret tunnel investigation, leaving Jeth and Vidya alone at the gate. Vidya pushed it southwest toward Herran while Jeth spun the crank to activate it. And they walked on through.

Once on the other side, Snake Eye rushed up to meet them. "It's about time, children," he said with an air of annoyance.

Jeth was still reeling from the revelations he had just learned. *He can kill his own gods, but if he thinks he can come after yours . . . You can't let that happen.*

"You fill him in. I have to get to Credence," Vidya said. She stepped off the platform and walked through the line of Herrani warriors Snake Eye had brought.

Jeth followed her. "Right this minute?"

"Yasharra's the one he's going after next. I need to warn the Council."

"How do you know he won't go to Fae'ren first? Garwin said the Crannabeatha and Yasharra came into existence at the same time." He also recalled what Anwarr told him about the scads of tradesmen in Lanore. Those men had been long gone when Jeth arrived there, meaning whatever they were building was likely complete . . . another secret warping gate perhaps.

"But the globe read: *ruins are overgrown* first, then *pain is washed away.* Yasharra is second." Vidya turned and kept walking.

"We don't know that he has the Champion of Elmifel," Jeth said while keeping pace with her.

Vidya spun around in a huff. "Even if he doesn't, we don't know where he or she is. We do know that he doesn't have the one to shut down the Crannabeatha because I'm right here."

"Stay with us, and we can formulate a plan of attack," Jeth posed.

"I left Nas'Gavarr in Rangardia. I need to get back home if not for any other reason than to do damage control."

Jeth sighed in frustration. "We should stick together and check Fae'ren first. In the meantime, you can send a pigeon with word to Credence."

"I can fly faster than a stupid pigeon!" Upon taking a breath, she continued more calmly, "You go protect yours, and I'll protect mine. Is that not what we Champions are supposed to do?"

Jeth rubbed the back of his neck. "Sure . . . unless your method of protecting yours is going after the dagger again and building your harpy army."

Vidya bit her lip. "There's no time for that anymore. The risk is too great. I realize that now. The best thing I can do is stay as far away from Nas'Gavarr and Fae'ren as possible."

"Alright," Jeth said, and put a hand on Vidya's shoulder. "Good luck then, and watch your back."

"You too. . . ." She looked down at Jeth's hand before awkwardly shaking it off. She backed up a few more paces before shooting up into the sky with a blast of air.

Turning back around, Jeth caught a confused look from Snake Eye.

"What in Sag's name were you two talking about?" he asked.

"Let's return to the city and gather all the warriors you have. We're marching for Fae'ren," said Jeth.

Snake Eye narrowed his serpent gaze. "I told you, I'm not ready—"

Jeth cut him off. "We're going to see the Spirit Mage I told you about, so bring your artifacts and arm your men and women with Magitech. You have to be ready, Snake Eye. The time is now."

32

What You Were Created For

Snake Eye had only thirty warriors at his disposal. The rest were still miles away in various Del'Cabrian or Fae'ren outposts, and word wouldn't be able to reach them all without causing suspicion among their generals. Jeth feared thirty men armed with Steinkamp Magitech wouldn't suffice in protecting the Deep Wood once Nas'Gavarr decided to advance upon it, even with the additional men under General Nadila in Fae'ren. The next two weeks were, therefore, spent trying to bring more fighters to their cause.

That was how Jeth and Snake Eye found themselves riding up to a line of fifty mounted Tezkhan raiders. A rather large troop had set up camp in the northern grasslands that had once been part of the Burning Waste. Now, there was nothing to stop all the raiders from riding unhindered into Herran, but they were likely holding back in fear of retaliation from the Overlord.

Jeth stepped down from his saddle, and the troop leader and one of his brothers did the same. Snake Eye awkwardly dismounted last. He was wearing bulky brigandine armor made for a man twice his size, though he'd insisted it was fine before setting out.

As the four of them stood face to face on the new grasslands, Jeth recognized the leader as none other than Genkhai.

Genkhai's face lit up with recognition. "Manservant? You are a Herrani warrior now?"

"Sort of . . . and you're a chief now?"

"The strongest of us divided up Ukhuna's riders, his wives, and his wealth, and went our separate ways." Genkhai spit some foul-smelling khat leaf on the ground. "Last I heard, he went after you and that imposter bride to regain his honor. I assume he did not find it."

Jeth shook his head and glanced down to Anwarr's tulwar at his hip. He had been unable to find another khopesh to match his remaining one, so he decided to retire it for the tulwar instead, to not only remind the Tezkhan that he had, in fact, killed their last chief but to carry a part of Anwarr with him into battle.

Genkhai nodded slowly to show he understood. "Did you bring this tiny army to challenge us for this land?"

Snake Eye said, "This land is not yours now, but it could be."

The two Tezkhan looked the effeminate Herrani up and down. "That armor is too big for you," said the other raider.

Jeth coughed a little to mask a chuckle.

"I say it is just big enough," he replied without a flinch. "I speak on behalf of my brother, the Overlord of Herran. He took the fires away from this land, and he can bring them back."

"You dare threaten us, woman?" Genkhai narrowed his gaze at Snake Eye.

"On the contrary. I offer you an opportunity to not only settle in these grasslands permanently but also to regain the treasure that inspired hundreds of Tezkhan to follow behind one great chief."

"And that chief can be you, Genkhai," Jeth finished, taking out the palm-sized Emerald of Dulsakh, having been removed from Ukhuna's sword, and holding it out for all to see.

"You still have it!" Genkhai exclaimed.

"It would look mighty nice on the pommel of that sword you're carrying," Jeth added.

Genkhai reached for the jewel, but Jeth jerked it away and gave it back to Snake Eye for safe keeping. "You need to do something for us first."

Looking past Jeth and toward Torrent, he replied, "I suppose for the man who could tame a wild beast like that, I'll at least consider it."

"We need men who can fight and ride with the best of them. Come with us across the world, help protect a little woodland area. Then the emerald and everything you see here—"

Genkhai snorted through his nose and put his hand out to stop Jeth from continuing. "That's enough. I was with you when you said fight and ride." The man flashed a half-toothed grin.

With Genkhai's troop of Tezkhan raiders behind them, the force of eighty strong arrived at the temple warping gate by midday. They spent the next few hours resting up and organizing their weaponry.

Jeth was sharpening the tulwar when Snake Eye approached and handed him a bow and quiver. "I found an extra one for you. Can't have Gershlon Reborn going without a proper bow, now can we?"

"Yes, yes, thank you!" Jeth jumped up to accept his replacement bow, having felt so naked without it for the last two weeks. Once he took it in hand, he frowned.

"What? Is it not to your liking?"

It was typical of Herrani made bows. The wood was poor quality and flimsy. But for a short bow, it didn't have to be perfect. It would do him well enough on horseback, but not for long range shooting.

"It'll do, thanks again." He patted the armored ashipu's shoulder.

Snake Eye smiled and went to join his other warriors. He helped them equip their Magitech—blast gel, ice powder, wind blades, and the like. "Make sure you are wearing your Steinkamp gloves, boys and girls, or your new magic weapons won't work," he sang.

Jeth spotted Genkhai with his riders, stringing lariats to their poles. "Do you think you'll even need those?" he asked.

Genkhai grinned from ear to ear. "Your serpent-eyed lady gave us some new leather straps that fuse to the skin. Should come in handy."

Jeth nodded, noticing that each of the Tezkhan were wearing a black glove on one hand as well. He sat down and helped them switch out the old ropes for the enchanted Steinkamp leather.

A few hours later, everyone lined up in twos before the gate with Dulsakh's Sarcophagus being carted behind them. When Jeth climbed up the gate's base, Snake Eye said, "Are you sure there's going to be a gate in Fae'ren?"

"Anwarr told me about tradesmen in the commune she was taken from. After Vidya found the secret gate in Elmifel, it stands to reason that's what they were hiding so close to the Deep Wood."

"I hope you're right."

With that, Snake Eye ordered three of his men to push the gate to face east. Jeth was relieved to find his hunch paid off as soon as the warp stone in the base began to chime.

"Stop there," said Jeth. "Now turn the crank."

The men went to work until the energy splashed into the ring, much to the astonishment of everyone waiting to ride through it.

"Time to go, my warriors," Snake Eye announced. He and Jeth left the platform and mounted their steeds, then led the warriors through the liquid energy.

The two were the first to emerge on the other side, and just as Jeth expected, they were surrounded by a thick forest.

Without a moment's hesitation, they rode off the platform and into a clearing to leave room for the others to pass through. A dozen Herrani warriors were standing guard. The one at the crank jumped down from the base and ran into the underbrush.

"He's going to warn someone." Jeth spun Torrent around and shot an arrow through the back of the man's neck where he had no armor.

A man at the other side of the gate also ran but was halted when Snake Eye's flesh whip found his neck. With a sharp yank, Snake Eye pulled the warrior to the ground and another yank ripped his throat right out. Jeth grimaced. Their own warriors, rode two by two from the gate and into the clearing, cutting or shooting down every last foe.

"Check the surrounding area thoroughly, there is certain to be more stationed nearby," Snake Eye ordered. He then turned his white steed around to face Jeth. "We will replace however many there are and hide and wait for your return."

"Are you sure you don't want me to stay and fight? You don't know how many warriors are beyond here," Jeth said.

"Not to worry, ours are aching to use their Magitech in real combat. Go find your fairies, and we will meet up with General Nadila near Fairieshome before trekking over to Ingleheim."

"Alright, I'll be back before sundown." Jeth nodded.

He kicked Torrent due east. His plan was to first warn Serra and the other fairies of Nas'Gavarr's pending arrival, then he and Snake Eye would try to enlist Jenn's help with the resurrection spell.

They could only hope the Overlord would not come to Fae'ren before then. *Just stay out of his grasp, Vidya, that's all you have to do.*

Vidya flew through the window of her dormitory to find no one there. That wasn't enough to alarm her, but everything she owned having had been cleared out certainly was.

"What in Yasharra's name?" she whispered, frantically looking around her small hovel of a living space. *They might be fine, I should check with Demeter,* she thought, willing her heart to stop pounding in her throat.

Diving out the window, Vidya flew across the city to her sister's estate. She soared over the heads of her personal guards and through one of the larger windows of the east wing. Her niece and nephew were there, playing with turtle doves, and giggling away. Both children picked up and ran out of the room as soon as Vidya landed on their sofa.

"Demeter!" Her voice echoed off the high marble domed ceilings.

A handsome long-haired man, lost in thought, walked down the hall toward her,.

"Camdus!" she called, taking brisk steps to meet him. He gasped in shock and halted his gait. With one look at Vidya, he spun around and took off running the other way.

What is going on here? She didn't bother chasing down the breeder and instead rushed to Demeter's bedchambers.

Violently shoving the door open, Vidya marched into the room. Demeter was sprawled naked on her bed, wings and dark wavy tresses free of her wig, fanned out over her lilac bedspread, as she received cunnilingus from her other breeder. The sound of her door flying open was enough to break her out of her pleasure-filled stupor.

Demeter screeched, her wings reflexively folding around her exposed form. A startled Rufios sprang up from between her legs and fell backward off the bed.

"Vidya, you came back!" Demeter gasped, grabbing for her silk robes hanging from the bed post.

"Where are Phrea and Daphne?" Vidya demanded. "Are they here?"

"Rufios, leave us," Demeter said to her breeder on the floor. He said nothing and scurried, bare-assed, into the lavatory. "You've been to your dormitory," said Demeter after climbing into her clothes.

"There was nothing there," Vidya's voice was shaking. "Tell me they didn't get found."

"You shouldn't have come here," Demeter said in a low voice.

"Where else would I go?"

At those words, the sound of several rapid footsteps echoed down the halls from every direction, all of them heading toward the bedchambers. Before Vidya could utter another word, several armed guards ran into the room and surrounded her.

"Demi, these are guards from the Citadel. What is going on?" Vidya said as the ten guards put up their round bronze shields and pointed their spears at her.

"I'm sorry, Sister," she breathed.

"Vidya, daughter of Sarta, you are hereby under arrest for war crimes, pertaining to mass murder and conspiracy at the detriment of the Republic," said the guard in front of her, voice muffled through his face plate.

"Why are you only arresting me?" Vidya asked, fearing the answer.

Tears flooded her sister's eyes as she said in a shaking voice, "Take her away."

One of the guards grabbed for Vidya's arm, but she smacked it aside. All at once, they closed in around her. She punched their shields, sending one flying over the bed, and another smashing through the vanity.

"Tell these buffoons to stand down!" Vidya bellowed.

"Don't fight this!" Demeter cried.

Vidya spread her wings and knocked all the guards back before running out of the room. With a burst of air, she flew down the hallway. A throwing net appeared in front of her, and there was no time to dodge it. The sinewy fibers clung to her, tangling in her wings. She hit the floor hard, skidding along the slippery marble and smacking into a pillar protruding from the wall.

She screamed as the guards surrounded her. All but one held her down, and the last approached her with a vial. He kneeled in front of her while she thrashed about on the floor and forced multiple drops of valerian down her throat. Three times the dosage that they had given any of the Rangarders.

It didn't take long for the drops to take effect. She fell in and out of consciousness as the soldiers took her to the Citadel's dungeon.

Once inside the dark, windowless space, they put thick iron shackles around her feet and wrists, and chained her wings together, forcing them flat against her back. After cutting her leathers off and replacing them with a thin backless tunic, they closed and locked the heavy barred door with an echoing clank. With a powerful bellow, she launched herself against the door. But even if her strength had been at full capacity, she couldn't hope to break it down.

Pain reverberated through her entire body as she collapsed and slid down the wall, shaking with rage and despair.

She bashed her shackled fists on the hard stone, screaming with each strike until all she could do was fall to her side and weep.

"Vidi? Is that you?" came a raspy voice from the next cell over.

"Phrea?"

"I'm here too," echoed the emotionless voice of Daphne from the other side.

"Daph! I thought something horrible happened to you two," Vidya said in breathless relief. "What in Yasharra's name is going on?"

"We've been betrayed," Phrea said, followed by the sound of a pebble hitting the wall of her cell.

"Demeter . . ." Vidya growled.

"We did everything you requested," Phrea said. "We uncovered the male uprising conspiracy—turns out, the Infantry Commander was behind it. The Supreme is claiming ignorance, but because he was crucial in preventing it, he won't lose his position."

"What happened?"

Daphne replied, "We observed them like you told us. He got wind of their plans to detonate dynamite in the Council chambers when a meeting was in session."

"They tried to assassinate the entire Siren Council?" Vidya gasped.

"We were going to stop it just before it happened, implicating them all," said Daphne.

"Then how did you two end up here?"

Phrea began, "Since you hadn't yet arrived with this special dagger, we had to bring Demeter in on our plan. She was supposed to convince the Council to sacrifice them to the Harpy to make an example of the traitors."

"She confessed to the Council everything," Daphne rejoined. "The missing infantrymen, even the Rangarders we sacrificed. She even went as far as tell her that we helped plan the uprising to get more harpies, under your orders."

"No." Vidya shook her head upon the hard, cold floor. "She couldn't have told them so much without implicating herself."

"She told everyone it was your idea, and that you threatened her children's lives to make her comply with your demands. Only when you left for the mainland did she feel brave enough to come forward," said Daphne.

Vidya clamped her eyes shut, squeezing the tears from them.

It had always been Vidya's fear that Demeter would betray her in some way. But now, hearing the truth told from her own harpies' mouths, she couldn't believe it. In early childhood, Vidya had never trusted the siren. Demeter had been so jealous of her relationship with their mother, only for that jealousy to wane as soon as Vidya left for Rangardia. In the last few months, however, Vidya thought she and Demeter could really be sisters. *The only sisters I have are the ones locked in this dungeon with me now,* she thought, her heart breaking.

"I'm sorry, Vidi," Phrea said. "But your sister is a coward and as power hungry as the rest of the sirens. She threw us to the vultures so she can keep her mansion, her breeders, and her seat on the Council."

A shadow formed above Vidya as she listened to Phrea, its dark wings stretched like sinister tendrils across the entire ceiling, its yellow eyes burning into hers. *"There is treachery afoot . . . ."*

"You're just figuring that out now?" Vidya scoffed at the shadow. "Where have you been?"

Phrea, believing Vidya was talking to her, replied, "You're the one who said we needed a siren on our side."

"Not your sister . . . Señor Ricardo. He wants to save our republic and his empire . . . be the hero . . . and get rid of you."

"He couldn't possibly know what we did in Venerra," murmured Vidya.

"Who would he have had contact with in the last few days?" The shadow harpy tittered.

Daphne called, "What are you talking about, Vid. . . . Vidya?"

The shadow dissipated from the ceiling and Vidya snapped back into reality. "I . . . I'm going to get us out of here. Do you hear me?"

"I sure hope so," Phrea said. "Because we already stood trial and tomorrow night they pass sentence."

"Are you sure you can do it?" Jeth asked Serra.

He hadn't gone far into the Deep Wood, calling Serra's name on the back of Torrent, when she appeared to him. After telling her everything that happened with Anwarr, the temple, killing the Serpentine Gods, and his plan to defeat Nas'Gavarr and save the forest, he was now ready to head back to the gate.

"It will take all us fairies working together, but it's what we were created for," said Serra. "However, it will take more than twenty-four hours for us to grow an adequate barrier around the Crannabeatha."

"He still needs Vidya to perform the ritual, so we should have plenty of time. If anything happens, I'll do my best to keep him and his armies as far from here as possible."

"We're on it," Serra said with a nod.

Jeth climbed into his saddle. "Remember, Ser. It's only a matter of time before Nas'Gavarr advances on this place. You're our last line of defense and the only hope we have in defeating him."

Serra batted her long eyelashes and said, "The power of a dead desert god is no match for the power here. Go now to Ingleheim. We have things covered." As Jeth gathered his reins, Serra fluttered over to him and hovered just before the horse's head. "I think I know what *you* were created for, Jeth."

"I'm Crannabeatha's Champion," he stated, puffing out his chest.

The pixie chuckled while rubbing Torrent under her chin. "Our Mother has never needed a champion. She has us fairies looking out for her. She didn't call upon you to protect *her*, but to protect *them*." She pointed her small finger back west.

"Them being the people that want nothing to do with me?"

Serra frowned. "She senses things are to get much worse for the Fae'ren people. They may not want you, but they're going to need you."

He turned his steed around. "How about I keep this forest alive a little longer, then I'll worry about the people who live in it."

Jeth waved goodbye to his fairy guardian and rode west. It was almost dusk when he came upon the warping gate.

As he approached the rendezvous point, the forest grew eerily silent. The smell of blood and viscera filled his nostrils before the clearing was even in sight.

Pushing Torrent into a gallop, he came upon a swarm of naja, tearing through the flesh of both man and horse. *Snake Eye!* Mutilated bodies were strewn about, all of them the Herrani warriors they had killed earlier. Snake Eye's warriors and the Tezkhan were nowhere to be seen. That realization did little to stave off his terror.

Torrent reared backward. Every naja snapped their heads up, entrails hanging from their blood-stained jaws. Jeth kicked his steed into the underbrush, the carnivorous reptiles leaping after them and snapping at Torrent's back legs. In the next clearing, more naja sprang out. The ones behind him emerged from the foliage while the others in front closed in, their growls rumbling from every direction. Torrent shrieked, jerking her head from side to side.

"Whoa, girl," he commanded his horse. *You can't go out like this, not now,* he thought in panic. The only way Jeth could see surviving was to jump over the armored shoulders of the naja, and try to outrun them on foot, leaving his loyal steed to be devoured. It sickened him to even consider such an idea.

Each yellow eye was fixated on him and his mare, but none of the naja pounced. They all backed away, forming a circle around him. Then, an armored Herrani man on a large black horse rode through the crowd of reptile beasts and stopped in front of Jeth.

"You must be the Desert War Traitor," the man said. "I thought I'd find you wandering around here somewhere."

"Saf'Ryeem." Jeth gave him a nod while nervously glancing at all the ferocious reptilian faces staring up at him.

It was hard to find the resemblance to the Overlord in Ryeem's leathery features. Up close, he appeared older than his father, his chin lacking but compensated for with an elaborate blonde goatee down the length of his chest. Tattoos of serpents wound around his partially shaven head, down his neck, and around his one bare arm. The other was fully armored to accommodate the trident spear he wielded.

"You've given my father a lot of trouble in these last few days," he said.

"Someone's got to give that Mage a hard time every now and again," Jeth quipped.

Ryeem smirked. "Step down from your horse, and I won't have my naja eat it from under you."

With a heavy sigh, Jeth did as he was told but wouldn't let go of Torrent's reins.

"Place all your weapons in the saddlebags and step away."

"Come on," Jeth whined as he removed his scabbard. "I just got these."

"You won't need them anymore," Ryeem said flatly.

Once Jeth tied all his weapons, including his knife, to his saddle, Ryeem motioned for one of his naja to take Torrent's lead. She whinnied and jerked away. Worried that they'd kill her, Jeth placed a hand on her neck and tried to soothe her, but to no avail.

She knocked the naja back with her front hooves and ran straight for the opening that Ryeem had made.

"Tor!" Jeth called after her. It was no use. His untamable mare disappeared into the forest with all his weapons. He put his palm to his forehead in shock.

Ryeem grinned. "Those Tezkhan breeds can be unpredictable." Another two naja tied Jeth's hands behind his back. "Come now, my father awaits."

Jeth's heart seized. *It can't be! He can't be here already!*

The next day, Vidya awoke to the jarring clank of her cell door. A Citadel guard peered in as she sat up from the floor. "Get up. The War Council awaits."

Another few drops of valerian later, she was escorted out of the dungeons and to the Citadel's third floor where the War Chambers were located. *Trials take place in the courtyard, on the ground level,* she thought with a strange dread creeping into her gut.

Meeting Vidya at the large round table was Supreme Commander Ariston, the Archon, and the Mistress of Foreign Relations and Trade. The Mistress of Law and Order was not in attendance. *Althea needs to be here to pass the judgment, not my sister.*

Vidya swallowed the lump in her throat as she was made to sit down in the chair opposite of Xenith, Ariston, and one empty seat. Demeter sat diagonal to her, right where her mother sat the day Nas'Gavarr broke her neck. She wasn't wearing her wig today. It was strange for Vidya to see her as a brunette. *She looks too much like Mother, it's not fair,* she thought with a bitter taste in her mouth.

For a whole minute, nobody said a word. They only stared down Vidya like she were some kind of lowly creature, weighed down by cast iron shackles, degraded by a colorless prison garb, and weakened by valerian.

She decided to speak first. "I don't know what Demeter told you, but everything I did was to protect—"

"Silence," Xenith's voice echoed off the marble pillars. "We did not bring you here to plead your innocence."

"Is this not a trial?" Vidya asked.

Xenith shook her head.

"You would deny me my Yasharra-given right?"

"We have more pressing concerns at the moment," Xenith began, her voice disarmed. "It broke my heart to learn of the atrocities you have committed in Credence's name. However, fault does not rest solely on your shoulders, but on mine as well."

Vidya's raised an eyebrow, unsure of where Xenith was headed with such a statement.

"The Siren Council had unanimously agreed, out of fear, to bring a harpy into this world. We believed it was the only weapon we had against a foe as powerful as the Immortal Serpent. We were wrong. And we will surely pay for that mistake."

"And how are you all paying for it?" said Vidya. "From where I'm sitting, it is only me and my harpy sisters who are being punished."

"You and the harpies you *spawned* have proven to be far more dangerous to the Republic than the Overlord ever was," Xenith countered in a sharpened tone.

"It is not the Harpy that poses the threat this time," Vidya spat, "but the Siren who does not have the stomach to do what must be done!"

"What must be done," Xenith exclaimed, "is not murdering our allies, unlawfully executing our own men, and flying off with Del'Cabrian traitors instead of forming an alliance we desperately needed!"

Vidya's heart skipped a beat. "How did you—?

"Spies were sent after you," Ariston interjected. "We had to make sure you were following orders. You have no respect for the Republic or Yasharra!"

"One of your commanders organized an uprising under your nose. You're in no position to lecture me, you incompetent fool!" Vidya hissed.

"Enough!" Xenith boomed.

"I demand a fair trial!"

"You have forced our hand, Vidya!" Xenith snapped.

"Forced it to do what exactly?"

"To form a treaty with Herran."

Her stomach lurched as the shadow harpy's message from her cell replayed in her mind. *'There is treachery afoot.'* It was then the chamber doors swung open, and the guards escorted someone else in. They moved aside and allowed Nas'Gavarr to take the empty seat next to the Supreme Commander.

It wasn't until he looked at Vidya, his serpent eyes narrowing to thin slits, that she knew she was not hallucinating.

"No! You cannot sign a treaty with him!" Vidya screamed as she tried to get out of her chair, but the guards beside her shoved her back down.

Xenith replied in her usual stoic voice, "We can and we must. Your actions have left us no other alternative. Now, let us begin."

33

You Killed Them

"How did he even get here?" Vidya asked in horror, unable to peel her eyes away from the Mage sitting across the table.

Finally, Demeter spoke, "The Emperador of Rangardia sent an urgent message a few days ago. Witnesses at their central gate saw you open a pathway and later throw Nas'Gavarr through it. You literally delivered our enemy to our ally's doorstep without warning. I know you've had issue with Rangardia from the start, but to pit them against us like this? What were you thinking?"

Vidya pounded her shackled fists on the table. "I had no choice. He destroyed the gods of the desert, and he will do the same to ours!"

Ignoring what Vidya said, Xenith cleared her throat and began, "Fortunately, what could have been an unmitigated diplomatic disaster has worked out in our favor. Thanks to the graciousness of Emperador Agustin and his administrator, and the peace-keeping efforts of Demeter, we have found a way to repair our damaged relations with Rangardia and end our war with Herran at the same time."

"Herran offers Credence a truce in which its elected leaders will remain in power and its sovereignty be respected," said Nas'Gavarr.

"At what cost?" Vidya asked, her fists clenching until her fingernails bit into her flesh.

"First, male citizens shall be granted the right to vote, and their freedom assured."

"The right to vote for Assembly representatives is for mothers only," said Xenith. "Therefore, we can grant that same right to fathers as well. No childless woman or man has right to vote in Credence. Only those in the Mothers' Assembly can vote for Siren Councilors."

"Then extend that right to their husbands, and I will consider that fair treatment of men under Crede law," concluded Nas'Gavarr.

"Agreed," Xenith said, tapping her fingers irritably on the table, lips pursed.

"In return," Nas'Gavarr continued. "Herran promises to come to the aid of Credence in any military altercation, and will ensure free trade among all allied tribes."

"Any military altercation?" Demeter asked. "Will this not conflict with your treaty with Del'Cabria?"

"Del'Cabria has agreed never to enact war on Herran or any of its allies. Credence will be one of those allies," he said.

"What is wrong with you people?" Vidya yelled. "The last time this man was in this room he broke the neck of one of your own!"

Xenith donned a somber expression. "Yasharra knows this was not the course of action we envisioned taking, but we must put desires for reprisal aside and do what is in the best interest of the Republic."

"This man doesn't give a shit about our best interest! He wants this treaty so he can access the Grand Altar. He will destroy Yasharra and our entire island with it." *Pain is washed away,* Vidya recalled, panic rising into her throat.

"Listen to yourself," Xenith said. "Nobody can destroy our goddess. What we are doing here today will not only save Credence but you as well, don't you understand?"

"You're all being fooled!" Vidya shrieked. Nas'Gavarr sat there, unflinching.

Demeter sniffed back tears. "Nas'Gavarr is going to take you with him as a final condition of this treaty. He claims that he can rid you of the Harpy's influence while allowing you to keep your wings. You will serve him for the rest of your days and never be allowed back on this island again. Consider it a mercy, Vidya. Your betrayal to the Republic rivals that of our former Mistress of Sciences Cosima who's been rotting in prison for thirty years." Vidya recalled stories her mother told of Cosima and her hideous crimes as the most atrocious abuse of a siren's power in over one hundred years. In what way could Vidya's actions be remotely comparable and how dare Demeter of all women suggest such?

"Do not speak to me of betrayal, you treacherous cunt!" Vidya growled, teeth gnashing. "You've wanted this all along—me gone, never to return! What of Phrea and Daphne?"

"They are not part of the deal," Xenith said. "They should never have been made in the first place. Once their wings are removed, they will spend the rest of their days in confinement."

"Let them come with me, please!"

A tear tumbled between the wrinkles of Xenith's cheeks. "I'm sorry for all this, Vidya. Sarta weeps in her tomb to know what has befallen you. I can only wish you find some peace."

The guards started dragging Vidya away as she struggled against them.

"You've doomed us all—he is here to destroy *everything*. I'm all you have!" she screamed, tugging against the guard's grip with all her might, but the sedatives made her weak. "By the Harpy's wrath, you will all pay for this mistake! You hear me? May Yasharra rip you all to shreds!"

The Council doors slammed shut, cutting off Vidya's last shrieking threat.

Led by naja with a rope around his neck, Jeth arrived in Lanore by nightfall. The small isolated commune was now a Herrani military outpost. Hordes of naja were living in pits dug along the outskirts several yards away, making the populous too terrified to venture out.

Saf'Ryeem's warriors had taken up residence in the people's homes. Even the midwives' cottages weren't safe from the invading soldiers. Jeth overheard accounts of Ingle forces having cleared the Herrani out of the northern borderlands, but they didn't go as far as Lanore. It was now up to Jeth and his makeshift army to free this place. *If you can manage to free yourself.*

The naja captors passed Jeth to General Nadila.

"Why are you here?" he asked, his spine tingling with worry.

"Nice to see you again, Fae'ren," Nadila said. "Getting yourself into trouble, I see. You should have taken your fortune and your woman to the far reaches of the desert."

"She's dead," said Jeth in blunt fashion.

"Oh." Nadila cast her eyes down and scratched at her blonde braids. ". . . and your child?"

Jeth didn't respond as they trundled through the dried mud.

The general shook her head. "I'm sorry."

"Never mind that," Jeth said. "I have to find Snake Eye. Has he been captured too?"

"I haven't seen him . . ."

As they trudged past a group of warriors, Jeth recognized a few. *Those were the men that came with you. Why are they not tied up?*

"You have to get me out of here," Jeth urged Nadila.

She met his eyes and shook her head. "You know I can't do that."

He cursed to himself. *It was worth a shot.*

They came to a large, round mud hut that normally served as a meeting place for the commune Elders.

"The Overlord and his son are right through here," said Nadila.

"You know that using the Elders' place of governance for anything else is a sacrilege to my people, right?"

Nadila shook her head and shrugged. "If it's any consolation, I hope that whatever it is he wants to do to you, he makes it quick. Then, you may see your woman and child again."

"Thanks . . . I guess," he muttered as she pushed him inside. *If he wanted you dead, the naja would have done so already,* he assured himself.

Nadila forced Jeth to his knees in front of a roaring fire pit with Saf'Ryeem and Nas'Gavarr standing around it, and Dulsakh's Sarcophagus between them. The general couldn't leave the hut fast enough.

"Hello, Jethril," Nas'Gavarr said. He was fully armored similarly to the other Herrani warriors, but with more elaborate shoulder plates, identical to what Snake Eye had been wearing.

"Aren't you supposed to be in Rangardia?" Jeth asked.

"I was."

"Then if you're here, I take it you have Vidya with you," said Jeth as his heart sank.

"The harpy is none of your concern."

"What of your brother?" Nas'Gavarr raised a questioning eyebrow as if he had no idea what Jeth was talking about. ". . . Or sister?"

Nas'Gavarr shook his head. "I brought you here to thank you once again."

"What favor did I unwittingly do for you this time?"

The Overlord stepped to the sarcophagus and delicately grazed his hands along the ancient carvings. "Your assistance in finding Dulsakh's artifacts."

"Don't thank me. Your wife was the mastermind behind it all," Jeth said through gritted teeth.

"Then, you shall accept my gratitude on her behalf." His jaw tautened and his serpent eyes darkened. *Does he miss her too?* Jeth wondered.

"What could you possibly want them for anyway?" he challenged.

"I wish to merge Dulsakh's spirit into my own and resurrect his flesh with these bones. Through his sentience, I will awaken all his ancient progeny from their slumber and bring them to my side."

Nas'Gavarr's words baffled Jeth more. "And how does this fit in with your plan to shut down all the Conduits?"

Ryeem turned to Nas'Gavarr with the same confused air. "Father, your plan is to destroy the ancient ones, not join with them."

"Is that what I said?"

"Yes!" Ryeem insisted. "After they've been weakened by the removal of the Serpentine Gods, they'd be made mortal. You'd be able to do what the Immortal One could not. Then, we were going to let Dulsakh's spirit disperse into the Spirit Realm and throw the bones into the Volcano of Verishten."

"Right, I like that plan much better." Nas'Gavarr tossed the emerald to Ryeem. "Release the spirit and let us begin."

The lid of the sarcophagus made a jarring scrape as the Overlord pushed it off and let it slide to the ground with a heavy thud. The bones within, browned by age, were smaller than Jeth would have guessed, no different than the remains of any naja.

Nas'Gavarr put his hands upon them and closed his eyes. He said to

Ryeem, "Have you released it yet? I wish to pull it from the Chamber before it disperses."

Ryeem didn't reply, only paled and backed away from the Mage before him.

The Overlord opened his eyes and looked to his son. "What are you waiting for. Extract it!"

"You should extract it," Ryeem replied, holding the emerald out to him.

Nas'Gavarr stared at the green gem, lines of unease forming upon his brow. "Are you incapable, Ryeem? Must I do everything for you?"

Why won't *Nas'Gavarr do it himself?* Jeth wondered as well.

"It is you who is incapable!" Ryeem spat.

"Ryeem!" Nas'Gavarr stood erect and burned his gaze into him.

"We have a rapport, *Father.* And you've just sent me a mind message. . . . You will be returning from Credence shortly with the harpy."

Nas'Gavarr looked to Jeth and shrugged. "We almost had him, didn't we?"

"Huh?"

Ryeem grabbed his trident spear, sticking out from the ground, and pointed it toward the false Nas'Gavarr. Three Herrani warriors rushed in.

"This man is an imposter. Subdue him!" His warriors backed him toward the far-left side of the round hut.

Nas'Gavarr's flesh started to peel away. It rolled in clumps down his face and arms, dropping in a series of splats on the ground. Wiping away the excess skin and blood, Snake Eye's striking features revealed themselves. Ryeem snatched the skeleton from the sarcophagus and threw it into the flames.

"No, don't!" Jeth protested.

Nadila and two of Snake Eye's warriors ran in a second later. She cut Jeth loose while the other two backed Ryeem into the opposite end of the hut.

"Whatever it is you wanted with Dulsakh, you can't have him now," Ryeem hissed. "The flesh required to bring him back will soon be cinders."

"Mere flame cannot destroy the bones of an immortal Najahai," said Snake Eye.

"Perhaps not, but once I've crushed them and fed them to my naja, they might as well be. Now, what to do with this spirit . . . ?" Ryeem held up the emerald.

"Why don't you let it disperse into the Spirit Realm?" Snake Eye posed.

"Not before the Najahai rise from their resting place so my father may destroy them. The flesh is meaningless, only the spirit is required to awaken them, and my spiritual strength is more than adequate to contain it."

The gem began to glow within Ryeem's hand. Vibrant green streams of light burst between each finger. The light went out as he fell to his knees, out of breath. When he lifted his head, something within his eyes changed.

They appeared serpent-like even though they were still human. Jeth swore he could see Ryeem's serpent tattoos come to life and slither over his skin. The warriors backed away in alarm.

That's when the high-pitched snarls of naja, followed by shrieks outside the hut made Jeth's chest seize with terror.

Ryeem let out a reptilian grin at the sound. Jeth ran out of the hut to find a river of naja flowing out of their pits from every direction and were minutes from flooding into the commune.

Blazing torch light illuminated the Grand Altar in an ominous glow. Most of Credence was gathered at the Citadel grounds to witness the unmaking of two harpies.

Vidya was chained to a balustrade on the garden terrace, overlooking the altar with Nas'Gavarr standing beside her. They both watched Daphne and Phrea, heads shaven and heavily sedated, be taken up the steps and chained by their feet to the platform between the two effigies.

Xenith stood under the Siren. With a single beat of her flaxen wings, she addressed the amassing crowd. "We gather here in both celebration of peace between two enemies, and to bear witness to the punishment of the women who stood in the way of that peace."

The Archon presented Phrea and Daphne to the crowd with her arm. To the guards accompanying them, she said, "Unchain their wings."

Phrea was the first forced to spread them. Wings as jet black and beautiful as her hair once was. Two large hooks at the end of thick chains were fastened to the statue's bases. Her dark bloodshot eyes could only stare at the macabre iron monstrosities before they were shoved through each wing. She grunted in pain and collapsed to her knees as Vidya's heart leaped from her chest. The guards pulled the chains taut, stretching her wings out to their maximum span.

Xenith continued, "Let this be a sobering reminder of why the Harpy must never be allowed to walk among the Siren, and when faced with the temptation to bring her forth again, we will remember the misfortunes that will befall us if we do."

"The Harpy can never rule Credence again!" the Mothers' Assembly recited in unison.

Phrea gritted her teeth and dug her dirty nails into the marble. *I promised I'd get them out of this, and I failed them*, Vidya lamented, tears trickling down her cheeks.

The Citadel Executioner walked up the steps carrying a large, curved scythe on his bulky shoulder. He took position behind Phrea and her outstretched wings as she trembled with rage, unable to look behind her.

"A harpy's power rests in her wings. As great suffering is required to give her that power, suffering is needed to take it away." Xenith's mouth formed a hard, thin line.

As the executioner placed the scythe at Phrea's back, Vidya wished to turn away, but her eyes remained fixed. With a somber nod from the Archon, the executioner raised the scythe and brought it down swiftly over Phrea's scapula. A shrieking roar burst from her as blood splashed out of the base of her left wing. The blade had not cut all the way through on the first strike.

The scythe came down again, and another pain-filled bellow ripped through the night as more blood poured onto the white marble. Vidya crumpled to her knees, screaming at the top of her own lungs. "Stop, please, no!"

Her mind kept flashing away from the gore on the altar and back to that bathtub from her past. *Don't look, don't look,* she clamped her eyes shut, listening only to Phrea's agonizing cries and the slicing of her flesh.

Vidya's entire bottom half felt numb, like it wasn't her own legs moving toward the tub. Water dripped from the decanter that had filled it. Each drop was an ear shattering boom from a flintlock pistol going off repeatedly in her mind. As she drew nearer, her throat seized. Two small bodies suspended in crimson water and pale as the porcelain cradle that held them. Dark, wet curls were plastered to a young boy's face—his throat slashed open. His little brother floated atop him face down—lifeless.

Falling to her knees, she grasped for them. Spyros, the youngest, was cold. Vidya's heart shattered into jagged pieces as she pressed his frigid cheeks to her own. Only a few hours ago she was saying goodbye to him. He was too young to realize she wasn't going to return for a long while. He had squealed with laughter and tangled his pudgy hands in her hair.

Grief-stricken shrieks rang in her ears, amplified by the porcelain as she desperately tried to lift her boys out of it. Her arms were weak gelatin. Alonz slipped out of her grasp, and she dropped Spyros back in as well.

"No, no, please . . ." she sobbed, the flood of tears blinding her from what was left of her sons.

Phrea was dragged off the altar by the guards, blood streaming down her back. Daphne's light brown wings were now stretched between the two effigies. The executioner took his place behind her, to start the whole gruesome process over again. This time, Vidya's airways were closed off completely by her grief.

While choking on her own sobs, Vidya heard heavy breathing from the corner of the lavatory that was not her own. Agustin stood there, unkempt, eyes bloodshot, his shirt sleeves rolled up with bloody water dripping from his forearms. He gripped a pistol in a shaking hand.

"What did you do?" Vidya croaked from the floor.

"Isn't this what you wanted?" he murmured, his jaw trembling.

Without waiting for her reply, Agustin put the pistol to his own temple. Vidya stared up at him, frozen in her horror. She watched him pull the trigger. A muffled click—a misfire, the flint must have gotten wet. He pulled the trigger once more, and again, nothing.

Agustin dropped the pistol, his face contorting in revulsion as he looked upon what he'd done.

Vidya's rage finally broke through her paralyzing despair. "What did you do, you bastard?"

She sprang up from the ground and tackled the large man to the floor. "They were my babies. My babies!" she wailed, smacking his head on the tile.

Agustin made no attempt to push her off. Guards rushed in. Firm hands grabbed her shoulders from behind, but she fought against them with all her might.

Vidya clawed at her husband's face, drawing blood. She was a whirlwind of pain and violence—all focused on him. "You killed them! my babies!" The guards yanked her away, keeping her from digging her fingers into his eye sockets.

Daphne's left wing fell to her side. Her face was wet with tears, her jaw clenched so tight Vidya could hardly recognize her, but she didn't scream, not the way Phrea did. Her big aquamarine eyes were dead—as if her spirit had gone somewhere else.

"You killed my babies!" Vidya's shrieking moans spanned the altar, causing many of the spectators to gape up at her.

Once Daphne's second wing dropped, the men unchained and carried her off. Vidya choked out sobs, images of her sons' pale faces were everywhere she looked. Everywhere except on the one who had been standing beside her. He had Agustin's face.

". . . You killed them. . . ." she cried, looking deep into those sinister serpent eyes.

"I think we've seen enough here. It is time for pestilence to devour the living."

34

One Confusing Battle

Jeth ran back into the Elders' hut. "Naja incoming!"

Nadila put her tulwar to Saf'Ryeem's throat. "Killing him should end his control of them, and the spirit will be released as well."

"Do that and their minds will be trapped forever in the bodies of vicious killers. I won't be able to stop them from slaughtering innocent civilians if I'm dead," said Ryeem.

"Leave him be," Snake Eye ordered. "I need you all out there forming a line, now!"

"Come on, boys, get your wind blades ready." Nadila ushered the other two men out of the hut.

"There are hundreds. You cannot hope to kill them all with some Steinkamp weaponry," Ryeem sneered.

"I'm hoping not to kill any," Snake Eye returned with a glint in his reptilian eye.

He pulled his flesh whip out from underneath his oversized armor, and Ryeem's warriors advanced. He cracked it across all three of their throats and tore them out in a split second. Jeth stood there wide-eyed as all three men hit the ground at the same time. Snake Eye sauntered over their bodies and outside while Jeth grabbed a tulwar from one of the dead warriors and went after him.

The horde of naja advanced from all sides. Lanore citizenry rushed to barricade themselves into their homes. All thirty of Snake Eye's warriors and eight more, loyal to Nadila, formed a perimeter of defense around him and Jeth while Ryeem's formed an attack perimeter. *Herrani warrior against Herrani warrior. This is going to be one confusing battle*, Jeth gulped.

"Please tell me you have another trick up your sleeve," he said.

"As a matter of fact, I do." Snake Eye donned a look of determination.

Right before Jeth's eyes, the Flesh Mage's skin began to flake off his face as glistening green and brown scales emerged in its place. Snake Eye grunted, clutched his stomach, and fell to his hands and knees, scales traveling down his arms, his fingers stretching into elongated claws. He tore off his bulky armor, revealing a massive ribcage and vertebrae worn around his body. Reptilian flesh rapidly formed over the bones, a protruding spine and long winding tail pushed through the skin. *He's resurrecting Dulsakh through his own body!* Jeth realized.

All the naja halted behind the line of Ryeem's warriors. They stood in witness of the ashipu's transformation, his bones cracking and contorting to form the literal embodiment of Dulsakh. The creature that stood in Snake Eye's place was no longer human. Its eyes were a brilliant emerald green and took up most of its face. Its elongated snout featured rows upon rows of sharp, pointed teeth.

Ryeem emerged from the hut with his spear in hand, pushing his way toward the ancient Najahai made flesh. "Dulsakh," he whispered in awe.

Snake Eye rasped, "Essence, spirit, and flesh always long to be made whole."

"You have the flesh, but only my father the essence," Ryeem said.

"Not only," Snake Eye growled with a subtle shake of the head.

Ryeem collapsed to one knee as his eyes widened, returning to normal. At that moment, an ancient force appeared behind the Najahai's eyes that chilled Jeth to the bone. Snake Eye wasn't there anymore.

"Attack!" Ryeem bellowed from the ground.

His warriors ducked down to allow the naja to spring over their backs and scramble toward Snake Eye's warriors.

Dulsakh put out his palm to halt the advance, but the naja didn't stop.

"Heed!" he snarled.

The warriors didn't wait for Snake Eye to make the order. They brought their round circular blades in hand and threw them. With a clench of their gloved fists, the wind magic within the blades activated, causing tiny cyclones to surround them and allowing the wielders to guide them at their will. Countless naja heads flew off in tandem, their bright orange blood spraying into the night air.

Naja left untouched by the blades crashed through the line of warriors who desperately fought them off with their swords.

"They won't heed to you, Dulsakh." Ryeem laughed as he stood back up. "They're humans!"

A shock ran through Jeth's spine. *Had he not considered this?* Snake Eye had dismissed him out of hand when he tried to tell him Jenn had learned the same thing while fighting them in Ingleheim.

Ryeem laughed again. "They won't respond to your Najahai spirit."

"No!" Dulsakh shrieked.

"All the real naja were driven to extinction over a thousand years ago. The

Serpentine Gods are gone . . . there is nothing left for you here, only the four deep in slumber on their faraway islands," said Ryeem.

Dulsakh released a rage-filled screech that deafened the whole commune. He took the first naja to come at him by the throat and tore it out. The rest of t

hem broke through the line, moving in slow motion. Jeth ducked low and slashed his tulwar across the bellies of the first two in front of him, leaped out the way of their claws, and stabbed others through their necks. He found the tulwar awkward to wield, and not having a second blade only added to his stress.

Numerous naja flew by, orange blood splashing everywhere. He bounded over the mounting corpses, then slid under arrows zooming past him, piercing through warriors while bouncing off the naja's tough hides. Jeth weaved throughout the battle, stabbing through naja's legs one moment, and slashing their throats the next. He narrowly dodged a naja flying toward him. Reptilian bodies filled the battlefield at an alarming rate.

Dulsakh, in his ire, slaughtered several naja at a time with flesh magic. Without even touching them, he ripped open throats, severed heads, and dismembered any reptilian in his immediate vicinity. Wherever naja managed to escape Dulsakh's wrath, Steinkamp wind blades made up the slack. Ryeem's warriors remained back, waiting for their beasts to complete the carnage.

The battle sped up again as Jeth exhausted his speed advantage. All he could do was avoid naja attacks and flying bodies, more and more finding their end by Dulsakh's brutality. Soon, however, the Najahai slowed down. He screamed into the night sky—a painful, grievous bellow that made Jeth's hairs stand on end.

Ryeem's warriors took the opportunity to attack. Snake Eye's remaining fighters clashed against them, but most still pushed past. One slashed his tulwar across Dulsakh's chest, and another drove his spear through the back of his shoulder. The mighty Najahai faltered as man and naja closed in around him.

Jeth rushed up behind the fray, stabbing several warriors in the back and shoving them aside, but more closed in behind him. Even with a new burst of speed, he couldn't kill enough to clear a path for Dulsakh. The air became stifling—the darkness blinded him. He could no longer determine if he was slaughtering friend or foe. His limbs were heavy and his perception of time hastened. Bodies piled up underfoot, making each step more uncertain. Dulsakh bled from countless gashes all over his body, but he wouldn't go down.

Then came a sharp pain in Jeth's forearm; a slash of a tulwar followed by a blow to the head forced him to the dirt. The tulwar, wielded by a wiry Herrani, came hurtling toward him, but he blocked it with his own sword, then jammed it into his attacker's neck before he could swing again. Shoving the dying man off him, another one jumped through the air, about to drive a trident spear through his neck. Jeth rolled to the side as the spear lodged into the blood-drenched earth where he had just been. It was Saf'Ryeem on the other side of it.

"My father was supposed to have killed you," he rasped.

"So, they keep saying." Jeth kicked Ryeem's knee out and sprung back up to his feet. Before he could slice his tulwar across Ryeem's neck, the man vaulted into the air using his spear, still stuck in the ground, and kicked Jeth in the chest with both feet, sending him right back down. He jumped up with a start and clashed his tulwar against Ryeem's spear, only to have it catch between two of the blades and be wrenched from his grip. Dodging the spear again, Jeth grabbed it and pulled hard. Ryeem's grasp was firm, and the two men struggled against each other for a time before Ryeem met Jeth's face with his forehead. Staggering backward, Jeth wiped the blood pouring from his nose.

Then, a series of hollers from the north alerted both men. Fifty Tezkhan raiders galloped full tilt toward the commune. Every warrior looked up from the battle, gaping at the wild riders standing in their stirrups and waving hammers and axes above their heads. Their horses raced like the wind down the northern hillsides and crashed through the enemy line. Their heavy axes cleaved through countless throats, reptile and human, burying them under their steeds' trampling hooves. Jeth and Ryeem stood in awe of the fearless riders quickly overturning the course of the battle.

Jeth spotted Snake Eye's flesh whip lying amongst some naja corpses. The Mage was still distracted, so he dove for it. Ryeem ran to stop him but was too late. Jeth cracked the whip around his ankles and pulled him to the ground. The Mage tried to wriggle free, but Jeth punched him down and tied his arms behind his back with the whip, fusing his wrists together by a squeeze of its leather grip.

Jeth picked up Ryeem's spear and put it to his throat. "Tell the naja you have left to go back into their pits and stay there."

"Kill me, and they will be even more unstoppable," Ryeem hissed.

Jeth pressed the three spear points harder against his neck. "Doesn't matter, I know another Spirit Mage that would be happy to cure them in your absence. If the Tezkhan doesn't finish them off first."

Ryeem glared at Jeth contemptuously, and the surviving naja began to retreat. General Nadila approached, her armor drenched in orange blood. "Nice work, Fae'ren. I'll take it from here."

With a powerful heave, the brawny woman forced the Mage to his feet and dragged him away.

Once the Tezkhan cleared the rest of the battlefield and the surviving naja were back in their holding pits, Jeth found some vera leaves to treat his and some of the others' wounds. That's when the people of Lanore slowly emerged from their cottages. Jeth saw Twilla and the other Elders, gazing upon the gore that had marred their peaceful settlement.

He decided to approach them. "The naja won't attack any of you now. You should all head to Fairieshome until it's safe to return."

"This is our home. We will not give it up to these Herrani demons!" exclaimed an elderly man with gray locks down to his knees.

"What curse have you brought upon us?" Twilla said in an accusatory tone.

"I know this doesn't mean much coming from me," he began. "But I promise you, Lanore will be restored."

"And why should we believe you? Why would you care about us when your loyalty is clearly with them?" She motioned to the activity behind Jeth.

He looked back at the Herrani and Tezkhan nursing their wounds and tending to the dead. *Loyalty. What does that word even mean anymore?* He thought.

"I don't care if you believe me," Jeth said curtly. "Lead your people to safety to rebuild later or stay here and watch them all die. The choice is yours. Just know, the destruction of everything you care for is upon you, and the only thing standing in its way is a Fae'ren orphan and his army of demons."

The Elders brought their eyes down. Jeth began to walk away but stopped mid-step. He didn't want to be so brusque with the woman who'd helped Anwarr during her pregnancy.

He turned back and said, "If you want to help your people, come to the Elders' hut and learn what is happening for yourself. We can no longer afford to keep our heads down and wait for the horrors to pass us by. Your old ways will be the death of you. . . ." He paused. *Why should you care about them?* The fact was, he did care, more than he wanted to admit. The Elders stared at him with solemn eyes. Twilla gave a nod and walked toward the hut, the rest of the group following hesitantly.

Jeth returned to the battlefield to find Snake Eye having reverted to his human form, now looking around in a daze. On his way over to talk with him, Genkhai rode up on a bay steed and a dapple gray on a lead. "Hey, Jeth, look what I found running around out there. As hard to wrangle as she ever was."

"Tor!" Jeth gasped, running for his mare like a little boy presented with sweets. "Don't ever take off on me like that again, you silly beast." He was even gladder to find all his weapons still securely tied to his saddle. He immediately strapped on his scabbard with Anwarr's tulwar in its sheathe.

"Guess you haven't tamed her yet, uh?" Genkhai chuckled.

Rubbing Torrent under her chin, he replied, "Don't suppose I ever will."

Back in the hut, the Elders, along with Jeth, Snake Eye, Genkhai, Nadila, and the restrained Saf'Ryeem sat around the fire pit as the morning sun seeped into the rounded space.

"Nas'Gavarr's through the warping gate," Jeth said to the group. "Ryeem tells us he has Vidya, which means he will likely go straight to the Crannabeatha."

"No one rides faster than the Tezkhan," Genkhai said. "If we leave now, we can get you there before him."

"Or we threaten to kill his son, forcing him to come here first," suggested the general.

"You would bring the Overlord to our home?" The male Elder was aghast.

"He won't stay long, but it would buy some time for us to get to the Deep Wood," said Nadila. "Either way, this commune needs to be evacuated."

"Many have fled already, but the Elders must remain," Twilla retorted.

"If there are no Elders, there is no Lanore," Jeth said.

Twilla's thin lips twitched. "If the Overlord of Herran cannot be defeated, and he is to destroy our Mother Oak as you say, then Lanore and every other commune is doomed anyway. If we are going to witness the death of our forest, then we will do it right here where we belong."

Jeth solemnly nodded. "Fine, stay, help the wounded. But when Nas'Gavarr comes, I won't be able to guarantee your safety."

"Alright then." Nadila took out a curved knife and turned to Ryeem. "Time to call out to daddy."

"Kill me and my father's wrath will ensure this overgrown cesspit shares its fate with the Death tribes," he seethed.

Imagining his forest home up in flames sent shockwaves of anger through Jeth's body. "Hold on."

He marched outside to the nearest dead naja on the ground. He bent down and yanked open the creature's mouth, then dragged the edge of his blade along the tongue, careful not to sever it lest he get blood on it as well.

Once back inside, he walked assuredly over to Ryeem and sliced his one exposed bicep before anyone could question him.

Ryeem growled, clutching his hemorrhaging arm. "What in the name of Sagorath . . . ?"

"There." Jeth sheathed his blade. "Now, your father has no reason to torch the whole forest if there's a chance he can save you. I know it takes a few days for naja saliva to kill someone, but I put *a lot* of it on my blade just now, so there's no telling how long it'll take to kill you."

Ryeem's arm shook uncontrollably, his skin already paling. "You're a fool!"

"I hope he'll make it in time. As for everyone else," Jeth addressed the other people in the hut. "Don't let this one anywhere near naja blood."

Nadila, still covered in it, backed away while Genkhai went to wrap up Ryeem's arm. "Ready to call to your father now?" he asked.

The Mage, quivering in pain, nodded. "It's done. He's on his way."

The general, Tezkhan, and Elders began to talk strategy as Jeth looked back at Snake Eye who had been sitting beside Dulsakh's skeleton against the wall. His wounds were gradually healing. They didn't look as gruesome after he transformed back to human form.

"Hey, Snake Eye, are you still in there?" Jeth asked, sitting down next to him.

He looked at him listlessly. "For now. Dulsakh has buried himself deep. I can still feel him festering. There is so much pain. I didn't know. I didn't think. . . ."

"That the naja were once human beings transformed into monsters against their will?" Jeth sighed. "Sorry, I thought you knew."

"It's not your fault. I should have been more upfront with you from the start, but I didn't know how much I could trust you. Nobody knew the full extent of my plans because I feared they'd talk me out of it. I told Yemesh to stay in Herran because I couldn't bear to have him witness the monster I was willing to become to stop Gavarr."

"That's understandable, but at least you could have brought me in on your scheme to take his form so that I didn't look like such an idiot."

Snake Eye sighed with levity. "Oh no, the plan had always been to go find your Ingle witch. But on our way to General Nadila, we came upon Ryeem. With you still running about in the Deep Wood, I had to improvise. I sent the Tezkhan away, used a dead body to give me the excess flesh required to become Gavarr, and attempted to trick my nephew into releasing Dulsakh's spirit for me. After I sent him out to find you of course. Apologies for making you worry."

"What bones did Saf'Ryeem destroy?"

"Some old naja remains I found on the way to the temple. I thought it would be easier if everyone believed the real bones were in the sarcophagus so they would protect it with their lives."

"What are you going to do with Dulsakh now?" Jeth asked.

Snake Eye's complexion paled even more. "I've never felt a grief quite like this. I fear that I have unleashed a terrible vengeance upon this world. I assumed that Gavarr would take the power of the artifacts for himself, and I was willing to do the same to stop him. This entire time he wanted to destroy them, which is what I should have done in the first place."

"When this is over, we can still find Jenn and ask her to get the spirit out of you," Jeth offered.

"I have a better way," Snake Eye began. "Since my brother is on his way, I will confront him, and he will extract the spirit for me." His breath shuddered. "The rest of you should go to the Deep Wood, and I will do what I can to hold him here as long as possible."

"What if he kills you?"

"I made the choice to unleash this spirit. I will face the consequences." He handed the emerald to Jeth. "Give this to Genkhai. I want nothing Gavarr can use to seal the spirit away. Now gather your riders and go."

Jeth put the emerald in his pocket and rose to his feet, expecting Snake Eye to do the same. Instead, the ashipu looked up at Jeth from the ground with a pained look. "I sure hope this isn't goodbye, Little Gershlon."

Jeth shook his head. "You don't hear me saying it." He then addressed the rest of the room. "Alright, Snake Eye will watch the Mage, the rest of us are going to mount up and head out before the Overlord gets here."

"We will make sure the rest of the commune is evacuated," said Twilla.

While discussing the specifics, a Herrani warrior barged into the hut. "A small contingent has arrived."

"Nas'Gavarr can't be here already!" Jeth rushed outside.

Marching in from the west were twenty Del'Cabrian soldiers on horseback being led by Major Faron, and to Jeth's utter shock, Olivier, riding at his right. *That impeccable timing of his.*

The two men's gaze instantly fell on him as they dismounted and made their way toward the Elders' hut.

Jeth's heart sank. *Great, just what you need.*

35

Stand in Your Way

Faron and his contingent approached with spears, swords, and bows at the ready. Everyone else exited the Elders' hut and stood behind Jeth.

Looking to the sky, Faron said, "Where is that winged woman?"

"Not to worry, Major." Jeth crossed his arms high on his chest. "You and your men are safe."

"It is time for you to face justice, Jethril of Fae'ren," the major announced.

"I'll say when it's time."

"Stop this, Jeth!" Olivier exclaimed. "I know that deep down, you are not the criminal everyone thinks you are, but the longer you evade justice, the more likely you'll be seeing the gallows."

"I am every bit the criminal, Oli," Jeth said. "And there is no scenario that doesn't end with a trip to the gallows for me."

"Aren't you tired of running?"

"Damn tired. That's why I'm here. I don't have time to explain, but the Overlord of Herran is hours away from this commune. This entire forest will be wiped out if we don't stop him."

"Ludicrous," said Faron. "The treaty states that neither Del'Cabria nor Herran can take up arms against the other."

"Nas'Gavarr signed the treaty so he could gain access to these lands. He destroyed the Serpentine Gods, and he aims to destroy the Mother Oak as well."

"Save your tall tales for the Royal Magistrate." Faron unsheathed his sword and took several steps toward him.

Several Herrani warriors took out their weapons as well, triggering the rest of Faron's men to do the same and every nearby Tezkhan thereafter. The only person without a blade in his hand was Jeth.

With his arms still crossed, he said, "Are you sure you want to do this? If so, you should have brought more men."

"If any of these men . . . or women attack mine, the treaty is null, and our people will once again be at war," Faron said in a loud, clear voice for all to hear. "Think hard on whether the freedom of one man is worth that."

"Freedom is always worth that," said Twilla, stepping out from behind Jeth.

"Madam, what grants you the right to speak here?" Faron asked with sanctimonious tone.

"I am a midwife and an Elder of Lanore, which gives me every right to speak here and more," Twilla responded curtly. She pointed to Jeth. "This man is one of the few who fights for us. Herran invaded our homes and Del'Cabria has done nothing. You come to arrest one of our own instead of offering to assist. Is Fae'ren not a province under the King's rule?"

Faron blinked a few times at the midwife's chastisement, but otherwise, his expression remained as stiff as always. "That is not relevant. This man, regardless of what he has done to make up for his crimes, still is and always will be a traitor to this kingdom."

"Like the Great Gershlon?" Twilla said. "Champion of Archers and Hero in the Golem Wars?"

"Precisely," Faron returned without pause.

The Elders grumbled among themselves. It was often said the Fae'ren people were never offended, always able to laugh at their own expense and take cruel jests in stride, *except* when it came to the subject of Gershlon's execution.

"Listen, fellas." Jeth put his hands out. "If you take me now, I'll find a way to escape. So, either you help me protect this place or go back where you came from."

"Only when you agree to come with us, will we leave," said Faron.

"I'm taking these warriors, and I'm heading to the Deep Wood. Once I've done what I came to do, I will gladly go with you. But, not before," Jeth said sternly.

The Del'Cabrians exchanged glances, and Faron returned with a hesitant look. "Very well."

Jeth blinked a few times and shook his head. "Wait, you're agreeing to that?"

"*We* will take you to the Deep Wood . . . as our prisoner," The major said. "If Nas'Gavarr does, in fact, wish to do it harm, then it is our duty to prevent that from happening. We will release you only for the purpose of fighting with us. Upon your survival, we will take you to the Capital. Try an escape, and we will consider that a final admission of your guilt. You will be executed on sight."

Jeth looked to the warriors behind him, many of them shaking their heads and urging him not to agree. Deep down, Jeth knew this was the best course of action. The Del'Cabrian contingent provided more bodies to stand guard of the wood, which after the last battle, were desperately needed.

"Well . . ." Jeth scratched the back of his neck. "There's a pretty good chance I'm going to die out there anyway, so why not?"

Herrani and Tezkhan alike put their palms to their faces as Jeth held out his hand to the major. Faron grabbed hold of it, gave him a stiff handshake, and slapped a manacle around his wrist.

Rain spat down from the gray sky, making Vidya shiver within her iron restraints. A hazy forested township gradually came into view as her heavy eyelids lifted. She was chained to a large wooden post near a well in the center of a Fae'ren commune, one she was pretty sure she'd never been to before, but they all looked the same to her. The ground was wet and muddy from the rain, the stench of dirt and blood hung in the air. *A battle has just been fought here*, she thought through her grogginess.

A donkey-pulled cart, carrying naja corpses, trundled by her, splashing mud upon her beige prison rags. Her hand stung as she tried to wipe the mud off. Her palm had a small cut on it and was bound with a soiled rag.

The cart stopped near Nas'Gavarr, standing ten paces away, conversing with Saf'Ryeem and a Herrani warrior woman in armor far too big for her delicate frame. Her long, wet hair was plastered to her head on one side, the other shaved. She undid the leather bindings around Ryeem's wrists and shoved him over to his father. Ryeem appeared near death, paled to gray and shuddering in the cold wet with a swelling, festering wound on his left arm.

Vidya watched Nas'Gavarr dig his fingers into a dead naja's open gash and smear blood into Ryeem's wound, causing it to foam. The man growled at the pain. Nas'Gavarr took his knife and made a hairline cut along his own bicep and placed a hand over his son's cut for a few minutes until both of their wounds closed.

Nas'Gavarr told his son to wait a short distance away as he addressed the female warrior. It was then Vidya recognized her as Snake Eye.

"Why do you continue to defy me?" Nas'Gavarr asked her.

"You are my brother, not my father. We are supposed to be equals."

"And we were," he hissed. "It was you who chose to undermine me. All those years I've healed you of age until you gained mastery of your own body and this is how you show your gratitude!"

Snake Eye scoffed. "Save me the 'I made you who you are' speech. You are not that man anymore. He has been dead to me for a century now; right around the day you decided to put an entire tribe to flame!"

Nas'Gavarr stepped up close to Snake Eye and said in a quieter voice that Vidya strained to hear. "Is it really the Death tribes you mourn for or is it her?"

"You *knew* she was there, but you didn't give a shit!" Snake Eye spat, fists clenched. "And as much as it pains me to say . . . she would have lived an eternity with you."

"Most people are not suited for immortality. You know that to live as long as we have, you must learn to let others go and accept that they all will perish," Nas'Gavarr said.

"Perhaps we should too."

Snake Eye took off her armor, revealing a massive skeleton worn around her torso. She began to transform into a harrowing reptilian beast and sprang to attack the Overlord. He immediately raised a shield of earth. Snake Eye clawed into it, digging through the wall of dirt and rock, whittling it down to nothing in seconds. She pounced on Nas'Gavarr and slashed at his chest, tearing his skin, blood splashing into the air.

Could she really kill him? Vidya hoped. She struggled against the chain holding her to the post. Had she been at her full strength she could yank the post out of the ground. However, Nas'Gavarr had put her in a spiritual slumber, something Vidya had read that Spirit Mages could do when the victim's mind was vulnerable, be it by unconsciousness or terror. She slumped against the post in exhaustion.

By now, Snake Eye had slowed her strikes and Nas'Gavarr was able to speak. "This rage you feel does not fully belong to you. Let me free you from it."

Nas'Gavarr grabbed hold of the creature's head with both hands and jammed his thumbs into her large reptilian eyes. A spine-tingling shriek blasted through the commune. Snake Eye flailed backward and writhed in the mud as she slowly began to revert to her original form.

As Nas'Gavarr's gashes healed, he rose to his feet and walked toward Snake Eye. She screamed in agony, bleeding from both eyes, one of them gouged out completely, leaving behind a weeping socket.

"To rip a spirit from a living vessel requires that vessel to experience great pain. For that I am sorry, but your eyes will return to you in time."

Snake Eye got onto her hands and knees as she blindly searched through the mud for her missing eyeball. "It makes me wonder, though" Nas'Gavarr went on, standing over her. "You could have refused to heal the aging process and let yourself perish like everyone else." He reached down and ripped Dulsakh's bones off her, breaking them apart and scattering pieces through the mud. He then grabbed her by the neck and lifted her right off the ground. "Yet here you breathe, just as I do."

"Do it!" Snake Eye hissed, saliva flying from her mouth. "Kill me! If you don't, you will never be rid of me. I will *always* stand in your way!"

With a powerful heave, the Overlord threw her straight down. The mud rippled like water and her bones audibly crunched.

Vidya gasped as she watched Nas'Gavarr bend to one knee over Snake

Eye's broken body. "I can't have you dying just yet. It's by your blood that the rivers will run dry."

"What are you talking about?" Snake Eye said, teeth clenching.

Snake Eye is the Champion of the Serpentine whose blood can destroy Elmifel, Vidya realized.

Nas'Gavarr rose to his feet and turned to his son. "Tie up this wretch and make way for Herran."

"Crannabeatha's Champion took a small army to the Deep Wood," Ryeem said.

"No matter."

"Do you require any of my naja to accompany you?"

Nas'Gavarr shook his head. "You've done enough. Take what's left of them and leave this place. You don't want to be here when the Conduit is closed. I have released Dulsakh's spirit, and it should disperse soon." Nas'Gavarr pointed to the broken skeleton in the mud beside Snake Eye. Vidya thought she caught her hiding an arm bone in her sleeve right before the two men turned back around. "Put those somewhere safe. We will destroy them later." He began to walk toward Vidya.

"Yes, Father," replied Ryeem, looking intently after him for a few moments too long.

The shadow harpy, perched upon the edge of the well, whispered in her ear. *"I wouldn't trust him with such a task. . . ."*

It then dissipated as Nas'Gavarr picked her up and flung her back onto the horse he led behind his own.

Ten Herrani warriors, forty-eight Tezkhan raiders, and twenty Del'Cabrian soldiers formed a line of defense at the only known entrance to the Deep Wood. It was a pathetic force to be sure, but it was all Fae'ren had left. Jeth could only pray that Serra would finish her part before the Overlord arrived. Thankfully, they had a few ideas of their own to keep him at bay for a time.

Seated on Torrent, Jeth's wrists were shackled in front of him and his weapons were in the safe keeping of Olivier who'd volunteered to keep an eye on him.

Jeth kept his gaze directed down the Lanore road ahead. "So, when did you decide to join the Desert War Traitor hunting party?"

"I volunteered the same day the major was put on assignment," Olivier said.

Jeth thought of a witty retort but decided not to say it. "You should know, I never meant for any of this to happen, but I did what I had to do."

"I know." Olivier sighed, smoothing his ginger mustache that had grown more impressive since they'd seen each other last. "Which is why I'm still willing to testify on your behalf, and perhaps you will be spared execution."

"Come on." Jeth scoffed. "You can't believe that's possible?"

"Stranger things have happened."

"Why risk your reputation defending a Fae'ren traitor?"

Olivier took his eyes off the road and looked directly at him. "Because you're also my friend."

"I was just a fellow bowman." Jeth cast his eyes down.

"It was more than that and you know it."

"Ah, sweet, Oli." Jeth chortled. "You're a great catch for sure, but I wouldn't want to make your Ludesan lady jealous. Best we keep things professional, don't you agree?"

His freckled face turned beat red, reminding Jeth how fun it was to tease him. "Oh, rats, my mistake," he said dryly, trying not to laugh.

Jeth continued, "Now if your name were Siegfried of Ingleheim . . ."

"Who?"

"Never mind." Jeth waved his shackled hands down at him.

Olivier cleared his throat to regain his serious composure. "Speaking of Ludesan ladies. I was tasked with finding people you had come in contact with in the past. The first place I went was Talbit's ranch where I had the pleasure of meeting a certain red-headed lady."

Jeth perked up. "Really?"

"You never told me she was the owner's daughter."

"Because you would have told me how stupid I was for thinking I had a chance with her." Jeth smirked.

"True." Olivier nodded.

"H-how is she?"

"Good, good. She married a Rangarder from the Tradesmen's Guild."

"Oh, I wonder which one," Jeth mused, trying to remember the many who had done construction projects at the ranch during his time there.

"You know what they say about Rangardian men, don't you?" Olivier went on.

"The ladies seem fond of them for some reason."

"On the coast, we call them girl wreckers. For her to experience the pleasures of one of them, wrecks any chance another man can satisfy her again."

"Oh, that's . . . uh . . . great." Jeth nodded. "Good to know she's in capable hands."

"I'm sorry, friend." Olivier patted Jeth on the shoulder.

"Don't be. I haven't thought of her in months."

"Right, you ran away with that gorgeous Saf. That doesn't have anything to do with why her father's coming here, does it?" Olivier gave Jeth a nervous glance.

His guts twisted painfully inside him. "Maybe someday while I'm sitting alone in a jail cell, awaiting my execution, I'll tell you all about her, and then some." His fingers fidgeted in his constraints.

"I may take you up on that. I've been aching to hear how you came to befriend the winged woman who riled up the major."

"Speaking of winged women . . ." Jeth mumbled.

Sensing movement down the forest road, he honed his vision to find the Overlord riding in their direction, leading another horse with Vidya tied to the saddle.

"Overlord approaching!" Jeth yelled down the line. He put out his wrists to Olivier. "Free me, quick!"

"That can't be him." Olivier squinted down the path. "Could be just some traveling tree worshiper."

Jeth gave Olivier an annoyed glare only for him to roll his eyes. "Right, right, fine . . . dammit." He took the key from his pocket and unlocked the manacles from his wrists.

"Weapons, weapons, weapons." Jeth snapped his fingers until Olivier handed him his still-poisoned tulwar and his short bow and quiver.

Once ready, Jeth rode across the line of soldiers. "Everyone stand guard and wait for my commands."

He cantered to meet the Overlord face to face, although he had no idea what he was going to say.

Nas'Gavarr spoke first. "Tell these warriors to move aside."

"You think I'm going to let you walk in here and take my home after you took everything else? You can turn right back around," he said in a stern voice while Torrent danced about, bobbing her head up and down and backing away.

Jeth jerked the reins to settle her down while the Overlord remained planted in his saddle with a blank expression.

"These men"—Jeth pointed behind him—"are Del'Cabrian soldiers. If you attack them, you will be breaking the treaty."

"They already broke the treaty by getting in my way."

"Right. . . ." Jeth cringed.

Vidya groaned. "You're not very good at this intimidation thing, are you?"

"Well, sorry, *Champion of Yasharra.* Thanks for getting captured by the way," he lashed. Vidya bit her tongue and turned her head away.

"You are wasting time," Nas'Gavarr said, taking out the naja teeth from under his armor. "If you won't move your men, I will do it for you."

He gripped the string of teeth as the naja scales began to appear from beneath his rapidly peeling skin.

Shit! Jeth spun his horse around and galloped back toward the line while Nas'Gavarr, in naja form, galloped after him. Luckily for Jeth, his Tezkhan mare was far faster than the Overlord's two Herrani stallions.

Once he reached the line of warriors, Jeth turned back around and waited. When Nas'Gavarr and his horses were the right distance away, he yelled, "Blast gel!"

All ten warriors clenched their gloved fists and ignited the blast gel they had spread over the path beforehand. The detonation caused a wall of earth and fire to erupt. The Overlord's steed's legs were blown apart, making Jeth wince. He was thrown back while the other horse tumbled to the ground. Vidya was tossed from its back and rolled through the dirt. Jeth could only hope she remained unscathed as he knew she had only one life left.

Fire and smoke obscured the road beyond. Nothing more than crackling flames and agonizing whinnies of the dismembered horse could be heard. Each soldier held their breath. *This is far from the end of it*, Jeth thought with a tingling in his spine.

A flaming reptilian beast burst through the smoke and sprinted full speed down the path, shrieking into the wet air.

"Tezkhan!" Jeth called.

Genkhai and his riders galloped out from the underbrush lining the path in every direction. They formed a tight circle around the fiery naja. Riders veered into the circle in crisscrossing clusters as if Nas'Gavarr were an untamable steed. They tossed ice powder into the circle, clenched their gloved fists, and instantly put out the flames all around them while covering the burning reptile in frost. *Good, now he can't use the fire against us*, Jeth thought with some relief.

The ice coating slowed the Overlord down so the riders could form a tighter circle with their new earth essence-infused lariats at the ready. One Tezkhan lassoed Nas'Gavarr around the neck and molded the leather to the bronze brace. He kicked his steed into a gallop down the path while dragging Nas'Gavarr behind him, away from the wood. The forest path beneath them formed a violent wave of dirt and moss, tripping the horse and swallowing it and the rider in mere seconds.

Nas'Gavarr rolled onto his knees, tore the lariat from around his neck brace, and struck the ground with his fists. More earth uprooted itself in a cataclysmic ripple effect. Most of the Tezkhan went flying off their mounts or got buried under mounds of loose dirt.

"Bowmen!" Faron ordered. "Aim!"

All the archers in Faron's contingent, as well as Jeth, took aim.

"Release!"

They each let go of their bow strings, catapulting their arrows straight into Nas'Gavarr. He halted his warpath to take them out of his tough, scaly flesh.

"Swordsmen. Spearmen. Attack!" Faron raised his sword, and he and his soldiers, save the bowmen, advanced.

"Major, not yet!" Jeth yelled after them, but they would not heed. *They're going to get slaughtered*, he thought, his heart pounding in his throat.

Nas'Gavarr, still with some arrows sticking out of him, swatted the soldiers and their horses away like flies. Spears snapped within his grasp, swords flung to the side, and shields shattered in pieces.

"Fall back!" Jeth shouted. None of them listened.

He kicked Torrent toward the fray. One of the spearmen got his throat torn out before his lifeless body was thrown at Faron, knocking him from his saddle.

The Overlord advanced toward the major rolling up from the ground, but Jeth dashed between them and slashed his tulwar across Nas'Gavarr's scaled face, splintering the few arrow shafts in the process. Faron remounted and gained some distance while his men rode in to attack again.

Nas'Gavarr sprang into the air, landed on an urling soldier, and sank his teeth into him. He slashed his claws down his back and took him to the ground.

"Bowmen!" Jeth yelled. He raised his bow as did the others. Again, a flurry of arrows pelted into Nas'Gavarr, halting him momentarily.

Faron shouted to his remaining men, "Regroup!"

Every Del'Cabrian, including Jeth, rode back toward the line where the Herrani warriors, behind General Nadila, moved in with their wind blades while the archers nocked another set of arrows. The retreaters were a few seconds away from the line when the ground gave way beneath everyone's feet. The trees in front of them groaned and fell over. Horses screamed and rolled down the steep inclines quickly forming. Jeth leaped off Torrent's saddle to prevent her from crushing him as she tumbled backward. Her terrified whinny made his blood run cold.

He landed on his back as a tree's trunk fell straight for him. Its descent was blocked when it landed on the other side of the newly created pit, saving Jeth from being flattened. Dragging himself out of the mud, he ducked under the half-fallen trunk in search of Torrent. She was struggling to get to her feet. He pulled on her reins with all of his might. Relief flooded through him when she returned to four legs, none of them appearing broken.

"How are we going to get you out of here, girl?" Jeth wiped handfuls of mud out of her mane.

Painful grunts from a few feet away turned his attention from his horse. Faron was on his back half crushed under the weight of his own broken steed while Olivier struggled to push it off him.

Jeth ran to them and pushed against the bay's withers as hard as he could, his boots slipping through the mud. Eventually, the horse shifted its weight enough for Faron to crawl out from under it and collapse to his back.

Olivier, now acting as field medic, took to Faron's side. "Can you get up, Major?"

"My foot . . ." he rasped. His left foot was bent in and flattened to the dirt.

"But I'll live, go tend to the other injured."

Del'Cabrian soldiers were strewn about the pit, holding their heads, some trying in futility to climb out. The Herrani had been mostly spared and now fought the Overlord with the Tezkhan on the surface.

Faron opened his mouth to shout more orders when the whites of his eyes turned red. Blood dripped down his cheeks and poured from his nose.

"Major?" Olivier gasped in horror.

Faron started to choke up blood onto his blue buttoned lapels. More screams of pain and sickening coughs could be heard. Every urling soldier collapsed and violently began regurgitating their own blood. Only Jeth and the other human soldiers appeared unaffected.

"What's going on?" Olivier screamed, his eyes filling with panic. It was a panic Jeth knew all too well.

"He ingested urling blood," Jeth said. "Now he controls it."

"*What?*"

"Stay with him," he said as he rose to his feet. "I'm going to end this." *Not one more death . . . not one more!*

Olivier picked up his bow lying beside him. "Take this. The Herrani one you have is shit."

"You're telling me," Jeth said as he took the Del'Cabrian military-grade bow from Olivier. It felt good to hold one in his hands again.

Faron coughed up more blood onto his chest, and he started to convulse. "Whatever your plan is, you best hurry." Olivier handed Jeth his quiver as well.

With a determined nod, Jeth strapped the quiver to his lower back. He ran past Torrent and scrambled up the muddy incline, using upturned roots and grasses to keep from slipping back down. He emerged on the surface, covered in dirt. Seven Herrani warriors, four human Del'Cabrians, and twenty Tezkhan were all that was left to hold the line. Nas'Gavarr used his blood magic to render every urling on the battlefield a convulsing mass and was still able to defend himself from further attack.

"Genkhai!" Jeth called. The Tezkhan Chief cantered in from the battle. Jeth tossed him the emerald. "You fought bravely. Take your riders and get out of here while you're still able."

"Are you sure?"

"Just do it!" he barked.

Genkhai hollered for his men, and they gathered their injured and galloped off the battlefield. Not having the Tezkhan riding around allowed Jeth and the Overlord to get a clear view of each other. Nadila slashed her sword across the Overlord's chest, catching the string of naja teeth and breaking them away. He then reverted to human form before shattering Nadila's arm and throwing her several feet into the bush.

"Gavarr!" he bellowed. The Mage turned his attention from the slaughter to focus it all on Jeth. "This stops now!"

The urling soldiers stopped convulsing.

"Are you finally ready to let go of your goddess?" Nas'Gavarr asked.

I sure hope you're ready, Ser, Jeth thought with a gulp.

"If you want the Crannabeatha, come find her!"

With that, Jeth took off running for the Deep Wood and vanished into the dense underbrush.

36

Path of the Masochist

The forest was a blur of green and brown hues as Jeth raced through it. He leaped over roots, running so fast he barely registered where each foot landed. Sometimes he was on the ground, other times he was running along the low hanging branches, swinging from vines, and springing off the tree trunks.

He wasn't alone. His ears picked up Nas'Gavarr's horse trampling through the foliage behind him, but far enough away to give him time to warn Serra. When he neared the Grove of the Crannabeatha, he found her, a wood nymph named Ami, and another forest pixie he didn't recognize, busily growing a thick wall of overgrowth made of winding roots, branches, and vines. A narrow path through it was all they afforded, which would allow someone passage, but offered little room to venture elsewhere.

"Jeth, you're here." Serra flew over to him. "We're still too close to the Crannabeatha. We need a few more hours at least."

"This will have to do. He's on his way," he said, trying to catch his breath.

"He can't come yet!" Ami protested.

"I can't distract him anymore. If we're going to end him, we need to do it now."

"Alright." Serra sighed. "Get in positions, everyone!"

Several fairies fluttered about in an array of colorful sparks to their hiding places amongst the high branches. No human eye would be able to spot them.

"Please let this work," Jeth prayed, clutching a strand of hair.

To the west, he could hear Nas'Gavarr getting closer but still couldn't see him. Undoing the tie that held his mud-slathered locks in a heavy bundle, he let them tumble down his back.

He waited.

Bouncing up and down over Nas'Gavarr's shoulder as he jogged through the heavy foliage made Vidya want to vomit. The Mage had left his armor and the horses behind when the forest grew too thick. The moisture of the air and the overabundance of odors put Vidya off more than she'd expected. *No wonder I'm supposed to destroy this place, I can hardly stand it,* she thought with bitterness. She shook her head and tried to think. For her to formulate her own plan of escape seemed impossible through the fog of her mind, so filled with images of the ritual that de-winged her best friends, her guts still twisted by her sister's betrayal.

They turned north and climbed up a steep incline. Then came the swish of an arrow cutting through the air. Nas'Gavarr grunted and dropped Vidya on the ground.

A long shaft stuck out from the Mage's chest. He yanked it free, and his wound healed over in mere moments. Jeth, caked in dirt from head to toe, stood on the path ahead. He turned and dashed down a narrow deer path into a dense thicket of spindly branches. *He's baiting him,* Vidya's heart picked up pace.

Nas'Gavarr grabbed her by the ankles and dragged her along the ground. The foliage closed in around them, and any daylight that managed to seep through the oak branches above was cut off entirely. Wet leaves and sharp twigs scraped against her arm as her backside and shoulders bumped over hard roots embedded in the earth.

Branches snapped and bushes rustled in every direction. Jeth was nowhere to be seen, but she knew he was close.

Nas'Gavarr looked around in search of him as well. "You may be resistant to blood magic, but you are still powerless in protecting your Mother Oak. You should give up now."

An arrow whistled through the trees, piercing Nas'Gavarr all the way through the shoulder. He stumbled back before ripping it out. "I've been planning this for nearly a century!" he growled, finally showing legitimate frustration. "Your little arrowheads are not going to do a thing to change this!"

Swish! Another arrow, coming from a different trajectory than the last, pierced through his calf just under his knee. Despite the rustling leaves and vines moving about, there were only brief flashes of whatever it was that had disturbed them. Vines crawled along the ground under Nas'Gavarr's feet and tickled Vidya's arms.

"I am not your enemy," Nas'Gavarr continued in a more controlled tone. "My aim is to save humanity."

"Yeah, you keep saying that." Jeth's voice was directly east.

Nas'Gavarr didn't hesitate in firing an electric bolt in that direction, lighting a cluster of bushes aflame. A few seconds after, an arrow zoomed from the north, impaling Nas'Gavarr through the abdomen. "I think you and I have different definitions of the word *save*," Jeth said from the northwest.

The Overlord let out another lightning blast, lighting a tree branch on fire. This time, he didn't bother taking the arrow out of himself. That's when Vidya noticed something peculiar. The wound on his shoulder and the other in his calf had not yet healed like the first.

"I understand why you resist. The damage done today will be irreparable, but necessary for future generations to survive in the long run," the Overlord said.

His pace through the path was starting to slow. He dropped Vidya's legs. The earth vibrated, the trees around them groaned, and they appeared to widen and bend as if the thicket was a living organism.

"I won't be fathering any future generations. You made sure of that!" Jeth shot another two arrows from some unknown spot to the west. One caught Nas'Gavarr in the side and another in his shoulder.

Now breathless, Nas'Gavarr said, "That is what is wrong with you mortals. You cannot see beyond your own short existence, and that has always been and will continue to be your downfall. Many must die now, so more can live later. It is that simple. The ancient ones will never allow us to reach our full potential. I have shown them what we are capable of and they tremble. This realm will belong to us."

"It belongs to no one." A flash of a figure dashed across the path, sliced open the Overlord's knee, and fled into the bush.

Blood squirted out from Nas'Gavarr's leg as he faltered. He gritted his teeth at the pain, something Vidya had never witnessed before. His old wounds were almost healed, but his fresher ones had not even started to close.

"You seem a little winded," said Jeth from the underbrush. "Hope I'm not tiring you out."

The Overlord remained on one knee—his breathing labored and his skin paling with every drop of blood from his fresh gash. "W-what's happening to me?" he rasped.

"You're going to have to heal faster than that if you hope to make it to the Mother Oak." Four more arrows zoomed out of the bushes almost simultaneously, piercing through Nas'Gavarr's shoulders and side.

"How are you doing this?" he wheezed.

More branches stretched out, hugging Vidya as she lay on the ground.

"*You're* the two hundred-year-old Mage, you tell me." Jeth finally appeared down the path in front of them, nocked two arrows on one string and drew back. Nas'Gavarr put his hand out as if he were about to shoot another lightning bolt. The two arrows released and Jeth was out of sight before an electric burst could form in the Overlord's palm.

Both arrows pierced straight through his hand, and he cried out. With a determined grunt, he slowly pulled them out and rose to his feet. He bent down to pick Vidya up, but she took the opportunity to kick him in the wounded leg. Growling in pain, he smacked her with the back of his bleeding hand. Her ears rang, and her jaw went numb, blood smearing across her face. He took hold of the bindings around her legs with his good hand and limped his way down the narrowing path.

Time was running out.

Nas'Gavarr's serpent eyes were wide and frenzied as he dragged Vidya's bound body through the thicket, growing more obtrusive with every morsel of life force it drained from him.

The fairies hid all around them, urging the trees to take their life force from the Immortal Serpent instead of them, and it was working. His wounds continued to bleed, and his gait continued to slow, his chest heaved with every step. *It's time to end this,* Jeth decided, having exhausted his quiver to one last arrow.

With Anwarr's tulwar in hand, he dashed along a low hanging branch and jumped off it, ready to bring the blade down over the top of Nas'Gavarr's skull and deliver the naja saliva into his brain. But Nas'Gavarr put his arm up to block the sudden attack, and the blade claimed his wounded hand instead.

The Overlord's bellow ripped through the trees as he fell to his knees, clutching his bleeding stump. The foliage closed in tighter. It was impossible for him to avoid touching it and find the life force to regenerate his hand. Jeth walked up to the blood coated Mage, getting paler by the second.

"You don't know what you're doing . . . I'm your only hope for salvation," Nas'Gavarr panted.

"You're no savior. You're nothing more than a zealot. You wish to kill our gods so you can replace them!" Jeth brought the tip of Anwarr's blade to his face.

"Not all of them." Each breath from Nas'Gavarr's lungs shook like a rattlesnake. "There is a sixth Conduit no one knows about, not even the ashray with all the world's knowledge locked in their monasteries."

"What are you talking about?" A chill ran down Jeth's spine.

"I found the source of humanity." Nas'Gavarr's face contorted in pain, fear filling his eyes. "I'm the only one who knows our true origins. I must change our Way before it's too late."

"There's no changing it. You said it yourself, 'We are all born to die.'" Jeth raised his sword.

"Don't you want to know where you come from?" Nas'Gavarr pressed.

Jeth presented the forest with his other arm. "Here is where I come from.

You are in my house now! So, get out!"

He swung his sword for Nas'Gavarr's head just as Serra's scream pierced his ears. "Jeth, get down!"

A sparking green energy flew into his periphery a second before he was knocked violently to the ground. At the same time, a searing flame exploded all around them. The flames of the burning trees from the previous lightning blasts had rapidly expanded. Fire magic, combined with wind, produced a blaze that blew out in all directions.

Serra lay on top of Jeth, protecting him from the flames while pushing Nas'Gavarr away with sparkling energy from her hands.

Smoldering pain throbbed in Jeth's left arm and face. *You're on fire!* Serra smothered the flames with her own wings even though she was covered in them as well. The entire thicket became a raging inferno, spreading ravenously through the underbrush, and cleaved a wide path to the Crannabeatha. Several screeching fairies, engulfed in flames, sped toward the surrounding creeks to put themselves out. Serra had no choice but to follow suit.

The stench of Jeth's own seared skin was nauseating—the hearing in his left ear was muffled. He touched it and found it gone. Only a stinging, weeping mass was left in its place.

Drawing on the spark within him, Jeth pushed through the pain and climbed to his feet, choking on floating cinders that singed his throat.

Nas'Gavarr marched out from the blinding smoke, dragging Vidya by the ankles again. The flames parted in his wake, pushing out on either side of the path and leaving charred, black foliage behind. Now with the thicket burnt away and the fairies scattered, his wounds began to heal slowly. His bloody stump, however, swelled and wept puss with no new hand in sight.

Jeth ran to stop him, preparing to disembowel him again, and slow his healing process as best he could, but one backhand strike sent him reeling through the bushes and into a burning tree trunk. A rib cracked on impact, taking the wind right out of him.

Too weak to get up, Jeth watched the Overlord continue his advance toward the Crannabeatha. *You can't let him get near it. . . .*

As he struggled to move, a small arrow whisked through the burnt underbrush and pierced the Overlord's lower back. He glared over to Jeth and his single arrow still in his quiver. Nas'Gavarr exhaled in frustration as he looked around.

Then, a disturbance in the air—a faint flicker of light, and a huge scorpion-tattooed Herrani materialized in front of Nas'Gavarr and embedded his pole axe right into his pectorals.

"Ash!" Jeth coughed.

Nas'Gavarr was knocked on his back only to have Ash rip the axe out and bring it down again, slicing him through the midsection. Blood squirted vertically into the air and poured from his mouth.

"Free Vidya!" Jeth shouted. "Without her, he can't complete the ritual!"

"On it!" Ash turned around as an ebony-skinned woman appeared out of thin air and thrust her staff through the opening Ash made in Nas'Gavarr's abdomen. The Overlord wheezed out a rattling breath.

A shrill screech tore through the smoke as a skinny boy, with a small bow and quiver at his back and a Del'Cabrian military dagger at the ready, charged for the fallen Mage. Nas'Gavarr put his arms up to defend his head as Khiri stabbed him repeatedly in a violent frenzy.

Tears stung Jeth's eyes as he ignited a second spark and found the vigor to force himself back to his feet and join his loyal crew.

One moment Vidya was being carried to her doom through a burning forest and the next she was on the ground with Ash, severing the leather bindings around her ankles.

She held the shackles around her wrists out to him. He shrugged and raised his tabar over his shoulder.

With her eyes shut tight, she bit her lip in anticipation for the large axe blade to possibly slice her hands from her wrists. A few jarring clanks later and she was free. She exhaled with relief as Ash went to do the same with the chains around her wings.

"You okay?" he asked.

Vidya placed a hand on his shoulder and pulled herself to her feet.

"Doing better than he is." She nodded to Jeth limping out of the blackened bushes.

His left arm was red, flaking, and oozing, as well as the whole left side of his face. His ear was burnt away with half his locks having singed off. *How is he still standing?*

"Jeth!" she called.

"Get out of here, Vidya!" He waved her off with his burnt arm.

"Come with me. You're badly hurt," she urged.

From the ground, Nas'Gavarr flung the Ankarran boy away by the arm. It snapped, and he gave a screech that made the mother in her sink.

"Khiri!" The Light Mage ran to the boy's aid, leaving Nas'Gavarr to recover on his own.

"Not until I'm finished with him!" Jeth finally replied.

With a jolt of adrenaline, Vidya took to the air, breaking off charred branches on her way up.

She hadn't made it beyond the smoke before a debilitating weakness came over her. White stars flashed in her vision, her wings seized, and she fell from the sky like a bag of rocks.

She hit the ground, but it was not the impact she'd expected.

"Got you," Ash grunted, and they both fell to the dirt. She looked up at his sweaty, smiling face only to see Nas'Gavarr's appear behind it. She opened her mouth to give warning, but she lacked the wind to speak.

"Ash, watch out!" Jeth wailed in her stead.

Nas'Gavarr grabbed hold of Ash's hair tail with his one hand, and swung him around like a giant ragdoll before letting go. The Bahazur flew at Jeth, and together they hit the ground in a heap.

As Jeth struggled to climb out from under Ash, Nas'Gavarr took Vidya by the neck and dragged her toward the Crannabeatha once again.

"No," she wheezed, starved of blood and close to passing out.

Nas'Gavarr stepped into a large dip in the massive tree's roots.

"Vidya!" Jeth yelled. "Don't let him take your mind to the Spirit Chamber. If you go there, it's all over!"

"I won't," she croaked.

"Vidya!" he called again. "Free the raven!"

"What?" she mouthed the words, but no sound escaped.

"Free . . . the raven!"

Nas'Gavarr dropped her into a cradle of roots and a ring of fire formed around the entire tree, blocking Vidya's view of Jeth and the others.

Confusion mixed with pure terror flooded over her as the Overlord took to one knee, and pulled out the Bloodstone Dagger. He placed his hand over her head, and everything fell into shadow.

Vidya was now hovering in a dark and empty atrium, feeling having returned to her limbs and wings. She was in the Temple of Sagorath before it had been transformed into forested ruins, except the statue of Sagorath and Salotaph lay in pieces on the floor. The last words Jeth said to her echoed in her mind. *'Free the raven. . . .'*

She glided about the atrium, not sure what she expected to find. But there it was . . . an actual raven, shackled to an iron ball in the corner of the room. Landing before it, she found it to be bigger than she was. *"SQUAWK"*—she backed away.

She winced at the burning pain at her side and looked down to find blood dripping through her tunic. It poured down her thigh, forming a puddle at her feet that grew wider and deeper until she started to sink.

"The blood will take you to the Crannabeatha, where the power of Yasharra will defeat her." Nas'Gavarr's voice startled her. She spun around, already up to her knees in blood, and found a giant snake slithering toward her.

"Not a chance!" With a flap of her wings, she sprang out of the blood and returned to the raven. She tugged at one of the manacles attached to its leg, but her strength was not adequate to break apart the thick iron.

The serpent slithered around her, and the raven retreated into the shadows, but Vidya yanked it back into the light by the chain.

The pool of blood spread, and she was sinking again. Taking the chain in both hands, she flew up into the air and forced the raven to fly along with her. The giant snake clamped its jaws on her wing and flung her across the room.

Vidya met the wall with two feet and jumped off it before the serpent could nip at her again. She weaved between the hanging cages as the cobra's head bashed through them to get at her.

The squawking raven flew by, and she grabbed hold of the manacle again. "Sorry, birdy, but this is going to hurt."

Drawing both feet back, she kicked the raven's legs as hard as she could. The creature's shrieks echoed off the empty temple walls, but she kept kicking and kicking, turning the leg to mush before finally yanking the manacle once more.

The serpent's jaws clamped around her legs and pulled her down. The shackles tore off, and part of the broken leg detached and splashed into the bloody pool, having now spread across the whole temple floor.

The freed raven dove toward the snake, landed on its head with its one good leg, and hammered its beak into the snake's scaly flesh. Vidya, released from the snake's mouth, smacked against the pool's surface. Her wings became drenched in blood, and the more she flapped them, the deeper she sank.

"Help!" she screamed.

The raven had grown to the size of the serpent, its massive black beak tearing into the reptile meat. The snake tried to smother the bird in its coil, but it flew to another spot atop the snake and continued picking apart its flesh and flinging it around the atrium.

Vidya gurgled another scream as blood filled her mouth, and she was sucked under. She was free falling—hurtling through an old growth forest so thick, no light could escape. She tumbled over branches and ripped down vines, spinning uncontrollably through the air until she made an abrupt landing on a large oak branch.

She coughed up the blood she'd swallowed and shook it off her feathers, only to find more of it raining down from the sky. Deep red drops bounced off the leaves, dripped down the tree's bark, then into an empty black abyss— no ground in sight.

"There has to be a way of out of here," Vidya whispered in panic, gazing back up to the bleeding red sky.

The tree branch she was on began to move like a living appendage. She sprang back up into the air, but vines wrapped around her ankles and tugged her down. They entwined around her arms and legs, stretching her body out like a starfish as the vegetation swathed over her torso, her wings, and even her neck. She released a shrieking roar, struggling against her natural restraints.

The branches in her vicinity bent and weaved amongst each other, forming a gigantic face that loomed above her. Vines and leaves acted like muscle and sinew, leafy green skin filling the hollow nooks in the bark serving as eyes, nose, and mouth.

A soft, yet powerful feminine voice floated through the trees like a swift wind. "Who are you to invade this sacred place?"

"I'm the Champion of Yasharra." Vidya thrashed furiously against her bonds. "Release me, and I will leave you be. I do not wish to hurt you."

The face of trees let out a dreadful weep. "You've come to bring suffering upon us?"

"No, no, I don—" The vines squeezed tighter around Vidya's neck, choking off her words.

"We will not allow it!" The Crannabeatha shrieked.

Vidya was pushed hard against a tree's trunk, and the overgrowth buried her. A sickening wrath rose within her. Something putrid climbed up her throat, making her retch. Vidya gagged on a crawling lump. Mounds of black maggots, followed by enormous flies, flooded from her mouth. The leaves around her browned and curled. Soon she was free of their grasp.

She gagged again, collapsing to her hands and knees. More insects flew out of her. The flies ravaged the leaves, the worms elongated and strangled the branches until they blackened and fell away. The Crannabeatha's moans vibrated through every branch.

As horrified as Vidya was, she felt a strange comfort in the decaying power, as if she were witnessing the natural order of things—a brutal truth. *"Pestilence devours the living!"* The giddy voice inside her said.

Perhaps this is what I was meant for . . . why fight it? Then, a shining light beamed down from above, making her squint. A hole in the sky sucked up all the flies and worms at the same time something large fell through it.

A giant serpent and a raven spiraled through the trees. The raven landed on a branch a few feet from Vidya as a bloody snake husk continued to plummet.

The pestilence no longer ate away at the plant life. Vidya yearned to continue the destruction, but this was her only chance at escape. With all her might, she pushed herself upward. Branches and vines tried to stop her, but she tore through them. The raven flew up beside her, allowing her to grab hold of its talons and lift her more assuredly toward the light.

The rain storm Nas'Gavarr created to fill the cradle of blood put out much of the flames that still burned in the thicket, except for the ring of fire surrounding the Crannabeatha.

Istari did all she could to direct the rainwater to it, but it kept replenishing. "I'm sorry, Jeth. His fire magic is too strong," she said breathlessly.

Jeth lay on his stomach. Having come down from his spark, a stabbing, burning pain radiated through his arm and face. All he could do was regard the magnificence of the Mother Oak and wait for it all to wither and die before his eyes. One desperate idea was all he'd had—*free the raven*—but he had no idea what such a thing would do, whether it would still be there, or make things worse. But that raven was their last hope . . . if it was any hope at all.

After a few minutes, the fire ring extinguished, and Nas'Gavarr fell to his back. He let go of the dagger and started convulsing. Floating in a pool of her own blood, Vidya's eyes shot open. *If she made it out, then that means . . .* Jeth couldn't allow himself to even think it.

Ash and Istari rushed over to help Vidya out of the blood pit. Nas'Gavarr stopped shuddering, blinked a few times, sat up, and with a groaning effort, returned to his feet. The Mage cringed, looking down at his own festering stump.

"A little worse for wear . . ." he muttered.

It was over. Jeth had nothing left. He was torn apart inside and out. But, if he were to die, he would die with his hands inside Nas'Gavarr, tearing out his viscera. Forcing himself to his feet, Jeth limped toward the Overlord, prepared to deliver the final blow before the entire forest succumbed to its doom.

Nas'Gavarr looked over to him as he approached and grinned widely, stopping him dead. *What is this serpent playing at?*

"Desert War Traitor, what a surprise," he said. "I was hoping you'd free me earlier, but no matter, this harpy came through."

Under Ash's arm, Vidya lumbered up to them, holding onto her still bleeding side. "Excuse me?"

"Huh?" uttered Jeth at the same time.

Nas'Gavarr limped past the group, grimacing with each step. "What did you do to this body? Its life force is so depleted I can scarcely heal enough to keep it alive."

From his strange and familiar dialect, it quickly dawned on Jeth that it was not Nas'Gavarr speaking to them. "Meister Melikheil? Is that you?"

The Mage nodded. "When the Immortal Serpent refused to fight me in the Spirit Chamber, I knew right then his spirit was not as powerful as mine. My challenge was figuring out how to convince him to enter a battle he knew he would lose. Luckily, I had a contingency plan, not altogether pleasant for me, but—"

"Your death was intentional." Jeth's mouth gaped, thinking back to that horrific day.

"Hmm, little did Gavarr realize that the torturous way he chose to kill me was just enough to boost the spiritual power required to possess his body after mine was torn apart."

"So, you weren't kidding when you said self-torture makes the spirit stronger," Jeth said.

"We call it the Path of the Masochist: the only true way to immortality for a Spirit Mage," he said with a glint in his reptilian eyes.

"Your spirit was in Nas'Gavarr this entire time?" Vidya asked as she stepped away from Ash. Red liquid tendrils of coagulated blood rolled down her skin in the rain.

"Yes," replied Melikheil. "It is rather disorienting to enter a live body for the first time. I was unable to gain full sentience before he and his son, together, pushed me down into the recesses of his mind."

"Couldn't they have forced you out?" Vidya wondered.

"Not without causing Nas'Gavarr severe pain in doing so. They would have found it easier to imprison me rather than get rid of me." He looked down at his severed stump and frowned. "I should be going. I have to figure out how to use flesh magic to get this hand back. Then, I shall return home."

Melikheil turned and took steps down the charred forest path.

"Do you mean Ingleheim?" Jeth called after him.

He turned around and replied, "That is my home, yes."

"You're probably not going to recognize it."

"Oh?" He raised an eyebrow. "Well, it's not exactly going to recognize me either," he said with a chilling grin.

"And what will you do when Nas'Gavarr decides to take his body back?"

"Won't happen. He opened a point of entry to the Spirit Chamber, and I sent him through it. Your Crannabeatha will certainly finish him off. This body is exclusive to me now. Thank you again." Melikheil cordially bowed and began walking away in Nas'Gavarr's body.

"I don't understand what's happening. We're just going to let him go?" Istari exclaimed.

Vidya joined, "I don't know much about the Raven Sorcerer, but I saw what he did in that Spirit Chamber. His spirit was stronger than Nas'Gavarr's, and now he has access to flesh magic on top of that."

"The man just helped save the forest and all our lives. We can't end his out of fear of what he *might* do . . . can we?"

Everyone stood amongst the blackened foliage, soaked by the rain, and watched the Mage disappear into the smoke.

After what felt like several minutes passing with no answer, Ash said, "So, to be clear, who we just let walk away was *not* Nas'Gavarr."

"That's right." Jeth nodded.

"You sure?"

"Pretty sure."

"Something tells me we might regret this," said Istari.

"Probably." Jeth sighed, the searing pain of his skin amplified by each rain drop that drummed on it. "But, we'll deal with that when—*if* the time comes. I'm just glad the forest is still here . . . more or less."

Serra fluttered into view, free of flames, her burns nearly healed already. "Not to worry, Jeth. In time, we can repair the damage. The important thing is that the Crannabeatha is unharmed, both physically and spiritually. Thank you, all of you, whoever you are."

"How did you all get here anyway?" Jeth asked.

"Yemesh came to us, worried about his master," Ash began. "He told us you and Snake Eye went to face the Overlord on your own. We couldn't allow that to happen . . . not this time."

Khiri, holding his arm, leaned against Istari and shook his head in agreement with Ash.

Istari continued, "We went to the temple warping gate just in time to see Saf'Ryeem and his naja coming back through it with Snake Eye in custody. So I cloaked the four of us, and we snuck Snake Eye away, stole some horses, and escaped through the gate before the naja could follow our scent. We came upon some Del'Cabrian soldiers who told us where to find you."

"We would have gotten lost looking for this Mother Oak of yours if the fires hadn't led the way," said Ash.

"I suppose we have Nas'Gavarr to thank for that," Jeth quipped, rubbing the back of his burnt neck and wincing in pain.

"Those burns look bad," Istari said with concern. "Snake Eye is back in Lanore. He can heal you."

"Perhaps we should give the ashipu time to heal himself first. He's in pretty bad shape," Ash reminded her.

"Vidya's the one that needs healing." The group turned to find she was no longer with them.

"Where did she go?" Ash asked concernedly.

"She was just . . ." Jeth trailed off, then murmured, "Shit."

Vidya was gone, and so was the Bloodstone Dagger.

37

Fairy Locks Grow Back

Clutching the Bloodstone Dagger in one hand and holding her bleeding side with the other, Vidya flew above the Deep Wood.

Now that the Overlord's spirit was defeated, the effect of his spell was gone, and she was more or less at full strength, apart from her stab wound. Hopefully, the dagger hadn't hit a major organ, but she was not about to slow down to find out.

Vidya had barely cleared the wood when Jeth, hanging from the arms of a green haired fairy, sidled up next to her in the air.

"Hey there, Vid, what are you doing?" he asked.

"What does it look like I'm doing?" She dove underneath him and turned southward.

The fairy zoomed overhead with a burst of green sparks and got in front of her. "Snake Eye should have the dagger," Jeth continued.

"You'd trust it with that freak? She could be worse than her brother for all you know," Vidya said.

"I trust him." The fairy zipped underneath her and brought Jeth up to her right side, nearest the dagger. "After what I've seen, I know he won't hurt anyone. Only he can ensure that thing stays hidden from Saf'Ryeem or Melikheil."

"It's safer with me." With a blast of wind, Vidya sped past Jeth and his fairy while blowing them off course. But another burst of sparks pushed them right up behind her, then engulfed her. Vidya felt like she was being pierced with a thousand tiny knives, and her body, including her wings, seized. She whirled through the air, out of control, and into the trees. She created a wind gust to level herself, but she couldn't get enough lift. She ended up meeting the ground hard with her backside.

"Bastard!" Vidya bellowed into the sky. Jeth and the fairy made a soft landing behind her.

"I know those fairy sparks sting, but they can't hurt you. Now let's talk about this," he began.

Vidya spun around, her face red with rage. "Why are you doing this? You know I need the dagger!"

Jeth slowly approached, palms held out. "Nas'Gavarr is dead, and the threat to Credence is gone."

"Don't be a fool. Saf'Ryeem will try to finish what his father started. My people still need this." Those words left a sour taste in her mouth. *I'm not going to be saving them all*, she thought darkly.

"Your people aren't alone anymore, Vidya. Del'Cabria, Ingleheim, and Snake Eye, all of them can help Credence finish this war. There's no need for an army of harpies."

"This isn't just about the Harplite. This is about righting wrongs!"

"Vidya, it's over." Jeth put out his unburnt hand. "Give it to me."

Vidya growled and sent a sharp gust of wind to push Jeth aside. His fairy rushed forward in a flash of green light and caught him. She lobbed another ball of sparks at Vidya, knocking her to the ground.

"I've had enough of you!" Vidya snarled, directing a small cyclone to the fairy, throwing her up into the trees and out of sight.

"Hey!" Jeth howled.

"She'll be fine," muttered Vidya before taking off into the air.

She flew up past the tree tops. *Zing!* A burst of loose feathers, and a shooting pain through her right wing rendered it useless. She fell screaming from the sky and landed in some moss. An arrow protruded from her wing. She clenched her teeth.

"I'm sorry, Vidya." Jeth approached, but he appeared about to collapse at any moment. "I can't let you leave with that dagger."

"You'd let Snake Eye resurrect the first Najahai, but you deny me the ability to protect my island?" she hissed, pulling out the arrow.

"Nas'Gavarr was a murderous fanatic, but he was right about the danger of the ancient ones. An army of harpies will threaten us all."

"Only enemies of Credence will come to harm. Will *you* be one of them?" Vidya rose, her wing dripping blood on the mosses.

"I'm not an enemy of Credence," he said, taking slow, limping steps toward her. "But, I'm starting to think you might be."

"Shut your idiot mouth!" Vidya's screeched and punched Jeth in the sternum. It cracked in the wake of her fist and Jeth was down again. He choked up blood, and his breath shortened.

"They betrayed me, every single one of them! After everything I've done to protect them, and they still hate me!" Vidya screamed, her eyes flooding with tears. "Do you have any idea what it's like to be reviled by your own people?"

"Yes . . . ?" he wheezed.

Vidya couldn't hear him. Her right hand was gripping the dagger so hard it cramped. "I finally found people who truly understood me, and they were *mutilated*. Everyone I have ever loved has been taken from me over and over again. No more!"

"Believe it or not." Jeth dragged himself to his feet. "I understand you too. I know what it's like. . . ."

A sharp cackle escaped Vidya. "What? We shared a few pints, had a few adventures together, and that's supposed to give you a special insight into my life?"

"You told me about your children. That wasn't nothing."

Vidya had never told another soul about the circumstances around her sons' deaths. *He never judged me . . . why didn't he judge me?*

"I had the chance to save Anwarr," she blurted. "The child wouldn't have made it, but she could have survived to have another. I'm not your friend, Jeth! This is all I care about." She held up the dagger for him to see.

"I'm not about to make you responsible for Anwarr's death. What happened to her was by her choices and mine, that's it. The fact remains, you helped me when no one else would. I don't give a shit what your motivations were. Just let me help *you*." He began laboring toward her again.

She backed away and put her hands out. "You've done enough. I will have my Harplite. Stand in my way, and you will come to know its wrath."

"I can't let you," said Jeth.

In a flash, he tackled her to the forest floor and clambered for the dagger in her hand.

She dug her nails into the burnt side of his head, making him scream foul curses. She spread her wings, but Jeth jabbed her in the wound before she could attempt to lift off, making her double over in pain. He tried for the dagger again, but she knocked him away with her good wing. Lunging for him, Vidya bashed him against a tree. Another crack from his ribcage and more blood dribbled through his clenched teeth. Taking his unscathed arm, she flung him overhead. His back smacked against a tree root sticking out from the soil, a third crack echoed off the old bark.

He cried out as he toppled over the root and landed on his back. Vidya shot over to him, forced him deeper into the earth, and held him down by the chest. He wheezed from the pressure.

She raised her dagger-holding fist above her head, ready to strike him unconscious.

"He will continue to stand against us . . . punish him. . . ." The voice whispered through the trees from seemingly every direction. She gasped at the shadow appearing right in front of her. It loomed over Jeth, its yellow eyes burning with a lust for his blood.

"He doesn't deserve it," Vidya whispered, suddenly sickened by what she had done to him.

"Who?" Jeth croaked from beneath her.

Vidya lowered her arm just as the fairy shot out of the underbrush like a bolt of green lightning. She bashed Vidya into a dying tree, splintering the old wood nearly in half.

The fairy was now accompanied by another four—some with brown and even blue matted locks. "Drop the dagger and leave this forest," the green-haired one said in a low voice.

Vidya gazed upon the broken man she left in the dirt and said nothing. She forced a swirling wind gust around her, launched herself into the air, and didn't look back.

Jeth lay there, staring after Vidya flying higher into the sky until she became lost in the clouds. His spark was wearing thin once again and every imaginable pain throbbed through his entire body . . . everywhere but his legs.

Serra's head eclipsed the blue sky above the trees. "Jeth, are you all right?"

"I-I can't feel my legs." He couldn't breathe either. It felt like one of his lungs had been ripped out through his aching back.

"Oh no," Serra gasped.

"Can you help me move them?" he asked, still looking to the sky.

"I am." Serra moved his left leg up and down.

He felt nothing—like they were someone else's legs. A horrible sinking sensation tugged his body into the soft earth as darkness swept over him. He yearned for the mosses to swallow him up . . . to make him part of the forest as he was in the Spirit Chamber.

"Any chance the forest can give back a little of that life force and help me heal?" Jeth asked.

Serra shook her head. Her big green eyes were saddened, but they were free of tears. Fairies didn't cry. "We can transfer life to and between plants, but never from plants to other living things. I'm sorry. It's not within our power."

"That's all right, Ser." He reached out and touched her soft green locks, small vines entwined throughout. "I know you would if you could."

She nodded and took him in her arms. He hugged her tight, allowing her to lift him up. Overwhelming agony weakened him, and he let go, the darkness looming ever larger above him. As Jeth's spark dwindled to nothing, he let that darkness overtake him.

When the black veil was lifted, Jeth found himself in a single bed in a log house that smelled of sweet pine. The first thing he noticed was the feeling had returned to his legs, and not only that, he could move them. They were as two sacks of bricks in bed with him, but he would take it.

A small fire flickered in a hearth. In front of it sat Snake Eye in a wheelchair and a blanket around his legs, one of them in a splint. *He's gone and done it again,* Jeth thought with guilt and relief at the same time.

Snake Eye was meditating when Jeth croaked, "Where are we?"

He opened his eyes and smiled. "Ah, welcome back. We're in Lanore." He called Yemesh in from outside the room who wheeled him closer to the bed. He placed a hand on Jeth's shoulder, his yellow eye filled with sorrow, the reptilian one patched over.

Jeth asked, "Are we going to have to come up with another name for you or . . . ?"

"What, this?" He pointed to his eye patch. "I'm still working on it. Repairing my spinal cord takes precedence."

Jeth placed his own hand over Snake Eye's. "Thanks. I haven't been able to repay you for the last time."

"Don't worry about that," Snake Eye said, his lips tautening. "Just confirm one thing for me. Is Gavarr really gone?"

"Yes." Jeth cast his eyes down. "In spirit anyway."

Snake Eye deflated back in his wheelchair, and gave an accepting nod.

"I know you wanted to be the one to . . . ." Jeth trailed off.

"I gave up the chance to end his life when I foolishly brought that Najahai back into this world. At least Dulsakh's spirit is dispersed, and his progeny can remain in slumber." Snake Eye's bottom lip trembled, and he bit down on it.

"Are you going to be all right?"

Snake Eye's features lightened a bit. "I suppose I . . . ." His eyelashes fluttered. ". . . I always believed that no matter what bad blood existed between my brother and me, we'd both die one day and meet again in spirit, not as bitter enemies, but as loving siblings . . . like we used to be." The ashipu swallowed hard and gathered himself. "You and Vidya did what needed to be done. I'm anything but comfortable with the Ingle Mage running around in my brother's skin, but at least the world has been spared his destructive machinations."

Jeth was not about to forget one of the last things Nas'Gavarr said to him. *'I found the source of humanity.'* He wondered if he should have let Nas'Gavarr tell him what that was. *Do you really want to know?* For now, he was content not to think on it.

"What are you going to do now? Take his place?" Jeth wondered.

With a breathy chortle, Snake Eye replied, "No, not yet. The chaos that will ensue among the tribes when they receive word of their immortal Overlord's death. . . ."

"Saf'Ryeem will figure it out sooner or later," Jeth warned.

"Yes, but he would not be so foolish as to let the rest of the populous know, lest other tribal leaders challenge him for power."

"And what about Vidya? She plans to use the Bloodstone Dagger to create her harpy army. Should we be worried?"

Snake Eye sighed and shrugged. "From what I know of Crede history, there is little chance their Siren Council would allow such a thing. For now, I will focus my energies on my nephew."

Jeth gulped, hoping Snake Eye was right, despite the gnawing discomfort in his gut. *'This is about righting wrongs!'* His stomach churned at the thought of how things ended between them. *There is more rage in that woman than anyone could have imagined.*

The door creaked open. Jeth's heart leaped from his chest. It then slowed upon seeing his crew, followed by the Elders, and a number of other Fae'ren he didn't recognize, file into the room.

"Sweet Mother, I thought you were the Del'Cabrians coming to take me away for good," he said, sitting up against the headboard.

Twilla took a seat at the foot of the bed. "The Del'Cabrians are content to believe you're dead for the time being. We all went to the Mother Oak to lend our support in prayer. There you were beneath her, fairies fluttering about you. They told us what you and your friends did." She put a hand on his leg through the blanket. "Cursed or not, you are always welcome in this commune."

"Don't I need a family name?"

"Jethril of the Deep Wood," said a Fae woman holding a toddler. "That's what those who fled to Fairieshome have started calling you. I for one had to find out if they were speaking of you."

"Henna? H-hi . . ." He hardly recognized her all washed of mud and healed of bruises.

"The people there don't believe a cursed one could have done what you did, but us fellow cursed ones do."

"You came all this way . . . ?"

"Us orphans need to look out for each other. The way you did for me," she said with a blushing smile.

All the other Fae'ren in the room nodded in agreement.

The child started to squirm so she put him down and walked closer to the bed. That's when Jeth noticed her red and peeling forearm, glistening with an ointment. The sharp odor of vera gel invaded his nostrils, and he instantly scaled back his sense of smell to near nothing.

"What happened to your arm?" He pointed to it.

"That's why everyone's here now," Snake Eye interjected. "When they saw how I was able to heal your broken spinal cord, they each sacrificed small amounts of flesh to heal your remaining injuries."

"It's nothing, really," Henna said, holding onto her burnt arm. "Your ashipu said having Fae'ren blood meant we didn't need to suffer injuries as severe as yours."

Istari added. "I singed the surface of her skin with concentrated light essence, not unlike the sunburns you used to get all the time."

Jeth chuckled. "I sure don't miss those." He scratched his head, realizing he could hear clearly out of his left ear again. "My ear!"

A tall Fae'ren, with vera smeared over his sunburnt face and ear, waved. "You're welcome, mate."

The door flew open wider and slammed against the wall. Khiri, wearing a sling, ran up to the bed. "Khir!" Jeth hugged the boy tight then inspected his broken arm.

"He'll have to wait until my arm is healed before I can break it again," Snake Eye said, raising his own sling.

Jeth rubbed Khiri's shaved head. "Ah, that's all right. A few broken bones build character."

"We didn't want him to get hurt, but there was no leaving the boy behind this time," Ash said.

"Anwarr would be proud of how you helped to avenge her. Nice job," Jeth said thoughtfully.

Saying nothing as always, Khiri hugged Jeth again, more than making up for the spitting incident. Khiri brushed his hand over Jeth's head and laughed at the absence of hair on the left side.

"I see no one volunteered to cut their locks off, though." Jeth chortled. "Do I look ridiculous?"

All eyes in the room wandered away. Istari bit her lip.

"Come on, Ash," Jeth pleaded. "You'd tell me the truth, right?"

"That hair style does not suit you," he confessed without pause.

"Hmm, I'd have to disagree with you, Ashbedael," said Snake Eye, giving Jeth a wink.

He reddened, unsure whether Snake Eye liked his look because he found it attractive or because it was a lot like his own.

"Fairy locks grow back," said Twilla. "But our forest would not have. Now the warpath of the Immortal Serpent has ended . . . because of you."

"But . . ." He rubbed the back of his recently healed neck. "I wasn't able to stop him—"

"Regardless of who dealt the last blow, you, a cursed one, risked your life for this forest. No Fae'ren has done anything like that for a long time."

"You should try to get more rest, little Gershlon." Snake Eye patted his knee under the blanket. "I must return to my meditation. I should be up and walking again in a week then it's back to Herran."

"We need to head back right away," said Istari. "We have a job lined up."

"No need. Just take the ninety-thousand gold note I left in the shop," Jeth offered.

Istari shook her head with a smile. "I'll stash it in a safe place for you."

"Thanks again," said Jeth. "Everyone . . . I can't begin to—"

"Stop." Istari put her palm out. "You're a part of this crew whether you like it or not, and this crew looks out for its own."

"As much as I appreciate that, I'm not going back to the desert," Jeth said. Khiri jumped off the bed with a pout.

"But we could really use you," Istari protested.

"I'm done with all that, Star. My place is here now."

"Most of your own people still shun you," Ash warned.

"I know." He sighed. "But they're stuck with me anyway. This is my home and no one, not even the people who live here, are going to tell me otherwise." Henna's eyes lit up at his words, and the Elders nodded in fervent agreement.

"Suit yourself. You know where to find us if you change your mind." Ash lugged his tabar over his shoulder and quickly started for the door as if to hide the emotions on his face from Jeth.

"This won't be the last you've seen of us, Fae'ren," Istari said with a subtle grin.

"I'm sure you're right."

Once everyone filed out, Jeth settled back down to sleep but was jolted awake by a panicked realization.

"Torrent!"

Flinging the covers off, he rose to wobbly legs. He used the furniture around the room to steady himself, eventually finding the wherewithal to exit the cottage and trundled to the stables.

"Tor?" he called. She wasn't there. Only Anwarr's buckskin.

"You're looking for the dapple gray?" the stable boy asked.

Jeth nodded. "Did she make it?"

"The Del'Cabrians were going to take her back with them, but I figured you'd want her, so I traded the black gelding for her. She's in the field now." The boy smiled proudly at his own foresight.

"Thank you, thank you, thank you." He hugged the skinny lad and ran back outside. His mare was cantering in circles around the pen. With most of his dexterity already returning to him, Jeth vaulted over the fence and sprinted after her. With a loud whistle, he got Torrent's attention, and she started toward him. Jeth flung himself on her bare back, gripped her wiry, gray mane, and steered her for the gate. The stable boy, having followed Jeth out, hastily opened it right before they reached it.

Jeth and his Tezkhan steed raced like the wind down the forested paths with no particular destination in mind. It didn't matter where he rode. He could already feel himself taking root.

(Three weeks later)

Lightning cracked across the gray skies over unruly seas. Rumbling thunder followed close behind. The wind whipped through Vidya's hair as she flew through the burgeoning storm toward the only women's prison of Credence.

It was a fortress built upon a tiny rock off the coast, as were the men's prisons. And like all those prisons it had one overlooked security flaw. The yard could be easily accessed from the sky. Back when she was learning to fly, she had flown over the prisons numerous times. Rain or shine, she knew the inmates were brought outside at noon every day. Today was no exception.

She descended upon the yard like a bird of prey, landing with such force, wet gravel sprayed out in every direction. The prisoners were hunkered down around tables under the shelters. They all stared at the winged woman who had dropped from the storm clouds.

"Daphne! Phrea!" Vidya roared.

For a moment, nobody answered. The thunder boomed, and rain pelted down, her curly hair flattened against her scalp and hung in dripping wet tangles over her shoulders. As she inhaled to try again, a thick boned woman with a unibrow stepped out into the rain. A thin, mousy woman followed. Both their heads were shaven, but there was no mistaking their faces.

"Vidi?" Phrea gasped.

"Hey!" a female guard barked. "What are you doing?"

Vidya directed the storm winds at the guard and knocked her back against the stone wall.

"You're both coming with me."

"Where will we go? We have no wings," said Daphne.

She turned slightly to reveal the indented scars running down her delicate shoulder blades. It made Vidya's gut wrench to see them.

Taking the Bloodstone Dagger from her scabbard, Vidya said, "You will have your wings back."

"With what sacrifices?" Phrea asked, crossing her arms and widening her stance.

"Don't worry about that. We need only direct our efforts to finding women like ourselves. The wingless, the childless, those left to rot by a republic that no longer values them. . . ."

Other prisoners started to come out into the rain to listen. The guards stood frozen in place.

Vidya blared her message out for the entire prison yard to hear, "Follow me and you will all have wings! The Harpy *will* rule Credence again!"

End of Book One

MAGIC TERMS

Aura - The energy that makes up each of the six essence (see Essence Mage).

Blast gel - Clear, highly explosive gelatinous agent enchanted by fire magic and is discharged from a small dispenser.

Bloodstone Dagger – an ancient dagger made of bloodstone used for ritual sacrifice and blood magic. The stone can absorb and store blood of one being and return one hundred times that amount.

Dulsakh's Sarcophogus - A coffin believed to hold the remains of the ancient leader of the Najahai.

Emerald of Dulsakh - An emerald that houses the spirit of the ancient leader of the Najahai. Currently in possession of the Tezkhan raider chief.

Essence Mage - A Mage who manipulates the six essences of wind, light, water, earth, fire, and life force.

Flesh Mage - A Mage who manipulates the physical tissues of living organisms.

Flesh whip - Whip wielded by Snake Eye made of enchanted leather that can take the form of human skin.

Gizelle's Sapphire - A sapphire shaped like an antelope owned by Snake Eye used for storing large amounts of aura.

Ice powder - Granular substance that freezes anything not warm blooded. It is useful in putting out fires and making objects more brittle.

Mage - A person, also referred to as a witch/wizard/sorcerer, who can manipulate one or all three components of existence: essence, spirit, and flesh.

Magitech - Items that a Mage has enchanted with magical properties for the use of people without magic abilities. Examples are: Blast Gel, Flesh whip, Ice powder, and wind blades.

Magus/Magi (plural) – An male-only order of the former Death Tribes who primarily worship Sagorath with the Immortal Serpent as their exalted master. Its high-standing members specialize in fire and water magic.

Naja Handler – a Spirit Mage who controls an individual naja contingent

Priming - The process in which a Spirit Mage readies a subject's spirit for manipulation (see Spirit Mage).

Spirit Mage - A Mage who manipulates spirit, the energy that gives all living creatures their sentience.

Wind blade - Round throwing blade enchanted by wind magic to allow the wielder to control its trajectory

NATURAL SUBSTANCES AND THEIR USES

Khat leaf - a gnarled plant grown in the dry Tezkhan Plains that acts as a stimulant for those that chew it. Has a strong and unpleasant odor.

Naja blood - contains the antidote for naja venom born out of their saliva.

Valerian - flowering weed extract used as a powerful sedative.

Vera - Gelatin contained in leaves used in Fae'ren to hasten healing of flesh wounds.

GODS AND ANCIENT BEINGS

Verishten
Form: Volcanic activity Ancients: Golems
Location: Volcano of Verishten, Deschner Mountain Range, Ingleheim
Role: Foundation of life
Dominant essence: Earth

Spirit of Elmifel
Form: Aquatic life Ancients: The ashray
Location: Sacred Spring, Holy City of Thessalin, Elmifel Province, Del'Cabria
Role: Source of life Dominant essence: Water

Crannabeatha (aka Mother Oak)
Form: Plant life
Ancients: Fairies and ogres
Location: Deep Wood, Fae'ren Province, Del'Cabria Role: Nurturer of life
Dominant essence: Life force

Yasharra w/ Daughters the Siren and the Harpy
Form: Aviary and insect life Ancients: harpies and sirens
Location: Grand Altar, Citadel, Credence Role: The suffering of life
Dominant essence: Wind

Serpentine (Sagorath and Salotaph)
Form: Reptile life
Ancients: Naja and their progenitors (Najahai)
Location: Temple of Sagorath within the Burning Waste, Herran
Role: Death of life
Dominant essence: Fire

About the Author

K.E. Barron wanted to be a writer her entire life but chose to be an accountant instead. Now she divides her time between writing books and balancing them. She grew up in Fernie, British Columbia and now lives in Red Deer, Alberta, working as a financial analyst and writing fantasy books in her spare time. Her interests are vast and varied, ranging from the aesthetics of eighteenth- and nineteenth-century period pieces to the scholarly realms of evolutionary psychology, anthropology, economics, and religion. These eclectic inspirations are all part of the magic and cultural realism of The Immortal Serpent, her second publication.

CPSIA information can be obtained
at www.ICGtesting.com
Printed in the USA
LVHW090134200819
628175LV00002B/7/P